The Child

JAN HAHN

Meryton Press

OYSTERVILLE, WA

Also by JAN HAHN

AN ARRANGED MARRIAGE

THE JOURNEY

THE SECRET BETROTHAL

A PECULIAR CONNECTION

THE DARCY MONOLOGUES

THE CHILD

Copyright © 2018 by Jan Hahn

All rights reserved, including the right to reproduce this book, or portions thereof, in any format whatsoever. For information: P.O. Box 34, Oysterville WA 98641

ISBN: 978-1-68131-024-4

Cover design by Janet Taylor
Cover image: Friedrich von Amerling, "Portrait of Princess Marie Franziska of Liechtenstein"
Layout by Ellen Pickels

Chapter One

I saw her for the first time in late September, on the twenty-second day to be exact.

The morning fog had dissolved, swept away by brilliant sunlight sent to bless the day and banish all shadows of the past. Rainfall from the night before had cleansed the normally fetid London air, or perhaps the fragrant soap with which I had washed yet lingered, making me believe the city smelled fresh. My clothing was impeccable, my linen freshly starched, my beaver new. I was prepared for this day in dress and thought, resolved to the change it would bring in my life—a new beginning. And then...I saw her.

I stopped as though struck, my feet unable to move. I inhaled sharply, holding my breath. Could it be? Impossible! But, I could never forget the particular play of her countenance, the manner in which her dark curls escaped and twined around the edge of her bonnet, and the way she tilted her head to the side. It could be none other.

Across the street stood Elizabeth Bennet, the one woman in this world who, when offered my heart, had cast it aside like refuse.

"Come now, Maggie, you must keep up," she called to the maid following her. "The carriage is waiting."

"It's the child, ma'am. She squirms so."

"Give her to me." She reached for the small girl, straightening the cap that had slipped askew on her chestnut-coloured locks. The babe howled in protest.

"I know, I know. You no longer wish to be carried; you want to walk, but you cannot. The pavement is far too uneven. You might fall and soil your pretty frock. Hush now. We will soon be home, and you shall have your bread and jam."

I thought of the last time I had seen Elizabeth—in the grove at Rosings Park, the scene seared in my memory. It had been morning then also, but springtime instead of autumn, the earth verdant and blooming with new life. My aunt's numerous, carefully tended beds of lilies had blanketed the grounds with their sweet aroma of Easter.

How shocked and hesitant Elizabeth had appeared when I asked her to read the letter I had laboured over all night! For a moment, I had doubted she would consent to my request, but when at last she took the composition from my hand, I had fled the place with as much dignity as I could summon.

And now, here we stood in the midst of Hanover Square on a morning filled with sunshine and promise…over two years later.

After Elizabeth had refused me with such incivility, had I not moved heaven and earth to escape her presence? I had spent the past years avoiding the very country in which she dwelt. Why, I had even skirted Napoleon's army to reach Naples and Rome. I had tramped through enough ancient ruins to drive me mad. At one point, I had sailed for Greece, so great had been my desire to conquer the pain that tormented me, and now it took but one glimpse of her light figure and lovely face to render me as undone as ever.

Unknowingly, I remained transfixed, so stunned that I forgot where I was and why. I had just walked past one of the reigning obelisks standing guard in front of St. George's Church, my head down, bent on making my way up the broad stone steps of the portico. What made me turn to look across the street? And why should she—of all people—be there at that point in time?

"I say, Darce, are you coming?"

I started at the sound of my cousin's voice, but I could not break my gaze. She wore a pale yellow dress I did not recall having seen before, a green shawl draped over her arms. I remembered the shawl. Had she not worn that to Easter services at Hunsford church? How pathetic was I! Even her clothing had taken up permanent residence in my memory.

Would she look up? Would she recognize me? At that very moment—as though something greater than ourselves willed it—she raised her head. Our eyes met, and I saw the disbelief that overtook her expression.

"The bride is waiting, Darcy!" Fitzwilliam called loudly, indicating that we must proceed into the church. "Why are you unsettled? You look as though you have seen a ghost!"

Instantly, I gathered my wits, tore my eyes from her, and determined to enter the sanctuary. Yet, when I reached the nearest great Corinthian column, I could not help but look back. I had to capture one last image. I had time only to see her board a carriage, holding the child close to her breast.

I KNOW THE BRIDE WAS BEAUTIFUL, THE CHURCH FILLED WITH GUESTS, and the wedding ceremony perfectly executed, but even under threat of death, I could not relate any of the details. I performed my role as expected, all the while my mind outdoors, across the street, rushing forward, speaking to Miss Bennet, and renewing our acquaintance.

How could I? Was not this wedding of utmost importance? Did not the bride mean more to me than any other person in the world?

Get hold of yourself, man! I muttered under my breath as the bishop proclaimed the final declaration. I smiled and kissed the radiant bride, accepted the good wishes and congratulations of our guests, and trusted I made appropriate remarks.

In my heart, I wished to bolt from the church and seek out the woman I had loved for almost three years. But she was lost to me. Had she not told me with absolute certainty that pursuit of her hand was senseless? And had I not gone forward with my life? Why should I entertain the thought?

"Darcy, this must be the happiest day of your life!" Bingley declared as we walked out the open doorway. "I know you have worried and stewed about the decision far longer than any man should."

"What?" I could not comprehend my friend's words. Of what did he speak?

"The wedding! Have I not watched you walk the floor night after night while considering the perfect match? You cannot deny the importance you have placed on your judgment concerning today's event, for I bore witness to your endless struggle while abroad."

"Yes, yes, of course! All is well." We had stepped out into the sunlight by then, and the carriages lined up like so many black boxes to carry the wedding party to my townhouse for the celebratory breakfast. Instead of looking after my guests as I should, I stood on the top step, examining the area across the street for any sign of her. Might she have returned to the house she came from in Hanover Square? Of course not, for her carriage was nowhere to be seen. But where had she gone? Did she now reside in Town?

And then, the thought struck me. Who was the child? Could it be hers? My heart sank like a heavy stone dropped into a pond.

"Bingley," I called, as he walked ahead of me, "have you had occasion to visit Netherfield since we returned from Italy?"

His eyebrows rose in surprise. "Netherfield? Why, no. Do you not recall I rued the day I had signed a five-year lease, and I was forced to let the property two years ago? I do nothing more than collect the rents now, and my solicitor handles that for me. Did you not advise me to do that very thing? As I recall, you cautioned me to stay away from Hertfordshire. You said it was best for all concerned."

"I did," I said grimly, regret furrowing my brow. "I simply wondered whether you had followed my recommendation."

"I have hardly had time for anything else, trailing behind you in your travels. It has been little more than a month past since we returned, so how could I have spent time at Netherfield?"

I sighed and put on my hat once again. "I just wondered whether you or Caroline ever heard what had become of Miss Bennet or her sisters."

Now, it was Bingley's turn to look cast down. I repented having spoken, seeing the discomfort that clouded his eyes. It was obvious he still cared for Jane Bennet. Never once during our absence from England had my friend fallen in love again. What dupes we were, carrying torches for matches undeniably unsuitable!

"It is of no matter," I said quickly. "Come, let us celebrate the day."

"I WILL WAGER I KNOW WHAT YOU ARE THINKING," CAROLINE BINGLEY SAID, standing closer than necessary and leaning towards me as though we were confidants, making the tall white ostrich feathers on her headdress tickle my ear.

I groaned inwardly, dreading whatever my friend's sister would shortly impart. How Bingley could possess two of the dullest and most meddlesome sisters in all of London baffled me. Their manners bore little resemblance to those of their brother, and it took but a brief amount of time in their company to drive me from the room. I was trapped, though, for I could hardly run from the wedding breakfast.

"I think not," I said quietly, moving slightly to avoid the feathers.

"You are thinking how beautiful the bride is and what a fortunate alliance you have secured, are you not?"

"I cannot fault your assessment of her beauty, and I am pleased with the union, but in truth, my mind has travelled some distance from this room."

"Oh? And just where has your imagination carried you?" She purred in that counterfeit tone of affected intimacy she seemed to delight in inflicting upon me.

"Back some years previous when we visited your brother's estate in Hertfordshire. I recall the pleasure a pretty face and a pair of fine eyes afforded me there." From the corner of my vision, I observed Caroline's expression as she attempted to cover her disappointment.

"I see." It was all she could manage to say.

"I was wondering about the Miss Bennets—Jane and Elizabeth, was it not? Have you seen or heard from either of them since Charles and I have been away?"

"Of course not, Mr. Darcy. We hardly travel in the same circles." She sniffed and straightened her neck. "Why ever would you think of such an unfortunate family?"

"Unfortunate? In what way?"

"Their connexions, that mother! Why, I thought you rejoiced when we persuaded Charles to abandon his attentions to Jane Bennet. As I remember, you provided inestimable assistance in that endeavour. Did you not persuade him to join you in that fearful journey abroad during wartime simply to overcome his infatuation?"

"I did." I placed my cup of punch on the table and nodded in greeting to an old friend across the room, encouraging him to join us. "Sometimes, I wonder whether I did Bingley a disservice by my actions."

"You did no such thing!" Caroline began to shake her head and sputter. "Especially in light of the uproar that beset the Bennet family after you left England. As it came about, we did my brother an even greater service than any of us realized at the time."

"What do you mean?" I turned to look at her directly.

By then, my acquaintance had crossed the room, and he claimed my attention, causing Caroline to bite her tongue. While I received his congratulations and compliments on the wedding, I could sense Miss Bingley growing agitated, no doubt alive with eagerness to relate some bit of gossip about the Bennets. I answered the man before me perfunctorily and attempted to keep my mind on the subject we discussed, but all the while I wondered what Miss Bingley wished to tell and whether it would be true or just another spate of her jealous venom directed against the Miss Bennets. Long ago, I had decided that Caroline's prejudice coloured her remarks in their regard. For that matter, I had been forced to admit that my own prejudice had done precisely the same thing.

Since that evening in Kent when Elizabeth Bennet had pronounced me uncivil and ungentlemanlike, I had spent countless nights considering the faults in my character she had brought to my attention. The memory of her censure disturbed my sleep no matter how many miles I had placed between us. It caused me to examine myself and eventually come up wanting. Oh, she had erred in her judgment of Wickham, but I had corrected her impressions of him in the letter I gave her the next day.

As for her other statements, with great dismay I realized Miss Bennet had spoken the truth. Although her accusations had been ill founded and formed on mistaken premises, my behaviour towards her at the time merited severe reproof. It was unpardonable, and I soon grew to think of it with abhorrence. I confess it took some time before I became reasonable enough to allow her words credit. After two years had passed, I knew without a doubt that, the day I had asked Elizabeth to be my wife, I could not have addressed her in a more unspeakable manner. My words assured her refusal. I wondered whether I would ever have the opportunity to beg her forgiveness.

"I thought he would never leave," Caroline said, pulling me back to reality as my guest concluded his conversation and joined a group at the table. "You must allow me to inform you of the dreadful scandal that has befallen the unfortunate Bennet family."

"Scandal?" If I had been reliving the past, that term awakened me to the present most painfully.

"Yes, you know—the Wickham affair."

A chill crawled up my spine. "You are mistaken. I have no knowledge of the matter. Is this purely tattle, madam, or do you know it as fact?"

"Oh, believe me, it is true. It happened here in London, so it could not be concealed."

"Tell me." I gritted my teeth, preparing myself for the worst.

"Mr. Wickham eloped with one of the Bennet sisters, but they never married. Instead, they lived together here in Town for months until he tired of her charms and deserted her, but that is not the end of the story. A child resulted from the union, and the family has been in disgrace ever since. None of them will ever marry well now, as though"—she gave a short laugh—"they ever entertained hopes of doing so."

I felt as though I had been flattened with one quick punch to the gut. Elizabeth and Wickham! She had eloped with him even after I had revealed all in my letter to her. She knew of his immoral character, his attempted designs upon Georgiana, and still she loved him enough to give in to him. Insupportable!

Suddenly, I felt the strongest urge to hit something, be it object or person. Lest I inflict my wrath upon Miss Bingley, who stood there smirking, I made the briefest of bows, turned on my heel, and left the room.

AMONG THE TRAITS I INHERITED FROM MY FATHER, THERE IS ONE IN PARticular I could do without. When I am bedevilled by a question or mystery, I am like a dog with a bone. I cannot leave it alone no matter what recourse I employ. Had I not fled the country to forsake all thoughts of Elizabeth Bennet and her refusal of my proposal? For all the good that had done me! One brief glimpse of her over two weeks prior to my present trip, and memories flooded my heart.

Again and again, I recalled the way her body had moved as she swayed to the music when we danced, how fiery her eyes had grown when angry, and the clever repartee with which we had fenced on most every occasion we had met. Oh, how often she had skilfully parried my verbal feints with challenges softened by a simple arched eyebrow or a sparkling smile!

If I were honest, I should admit that those memories did not prove difficult to recall, for they were never far from my mind. In fact, they hovered about me most every day no matter where I travelled. And now, every word Caroline Bingley had uttered at the wedding breakfast bore witness to the fact that I should consider any attraction to Elizabeth Bennet with repugnance. How could she have given herself to Wickham? She was far too intelligent, far too wise, and far too solicitous of her family to have run away with him. And yet, the fact remained that she had been the sister Wickham had pursued when we were all together in Hertfordshire, for no one could fail to observe how she had been taken in by his charm.

I should forget all about her. I should cast her from my every thought. Had I not almost pulled out my hair trying to do so? Had I not waged that same argument within my soul over and over again? Now, there was even more reason to do so.

Still, I had to know the truth.

To my shame, during the weeks following the wedding, I confess I resorted to every scheme I could think of to find Elizabeth in London. I questioned my friends at the club as to whether any of them had occasion to do business with a Mr. Gardiner, for I had not forgotten the name of her relations in Town. I regretted not having learned two years earlier exactly where the family dwelt or where he maintained his business. Bingley's sisters laughed about Cheapside. That was all I could recall. Upon social occasions, I paid excessive attention to the society doyens in hopes of learning whether any of them were acquainted with Hertfordshire society. I introduced the name of Sir William Lucas. I could not bring myself to ask outright about the Bennets for fear of reviving talk of the scandal.

I even went as far as to ask Caroline Bingley to accompany her brother and me on a ride through Town one day. I desired to visit the music sellers in Leadenhall Market and purchase a new selection to send to Georgiana. Seeking Caroline's advice seemed prudent since she was far more musical than I. With the suggestion that we could end our mission by calling at Gunter's to enjoy a sorbet beneath the shade of the sycamore trees, Bingley's sister readily agreed. Her feelings of flattery at the invitation evolved into frustration when our driver took the long route and progressed through the less fashionable portion of the city until we arrived in Cheapside. When I attempted to casually ask whether she had ever visited Miss Bennet at the home of her relations, I saw instantly what a blunder I had made. Caroline had never confessed to her brother that Jane Bennet had been in London or that she had kept the news from him.

"Whatever do you mean, Mr. Darcy?" she said. "Why should I have occasion to visit Jane Bennet's relations?" Her eyes darted frantically towards her brother, who sat beside her in the carriage, in a desperate signal for me to change the subject, but I could not let it be.

"I thought she might have come to visit them and, in so doing, written to you, as you seemed to be friends at one time."

"Friends? I thought her a pleasant enough diversion in the country, but I hardly think we should ever be called friends."

"But when she fell ill at Netherfield, did she not confide in you as to where in London her connexions lived? I thought I heard you mention Cheapside, and surprisingly enough, here we are."

"Actually, I believe she said *near* Cheapside." Her eyes grew wider and her eyebrows even more animated, attempting to persuade me to cease asking about Miss Bennet before her brother learned of her deceit.

"Near Cheapside, I see. And did she happen to mention how near?"

Caroline sat up straighter as though a pin pinched her back. Lifting her chin, her speech came forth stiff and terse. "In Gracechurch Street if memory serves correctly."

"Ah, Gracechurch Street." I enjoyed her perturbation, and if not for fear that Bingley would discover my part in the prior deception, I would have continued baiting her just to watch her squirm.

"Darcy, why all these questions about the Bennets' relations?" Bingley interjected.

"No reason—simply passing the time since I assume my driver has made several wrong turns and we are confined to a longer excursion than expected."

"I would think the Bennets the last persons you would wish to see after learning of their misfortune," Caroline said.

Bingley's demeanour altered visibly. "Misfortune? What misfortune? Miss Bennet is not ill, is she?"

"Nothing of the sort, Charles," his sister said with a disapproving sneer. "I refer to the fact that Mr. Wickham left one of the sisters with a child born outside of marriage."

He startled, his colour heightened, and he sat forward and turned to face his sister. "When did this happen?"

"While you and Mr. Darcy were travelling. I thought I had written to you about it."

"You did not. Which sister was it?"

"I am not sure. Lucy Stephens told me about it some time ago, but she did not know the girl's given name. I believe, however, that we all remember which sister Mr. Wickham favoured"—she smiled at me like a Cheshire cat—"and which sister favoured him."

I wished I had never brought up the subject.

The next day, I passed up and down Gracechurch Street for some time, even having my footman inquire at the hackney carriage stand as to whether any of the drivers knew which home belonged to a family named Gardiner. It took little more than a few farthings to discover the house. I did not call upon them, though. How could I since we had never been introduced?

Instead, I instructed my driver to repeatedly drive up and down the street until I suspected he thought I had lost my wits. It was all for naught, however, for Elizabeth Bennet did not emerge from any door. I wish I could say I ceased my efforts thereafter, but alas, I repeated my actions for the better part of a week.

As I said, a dog with a bone…and a bone was all I possessed.

At the end of that week, however, I received an unexpected stroke of luck, although it arrived in the form of a bit of ill fortune for my friend Bingley. He called on me early in the morning, waiting with such impatience for the servant to announce him that he almost ran over the man upon entering my study. Clutching a letter in one hand, he raked the other through his hair and fidgeted in a nervous manner as he greeted me.

"Whatever is the matter, Bingley?" I offered to order tea, but he refused, and I was surprised to see him eyeing the bottle of brandy on the table with unfeigned interest. Had it not been so early, I should have offered a glass just to hear his answer.

"Netherfield!" he exclaimed, thrusting the paper onto my desk. "The tenant has vanished without paying the last quarter's rent…and absconded with"—he drew himself up with the drama of a second-rate actor—"three valuable paintings that have been in my family for generations!"

One eyebrow shot up before I could control it, and I gave him a piercing look before picking up the letter. "Generations, Bingley? I seem to recall, only one generation removed, that your family was in trade, and yet you possessed family heirlooms of that magnitude?"

"Well…well," he sputtered, "perhaps not *generations*. But they are valuable, Darcy, mark my word!"

"Why did you leave them at Netherfield, then?"

"I never imagined anyone would steal them, especially not a man who had the means to afford that house! Read the letter. It is all there plain to see." He gestured towards the paper in my hand, and I leaned back against the chair and began my perusal of the document. Bingley's caretaker reported all my friend had related, save the fact that the paintings were as old as Charles had asserted.

"Hmm, so what do you propose to do about the matter?"

"I…I propose to proceed henceforth directly to Hertfordshire to conduct a thorough investigation of the matter, not only with my steward but with the local constable!" Bingley lifted his chin as though he expected me to challenge his declaration.

I felt my pulse quicken at the thought. "A sensible solution, and should you ask me to go with you, I should be glad to do so."

My friend blinked several times as though he could not believe what he had just heard. His mouth remained open as though prepared to refute my expected arguments against such an idea. "Why yes, that would be helpful, Darcy, very helpful, indeed." He sat down suddenly as though my agreement had flattened him.

"And now would you care for a cup of tea?" I could not help but smile at his consternation, but when he nodded, I rang the bell.

And thus, some eighteen days after I had happened to see Miss Elizabeth Bennet across the street from St. George's Church, I now travelled the road to Hertfordshire on the pretext of aiding my friend but all the while in fervent hope that I might put to rest the mystery concerning her fate. I suspected, and rightly so, that Bingley also hoped our paths might cross that of the Miss Bennets before our visit concluded.

Little did we know how quickly that unspoken wish would come to pass.

THE SKY WAS OVERCAST WITH DARK CLOUDS THE DAY WE SET OUT FOR Netherfield, rain having fallen for three days previous. Once we left Town, the country air smelled of mud, mould, and freshly turned earth. Most of the fields had been thoroughly ploughed before the rains came, and many of the furrows had turned into puddles.

Bingley chattered relentlessly from the moment we boarded his carriage —so continuously that I surmised he was much more nervous about the trip than he wished me to detect. More than once he assured me that, upon his written orders, the house would be prepared for our visit, that he thought autumn the perfect season in which to visit Hertfordshire, and that he recalled with delight our last days spent there some three years previous.

When he began to list the names of various local gentry, I thought it time to caution him.

"Do not expect to find people or situations unchanged since we were last at Netherfield," I said. "Much can happen within three years."

"Of course, of course," he answered too quickly, "but do you not wonder whether the Bennets' daughters still reside at Longbourn?"

"I had not given it much thought." I shifted uncomfortably, wondering how I had learned to lie with such ease.

"Have you not? Ever since Caroline related that terrible story about them, I have thought of little else. Do you truly believe one daughter's disgrace should prevent any of them from marrying?"

"Perhaps not marriage in general, but suitable marriages? Yes, that I do believe."

"It is hardly fair for all the sisters to pay the penalty for the transgression of one."

"True, but disgrace is the relevant point, Bingley. It taints the entire family."

He quieted for a while, staring out the window as though deep in thought. I observed the lines between his brows increase the longer he remained silent.

"Tell me, Darcy," he said at last, "do you think Miss Elizabeth Bennet is the sister who involved herself with Wickham?"

Immediate heat tempered my face, and I felt my neck cloth grow uncomfortably tight. "Why do you ask that question?"

"Caroline inferred as much. I wondered at your opinion. Her preference for Wickham did appear obvious as I recall."

"Dog that he is, I cannot believe he could successfully impose himself upon a woman of her intelligence!" I spoke with more force than I intended and regretted that the impact was not lost on my friend. Before he could respond, I attempted to mend my mistake. "Besides, I confided the details of Wickham's unfortunate attempt on Georgiana to Miss Elizabeth. She had every reason to spurn the scoundrel."

Bingley's eyes widened. "You told Miss Elizabeth all you related to me during those late-night conversations in Naples—everything involving Wickham and your sister? How and when did that come about?"

Deuce take it! Why had I revealed that? I had never told anyone of my wretched proposal or of the letter I had written to Elizabeth afterwards. I cleared my throat.

"I had occasion to meet with her at Rosings some months before you and I sailed from Portsmouth. She visited her cousin the Vicar Collins and his wife. Wickham's name came up, and I took the opportunity to enlighten her about his character."

"And how did she answer?"

"I do not know as Fitzwilliam and I were called back to London almost immediately thereafter, and I have not spoken to her since that day."

He seemed to be contemplating the matter, for he remained quiet for a while, and I hoped fervently that I had successfully put the subject to rest.

"Then I hope Caroline spoke in error," he said finally, "for she seemed quite certain it was Miss Elizabeth who bore Wickham's child."

I ground my teeth together and leaned forward to peer out the window, searching the sky for rain, hail, or pestilence—anything to change the subject —for I did not think I could discuss the matter further without resorting to foul language. Suddenly, Bingley gave forth a shout with such passion that my interest was jolted back into the carriage. He pointed out the opposite window, his mouth agape.

"Look, Darcy! It is Miss Bennet and her sister!"

"Where?"

"On the side of the road."

It was true. Some six miles out of London, there stood the Misses Jane and Elizabeth Bennet beneath an arbour of birch trees.

"We must stop!" Bingley ordered, quite excited. "They appear to be stranded."

"I fail to see how we can do anything less," I agreed, all the while my heart beginning to thud a great, drumming cadence in my ears. Bingley tapped on the ceiling with his cane, and as the carriage turned around at his instruction, I felt both apprehension and longing begin to battle within me.

Chapter Two

Bingley descended the carriage first, that familiar, eager anticipation already shining forth from his eyes as he strode towards Miss Bennet. It took fervent concentration for me to descend the vehicle in a more reluctant manner and walk slower by far than my companion. Within my heart, I wanted to race to Elizabeth's side.

Will she greet me with any degree of cordiality? Of course, she would. She had never been less than polite but for the evening I had proposed, and I knew my pompous insults had prompted that lack of civility.

"Miss Bennet," Bingley said with evident delight, "and Miss Elizabeth. With what chance do we meet in this of all places?"

The ladies murmured their greetings and curtsied. I straightened my shoulders and bowed slightly, but I did not speak. I feared my emotions might be revealed if I did. I could not refrain, however, from fixing my eyes upon Elizabeth in the same manner her presence had always provoked in me. How I wished I could perceive her thoughts.

"I fear your carriage has met with a mishap," Bingley continued. "May we be of assistance?"

Miss Bennet blushed before she spoke. "One of the horses threw a shoe."

"Then you do need our help."

"No, sir," Elizabeth said, and my heart beat double-time at the sound of her voice. "That will not be necessary. Our driver has taken the horse to a farm we passed. He will return shortly with the animal re-shod. There is no need for you to delay your journey, Mr. Bingley."

Miss Bennet smiled and nodded in agreement.

"I see," Bingley said, his brows knitting together.

I cleared my throat. "The last farm I saw was at least three miles back. It will take some time before your driver returns."

"All will be well, sir," Elizabeth answered firmly, her eyes meeting mine for the first time. "When we tire of walking in this grove, we may return to the carriage, and as you see, our uncle's manservant accompanies us. We are not unprotected. We will be perfectly well." She met my gaze without flinching. Her meaning was obvious. She did not want our assistance.

"Well," Bingley said. "I hardly see how we can leave you here by the side of the road. Why, any passing band of ruffians might come along."

"Yes," I agreed, taking a step nearer, "and the clouds remain threatening. I fear a storm may overtake us before your man returns."

Just then, a cry arose from the carriage, the plaintive howl a child makes for her mother. Bingley appeared taken aback at the sound, and he and I turned in the direction of the carriage.

"We travel with a child, sir," Miss Bennet said. "You must pardon us so we may attend her." The ladies curtsied briefly and walked quickly towards the carriage. The babe's wails began to grow in intensity until the nurse emerged from the conveyance, whereupon the child shrieked even louder, stretching forth her chubby little arms towards Elizabeth.

"There now, Fan, hush your crying." She took the child from the nurse and placed the little girl's head on her shoulder while patting her back. "There's a sweet girl."

The dead weight that had been my companion of late pulled my heart low once again. It must be true. Elizabeth comforted the baby with manners and expressions that could only be deemed experienced. My disappointment increased as I watched her walk back and forth, continuing her efforts to quiet the child. Her sister directed the footman to fetch a basket from inside the carriage. From within, the maid drew forth a small cup and a bottle of milk. Elizabeth kept her back turned towards us, and I felt as though I could read her thoughts. *She wants nothing more than for us to depart. If we linger, her shame will only worsen.* My heart went out to her, and I wanted to lighten her burden.

Even more, I wished I had slain Wickham when I had the chance!

"Here it is." Miss Bennet handed the cup of milk to Elizabeth. She cradled the child in her arms and placed the cup to her mouth. In doing so, she turned to the babe, and we could see the child begin to slurp like a greedy little piglet. I longed to run from the scene. I had no desire to watch Elizabeth feed Wickham's child, for it provoked unwelcome images of how the child had come to be. In the background, I heard Miss Bennet murmuring her thanks to Bingley and assuring him once more that they would manage if we went on our way. But how could we leave them?

"Miss Bennet," Bingley said, "Darcy and I cannot in good conscience desert you when we have a perfectly adequate carriage in which we might all travel."

"We could not put you to such inconvenience," she protested, and I heard the desperation in her voice.

"It is no inconvenience. Our destination is the same as yours, for I assume you are on your way to Longbourn?" When she nodded, he continued. "And we are bound for Netherfield. Could our meeting be more fortunate? Come now, you and your sister must go with us...and the child, of course."

I looked up to see the expression on Jane's face, and I realized how much she wanted to go with Bingley. It was written all over her countenance. He quickly went on to say that our servants' cart was approaching as he spoke and there would be plenty of room for the nursemaid to ride thereon. He would also tell a footman to remain behind with the abandoned carriage.

"Your uncle's manservant can ride alongside my driver on top until we reach Longbourn so that you will not travel unattended. There, is not that a sensible solution?"

Miss Bennet seemed to direct a beseeching look towards Elizabeth, and she shrugged. I felt relieved. Even though watching her hold Wickham's child made my heart ache, still I did not want to leave her presence. As they accepted Bingley's offer, I struggled to restrain the expression of satisfaction I felt from settling on my face.

One look at Elizabeth's frown as they proceeded towards Mr. Bingley's carriage told me that she dreaded the journey awaiting us. For her sake, part of me hoped the miles flew by, but another part of me wished the trip might never end. Bingley assisted Miss Bennet into the carriage, and in my opinion, his hand seemed to linger upon hers longer than needed. Elizabeth handed the little girl to her sister in order to board the carriage, and that action provoked another cry from the child. Miss Bennet rocked her to and fro, all the while murmuring soothing words while Mr. Bingley offered his hand to Elizabeth. It took all the strength I could muster not to step forward and assist her myself. Instead, I gave pertinent instructions to the manservant and footman travelling with the ladies. Then, I made certain the nurse climbed aboard our luggage cart before heading towards Bingley's carriage.

I heard Miss Bennet speak as I entered.

"Here"—she handed the babe to Elizabeth—"she wants you, as expected."

I watched the child nestle into the crook of her arm, content for the moment with one hand clutching her cup of milk and the other playing with the untied ribbons hanging from Elizabeth's bonnet. Bingley sat directly across from Miss Bennet, his attention rarely drifting from her face, causing me to sit opposite Elizabeth.

"Is everything satisfactory?" Bingley asked me, and upon my affirmation, he returned his smile upon Miss Bennet. "There, now, this solution is agreeable to all parties, is it not?"

Miss Bennet smiled her acceptance while I noted Elizabeth kept her eyes upon the child in her arms. Bingley signalled the driver to commence.

"Tell me, sir, do you plan to stay long at Netherfield?" Miss Bennet asked shyly.

He glanced at me with a somewhat uneasy expression. "I should like to do so. I hope we may stay for some time."

"I suppose sport is exceptionally plentiful this time of year," she said.

"It is, and then I have business with my steward."

Elizabeth cleared her throat. "You have not visited your estate for some time, Mr. Bingley."

"No...we—that is, Darcy and I have been travelling."

"Ah," she murmured.

"Yes," he went on, "for the better part of two years now. Darcy had often told me of the glories of Europe, but because of the war, of course, I had not been able to make the tour. However, with the cautious direction of Darcy's cousin Colonel Fitzwilliam, we were able to avoid the areas of conflict and visit the countries to the south. We have seen many ancient ruins and displays of art—in truth, more than we wished to see—from Athens to Rome to Naples. Would you not agree, Darcy?"

"Indeed? I found myself satisfied with the itinerary."

"I would think two years a long time to be away from one's home," Elizabeth said, "even for a man of the world such as you, Mr. Darcy."

I watched her eyes, wondering at her meaning. They still sparkled as I remembered, yet there was something about them that had not been present two years earlier, something I could not identify. "I do not consider myself so much a man of the world as not to miss my mother country, but yes, I did want to travel. I found it necessary at the time."

"Necessary?" She raised an eyebrow.

"I had a great need to get away, Miss Elizabeth. Surely, you can understand my feelings." I could not help but glare at her. Was it not evident that her rejection of my proposal had sent me racing as far away as possible? I noted with some satisfaction that she sank back against the seat as though I had put her in her place.

"But now, I understand you returned for the wedding," Miss Bennet said. "Allow us to congratulate you, Mr. Darcy, on your good fortune."

"Thank you. That was the uppermost reason for my return."

"And did you meet the bride while on your journey?"

I frowned, for I did not understand Miss Bennet's question. "No," I said slowly, "she remained in England. I admit, our long separation was a great sacrifice, but all turned out well in the end."

Elizabeth sat up straighter, a curious expression upon her face. I could see her unrest growing. What had transpired? Was it something I had said? The child stirred uneasily in her arms as though she sensed her mother's ill humour, and Elizabeth began to rock her in a more animated fashion than necessary. Mr. Bingley and Miss Bennet's conversation faded into the background as I searched for a possible cause for such emotion.

"So, you were well acquainted with the bride before you left England?" Elizabeth suddenly blurted out. "You certainly concealed that fact from Hertfordshire society when you tarried in the country, sir. And again, at Rosings during Easter, I do not recall your having mentioned you were engaged. Just where is Mrs. Darcy? It seems exceedingly early in her marriage for a bridegroom to leave his bride!"

I could not comprehend what she meant. I glanced at Bingley and saw his mouth standing open, as though he had been interrupted mid-sentence. The air in the carriage fairly crackled with tension, and I struggled to recover.

"I beg your pardon?" I said. "I do not understand to whom you refer when you say 'Mrs. Darcy.'"

"Your wife, sir!" Her eyes now flashed with feeling. "Did you not just declare to us with what difficulty you left her when departing for Rome, and here you are, leaving her once more?"

I could not help it. No matter how hard I tried, I know an amused, somewhat smug expression settled upon my countenance. Bingley stuttered something irrelevant. I cannot recall what he said, for my eyes were fixed upon the indignant person in front of me.

"I believe you suffer from the misconception that I am married, Miss Elizabeth," I said at last.

"Misconception? I saw you, sir, outside the church the morning of your wedding."

I did smile then, for I lacked the ability to contain it. "And I saw you across the street, but you are mistaken if you think it was *my* wedding that took place."

"But Colonel Fitzwilliam called to you. He said the bride was waiting."

"She was. My sister, Georgiana, was ready and waiting for me to escort her down the aisle. She is the bride to whom Fitzwilliam referred."

"Your sister?" Her voice emerged barely above a whisper.

"My sister."

Her cheeks flamed as she closed her mouth.

She cares whether I am married! That thought warmed my heart as we travelled on to Longbourn.

Little conversation escaped my lips once the fact of my non-existent marriage had been established. Perhaps Elizabeth felt safer thinking I was permanently entrenched in a marital union. Heaven forbid she might suspect I would renew my addresses to her after she had deemed them so odious at Rosings! On the other hand, if she did fear I would seek to further our acquaintance, that fact might have caused her reticence thereafter.

I do not recall much of the subsequent discussions that took place in Bingley's carriage. I know for certain the one subject that never arose was the child. It was as though all of us pretended she did not exist—much like the proverbial great elephant sitting in the midst of us—and each of us ignored the fact. Naturally, Elizabeth tended to the little girl, and I observed she was a most proficient mother. How tender were her touch and her tone as she petted and soothed the little one!

Just the kind of mother I had envisioned her to be. I remembered dreams of old that had contained a child of mine suckling at her breast. *Long vanished now, man!*

Bitterness rose in my throat until I tasted it. I closed my eyes, hoping to banish my thoughts, and wondered whether my companions thought my silence strange. In truth, it mattered not at all, for Bingley and Miss Bennet continued to converse as though their long separation had lasted no more than a day.

Eventually, I was curious enough about one matter to once more broach conversation. "Miss Elizabeth, since I saw you in Hanover Square on the morning of my sister's wedding, I have long wondered whether you have acquaintances in that section of Town."

She bristled visibly. "And do you find it strange, sir, that I would?"

"Not at all. I wondered whether we might have friends in common since many of my associates live in that area of London."

"We do not," she said pointedly. "Our nursemaid's sister happens to be employed in a residence down the street from St. George's Church. Maggie had requested an opportunity to make a visit while we were in Town, and since she was willing to take Fan with her, I agreed. After I completed my errands, I called to collect them, so any apprehensions you have that we share connexions may be safely laid to rest." She smiled sweetly with that last barb.

I bit my tongue before replying. *Why must she be ever ready to take offense?* "On the contrary, I entertained not the slightest apprehensions," I said evenly. It had the desired effect as I saw an expression of annoyance settle about her countenance.

"Lovely weather we have had lately, do you not agree?" Bingley said, and Miss Bennet immediately nodded, evidently oblivious to our three days of rain.

LATER THAT NIGHT AT NETHERFIELD, I SIGHED, TAKING NOTE THAT ELIZAbeth's scent still lingered about me even while the sting of our conversation remained. It had always attracted me—that hint of fragrance surrounding her—from the first evening we met and I snubbed her at that unfortunate assembly in Meryton.

When had it all changed? When did I begin to find myself obsessed with a need for her like no other I had ever known? I could not remember when or how, but I felt drawn to her before I knew why. And during that journey to Longbourn, sitting in such close proximity, her scent had reawakened that physical longing I hoped to have buried. That is not to say she wore a heavy perfume—quite the opposite. In the past, I had heard her answer Caroline Bingley in the negative when she asked for the name of her perfume, stating she wore none. How remarkable that her natural essence should prove so enticing.

"I say, Darcy," Bingley said with impatience. "Did you hear what I asked?"

I shook my head slightly, surprised that I had not heard his voice. How I regretted leaving thoughts of Elizabeth to return to the drawing room at Netherfield, where we sat following the evening meal. "Forgive me. My mind wandered. What did you say?"

"How soon do you think we might call again at Longbourn?"

I took a swallow of brandy and contemplated how I should answer. While holding my other hand out to the fire as though to warm it, I bided my time. I knew Bingley desired nothing more than to renew his attentions towards Miss Bennet. What should I advise him? For that matter, *why* should I advise him? My poor counsel was the last he needed.

"You are well-suited to make your own decision, Bingley. I think you might visit whenever you wish."

"*I* might visit? Shall you not join me?"

I took another long swallow, finding the warm liquid soothing. "I fail to see why. Miss Bennet is the object of *your* affection, not mine."

"Well…that is…you do approve, I take it?"

"Do you need my approval?"

"Well, no, but I should like to have it all the same."

I smiled slightly.

"I still cannot believe Jane Bennet was in London all that time and you failed to tell me until tonight."

"A gross disservice to you, my friend, and one of which I am ashamed. I have asked your forgiveness, and I trust I have it."

"Of course," Bingley replied. "I simply worry that Miss Bennet no longer holds me in the same regard she did earlier."

"From what I saw in the carriage, you need have little concern. She appears as pleased with your company as ever. As for her sister, well, that is another matter. Feel relieved that you do not seek her approval."

"But they are close, the Miss Bennets. Do you not think Miss Elizabeth's opinion matters to her sister?"

"As I recall, Bingley, upon the one occasion when the matter arose between Miss Elizabeth and me, she expressed the ardent desire that no one should separate you and Miss Bennet."

Bingley's brows knit together. "Then, I do not understand your earlier statement. Why should I feel relieved, as you put it, that I do not seek Miss Elizabeth's approval?"

Blast, I had revealed more than I should! I had been thinking how foolish *I* would be to seek Elizabeth's good will.

"You misunderstand. I meant it is fortunate you do not pursue Miss Elizabeth's *affections*."

"Miss Elizabeth? Of course not!"

"And that is a good thing on your part, my friend, for the man who seeks her hand in marriage...well, let us say, he has my sympathy." *There*, I congratulated myself silently, *I handled that smoothly enough.*

"So, you still think less highly of Miss Bennet's sister, Darcy? That does not surprise me because of the Wickham affair. But, I must say you seem unduly interested in what occurred between Miss Elizabeth and Wickham."

I shifted my stance and turned my attention back to the fire while I struggled to gain control. It would not do to show Bingley exactly how much interest that connection held for me. I placed my glass on the table and moved to sit upon the couch, attempting to compose myself before speaking.

"My interest in that affair matters only in regard to *your* welfare. You must comprehend that a possible union with that family will diminish you in society. It cannot help but do so."

Bingley sighed. "The Bennets have never mingled among the *ton*, and I failed to hear anyone speak of their distress while we were in Town. Do you not think that before long talk will fade away completely, especially if one of them decides to marry and dwell in the country much of the year?"

I knew full well what he contemplated. Had I not amused myself with the improbability of that same state of affairs upon my own part? I felt compelled to warn him. "And what of Caroline? She remains unmarried. If you pursue connexions with such a family, will it not discourage all eligible suitors from calling upon her?"

Bingley sighed again and swirled the brandy in his glass. "I fear Caroline's chances lessen every year. Her false manners have failed to please any suitable man who has ever looked her way. Only the fortune hunters continue to call, and naturally, she will not have them. In truth, Darcy, I think my sister shall remain a spinster and a bitter one at that."

My friend could not have spoken truer words. Caroline Bingley possessed a most disagreeable disposition, one that would require more than the modest fortune she owned to persuade a man to share the remainder of his time on earth with her. I could foresee her living out her life with either Charles or his sister Louisa, but I could not see her securing a husband, especially not if Bingley made an unpropitious marriage.

"Well, then, you have a dilemma before you. Does not duty require you to place your sister's well-being ahead of your own ill-advised pursuits?"

"Must you remind me?" Bingley groaned.

"In good conscience, I cannot do otherwise, my friend. For now, I shall leave you to your own counsel. As for myself, I fail to see any benefit in calling upon the Bennets." Rising, I bade him good evening.

In the sanctuary of my chamber, I opened the drapes and watched the wind and rain beat the leaves from a nearby stand of beech trees. Fortunately, we had delivered the ladies to Longbourn and then made our way to Netherfield an hour before the storm broke. I listened to the torrent hammering a barrage on the roof and caught glimpses of lightning streaking across the sky. If I could view the thoughts in my head, would they appear as irrational as the fury outside my window?

Refrain from visiting Longbourn—would I truly abide by my decision? The estates were situated but three miles apart. How could I dwell so near and forfeit the opportunity at least to gaze upon Elizabeth? If I accompanied Bingley, it would not signify I had renewed my affections for her. I would be supporting my friend, and he would feel more at ease if I went with him. I knew that for a fact. But had I not warned him to avoid Jane Bennet? Would he see my change of heart as approval of his regard?

As my valet assisted me in undressing for bed, my mind continued to wage war back and forth. By the time I dismissed the servant, I had reversed my decision. If truth were told, I was not called upon to argue long. My reserve was easily defeated.

Calling upon the Bennets was the only proper course of action. Mr. Bennet was a gentleman, but everyone knew his lax social habits, and I assumed he would take his time before visiting Netherfield. Did the family not deserve our condescension, seeing that their stature in the neighbourhood had suffered much while we were gone? My persuasive powers in favour of the visit were irresistible.

Face it, man, you cannot wait to see her again. You are as helpless as those beech trees outside in the storm.

ALL OF THREE DAYS PASSED BEFORE WE SET OUT TO CALL AT LONGBOURN. Bingley behaved oddly for much of that period, uncommonly impatient with the servants, unable to sit still for any length of time, and determined to discover new channels whereby he might expend his repressed energy. He entered the fields to shoot hours before I went down for breakfast. I was thankful Bingley's business with his steward that had precipitated our trip to Hertfordshire required much of his attention. Otherwise, he might have decimated all the birds in the county. He exhibited the worst case of nerves I had ever seen. To my mind, he had perfected the art of fidgeting.

Fortunately, several men of the community called at Netherfield during those three days—Sir William Lucas on the first day and Mr. Long and Mr. Phillips on the second. I made a valiant attempt to remain amiable during the visits. I was truly grateful the men had come, for they proved a diversion for Bingley, compelling him to concentrate on something other than his urgent need to see Jane Bennet.

Once I had agreed to go with him on the visit to Longbourn, I cautioned him against singling out Miss Bennet. It would only encourage her. I suggested he direct more effort towards Mr. Bennet. I had little doubt of the mother's welcome, but I had noticed a certain judicious reserve upon the part of Mr. Bennet when we had delivered his daughters from their difficulty on the London road. Perchance, he mistrusted Bingley after such an abrupt cessation of his attentions towards his daughter three years earlier. I certainly would if I were a father.

If I were a father...

Thoughts of the father of Elizabeth's child had failed to leave me no matter how forcefully I attempted to banish them. Wickham! Where was he now? And how could he have deserted Elizabeth and his child? No man in his right mind would have done so. Except a man like Wickham—the faithless scoundrel, seeking no one's good other than his own, determined to use and abuse every woman he could. I should have challenged him when I discovered him with Georgiana at Ramsgate. Why had I failed to do so?

All of this could have been prevented. I gnashed my teeth, regretting I had not acted. At least, I should have warned Mr. Bennet and the other fathers in Hertfordshire society. But no, I had felt too far above simple country folk. I had lacked feeling for my fellow man. I had been too concerned with my own injured pride upon seeing Elizabeth's preference for the blackguard to do the right thing.

"I do hope Miss Bennet is in," Bingley said, as we dismounted in front of Longbourn. "I so long to see her face again."

The day was lovely, the sky a vista of blue, interrupted with naught but traces of wispy clouds dotted here and there. I sighed. Bingley was besotted with Miss Bennet, and I prayed that he gained control of his feelings before he acted foolishly.

Bingley did receive his wish, for upon our entering the parlour, Miss Bennet, her mother, and her younger sister Kitty rose to greet us. The object of my friend's affection blushed a lovely shade of pink when met with his lingering gaze. I found myself irritated to see that Elizabeth would not attend us. Had I made the trip in vain? Would I not even be granted a glance at her fine eyes?

Mrs. Bennet raved over Bingley as much as—if not more than—ever and promptly ignored me. While my friend sat stiffly on the walnut armchair she offered, I remained standing, searching the room for an unobtrusive corner in which I might conceal myself well enough to fade into the background. I looked about. Where could she be? Since entering the house, I had not heard a sound of the child either. Perhaps Elizabeth was above stairs, putting her down for a nap.

After several minutes of trifling conversation, during which no mention of Elizabeth was made, I felt compelled to speak.

"Are your other daughters away from home?" I blurted forth.

Mrs. Bennet appeared startled that I could actually speak, but she quickly recovered and assumed her most imperious pose. "Elizabeth is without, and perhaps you have not heard that Mary is lately married to Mr. Simpkins, a curate from Shropshire."

When I did not answer, Bingley said, "Ah, and Miss Lydia? Is she visiting her married sister?"

Mrs. Bennet drew back as though she had been struck, and I was surprised to see her eyes fill with tears.

"Sadly," Miss Bennet said hastily, "my sister, Lydia, has passed from this life."

Bingley's countenance flushed. "Oh, I am sorely grieved to hear of your loss. Do forgive me, Mrs. Bennet. I...that is, we—Mr. Darcy and I—have been out of the country for some time, or I am certain we would have known of your great misfortune."

"Yes," I murmured, unsure of what else to say. How could such a young, lively girl have died? It must have been a severe fever or some other violent illness. Thank God, Elizabeth had been spared!

Mrs. Bennet sniffed into her handkerchief. "You have no idea how I have suffered from her loss, Mr. Bingley, or how good it is of you to call upon us and offer your condolences. I remember saying at the time, 'If only Mr. Bingley and his sisters were here to bring us comfort.'"

A look of surprise passed over the faces of both Miss Bennet and Kitty at their mother's words, and I could not help but marvel at how the woman could use even her daughter's death as a means of flattering her oldest daughter's former marriage prospect. *I do believe the woman would stoop to any level to secure a husband for her daughter!*

I crossed the room to the window on the pretext of viewing the lawn, but in truth, it was to hide my disdain. Yes, Elizabeth had been correct to call me arrogant and proud, but even she had to admit her mother could provoke a saint.

But then, I caught my breath at the prospect outdoors, for there in the far corner of the park, beneath a golden-leafed chestnut tree, Elizabeth sat in a swing, her daughter in her lap. I watched as the afternoon sun lit up her dark hair with strands of brilliant auburn. An errant curl or two had worked loose and lingered about her shoulders in lovely ringlets. What I would not give to unpin all those curls!

I heard Bingley rise, and knowing our visit was drawing to an end, I could not resist the urge to have a closer look at Elizabeth's face.

"Mrs. Bennet," I said, once again causing her to startle somewhat at my unexpected entrance into the conversation, "would you and your daughters care for a stroll around your park before my friend and I leave? The weather is uncommonly fine today."

Bingley looked like a starving dog that had been thrown a haunch of venison. "Capital idea, Darcy! Shall we?" He looked expectantly at Mrs. Bennet, and I was relieved to see her acquiescence.

"By all means! You must see the garden, Mr. Bingley, for I fear winter will be upon us soon, and the flowers will all fade. I confess I am too tired for a walk, but Jane, Kitty, show our friend the way, and...I suppose you may go too, Mr. Darcy, if you like." She looked me up and down as though I had just emptied the cinders.

I overlooked her obvious slight, bowed stiffly, and followed the others from the room.

What I suffer just to be near Elizabeth! I must be mad!

Chapter Three

Naturally, Longbourn's garden failed to compare to that of Netherfield, much less Pemberley, but the entrance steps were lined with early blooms of scarlet Guernsey lilies amidst remnants of yellow and lilac Georgina dahlias. Across the length of yard, I glimpsed clusters of white buds making an early appearance on the green viburnum leaves against the rock wall. I hardly noticed them, for my eyes were drawn to the sweet chestnut tree where the object of my attention failed to see us approach.

Elizabeth sat in the swing, facing the opposite direction. I assumed the light conversation passing between Bingley and Miss Bennet would have alerted her but for the fact that the child chose that moment to cause a commotion. She began to wail and squirm, determined to depart her mother's lap.

"Very well, Fan," Elizabeth said, "I can see you have had enough swinging for today. Let us see how well you can walk, but take care. The ground is uneven. It is not smooth like the floor in the nursery."

The little one toddled off, her legs moving faster than her equilibrium. Before she could fall, Elizabeth ran, bent over her from the back, and caught her hands to steady her. "You must slow down, or you will fall on your face."

The child would have none of it, though, and continued to push ahead, turning in our direction and walking straight towards us, forcing her mother to follow closely behind. Because she was engaged in protecting the babe, Elizabeth neither straightened up nor let go of the little girl's hands, and thus, she failed to take note of our presence until she could not help but see our feet. I saw the surprise in her eyes when she lifted her head, but even better, I saw the lovely view the bodice of her dress provided. Motherhood certainly had not altered her figure, for it pleased me even more than before. One could not tell she had ever given birth.

"Mr. Bingley, Jane!" she said, standing erect. "And Mr. Darcy." She curtsied and we, of course, greeted her. Kitty picked up the child, provoking a howl of protest.

"Shall I take her in?" Kitty asked, and at Elizabeth's nod, she returned to the house, the babe continuing to utter great wails of anguish.

"I was unaware you had called," Elizabeth said, obviously ill at ease.

"The gentlemen expressed a desire to see the garden," Jane said.

"Ah." Her sister folded her hands and turned to walk with us. As Bingley and Miss Bennet paired off in front, Elizabeth was left to fall into step beside me. We remained silent, and I searched my brain for some disinterested topic of which to speak. Although we now wandered among the asters and near the honeysuckle vines climbing the fence, Bingley and Jane failed to notice or mention them. How they could escape the overpowering sweet aroma of the flowering vine astonished me. Yet, they continued to converse on other subjects as though they had all things in common.

Well, why would they not, I thought. *They love each other.*

I, on the other hand, walked beside the woman I loved but who did not return my affection and with whom I knew the thought of sharing time together was insufferable.

"Have you heard from your sister?" Elizabeth asked suddenly.

"I have. I received a letter this morning. They have reached Bath, and she seems quite content."

"I am pleased to hear it. I hope she will be happy."

I glanced at her and saw her words were sincere. "I believe she will be. Harry is a good man, not good enough for my sister, of course…"

"Of course," she said, laughing lightly. "Judging by the little I know, you hold her in the highest regard."

"If you met her, I believe you would as well."

"No doubt."

"I always wished to introduce you. I regret circumstances never arose that allowed me to do so. I might add that Georgiana expressed the same desire more than once."

Elizabeth turned her head to the side in that way I had always found enchanting and looked up at me. "Your sister sought to make my acquaintance?"

I nodded. "She had oft heard me speak of you, and I am sure that is why."

She stopped and turned to face me. "You spoke of me often, Mr. Darcy?"

Immediately, I realized how I had exposed my feelings. What in blazes had I been thinking? That was the problem: I had not been thinking at all. I had been caught up in the pleasure of walking with Elizabeth and basking in the delicious scent that wafted over me when we inadvertently stepped too close to each other.

"I...that is—naturally, my sister was interested in the people I met while at Netherfield."

"I see," she said, turning back to continue our stroll. "And did you tell her of all my sisters?" The tone of her voice no longer sounded light and pleasing.

"Your sisters? I do not follow your meaning. I suppose I may have mentioned them in passing."

"Did you tell her how Mary embarrassed us by playing the pianoforte so poorly at Mr. Bingley's ball and how shockingly my younger sisters flirted with the gentlemen from the militia? And, oh, yes, how both my mother and my father humiliated our family with their improper conduct at that same ball?" Her eyes flashed with anger. "With such striking descriptions, I am surprised your sister wanted to meet me. But then, perchance, she wished to personally observe such a curiosity!"

I was stunned. I could not reply, for I found it astounding she should still harbour such ill feelings against me after all the time that had passed and after all that had occurred in her life. I struggled to recover.

There was little need, for she gave a deep sigh. "I must return to the house. I am certain Fan will be calling for me by now. Good day, Mr. Darcy." With the briefest of nods, she walked away from me, crossed the lawn, and went into the house.

I let out my breath, exhaling long and hard. Why had I even bothered to renew our acquaintance? Her prejudice against me ran so deep it would be impossible to overcome.

THAT SAME DEEP SADNESS I HAD EXPERIENCED OVER TWO YEARS EARLIER settled about me during the following days.

I spent long, solitary hours recalling the despair that had overtaken me upon first departing Rosings Park. At the time, Elizabeth's rejection had driven me to drink until both Georgiana and Fitzwilliam became alarmed, especially when I refused to reveal the reason for my unusual behaviour. My conduct had been bearish in those days; I shuddered anew at the memories. Tearing about my townhouse in London, barking at the servants in a manner they had never heard from me, short and irritable with my young sister, and refusing to see my friends, I had frightened those who cared for me until they were ready to summon a physician.

If not for the fear I saw in Georgiana's eyes one evening, I know not what might have happened to me. When she begged me to quit drinking, I had threatened to banish her to Pemberley. Thank God, the sight of her tears awakened some sense of decency within me. I had never mistreated my sister, and I abhorred any man who behaved with cruelty towards his family.

From that night on, I settled for a rational amount of brandy in the evening. Still seeking to divert my broken heart, I turned to sport. Daily bouts with my fencing master soon caused him to cast a nervous eye upon my arrivals. No doubt, the ferocity with which I attacked appeared menacing rather than sporting, but not even the expenditure of excessive amounts of energy tired me enough to sleep. Therefore, the evenings found me attending every social function to which I was invited. I knew I was the talk of London society, for rarely during the season had I accepted more than a handful of invitations. And not only did I attend. I danced almost every dance—a novelty that caused more tongues to wag than the Crown Prince's latest peccadillo. Oh, I could hear their whispers: *"Darcy dancing with such abandonment? Impossible! What has taken hold of him?"*

When those efforts failed to assuage my grief, one evening I had recklessly extended an open invitation to Bingley, Caroline, and Mr. and Mrs. Hurst to visit me when I returned to Pemberley. Caroline, naturally, anticipated that my unusual generosity meant only one thing: I wished to further the possibility of an attachment between us. For although Bingley had oft times visited my Derbyshire estate, I had never before included his sisters. Her mistaken notion caused me to turn around mid-way during my journey from Town to the country and go back to London. I had left the city several days before Bingley's family was scheduled to set out, wishing to reach my home alone and have the house to myself for a day or so. I had chosen to make the trip on horseback rather than carriage. Just outside Northamptonshire, I realized how my actions would encourage Caroline's false impressions. I could not do that to her, for I felt an unexpected sympathy towards one who desired someone she would never have. I understood her feelings all too well.

Upon returning to London and after making my apologies to Bingley's family for cancelling the invitation, I made plans to go abroad. Bingley had been only too happy to attend me as he, too, sought to overcome his disappointment. Fortunately, I left an excellent steward in charge at Pemberley, one who promptly kept me apprised of matters without fail.

Leaving Georgiana had not been easy, but I had called upon my uncle, the Earl of Matlock, and his wife to care for her. Fitzwilliam would also see to her, and even though he was sometimes called away on military duties, for the most part, he remained in England while I was gone. When, at Easter last, he wrote to say my young sister had fallen in love, I found myself beset with guilt that I was not present to judge her suitor. My family assured me that the man was worthy, the alliance was fortunate, and even though Georgiana was but eighteen, she was ready for marriage. Still, I had wrestled with the final decision, but after much correspondence, I had agreed to the union, for I could not inflict a broken heart upon my dearest sister.

Now, roaming the halls of Netherfield House, I realized my own heart was caught in a predicament, but I knew for certain that running away would not absolve the pain gnawing deep within me. It had failed to do so two years ago, and it would fail again. So, I plunged into sport. Daily rounds of shooting with Bingley filled the days, and I read as much as possible in the evenings while my friend vacillated in his decision about Jane Bennet. His visit to Longbourn had only increased his reawakened ardour for her. He struggled over whether to continue to see her, and I searched deep within myself for the strength to finally put aside the feelings I felt for Elizabeth.

To begin with, I knew I had come to Hertfordshire on a fool's errand. Her disgrace forbade any future with her I might ever have contemplated. Once again, I could see my decisions had been ruled by my heart and not my head. My desire to see her had robbed me of the good sense with which I had been born. Even if she cared for me, we could never marry. If my relations, especially my aunt Lady Catherine de Bourgh, had disapproved of Elizabeth Bennet years earlier—and I suspected she had—I could imagine their horror to know I would even consider such a union now that her reputation had been tarnished beyond repair.

I began to feel as though part of me had died. The knowledge that

Elizabeth still held me in contempt because of my previous censure of her family sealed my tomb. She had not forgiven me, and I knew without a doubt she never would.

The facts were clear: she chose Wickham, and now we both must bear the consequences.

"I have made up my mind, Darcy," Bingley announced at the table a week after our visit to Longbourn. "I cannot pursue my present course of action. Your judgment is true and right. I must not cause Miss Bennet to hope for a proposal when to do so would harm Caroline's chances at marriage."

I placed my fork upon my plate.

"Have you nothing to say?"

I shrugged. "It is your decision. I know you have given it much consideration, and I regret I must agree. To lead a lady of Miss Bennet's worth into unfounded anticipation would result in disappointment and possible heartbreak."

He appeared resigned but disheartened as he sipped from his cup of coffee. "I fear she will mistake my absence. She may think I do not consider her worthy of my attentions. I thought I might call on her today and give her some explanation."

"You enter a precarious path, Bingley. I fail to see how you can give an account that will not sound like rejection."

We left the table and walked down the hall to the billiards room before he answered. "What else can I do, Darcy? To cease calling upon her without giving a reason is cruel. And yet, elucidation of my thoughts may cause her further unhappiness. Whatever I do, she will hate me, and without her, I know that I shall never be happy in this life."

I nodded and chalked my cue stick. "Believe me, my friend, I understand."

"Seldom have I heard an expression of sympathy come from you concerning matters of the heart. I find your understanding remarkable."

"In what way?"

"One would almost think you possessed a romantic nature—you, who have always put duty first. Can it be that the great Fitzwilliam Darcy has lost his heart to one beneath him, and if so, to whom?"

I leaned over the table and lined up my shot. "Do not fear, Bingley. No woman owns my heart."

The only woman to whom I offered it threw it back in my face.

"One day," he said after I missed the shot, "I suspect you will fall in love, and when you do, it will be forever."

There was no need to reply. Bingley spoke the truth.

ON THE MORROW, BINGLEY CLIMBED INTO THE SADDLE TO EMBARK UPON his sad obligation. I mounted my horse and determined to ride until over-come by exhaustion. Perhaps then, I might be able to sleep. I set out for the country lanes south of Netherfield. I had not explored them in a long time, and I hoped they would be deserted so I might race my steed a good, long while. I needed the wind in my face to blow away the cobwebs of misery that consumed me.

I rode hard until my horse tired. Slowing the pace, I turned back in the direction from whence I had travelled, but rather than taking the road to Netherfield, I skirted the estate and continued my ride to the north. I was more than familiar with that area, for the road that led to Longbourn joined it soon enough. I had no desire to travel in that direction, so I wandered through a heavily wooded area onto a path that led to Lucas Lodge.

I allowed the horse to walk at will. The mild autumn had caused many of the trees that normally changed colour to remain green, intermingled with a scattering of willows turning yellow, maples slightly red, and beech trees becoming gold and purple. Hertfordshire was a pretty county—that fact I could not deny. Still, I preferred the wild peaks and dales of Derbyshire.

I should go home, I thought, *and Bingley should return to London. The longer we remain at Netherfield, the greater our melancholy.*

Yes, I would go home, for a proper master should never have remained absent for as long as I had. It would be a relief to be at Pemberley again… away from Elizabeth.

My mind made up, I was about to turn the horse to the left when I saw Sir William's house ahead. *I should call on him,* I thought. Bingley had returned his visit the day before, but I had begged off from going with him. Unfortunately, I still struggled to renounce my arrogant attitude towards the country society of Hertfordshire as I had vowed I would do. A visit to Sir William was in order, but I dreaded the tedium awaiting me at Lucas Lodge. Taking a deep breath, I squared my shoulders and picked up the reins.

"Kitty, wait!"

I stopped short. *That is Elizabeth's voice.* Looking around, I saw Catherine Bennet advancing upon me, carrying an archery bow and a quiver of arrows. Down the road behind her ran Elizabeth, waving her arm to alert her sister.

Upon hearing her name called, Kitty turned to wait for Elizabeth to catch up. I was some distance from them but near enough to hear their conversation.

"Kitty, you forgot my letter to Charlotte. Pray, give it to Maria so she may send it with hers when she writes her sister. You know I cannot correspond directly because Mr. Collins will no longer allow it."

"The old cavil-coot," the younger girl said. Turning in my direction, she took a step and then stopped, her mouth agape when she saw me. "Look, Lizzy, Mr. Darcy is up ahead."

Elizabeth raised her eyes to recognize me, looking much as she had when once I had happened upon her in Rosings Park. She wore a soft, pink-sprigged muslin dress with a spencer the colour of dark wine that complimented her cheeks made rosy by exercise. She gazed towards me with an irresolute expression as though she dared me to ride by without speaking as I had done upon that previous occasion in Kent.

Just do it, I thought. *Turn and ride away. She already thinks ill of you and most likely will welcome your departure.* But then, her eyes yet fixed on mine, she gave the briefest of curtsies.

Oh blast, I cannot leave her!

"You have wandered far from home," I said, dismounting slowly.

"My sister is calling on Maria Lucas," Elizabeth said.

"I was about to visit Sir William. Shall you come with us?"

Elizabeth lowered her gaze to the ground. "No, I—Kitty, go on your way."

The young girl looked from her sister to me, hastily bobbed a curtsy, and turned up the lane to Lucas Lodge.

I watched her go but made no movement to follow.

"Do not let me keep you, Mr. Darcy," Elizabeth said, turning back towards the direction from whence she had come.

I spoke quickly before she could walk away. "Do you not wish to visit Lady Lucas?"

Elizabeth sighed, keeping her eyes on the ground. "We…we are no longer invited to call. Lady Lucas allows Kitty to practice her archery skills with Maria in the back of the garden when no other company is present. No one will see them there. The girls have been friends since they were children."

I did not know what to say. Her family's embarrassment hung suspended in the air between us like an ugly, menacing cloud.

"Forgive me," she said. "If we had known you were going to Lucas Lodge, Kitty would not—"

I shook my head. "It does not matter. I simply found myself in the neighbourhood. I will visit Sir William another day." Holding the horse's reins, I led the animal behind me and crossed the length until I stood beside Elizabeth. "We are enjoying a beautiful day."

"I love this season of the year."

"As do I. I recall it was autumn the first time I arrived in Hertfordshire." She glanced at me, and when I smiled, she did so in return.

"I am surprised to find you out without the child. Have you been granted a reprieve from motherly duties?"

"In truth, I left the house without seeking anyone's permission."

"I suppose even the most caring person needs some bit of solitude."

We fell into step as though it were natural. The horse began to nibble at the available grass carpeting the side of the road. I allowed the reins to slacken as the animal followed us at his leisure. Leaning forward, I pulled a reedy stalk and occupied myself by stripping it into long uneven strands.

"I know not why Fan demands so much of my time. Jane is more capable than I, and Kitty delights in playing with the little one."

"Fan is an unusual name," I said, measuring my words. Elizabeth's mood appeared lighter than the last time we had spoken, and I did not wish to unwittingly spark her anger again.

"It is short for Fanny—Fanny Georgina—Fanny for my mother and Geor— Well, there is no need to speak of whom, for it is obvious." She sighed and turned her face away from me.

I wondered whether she often thought of him. How could she? How could she love Wickham after all I had disclosed about him? Despite my resolve, anger and bewilderment rose within me. I knew I should not speak of it, yet since she disliked me anyway, why should I not ask the question that tormented me day and night. Matters could hardly worsen between us.

"Does Wickham see the child?" My voice sounded harsh—harsher than I had intended.

Elizabeth startled visibly at the mention of his name and shook her head. "He has never seen her."

"Never?" I was incredulous.

"He left for parts unknown before she was born."

"Knowing you were with child? Wickham deserted you before you even gave birth? He should be drawn and quartered!"

Pulling another reed and holding it like a sword, I beat it back and forth against the tall grass while we walked. "I knew he was faithless, but I cannot conceive of a man leaving you in such distress! What is more, for the life of me, I cannot understand why you acted in the manner you did, Elizabeth! How could you turn to him after I revealed his behaviour towards my sister?"

When she did not answer, I stopped walking, suddenly realizing I had outpaced her in my anger and left her behind. Unable to disguise the fierce scowl on my face, I turned to see her standing in the middle of the road. Her hands placed on her hips, she glared at me in horror, her eyes burning with disbelief and her lips tightly pressed together.

"Allow me to understand, sir. You think…you actually think that I—" She moved her hands from her hips and balled them into fists. "Evidently, you regard me with even less esteem than I thought. Tell me, were you taunting me at Longbourn when last we spoke? Did you expect me to believe that you presumed to introduce someone like me—a person of whom you think so little—to your sister?"

I began to feel confused yet apprehensive, as though darkness had fallen and I could no longer see and that somehow I had stepped in something I should have avoided.

"I do not understand. I have never taunted you. I spoke of a time over two years ago when I wished for my sister to meet you…before—"

"Before I plunged my family into disgrace? I see." She took several steps, as though she might strike out through the woods, but then she halted, whirling around in obvious fury. "Mr. Darcy, I am not Fan's mother!"

A noisy buzz began ringing in my head, and I rubbed my hand across my forehead, attempting to make it cease.

"But…the child cries and clings to you."

"And thus, you think she is mine—" She shook her head. "You assume I would forsake all my friends and family and elope with a man like Wickham? And give birth to his child outside of marriage?"

I stood there stricken. Could I have been so easily misled by Caroline as to insult Elizabeth in an even more horrid manner than I had done at

Hunsford when I proposed marriage?

When I spoke, my voice came forth in a ragged whisper. "Then, who is the child's mother?"

Slowly, her countenance altered, its bright colour fading to ash as though her rage was dissipating into shame.

"My sister Lydia," she said softly, casting her eyes to the ground.

"Lydia," I echoed.

"While I travelled with my aunt and uncle that fateful summer, Lydia went with Colonel and Mrs. Forster to Brighton…where Wickham—"

"—seduced her," I finished bitterly.

Her eyes remained downcast. "He convinced her to elope—said they would wed at Gretna Green and, foolish girl, she believed his promise of marriage. They travelled no farther than London. My uncle's investigator followed numerous leads that turned up false. I am sad to report that some three long months passed before my uncle and father found my sister."

"And did your father not insist on marriage?"

"He never had the chance. Wickham had disappeared a fortnight earlier. Instead of seeking out my uncle's house, Lydia had remained in the seedy hotel where Wickham left her, hoping for his return. She was convinced he would come back, that he loved her. My uncle employed detectives to search diligently for the man, but he seems to have vanished from all England."

"And Lydia's passing? When did it occur?"

Elizabeth turned her back to me, and her voice was barely above a whisper. "Shortly after childbirth."

I watched her shoulders shake and knew she had begun to weep. How I longed to take her in my arms and comfort her, but I knew she would not permit it, would hate me even more if I attempted such liberties. I crossed the path to her side and offered my handkerchief.

"She lived long enough to name her baby before she died. She had turned sixteen by then but was still little more than a child herself."

"Forgive me," I said gently, "for thinking it was you who ran away with Wickham. I deserve your reproach for speaking of the matter, but I do feel responsible. I should have warned your father about the rogue when I had opportunity."

She wiped the tears from her cheeks. "It is I who should have warned my father! I, who knew of what the man was capable. You told me in your letter, but I was a fool. I told no one other than Jane, and together we determined we should not blacken Mr. Wickham's reputation needlessly. Needlessly! I am responsible, sir. I urged my father to refuse his permission for Lydia to go to Brighton, but I did not reveal Mr. Wickham's true nature. I never thought he would pay serious attention to my sister, for she had no fortune, no connexions, but I was wrong—terribly wrong. And now, we all must pay the consequences."

Without thinking, I reached out and took her hand in mine. "No, no," I murmured. "I am at fault. If I had only known! If I had not recklessly sailed away, I might have remedied the matter. Instead, I fled the country as quickly as that scoundrel fled London."

Still holding her hand, I could not help but rub my thumb back and forth across her palm. It was small and soft within mine, and I tucked her hand inside the crook of my arm and held it there as we resumed our walk. A blue jay fluttered overhead, and my horse snorted.

"How could you have learned of it?" Elizabeth asked quietly. "It was already too late, for I was in a small village in Derbyshire before I received Jane's letter informing me of the matter. Wickham and Lydia had run off some weeks prior."

I stopped and looked at her. "Derbyshire? You were in Derbyshire? When and where?"

"At Lambton, in early August of that year."

"Why, Lambton is not five miles from Pemberley. In early August, I was on horseback, making my way to my estate. In truth, I had ridden almost half-way there before I changed my mind and returned to Town and from there travelled to Portsmouth to catch a ship to Naples. If only I had found you at Lambton, all might have been avoided."

We gazed into each other's eyes, and I wondered whether she could see that the anguish in mine equalled hers.

"How, sir? How could you or anyone have found them in time?"

"You forget: I know the blackguard well. I know Wickham's habits and the sordid parts of Town he prefers. I should have found him if only I had known."

"And if you did? How could it have been made right? There was nothing to be done. Lydia was ruined and our family along with her."

"Did your father not remove Lydia from your house to await the birth of the babe?"

She nodded. "He found a family living on a farm some ten miles from Longbourn to take her in, but my mother insisted on visiting often. And when Lydia…" Once again, her eyes filled with tears. "When she did not survive, our grief was so great that we could not let her little one go. Fan is the image of my sister, and even though we knew it would be far better if she were reared separate from us, Mamá would not have it. So intense was her distress that my father eventually consented to bring the babe home with us."

A flock of geese overhead flew south, calling to each other. We both raised our gaze to watch the beauty of their symmetry. When they vanished, Elizabeth lowered her eyes to the ground once again. We turned and continued our walk.

"My mother made some attempts at pretence, saying Wickham *had* married Lydia, but since he has never appeared at Longbourn—and soon it will be two years since his daughter's birth—I doubt anyone believes the story."

Abruptly, she withdrew her hand from mine. I realized she could not bear the shame of my disapproval, for I represented society, the same society that condemned her and her family. *Our hypocrisy be damned!* Neither Elizabeth nor her sisters should suffer the degradation Wickham had inflicted upon them.

"You said you do not call at Lucas Lodge," I said. "Is it the same with all of Hertfordshire?"

She nodded. "But for my Aunt Phillips's house, of course."

I felt a tightening in my chest and struggled to breathe. What could I do? How could I right this terrible wrong? I could not bear to see her pain, and I longed to be the one who vanquished it. The fact that I had now forced her to experience the humiliation anew only added to her sorrow. How she must resent my presence!

I looked up to see we had reached a fork in the road. One path led to Longbourn and the other to Netherfield.

"I fear you have long desired my absence," I said. "I shall leave you now."

She raised her eyes to mine and swallowed. "Yes," she said, nodding. "I am sorry you have borne witness to my emotion. Forgive me."

"No, no, there is nothing to forgive, nothing at all." I bowed and mounted my horse. With one final view of her lovely, sad face, I guided the animal in the direction of Netherfield.

Heedless of the horse's fatigue, I flicked the reins and began to race him once again. I needed the wind in my face now more than ever. I yearned for it to drive away all traces of the horror that consumed me. Why had I not been present in Elizabeth's time of distress? Why had I put my own selfish needs first?

I knew those questions would haunt me until I made things right.

Chapter Four

Upon entering Netherfield House, I immediately directed Rodgers, my valet, to pack my bags. Although I was unsure what to do, I determined to act. Somehow, I would correct the wrong that had been done to Elizabeth and her family. To restore their honour, the child needed to be removed from Longbourn, and that involved Wickham!

I knew my best chance of tracing his whereabouts would be to start in London. Of that, I was certain. But what then? Even if I found him, it was now impossible to force Wickham to marry the girl he had wronged. But could I not insist he take responsibility for his child—that he provide for her? I entertained no delusion that he desired to rear the girl on his own, but could he not place her in a proper school? Children born on the wrong side of the blanket commonly grew up in such establishments.

I soon recognised my folly. Wickham would possess insufficient funds to support a child much less schooling. His habits led to numerous debts wherever he lived. And should he somehow stumble into adequate means, he would have no desire to spend them on his daughter.

I sank down in a chair, my urgent call for action suddenly halted. I drummed my fingers on the curved arm. A solution existed; I simply needed to discover it.

My fingers stilled as the idea began to take form.

If I could force Wickham to acknowledge the child, remove her from the Bennets' house, and place her in a suitable school, I would assume the expense, and Elizabeth's family need never know my part in the scheme.

Yes, a plan like that would work, but only if I found Wickham.

Then another thought intruded. Would the Bennets release Fan to her father? But why should they not? Her presence was a burden and humiliation. The circumstances of her birth were hindering their daughters' future chances, but in time and with luck, all memory of the child might fade from society. Would not the Miss Bennets find suitors then?

In my chamber, I nodded at my reflection within the mirror. Yes, I could correct the wrong my arrogance and negligence had allowed to transpire. I must not waste another moment, for far too much time had already elapsed.

While hurrying downstairs, I listened to the sounds of the house, hoping Bingley had returned, for I hated to take my leave by no other means than a note. I heard the front door being opened and smelled the rush of fresh air sweeping into Netherfield's vestibule. I rejoiced to see my friend had come home and was now shedding his hat and coat to the hands of a servant.

"Bingley, I am glad you have returned. I would have a word with you."

He nodded and led the way into the parlour. I could see by the drooping of his shoulders that his mood had not lightened. "And I would have a drink," he said. "Will you join me?"

"Make it small; my time is limited."

He frowned as he poured the brandy. "Why the haste?"

"I return to Town."

"Tomorrow?"

"Tonight."

"Tonight? Whatever for, Darcy?"

"I shall tell you all in a moment. First, tell me of your visit with Miss Bennet."

Bingley sank down on the sofa, laid his head back, and closed his eyes. "I failed."

"Failed? What do you mean?"

"I could not do it, Darcy. One look in Jane's beautiful eyes and I was as lost as ever. I love her, and to speak words that would give her pain…I could not tell her I shall not return."

"Did you not conclude that to do otherwise will contribute to even more unhappiness on her part?"

He sighed and gazed towards the fire. "I am a coward. I cannot bear her sadness. She was so pleased to see me that I recall little else of the visit. I know full well that her mother must have gone on and on with her senseless tattle, but I did not hear it. I could do nothing but gaze upon Jane. Oh, Darcy, what am I to do?" Leaning forward, he held his head in his hands.

I placed my glass on the table. "Bingley, you are your own man. You can decide what you shall do without my counsel. I take but one course of action: I am leaving Hertfordshire. It benefits no one for me to remain."

"How can you say that? You know I desire your companionship, and I certainly need your counsel."

I shook my head. "No, you do not. Your will is your own. You will do what you determine is best, just as I do."

"But what good will come from your departure?" Bingley rose and followed me to the door.

"It was made plain to me today that my presence distresses Miss Elizabeth. I feel certain she desires my absence."

"Miss Elizabeth? I do not understand. Did you meet with her?"

"We met by chance on the road, and she made known to me that she is not the child's mother. Her youngest sister was the one whom Wickham betrayed."

"Lydia! I wonder that Jane did not tell me."

"I do not think it a subject upon which she cares to dwell." I took my hat and coat from the servant. "Mind that you think long and hard whether you proceed with Miss Bennet."

He bade me farewell, a frown still wrinkling his brow. In the carriage, I turned for one last glance as we passed through the gates of Netherfield. Bingley remained standing on the same step, his countenance unchanged.

FOR TEN DAYS, I CANVASSED THE LOWER REALMS OF LONDON WITH THE aid of Harrison, a former Bow Street Runner who had been recommended by my barrister. We combed through unsavoury neighbourhoods, inns, and gambling dens without success. Each night I returned to my townhouse, feeling soiled, weary, and disappointed. It took all within me not to despair. I feared I might never discover Wickham's whereabouts.

Why should I even think he dwelt within the city? From what I had learned through Elizabeth, he must have fled London when he deserted Lydia. Still, that had occurred two years previous. He could have returned by now, and I knew the one person with whom he maintained contact—

Mrs. Younge!

Years earlier and unaware of her true character, I had employed the woman to care for Georgiana the summer she travelled to Ramsgate. Thank God, my sister told me of Wickham's intentions before he could make off with her.

Mrs. Younge had been privy to the entire plot and had aided Wickham's endeavour to elope with Georgiana. I knew the woman had resided in London in earlier times, and I hoped she had returned. Even more so, I hoped Wickham had been restored to her bosom.

I turned the task over to Harrison, for I could no longer stomach the stench of the area in which we had searched. Populated with beggars, many of them mere children dressed in rags, unwashed and unfed—the desperate results of poverty and vice depressed me. Why must it always be the youngest and most helpless who suffered the most? And what was the answer? The coins I gave fed them for a day or so, but it did not provide the solution.

Within three days, Harrison called upon me late in the evening. He had spotted an establishment that might be the one we pursued.

"What makes you think it is the place?" I asked as my servant assisted me in donning my coat.

"A number of young women have been seen frequenting the house, and they are not women of quality, sir. Men call at all hours and are allowed entrance. An older woman, possibly fitting the description of Mrs. Younge, grants them admittance at the door."

We hastened into my waiting carriage and made our plans as we descended into the netherworld of London after dark. Down the street from the house in question, we sat for some time and watched the activity before us. Harrison's description proved apt, and after an hour had passed, I signalled we should approach the house.

"A word of caution, sir," Harrison said. "Would it not be more prudent to call upon the woman in daylight when 'tis more likely she and the other women will be alone with no man to protect them?"

I could see the wisdom in his words, but oh, how I hated to wait! How could I go home to pursue sleep, suspecting the means to my end lay but a few miles across Town? After giving it adequate consideration, I consented, and we returned to the other side of London but not without an assurance from Harrison that he would be on my doorstep early the following day.

Fortunately, the man I had hired was punctual as well as efficient. I knocked on the house of ill repute at seven o'clock that morning. Some time passed before a slovenly young woman peered around the door. Her wrapper hung open, exposing her rumpled nightclothes.

"Come back tonight," she whined. "We ain't slept more than two hours."

Ignoring her plaint, I pushed open the door, and my companion and I brushed past her.

"'Ere now, you cain't come in. I told ya—"

"Where is your employer?" I said roughly.

"Where'd ya think she is? In bed!"

"Then, wake her."

When the girl opened her mouth to refuse, Harrison moved in. "Now!" he barked.

We walked into the garish parlour, reeking of stale tobacco, spilt alcohol, cheap perfume, and body odours. Scarlet, floor-length drapes hung from the windows, their fringe torn loose in places. Stuffing protruded from splits in several of the cushioned couches. Dirty glasses and overfilled trays littered the tables along with empty bottles strewn about the floor. A woman's gown was draped over the back of a settee, and several pair of dingy stockings sagged from the arms of chairs, much like a woman's stringy hair in need of a wash.

Revulsion rose in my throat, and I wondered what depth of poverty led women to degrade themselves in such a profession. For that matter, what lack of self-respect induced men to frequent an establishment like this one?

Quarrelling, angry voices announced the entrance of the woman I sought. I was gratified to see that my pursuit had not gone unrewarded, for there stood Mrs. Younge, hurriedly tying her robe, her henna-rinsed hair in disarray and the lines on her face more pronounced than I remembered.

"Mr. Darcy," she said in a scathing tone after recoiling at first sight of me. "How dare you invade my home at this hour?"

"Your home?" I looked around with withering disdain. "Is that what you call it?"

Her chin rose in defiance, and she straightened her stature. "State your business, sir."

"I believe you know what business—the only business we have ever had in common—the whereabouts of George Wickham. Is he here?"

Her eyes darted about the room before that familiar mask I had seen before descended over her countenance. "No, and I don't know anything about him."

"I do not believe you." I took a step closer and bore down upon her with the strongest, most fearful stare I could manage. Doing so did not prove difficult, for I held the creature before me in utter contempt. "If he is not here, you know where he is, and I shall not leave until I obtain that information."

"I tell you I don't hear from him," she insisted, backing towards the door from whence she had entered. "He's sailed to America, for all I know."

"He has done no such thing, for I have examined the shipping records in detail."

"Then...perhaps he returned to his previous haunts somewhere in Britain —maybe even your precious Derbyshire."

"He would not dare show his face near Pemberley, madam, for my steward would alert me to the fact immediately."

"Well, I don't know where he is, and I insist you leave my house." Although her words sounded brave, they were betrayed by the tremor in her voice.

I made no effort to comply with her order or even to answer her. In a nonchalant manner, I strolled to the window as though she had not spoken. I would have sat upon one of the chairs but for my sheer repugnance at the thought of touching it.

After some moments had passed, she appeared even more anxious. "Why do you plague me like this? I can't help you."

Slowly, I turned to stare at her once again, curling my lip in reproach. "You can, madam, and you will. I shall not leave until I have what I came for."

"Then...then I shall send for the constable! You can't inflict yourself on my house in this manner when I asked you to leave me in peace."

Harrison coughed and gave a low chuckle. "The constable? It should prove entertaining to see you bring the law into this establishment. I should very much like to witness that. Would you not like to see it as well, Mr. Darcy?"

She whirled around to face him but could not speak. The girl who had opened the door for us cried out behind her. By that time, two more women in various forms of undress had crept down from the landing above and hung over the stair railing, transfixed by what they observed. They, too, drew in their breath at the possibility of the constable's arrival.

I simply smiled. "Mrs. Younge has not the least intention of fetching the authorities, do you, madam? She would much rather line her pockets by telling me what I wish to know."

Instantly, the expression in her eyes altered.

"How much? How much will it take for you to give up Wickham?" I withdrew money from inside my coat pocket and fingered several pounds. "Will this amount buy your information?"

Stepping closer, she watched carefully as I extended the money towards her. "He...he's down the street at number six." With great haste, she grabbed for my hand, but I proved faster and pulled it up and away, out of her reach.

"Not until your information proves correct," I said. I nodded at my companion, and we walked out the door.

Mrs. Younge ran behind and called to us on the street. "If you tell him I sent you, I'll deny it."

Ignoring her, we strode briskly down the walkway, searching the doors until we found the number six hanging loosely from a nail. With the horse's head of his cane, Harrison rapped sharply on the door. All was quiet within. Again, he knocked, this time even louder. When no sound of movement was heard, I indicated that he should continue. He began to bang on the door incessantly. We would not let up until someone responded.

At length, we saw the doorknob turn, and a slip of a girl, no more than sixteen at most, allowed us a glimpse of her head.

"What'd ya want?" she said sleepily through the crack in the door.

I did not bother to answer but pushed past her with Harrison close behind. There were only two rooms, but we did not have to invade the second to find our prey. Lying there in bed, barely awakened by the intrusion, lay the companion of my youth, George Wickham.

I WISH I COULD SAY I PERSUADED WICKHAM TO DO THE RIGHT THING simply by appealing to his higher nature, but anyone who knew him would realize that was unachievable. I was certain the man's character was now at its basest. It took threats, coercion and, I confess, the promise of payment to convince him to do as I asked.

Somewhere in the farthest parts of my memory, I recalled a young lad who at one time possessed a kinder, more tender soul. That soul had long been blackened by a life of dissipation, and I no longer could detect any trace of the former within the man before me. Upon learning he had a child, he displayed but the slightest interest.

"Is it a boy?"

With the knowledge it was a girl, he turned up his nose in disgust. "What do I want with a female brat?" he said with a sneer.

"She is your daughter," I said, "flesh of your flesh. Does that not mean anything to you?"

"All the worse she will turn out and the sorrier I shall be to know her."

His refusals filled me with outrage, but I would not give over. I remained a dog with a bone. Over the course of the next week, I hounded him without mercy, and during the hours I needed respite, Harrison took my place.

Wickham possessed numerous reasons to refuse my proposal. He feared returning to Hertfordshire because of Mr. Bennet's anger, the myriad debts he had left unpaid in Meryton, and the fact that he still owed debts of honour in his regiment. I assured him the militia no longer resided in the county and that I would satisfy his local debts in that community. As for facing Mr. Bennet—until I offered sufficient funds to set him up to his satisfaction, Wickham would not dare to beard the den of his offspring's grandfather. Naturally, the rogue wanted more than he could get, but at length, he was reduced to be reasonable. Straightaway, I wasted no time in laying out the plan he was to undertake.

THE DAY I RETURNED TO NETHERFIELD WAS ONE OF AUTUMN'S FINEST. Although cool, the sun reigned supreme, and not a hint of rain lingered in the air. The clouds had vanished.

I was surprised to discover that Bingley not only had houseguests— Caroline and the Hursts—but he was hosting a ball that very evening. Part of me groaned at the thought of enduring the disdain of the local gentry for an entire evening, for I knew they still harboured dislike for my previous arrogant behaviour, yet another part of me thrilled with anticipation at the possibility of seeing Elizabeth once again. Had Bingley dared to invite the Bennets? Would she come?

Fortunately, my arrival in late afternoon precluded spending much time in the presence of Bingley's sisters. My valet required my time to prepare for the evening festivities. I was badly in need of a haircut and, of course, a shave and a bath. Dressing took more than two hours, for I deliberated long and hard on which evening clothes to wear. One would think I was a woman for all the time I wasted on a decision that normally took but a moment's attention. I had no desire to answer the questions I saw reflected in Bingley's eyes or to endure Caroline's fawning attentiveness. No doubt, she would bestow her concentration upon my person throughout the course of the evening. That alone was reason enough to dally in my chamber.

The night's festivities clearly signalled that Bingley's attentions towards Jane had not ceased while I was in London. The Bennets had been invited. If not for the child and Caroline's unmarried state, I could envision him proposing immediately after the ball. Had I made the right decision with my plot to bring Wickham back in order to remove the child? Would I have been wiser to consider stepping in and offering marriage to Caroline?

Insanity!

The hair on the nape of my neck stood up at the very idea! I was a friend to Bingley, but friendship had its limits. No, Wickham claiming the child was the only solution to the problem.

As I made my way into the ballroom, I was relieved to see the evening had already begun. Bingley and his sisters were busily occupied receiving their guests. I avoided the crowd, strolled around the edge of the room until I found a servant with a tray of drinks, and swallowed my first sip of brandy. Hurst soon slipped away from his wife's side and also signalled for a drink. The man imbibed far too heavily, but I had to admit I could understand why.

The throng swelled as more and more of Hertfordshire society arrived. I acknowledged brief greetings from Sir William Lucas and Mr. Long. Relieved that they contented themselves with little conversation on my part, I continued my way around the spacious room. Perhaps, if I kept moving, I might avoid all attempts at exchanging meaningless banter with anyone.

Still arrogant, I thought suddenly. Now, where had that come from? Did I truly believe I was above country society? I told myself I did not—that I simply had nothing in common with them—but the memory of Elizabeth's condemnation echoed in my mind. I swallowed another sip of brandy.

On my right, I heard a bustle of activity and familiar shrieks of delight. Sure enough, Mrs. Bennet had arrived. I watched her flatter Bingley and his sisters while her patient husband suffered behind her. Jane and Kitty Bennet curtsied—but where was Elizabeth?

I moved closer, straining to see over the crowd when, at last, I caught a glimpse of her dark hair. She wore a gown of white, simple but elegant when compared to Caroline's feathers and Mrs. Hurst's velvet. She was so lovely that I felt my senses heighten. I watched the false welcomes of Bingley's sisters and, as soon as she had passed, how they rolled their eyes at each other. Why did Caroline dislike Elizabeth as she did? Was it because she was prettier, more intelligent, and wittier than either of Bingley's sisters, or did it have to do with me? I recalled I had not failed to remark upon Elizabeth's fine eyes and lovely face, but I had never revealed the depth of my feelings for her within the Bingleys' company. At least, I hoped I had not.

The music began, and I dismissed such questions. Bingley asked Miss Bennet to dance. Someone might as well have fired off a shot in the crowd! Throughout the room, audible gasps and murmurs could be heard above the sounds of the musicians. The dowagers around me drew their heads together behind their fans to discuss the dancers, their feathers bobbing ahead of the rhythm while they waved their fans furiously. I dreaded the impression my friend created. With Mrs. Bennet's imagination and the barest hint of gossip, all of Hertfordshire would believe Bingley would ask for Jane Bennet's hand, just as it had years earlier. And now, it would cause even more rumours because of the family's disgrace.

"Look there," a lady whom I did not know said within range of hearing. "Since Mr. Bingley deigns to dance with Jane Bennet, Mr. Perkins has asked Elizabeth to dance. And what is this? Is that young Jenkinson leading Kitty Bennet to the floor?"

I craned my neck to see the man who dared to dance with *my* Elizabeth. He appeared presentable, and my neck cloth grew tight when she favoured him with one of her sparkling smiles. It was all I could do to refrain from marching across the room and snatching her away from him in front of everyone! Of course, that was a scene to be enacted only in my dreams. Still, the fact that she obviously enjoyed his company provoked me. What would I not give to take his place! Instead, I returned to my new occupation of listening in on conversations not meant for my ears.

"It appears Mr. Bingley has overlooked their misfortune, for he did invite the Bennets to the ball," said the woman sitting next to the former speaker.

"And if a man of Mr. Bingley's wealth can deem the girls worthy of attention, then every man in attendance will want to dance with them, for they are still some of the loveliest in the county."

"Hmmph! Men may dance with the Bennet girls, but mark my words: no man of worth will ever marry them."

"You forget Mary Bennet did secure a husband—and she the plainest of them all."

"He is but a poor curate. I hear they hardly have enough to get by. And he would not have married her if he had remained in Hertfordshire, you know. It took an offer of a position in Shropshire where the Bennets' story is most likely unknown before he proposed. I know that for a fact, for I have it from Mrs. Marigold, and she heard it from her cousin, Sally James, who heard it from her cook's daughter who works for our vicar."

I had heard enough. Loudly clearing my throat so they could not miss the sound of it over the music, I glared at them before striding away, but not before I saw with satisfaction the shock registered on their faces.

Immediately, upon conclusion of the dance, I approached Miss Bennet and asked her for the next set. Bingley appeared rather surprised, as he knew my aversion to the art, but he beamed with approval as I led his beloved to the floor.

With a slight blush upon her cheeks, Jane Bennet smiled, and I must admit I appreciated my friend's dilemma, for her classic beauty could not be denied. Her blonde hair glistened, and the sparkle in her blue eyes would have tempted any man if he were not already in love with another.

"I am pleased to see you have returned to Netherfield, Mr. Darcy," she said. "I trust your journey was successful."

"It was," I said and wondered what else in the world I might converse about with her. Fortunately, the dance proved spirited, and with all the skipping and turning required, conversation did not seem necessary. I took the opportunity to glance down the line of participants and saw Elizabeth twirling around with another gentleman.

Now, who in blazes is that man was my first thought, but upon further reflection, I saw that good had been accomplished because Bingley and I had set the example. I did not know how they had fared at previous assemblies since the child had been born, or whether they had even attended any, but I felt certain Mr. Bennet's daughters would not lack partners at this evening's ball. When the final chords of the song were played, I escorted Miss Bennet from the floor and returned her to her family. Her mother appeared shocked at her daughter's companion, but she did not hesitate to call Mrs. Phillips's attention to the fact that I had been her partner. I know what was being said, for she gestured towards me with her fan. All the while, her mouth moved almost as rapidly as her eyebrows danced up and down.

"Well, Darcy," Bingley said, appearing at my side, "what has come over you? Dancing with Jane Bennet without prompting from me? What next? Shall you select another of Mr. Bennet's daughters for the following sets?"

"I believe a breath of air is required before I endure another."

"That is the Darcy I know! I venture you are the only man present who would describe dancing with Miss Bennet as something to be endured."

I smiled slightly. "I meant no discredit towards the lady. She is quite comely."

"She is an angel, man, and you know it."

"How could I fail to acknowledge the fact, for have you not called her by that term most every time we speak?"

"Can you blame me? Was she not light as a feather in your arms? Did not her charms sway you with…"

I smiled again, shook my head, and walked towards the balcony, leaving him to continue rhapsodizing. I felt relieved when the couple standing without left the area as the music began again. I would have the place to myself. Inhaling deeply, I recognized the season would soon change, for the temperature had dropped considerably since the evening had begun. I leaned against the balustrade and stared up into the night sky. Only a star or two blinked in the dark expanse, for a full moon hung high above my head.

Hearing footsteps behind me, I turned just in time to see Elizabeth suddenly halt when she saw that I stood before her. Lowering her head, she turned back towards the ballroom. Not wanting her to leave, I called her name, forcing her to stop and acknowledge my greeting. Slowly, she turned towards me, her face half in shadow. How beautiful she was! That familiar tightness in my chest returned like a well-known friend. Why did I find it hard to breathe when she was near?

"Mr. Darcy," she murmured, "Jane told me you had returned from Town. I am surprised, for I did not expect to see you again. Please do not let me disturb your reverie."

"My reverie is not disturbed." If I had spoken honestly, I should have declared that she disturbed my thoughts, my dreams, my entire life, but I restrained myself. "Do not leave on my account. You will find the coolness of the night air refreshing after the heat of the ballroom."

Seemingly with reluctance, she joined me beneath the moonlit sky. My heart hammered in my chest, and I turned my face away, seeking some topic with which to engage Elizabeth in conversation. "I must admit I did not expect to see you out here."

"Why is that?" she asked quickly. "If I intrude—"

"No, no, that is not what I meant. I wondered how you managed to elude the crowd. Your popularity has certainly reigned tonight. Is this not the first dance you have forfeited?"

She smiled slightly. "I did not know you kept account of my partners, sir."

I shrugged. "I am pleased to see you participate."

"And somewhat surprised?"

"In what way?"

"Are you not astonished that my sisters and I do not lack for partners, given the unfortunate state of our family's reputation?"

I had hoped to hide my presumption. "If you failed to notice, I danced the last with your older sister. I would request the favour of your hand for the next."

She raised her eyes as though to see whether I spoke in jest. I met her gaze with my own, undaunted and without the hint of a smile.

"Mr. Darcy, pray do not think I am ungrateful that your friend extended invitations to my family for tonight's ball. I understand what it signifies, and Mr. Bingley's generosity is to be greatly commended. You, however, must not feel obliged to dance with me or any of my sisters. We will do perfectly well on our own."

I nodded in acknowledgement of her words. "But I, Miss Elizabeth, shall not fare so well if you will not consent to be my partner."

I held out my arm, willing it to remain steady. Ever so slowly, her eyes travelled up to mine where they lingered, seeming to search deep within until at length, she placed her hand on my arm.

Inside, we joined the line forming for the next set as the music began. The musicians had selected a favourite of mine, and I wondered whether Elizabeth shared my feelings. Instead of asking her, however, I remained as mute as a block of wood. The truth is, I could not think of one single subject on which to converse. I was swept into the enchanting and graceful way her body moved as we dipped and swayed and repeated the steps. Her skin glowed in the candlelight, and the blush on her cheeks rivalled that of a perfectly ripened peach. Throughout the dance, my eyes locked upon hers, and she did not avert her face. And at the end, when I was forced to give her up, Elizabeth favoured *me* with a smile.

During the course of the evening, I made every effort to participate in the dancing. Kitty Bennet became quite flustered when I requested a set, and I even forced myself to ask Caroline to join me. I did all of that to insure I did not give the appearance of singling out Elizabeth, for I wished only to demonstrate that she was an agreeable partner. Evidently, I achieved my purpose too well. By the end of the evening, I felt myself sinking into a morose mood, for Elizabeth danced every dance. I know, for I could not fail to observe how she smiled when each man took her hand. I retreated to a corner to nurse my snifter of brandy.

If only she reserved her smiles for no one other than me! If only she felt the same thrill I did when our hands touched!

What if my wishes came true and Elizabeth loved me as I do her? Circumstances disallowed any greater relationship between us because her family was trapped in scandal. Silently, I cursed Wickham anew. His selfishness had ruined much more than Lydia Bennet.

Chapter Five

I t was late in the afternoon, three days following the ball, when a courier arrived bearing a message from Wickham. I snatched up the letter and hastened to Bingley's library, for I knew neither he nor his sisters made much use of the room.

Upon my instructions, Wickham was to have arrived in Meryton within the past two days and rented a room at the inn. At the first opportunity, he was to visit Longbourn and make the offer we had agreed upon to Mr. Bennet. I had cautioned him more than once that no one was to know of my part in the plan.

Tearing open the seal, I hastily read the message and sank down into a chair beside the fireplace.

It will not work. The old man might give up the child eventually but for his daughter, who is adamantly opposed to the plan. I have fulfilled my end of the bargain, and I expect to be paid.

—GW

His daughter! Which daughter objected to removing the cause of the Bennets' shame? Why had the family not welcomed the solution set before them? Did the daughters not wish to marry well?

"Insupportable!" I said aloud.

"What is that, Mr. Darcy?" Caroline Bingley asked, sweeping into the room unexpectedly. "What could prove so vexing to make a frown crease your forehead? I do hope you have not received unfortunate news from Pemberley."

I gritted my teeth. My last desire was conversation with Bingley's sister. I stood, bowed briefly, and muttered, "Pardon me," before exiting the room. I cared not whether she thought me boorish. I had to find Wickham and discover what had gone awry.

Urging my horse through the gates of Netherfield, I galloped down the road to Meryton, but a few miles before I entered the village, I realized my first reaction had been unwise. It would not do for me to be seen in conversation with Wickham. I slowed the animal to a walk and dismounted outside the inn in which he stayed. I strolled along the path with deliberate nonchalance, taking time to study the goods displayed within the windows of the shops, although I had not the slightest interest in ladies' bonnets and gloves.

At the end of the street, I stepped into the Black Stallion, selected a table at the back, and ordered a glass of ale. When the maid brought the drink, I asked her for writing materials, placing some coins on the table. Her eyes widened, and she broke out in a grin as she swept them into her hand. Within moments, she returned with the requested paper, quill, and pot of ink.

I hastily scribbled a note and paid the young boy sweeping the floor to deliver it to Wickham post-haste. After taking a deep swallow from the glass, I left the establishment, mounted my horse, and rode away from the village. Upon reaching Oakham Mount, I paced back and forth, examining the horizon for Wickham's arrival. He took his time complying with my order, leading me to suspect that the lad, upon delivering my note, must have found him in bed.

The sun was setting when I finally heard footsteps approaching.

"Must you select the farthest place from the village for us to meet, Darcy?" Wickham fumed, as he removed his hat and swatted at the dust on his boots.

"It is not far by horse."

"Does it look as though I own a horse?" He shot a scornful sneer in my direction.

"It is essential that we do not meet in public."

"Have you the money?" He sank down on a tree stump, obviously fagged.

"Contrary to your message, you have not fulfilled your charge. Other than the funds I have already given you to cover your passage from Town and room at the inn, payment will not be made until the deed is done."

"Blast it, Darcy! That is just like you! Cheating me again just as before. I did my utmost to secure the child from the Bennets, but it is not to be. Would you have me kidnap the brat?"

"Who will not give her up? Mr. Bennet possesses the authority to hand over the child."

"He is willing to listen, but his daughter Elizabeth refuses."

"Elizabeth! But why?"

"I do not pretend to know what goes on in the female brain. All I know is that she threw a terrible crab! She uttered endless entreaties for her father not to grant my request, and whenever she paused to take a breath, her mother and sisters joined in. Heaven help the wretched man who dwells in a house full of women!"

I began to pace again. Why would not Elizabeth give up the child? Surely, she could see the benefit to her family. Would she doom her sisters and herself to spinsterhood because of Lydia's mistake? No, she was far too intelligent to fail to see the foolishness of her actions.

"You must make a second attempt," I said. "Convince the family that you care for your daughter—that you wish to do right by her, that you demand your privileges as her father."

"And how shall I do that? I am none too popular in that house. Upon my arrival, their old housekeeper came at me with a broom, and the first words out of Bennet's mouth were threats against my life! It took some time before I convinced him to see the reasoning behind my argument."

"Did you even ask to see her?"

"Who?"

"Your daughter!"

"Why should I? If the chit is not to bring me wealth, of what use is she?"

I stopped short. "There! That is why you failed. Why should the Bennets release the girl to you when you show not the slightest interest in her?"

"I offered to send her to school as you said."

"Wickham, use your wits. You know how to charm. God knows you have had years of practice. If you want the prize I have promised, call at Longbourn again, and this time, do more than reason with them. Use your good temper, flattery—whatever it takes to achieve the goal. If you fail, you will not receive one brass farthing from me. Do you understand?"

A scowl drew his mouth down and narrowed his eyes as he stood and replaced his hat. "I might have known nothing you promised would come easy."

"Send word as soon as the task is accomplished."

I swiftly mounted my horse and galloped away before he could utter any further complaint.

FOUR DAYS LATER, I AWOKE WITH A NOW-FAMILIAR SENSE OF DREAD SQUEEZing my head like a tight band. I had little confidence in Wickham, and the more time that passed without word from him, the more I feared he would not follow through with our agreement.

After completing my morning ablutions and dressing, I joined Bingley at the breakfast table. With relief, I saw that neither of his sisters attended him—only Hurst before a plate piled high with biscuits, sausage, eggs, and bacon.

"Good morning, Darcy," Bingley said with a smile, placing his cup in its saucer. "What does the day hold for you?"

"Other than the completion of a letter to Georgiana, nothing of importance," I said, pulling out a chair. The servant poured coffee into my cup, but I decided to forego the dishes on the sideboard. I found I had little appetite.

"Shall we have some sport?" Hurst mumbled between bites.

"Darcy may, but I plan on calling at Longbourn," Bingley answered.

I forced a smile. "And how is the lovely Miss Bennet?"

Bingley's cheerful countenance turned into a frown. "I found the family in an uproar earlier this week."

"Oh?" I sipped my coffee, attempting to feign an air of innocence.

"You will not like what I tell you, Darcy, so brace yourself. It seems Wickham has returned to the county, and he actually called at Longbourn!"

"Wickham?" I strove to appear shocked. "Whatever for?"

"He has come for his child. Jane said he desires to raise her on his own. I find his reason extremely hard to believe, do you not?"

"It does seem out of character, but perhaps he has had a change of heart."

"Wickham? Come now, man! Are we speaking of the same rogue you detest with such vehemence?"

I shrugged. "People have been known to change."

"I cannot believe you think that! After the ill he did you, how can you believe he would come on a mission of merit?"

"I did not say I believed it, Bingley. I simply expressed a familiar truism. People do change."

My friend peered at me as though he suspected I had lost my wits. *I need to retreat*, I thought, *or he will know something is amiss.*

I shrugged again. "But then, as you say, it is highly unlikely of the scoundrel. Tell me, does Mr. Bennet intend to give him the child?"

"No!" Bingley sputtered, sloshing his coffee. "Jane said her father was somewhat willing, but Miss Elizabeth protested to such a degree that he relented and changed his mind. I think the entire family finds the idea abhorrent."

"Humph, I shall be in the stables," Hurst said, rising abruptly, obviously bored with our conversation. "I told Carson to doctor my spaniel's ears, and I must warrant he is not dilatory in his duties." I waited until he walked out the door before speaking further.

"It would solve your dilemma," I said quietly.

Bingley looked up quickly. "What do you mean?"

"Well, think on it. If the child leaves the Bennet household, it may be that their daughters' reputations will gradually return. People have a way of forgetting what is not right in front of them. After Caroline marries or perhaps even before, you might succeed in asking for Miss Bennet's hand with but minimum gossip."

Bingley sank back in his chair. "I had not considered that."

"Had not considered what, Charles?" Caroline asked, coming through the doorway with Mrs. Hurst trailing behind.

"Good morning," I said quickly, rising along with Bingley until the ladies were seated. My sudden and more than usually cheerful greeting succeeded in drawing her attention from her brother's words.

"Why, good morning, Mr. Darcy," she sang, and Mrs. Hurst smiled and echoed her words.

"The blue sky promises a beautiful day," I added. Caroline's eyes lit up when I continued to converse with her. She began some idle chatter, and Mrs. Hurst joined her. Within a short time, I was able to make my escape.

Walking outdoors, I saw my weather prediction had not been false, for although a distinct chill lingered, the sun had climbed well into the sky and had begun to warm the land below. I walked towards the stables, but upon seeing Hurst exit therefrom with the dogs while loading his gun, I decided against riding my horse. I was too restless for a day of sport with

Hurst, and I knew he would argue in favour of it. I was not in the mood to listen to his curses each time he missed a shot, which happened frequently. I preferred a long walk through the Hertfordshire countryside.

Leaves of russet and gold littered the lane all about me. Most of the trees had now shed their glory and stood almost bare, causing what had been former patches of sunlight to burst into full-blown brilliance. The freshly turned fields smelled strongly of nature's scent. I missed Derbyshire. Autumn always reigned majestically throughout the park at Pemberley, and I regretted not seeing it.

Thoughts of home caused me to recall recent correspondence from my steward. I began to go over the accounts in my mind. Fortunately, I had always had a head for numbers and a good memory, so it was easy for me to mentally review the information he had sent the week before. In doing so, I soon became unmindful of my surroundings.

Thus, I was surprised when a distinct sound recalled me to the present. I was not alone. I could hear the voices of a man and a woman coming from around the bend in the road. I was amazed to see how far I had walked, for I found myself a distance from Netherfield Park. Less than a half-mile ahead, I recognized the road to Longbourn crossing the rough path I trod. The bridge over a shallow stream lay but a few yards in the distance, and it was from there that sounds of conversation stemmed.

I heard Elizabeth's voice. I ceased walking and stood perfectly still. Contrary to my previous behaviour at the ball, it was not my nature to eavesdrop, but when I heard Wickham's low rumble, I could not ignore the scene I had happened upon. Quickly, I stepped off the road into a grove of trees so I was hidden from sight lest they walked in my direction.

Unfortunately, even though I strained to hear, I found it necessary to either step out into the open to distinguish their words or move through the wood until I was closer. I chose the latter. I walked from tree to tree until I had a better view. My back stiffened in anger to see Wickham standing far too near Elizabeth, so much so that she took several steps back from him. All the while, they engaged in an exchange that grew more and more heated.

By the time Wickham backed her up against the side of the bridge and leaned towards her, I was about to tear through the bushes and race to her rescue. Instead, Elizabeth pushed away from him and turned her back on Wickham, her face towards me. I could see the anger blazing in her expression even from where I stood, and I heard clearly when she raised her voice.

"I have nothing further to say to you, sir. Please do not detain me any longer." She walked up the lane, away from Wickham and towards me. He slapped his hat against his leg in anger, placed it on his head, tugged at the brim, and strode hastily down the opposite path.

Instead of proceeding in my direction, as soon as Elizabeth heard Wickham's departure, she turned as if to ensure it was so, and then left the road and descended the riverbank. I ventured forth to determine her whereabouts, only to see her standing beneath the bridge. There, hidden from the view of most, she leaned her head against the underside of the stone structure as though her spirit had been trampled.

What should I do?

My mind whirled with the impossibility of the matter. What new scheme had Wickham proposed to cast Elizabeth in such high dudgeon? I had to know. Did the thought of giving up the child yet render such great distress, or had Wickham deviated from our agreed plan?

I removed my hat and smoothed my hair. I glanced up through the branches, searching for an answer. Why must Elizabeth insist on keeping the babe? I had to know the reason before I progressed. Her distrust of Wickham was pronounced, but if she was assured the girl would be placed in a proper school, not one where she would be mistreated, perchance she might change her mind.

And if she does not, what then?

I continued to survey the treetops as though the answer rested upon the tallest limb. Bingley's hopes had risen this morning when I suggested Wickham might provide the means by which he could marry Miss Bennet. I had seen my friend fall in and out of love numerous times over the years, but never had one girl held his heart as long as Jane Bennet. Elizabeth had been right. Bingley and Jane were truly in love.

Stepping out from my refuge, I walked towards the bridge. I took my time, hoping it might appear that I happened upon Elizabeth by chance, but keeping her within sight all the while. My efforts were not in vain, for she did not see me until I had descended the bank and appeared before her within speaking distance.

"Miss Bennet," I said, feigning surprise, "how unusual to find you lingering beneath the bridge."

Hastily, she averted her face, but not before I saw her wipe tears from her eyes. "Mr. Darcy, whatever are you doing here?"

"Exploring the river. It twists and turns some distance."

"It does." She nodded but added nothing more.

"Are you well, Miss Bennet?" I asked cautiously.

She nodded again.

"I beg your pardon, but your distress is evident. Is there some way in which I might be of help?"

She would not look at me but kept her eyes on the ground. "There is nothing you can do, sir. In truth, there is nothing anyone can do." She turned, leaving the shelter of the bridge, and began to walk along the river. I followed, quickly catching up to walk beside her.

"Are you fixed in that opinion? I find it rare that some solution cannot be found to repair almost any situation. Will you not tell me the cause? Is it your family? Is someone ill?"

"No," she answered, "everyone at Longbourn is well. I have just had an unpleasant encounter."

"Have you been injured?" I stopped slightly ahead of her and turned so that we faced each other.

"Not bodily, but if you have a remedy for an illness of the heart, I would welcome that." She smiled slightly.

I wanted to cry, *Oh, Elizabeth, if only I could ask you to give me your heart and allow me to hold it within my safekeeping!* But I did not.

"I believe you must tell me," I said gently, "for it saddens me to see your countenance downcast. Will you not rest a moment? You truly do appear troubled." I indicated a patch of green slightly up the incline where the last of the season's grasses had yet to turn brown.

She took my outstretched hand and made her way to the place indicated where we sat side by side. "It grieves me to tell you, Mr. Darcy, but your enemy has returned to Hertfordshire."

"My enemy?"

"Mr. Wickham has been in residence in Meryton for at least three days."

"Wickham! But why?" I regretted having to affect pretence, but I dared not tell her that he had come on my orders.

"For some reason, he has decided to claim his child."

"Ah, but is that not a good thing?"

"Good? To hand Fan over to the likes of such a man—I cannot believe you, of all people, would sanction that, sir!"

In the face of her anger, I found myself shocked by the depth of it. I struggled to find words that would not cause her more offense. "I admit Wickham's character does not merit fatherhood, but could it be that he has changed? Will you tell me more of what he said?"

"It seems his situation has changed, and somehow he has made his fortune. He claims he now wants to right the wrong he did poor Lydia by taking charge of the child. He means to place her in one of those schools for children…like her." A blush crept up her cheeks.

A slight breeze ruffled her curls, and I longed to reach out and smooth them back. I forced myself to look away and study the ripples the wind provoked upon the water.

"It would benefit my family," Elizabeth murmured. "Papá says my sisters and I might entertain better chances for good marriages if little Fan no longer dwelt with us."

"Your father makes a practical observation. Rumours and gossip have a way of fading once the evidence of disgrace no longer remains within sight."

Elizabeth sighed. "I see your point, but I do not trust Mr. Wickham, and I cannot subject Fan to the misery of leaving the only family she knows, the only people who love her. What would become of her?"

I looked down at the grass and pondered my answer. "I have little knowledge of these things, but from what I hear, girls from those schools often find employment as governesses or ladies' companions."

"I do not wish that sort of future for my niece."

"Of course not." I leaned back on my elbows. "You love the child. It is understandable that you want the best for her, but what future will she have growing up in her present circumstances? Even in the bosom of your family, she will bear the stigma of her unfortunate birth, and of even more importance, her existence bars any successful unions your sisters might make. Once your father is gone—"

She turned quickly and looked directly at me. "Do you think I am not aware of that, sir? Believe me; I have been intimately acquainted with the fact for over two years now."

Her voice had risen in anger, and I sensed I must tread lightly.

I rose and stood before her. "At your cousin's parsonage in Hunsford, you informed me that I had caused the separation of two people who loved each other—your sister and my closest friend. As I recall, you were exceedingly angry in your accusations."

Once again, she blushed. "Pray, Mr. Darcy, do not bring up what I said then. I regret the harshness of my language."

"Your words were just. Since then, I have struggled to right the wrong I committed."

She looked up at me, amazement apparent on her face. "I had no idea."

"Do you not find it curious that, since our return, Bingley courts your sister's favour with such vigour?"

"I…I thought he had come to that attitude on his own—that his actions still met with your disapproval."

"Your rebuke changed my behaviour, Miss Bennet. I could not help but see the harm I had caused, and eventually, I confessed to Bingley my part in separating him from your sister. You were correct to term my friend's feelings as love, for he will have no other. Unhappily, he cannot ask for your sister's hand because of…well, because of the child. He must think of his own unmarried sister and restrain his desires for her benefit. I confess I find him quite miserable much of the time."

She made to stand, and I took her hand to assist. Once she had risen, she raised her lovely face and looked up into my eyes. Reluctantly, I released her.

"What you have said only adds to my distress, Mr. Darcy, for I am caught amidst a great predicament. As long as Fan lives at Longbourn, Jane and Mr. Bingley can never be happy. But if I consent to release Fan to Mr. Wickham, she will be banished to a school and grow up a lonely, unloved child. Can you not see the desperate choice before me?"

"I can." I forced myself to be composed, for the band now tightening 'round my chest left me breathless.

"There is but one remedy before me, sir."

"And what is that?"

Elizabeth turned away, stepped closer to the water, and peered at our reflections therein. "I can marry Mr. Wickham," she murmured.

I staggered, suddenly fearful that I might possibly pitch head-first into the river! "Marry? Wickham? No!" My voice erupted in a roar.

"He offered for my hand a short while before you happened upon me. If I agree to be his wife, he said we could raise Fan far from Longbourn. We could simply disappear. Kitty will have the chance to marry, and of greatest importance, Mr. Bingley might feel free to propose to Jane. I confess I see no other way."

I thrust my hands behind me so she would not see them clenched into fists. A noise roared in my ears, and the thought of Elizabeth married to that rogue turned my stomach to acid.

"There must be another answer. You cannot sacrifice yourself in that manner, Miss Bennet. Marriage to Wickham is abhorrent! Think on it. You could never return to visit your family with that man as your husband. You truly would have to disappear, and how could you bear never seeing your loved ones again?"

"What else can I do, sir? I cannot give up Fan."

"You would rather condemn yourself to a union with that blackguard? Insupportable!"

We stared into each other's eyes. Unconsciously, I had taken a step closer and without thinking, I reached for her hand again. "Elizabeth, no, a thousand times no! You must not do this! I cannot allow it!"

"You, sir?" she said softly, removing her hand from mine. "What is it to you whom I marry?"

I faltered, struggling not to pull her into my arms. I took off my hat and raked my hand through my hair. What had I done by inflicting Wickham on this family? How could I thwart his devious plan? And how Elizabeth would hate me if she knew my part in the stratagem that provoked his proposal! What could I say? I needed time to think.

"Miss Bennet," I said, turning back to face her, "you did not accept Wickham's proposal, did you?"

She shook her head. "He will ask again, though. He is determined to have the child."

"Pray do nothing until I have had time to consider an alternate solution. Will you promise me that much? Marriage to Wickham is a sentence no woman deserves, especially not one as fine as you."

She raised her eyes to mine, and I could see them fill with tears. "But did you not say you thought he might have changed?"

"In fortune, perhaps, but not in essentials—and never enough to deserve you as his wife. Give me time—at least until the morrow—before you make your decision. I shall come to some determination and call at Longbourn."

With a brief bow, I adjusted my hat, turned away, and left Elizabeth standing there.

Chapter Six

The night sky seemed darker than usual when I rode my horse into Meryton. Clouds had moved in and covered the moon. I hoped the animal's vision was sharper than mine, for I could hardly discern the path before me. I passed no one—not unusual that late at night—for I had tarried long at Netherfield, waiting until Caroline and her sister retired before setting out. Hurst was deep in his cups by then and nodding by the fire. Fortunately, Bingley had gone to a card party at the Gouldings. All of us were invited, but I had declined, a fact I could see pleased Caroline no end, for naturally, she had refused to go as well, assuming I preferred her company to that of Hertfordshire society. I, however, foiled each of her attempts to draw me into a card game with the Hursts by toiling long over correspondence to Colonel Fitzwilliam and his father. At last, she and Mrs. Hurst conceded defeat and said goodnight.

Now, I urged the horse forward, for I knew it would be rare to find Wickham yet sober by that time of night. Outside the Black Stallion, I paid a man to go inside in search of him. Within a few moments, Wickham appeared at the door and followed me up the street and around the corner of the building.

Dismounting from my horse, I looped the reins over the metal ring hanging from the nearby post and placed my hat on a nail that had been hammered into the wood. I walked towards Wickham, my head down, but not so low that he failed to see the fire blazing in my eyes. With one swift move, I slammed him up against the side of the brick building, my hands at his throat and my face but inches from his.

"How dare you propose marriage to Elizabeth Bennet!" My voice was low but deadly. "Have you not damaged that family enough?"

"How…how did you know?" he gasped, clawing at the hold I had on his throat.

"That is not your concern."

"Let up, Darcy. I cannot breathe!"

"You will not be able to stand by the time I finish if you fail to tell me the truth!"

"I…I was desperate. Come now; give over. I cannot speak like this."

I loosened my grip slightly but still held him against the wall. He swallowed, taking in a huge gulp of air.

"The old man is not the problem. He agreed to release the child to me when I assured him that she would never live with me, but be placed in a school until she is of age. But the daughter, Darcy! Elizabeth will not be parted from the girl, and her father will not go against her wishes. Because of her objections, I see no other alternative."

"This *alternative* you conjured up was not part of our agreement. I never authorized you to propose marriage to any of Mr. Bennet's daughters. You were simply to convince him that you would see the child properly cared for."

"I tried; believe me. I tell you, he will not release her. You can beat me to a pulp, but it will not get that brat out of Longbourn while Bennet listens to Elizabeth."

I turned away in disgust. I never should have enlisted Wickham's assistance. The man was useless.

"I thought if I could persuade Elizabeth to be my wife, it would solve the problem."

I shook my head. "And how did you think you could ever persuade her to accept the likes of someone like you?"

Wickham brushed his sleeves and straightened his coat. "No need to be nasty. I still have a chance, for she and I have been friends in the past."

"Oh, have you? After you abandoned her youngest sister with child, how can you still think Elizabeth Bennet is your friend?"

"Give me time, Darcy. Some years earlier, I think she preferred me. If I work my charm on her, I see no reason why I cannot bring her 'round again. Women are like horses; a bit of gentling and I'll have the filly eating out of my hand."

My indulgence of the wretch suddenly ended. I would not suffer another word of his insolence. With a single blow, I knocked him to the ground. I braced myself, waiting for him to rise and return the fight, but he lay there moaning and rubbing his jaw.

"Do not go near Elizabeth Bennet or any of her sisters again. Do you understand? Our pact is broken. You have made a thorough blunder of it."

Wickham rose to his knees as I retrieved the reins and began to mount my horse. "Wait, Darcy, we had a bargain. I can still deliver."

"I do not care for your means of delivery. Return to Town and the gutter out of which you crawled. I shall conduct no further business with you."

He continued to beg, and his plaintive wheedling grated on my nerves. As I turned the horse towards Netherfield, I regretted the day I had ever contacted the man.

ON THE MORROW, I EXHIBITED GREATER ILL HUMOUR THAN I HAD EVER displayed as a guest in my friend's house. Bingley's inevitable cheerfulness drove me from his presence while Caroline's playing the coquette provoked me to harshness. Without giving a reason, I bluntly refused Hurst's invitation to join him in sport, and I cannot recall a word of Mrs. Hurst's tedious prattle at the breakfast table. I must have ignored her entirely.

How could I prevent Elizabeth from sacrificing herself in marriage to Wickham? The devilish quandary consumed my every moment, for I did not delude myself into believing the scoundrel would give up on the prize. The possibilities of his further pursuit tormented my dreams, waking me repeatedly until I repented my attempts to sleep and rose from the bed long before the cock announced the dawn. I determined to do whatever it took to spare Elizabeth a lifetime of misery with Wickham. The image of their union was so horrendous that I shuddered more than once.

I thought of approaching Mr. Bennet on my own and attempting to convince him to allow *me* to finance the boarding of his granddaughter at an appropriate establishment. Might Elizabeth be willing if I could personally assure the family that Wickham would have no part in his daughter's life? Mr. Bennet would wish to know why I extended such a generous offer, and what possible reason could I give him? Did I make a practise of going about the country rescuing Wickham's bastards wherever they might be? I could just imagine his commentary on that supposition: *"Mr. Darcy, if you do, I fear the numbers will soon plunge you into financial ruin."*

No, neither Mr. Bennet nor Elizabeth would believe I felt obligated to right Wickham's wrongs. They would suspect I had other motives.

Why did I not listen to the thought that dwelt in the deepest recesses of my heart? If I gave in to my true desire, I would declare my love for Elizabeth and beg her to marry me.

My better sense assured me that a passionate declaration would be rejected. I shuddered anew at the memory of Elizabeth refusing my first proposal. Did she not still feel the same? Could I dare approach her with such an idea?

And then there was the child. Rearing Wickham's child as my own left a bitter taste in my mouth that turned my stomach. Did I love Elizabeth enough to take the child too?

I had been pacing up and down in the gardens at the rear of Netherfield when the possibilities began to take root in my imagination. I loved Elizabeth; there was no denying it. No matter how hard I endeavoured, my ardent feelings for her would never die. Now that Georgiana was safely married, why should I not follow my heart's desire?

Oh, the idea would incense Lady Catherine—I knew that well—but she could either accept my bride or forfeit my company. Fitzwilliam could take my place and suffer our aunt's oppressive favour. I was only too willing to relinquish it.

Nor would the idea sit well with Richard's parents, especially if I were rearing a child born under such circumstances, but the Earl and Countess of Matlock were fair-minded people, not excessively demanding like Lady Catherine. I hoped they would eventually accept the marriage. As for Georgiana's husband, well, that was another matter. They were to make their home far from Pemberley in the North Riding of Yorkshire, so we would not be constantly in each other's company. I felt certain Georgiana would grow to love Elizabeth, for my sister possessed the kindest of natures. When she witnessed my happiness, her affection for me would overcome even her husband's objections, if he had any.

I smiled at the vision of how it could be, how all could turn out well, how ultimately, I could even tolerate the child. Of a sudden, my smile vanished, and my old fears returned. What if Elizabeth refused to marry me? I sank down upon a stone bench in dismay. The cloud on which I had been floating fell apart like pieces of down scattered in the breeze.

I remained in Bingley's garden for much of the afternoon, deep in thought, my fear of rejection doing battle with my hope of happiness. Surely, Elizabeth would see the advantages to my proposal. True, she had spurned me years ago. Her words still echoed in my memory.

"You are the last man in the world whom I could ever be prevailed on to marry!"

Circumstances, though, had changed severely since that day in Mr. Collins's parlour. She was older now and, hopefully, wiser. I dared not dream Elizabeth loved me, but her practical nature had to admit that my offer provided the answer for her sister and Bingley. She could not refuse me in favour of Wickham. I might not be the man she hoped to marry, but I offered more than a wretched life with him.

Wickham! With sudden force, the thought struck me that perchance he had failed to heed my orders and even now proceeded to Longbourn to seek Elizabeth's hand from Mr. Bennet. I raced into the house and up the stairs two at a time. Barking orders at my valet to fetch one of my finer jackets, I changed and strode forth to mount the horse waiting at Bingley's front door.

"Goodness, Mr. Darcy, you do make haste. Shall you return in time for supper?" Caroline Bingley asked, hurrying after me until we stood outdoors.

"Excuse me," I said as I ran down the stone steps, put the spurs to my horse, leaned into the wind, and urged him to race like lightning.

WHEN THE MAID GRANTED ME ENTRANCE TO LONGBOURN, I COULD SEE the door to Mr. Bennet's study was open. My heart sank when I heard Wickham's voice therein.

"Do you not see the advantage to such an arrangement, sir? You are unwilling to part with the child because of your daughter's pleas, and I am unwilling to forsake my quest to provide for my daughter. My marriage to Elizabeth will solve the impasse. Come now, Mr. Bennet, you must acknowledge there is wisdom in my proposal."

Without knocking, I strode into the room, bristling at Wickham, wondering how I was to restrain myself from taking him down then and there.

Mr. Bennet looked taken aback at my unexpected appearance, but as always, he maintained his composure. "Mr. Darcy," he said, rising from the chair behind his desk.

"Mr. Bennet," I said, bowing towards the older man. I did not bother to greet Wickham, but I saw beads of sweat pop out on his forehead at the sight of me.

"See here, Darcy," Wickham began, "you intrude upon a private meeting."

I glared at him before addressing Mr. Bennet. "Sir, you must not give serious consideration to this man's request. I know he proposes marriage to your daughter Elizabeth, and I urge you to refuse him and order him from these premises."

Mr. Bennet knit his brows and cleared his throat. "And might I ask how you have knowledge of this business, sir?"

"Yesterday, I came upon Miss Elizabeth by chance shortly after this man offended her by asking for her hand. She made it quite clear that she has no desire to enter into such a union."

"I have found that a common ploy among women," Wickham interrupted. "They turn down a first proposal to spur on a man's declarations of love. I feel certain that, with a little persuasion on my part and the approval of her father, Elizabeth will come to accept me. After all, we were good friends in the past."

"That is undeniable." Mr. Bennet removed his glasses and carefully laid them on a stack of books. "My daughter did consider you a friend at one time, Mr. Wickham. Indeed, we all welcomed you into our house, but in light of your monstrous behaviour towards my youngest daughter, you must know that neither Elizabeth nor any member of my family would call you friend today!" The gentleman pounded the desk with his fist.

Wickham swallowed.

Mr. Bennet clasped his hands behind his back and began to pace. "The babe you left behind will soon celebrate her second birthday, and you would have me believe that you actually care for her? That you wish to rear her as your daughter? This past week is the first time we have seen you since long before her birth—the first time you have even inquired as to her health!"

"A fact I, uh, I regret, sir. Formerly, my situation was inconsistent at best, and until recently I could not have provided for the child in the manner to which she is entitled."

"Ah yes, that fortune you keep saying you have now acquired." Mr. Bennet ceased pacing, folded his arms, and turned his full attention towards Wickham. "Pray, tell me how that uncommon occurrence can be? But for the amount you owed at the inn, I understand your debts in Meryton from two years prior remain outstanding. On a previous occasion, I also understood your only hopes of securing a living were to marry well. Were you not engaged at one time to an heiress, Miss King? You cannot have married her, for here you are asking for my daughter's hand."

I heard the mockery in Mr. Bennet's voice and watched Wickham begin to squirm.

"It is a peculiar manner under which I have come into means, but rest assured, sir, the amount is substantial. Elizabeth shall want for nothing, and as we discussed before, the child will be enrolled in a fine school."

"And just what type of school would that be?" I interjected. "One of those establishments that so conveniently solve the problem of a gentleman's unwanted child?"

"Where is the harm in that?" Wickham retorted angrily, his voice rising. "It is common practice. Being a gentleman, Darcy, surely you are acquainted with such places."

I took a step towards him and struggled to breathe. My hands were balled into fists, and it was all I could do not to knock Wickham to the floor.

"Gentlemen, let us lower our voices," Mr. Bennet said, walking out around his desk to close the door to his study. "My wife's nerves remain on edge, and I would not cause her undue excitement."

I was embarrassed to have stooped to argue with Wickham in front of Elizabeth's father. To allow myself time to regain control, I walked across the room and gazed out the window.

"As for your proposal, Mr. Wickham," Mr. Bennet said, "my first instinct is to roust you from this house with all the force I would use to club a rat! I made it quite clear when you called earlier in the week that you are not welcome under my roof. What possesses you to think I would consider giving my daughter to you in marriage? I find the very idea repugnant! However, because you are the father of my granddaughter and because I am convinced that removing her from this house would benefit my daughters, I shall discuss the matter with Elizabeth. Meanwhile, do not approach her until after she and I talk. Now, Mr. Darcy, I assume you have business with me, or is this a social call?"

"I would discuss a matter of great importance with you," I said.

"Then I shall ring for the servant to see you out, Mr. Wickham."

Wickham eyed me nervously, opened his mouth as though to argue further, but then bowed towards Mr. Bennet and exited the room. I could not help but expel a great sigh of relief.

"Mr. Darcy," Mr. Bennet said, pulling out his chair and sitting down, "will you take a seat and tell me the nature of your call? I trust I shall not find it as alarming as the one I have just encountered."

Pressing my lips together, I straightened my shoulders and sat down in the chair facing his desk. I knew Mr. Bennet cared only slightly more for me than he did for Wickham, and it would take some doing to convince him that my offer of marriage was any more palatable than the one he had just heard. I cleared my throat and plunged into my solution to his family's difficulty.

I spoke for some time, longer than I had ever talked with the man. I began with the utterly insupportable idea of Elizabeth's marrying Wickham, an argument with which I knew Mr. Bennet agreed. I then raised the possibility of Bingley's attachment to Miss Jane Bennet if the child no longer resided in Hertfordshire. The older man said nothing, but I could sense his curiosity at what I would say next. Clearing my throat, I broached the subject of *my* marriage to Elizabeth with the understanding that we would take the child to be reared at my estate in Derbyshire.

"She will have every convenience that a child of my own would enjoy, and Miss Elizabeth will not suffer the anguish of parting from her. From what I have observed, the child looks upon your daughter almost as her mother."

Mr. Bennet's eyes narrowed, and an amused expression played about his mouth as he peered at me over his spectacles. "Are you saying you will assume the role of father to Wickham's child, Mr. Darcy?"

At the thought of nurturing Wickham's offspring, I felt as though someone had placed my head in a vise. "I…I had not advanced to that point in my plans, sir."

"I see. And what makes you think Elizabeth will accept you? I have never heard her speak of you as a possible suitor she would encourage."

His words caused me to wince, but I prevailed. "She loves her sister—both her sisters; and I believe she will see the opportunities afforded them by removing the child from your house."

Mr. Bennet's eyebrows shot up. "Enough to settle for a marriage she does not desire?"

"I shall do everything in my power to convince her that our marriage will not constitute a hardship on her part. I am a man of resources, sir, and I shall provide adequately for Miss Elizabeth."

"More than adequately, I am sure." Mr. Bennet leaned back in his chair and folded his hands. "Mr. Darcy, I do not doubt your abilities, for rumours of your fortune are well known in the county. What I do doubt is that Elizabeth will consent to be your wife."

I swallowed. My neck cloth suddenly seemed tied far too tightly. "Do I have your permission to ask for her hand, sir?"

He shrugged. "Naturally, I cannot refuse a man of your means, but do not think the task before you a simple one. My daughter has a mind of her own."

"I am fully aware of that fact, sir."

We stood, and I bowed, for it was clear to see he was dismissing me. Mr. Bennet did not offer his hand, but he rang for the servant to see me out, and thus I left the room in search of Elizabeth. A word from the housekeeper indicated I would find her within the walled garden at the far left of the house. Heavily shaded by massive, ancient trees, the grounds beyond the wall had been left much to their natural state, almost like a little wilderness, with various grasses and weeds mingling freely in obvious content. There, sitting on a bench, I found Elizabeth reading a book.

Once inside the environs of the stone walls, I cleared my throat, for I did not wish to startle her. Still, surprise filled her eyes when she looked up to see me standing there. At our previous meeting, I had told her I would call, and yet she wore a pensive expression. Perchance, she did not believe I would keep my word. She rose, and we greeted each other, after which I bade her be seated once more.

"I did not mean to interrupt your reading," I said, stepping closer.

She smiled ever so slightly and waited for me to continue, but of a sudden, I felt completely tongue-tied and gazed at the grass below, remaining silent.

"Did you come alone, Mr. Darcy," she asked at last, "or is Mr. Bingley with you?"

"Alone," I answered, nodding vigorously. *Get hold of yourself, man,* I admonished myself silently. *She will think you a total fool!* "I feel certain he will call within a day or so, for I believe Bingley's horse knows the path to Longbourn almost as well as the way to his own stables."

She smiled again. I walked a few steps away and pretended great interest in the height of the oak trees encircling the garden. I removed my hat and, unconsciously, began to twirl it round and round in my hands. A glance in Elizabeth's direction gave evidence that she considered my actions unusual to say the least, and the longer I remained silent, the more awkward our situation grew. The time was upon me. I had to speak, or she would soon rise and excuse herself from my presence, concluding I *was* an idiot.

I swallowed. "Elizabeth…Miss Bennet, have you given further consideration to Wickham's proposal?"

She sighed. "I have thought of little else since yesterday."

"That is understandable. And have you reached a decision? No, wait —before you answer, allow me to offer my thoughts, for I promised you I would find an alternate resolution." I could not determine whether the look she gave me was hopeful or sceptical. "I think we both agree that marriage to such a scoundrel as Wickham is impossible."

"It would improve my sisters' chances."

"But it would doom you to a life of wretchedness. I know you recognize that fact!"

"Of course, but what else can I do? I refuse to relinquish Fan to Wickham's control. There is no telling what might happen to her!"

"I acknowledge that truth, but there is another way."

"And what might that be, Mr. Darcy? I have searched and reasoned, and I have failed to find another answer. If Fan remains, most likely my sisters and I will never marry. Although Mr. Bingley calls on us, he does not make an offer for Jane's hand."

I took a deep breath, and the words tumbled forth. "You could marry me."

Elizabeth could not have looked more shocked. Her eyes widened, her mouth fell open, and she drew back.

This is not the effect I desire!

I spoke more rapidly than before, hoping to persuade her with my favourable arguments before she had a chance to refuse me. "I know my proposal is not what you expected or desired. I am well acquainted with your feelings on the matter. Be assured I no longer harbour any romantic fancies towards you. Those are over, long dead and buried, but…I propose a marriage of convenience that would offer you a life of ease and solve the problem of removing the child from Longbourn. Your sisters would be freed from the taint of scandal that has plagued your family since Wickham's daughter was born."

When she remained speechless, I grew anxious. "Let us speak with practicality, Elizabeth. I can count on one hand the number of love matches

I know of that led to happy marriages. On the other hand, I have seen countless unions contracted for various reasons other than love, and most have proved satisfactory to both parties."

"I confess, sir," she said slowly, "that your proposal, as you stated, is not at all what I expected. After the words that passed between us in Kent, I never thought you would make an offer for my hand again. As I recall, my language was more than sufficient to preclude a second occurrence."

I closed my eyes for a moment. *So, she still feels the same towards me. How can I overcome her innate dislike?* Taking another deep breath, I continued. "Our situations have altered since then. I no longer make those declarations of love and adoration that you found so…odious, Elizabeth."

"So I noticed," she said softly.

What does that mean? Have I erred again? Does she fear that I think less of her because of the scandal?

"That is not to say I have ceased to admire you," I said quickly. "I have considered anew the prospect of our marriage, and I think you would make an excellent mistress of Pemberley, an honourable wife to preside over my table."

"I see," she said, looking away, "and what about Fan?"

"Naturally, you may bring her with you."

"I understand that much, sir, but will you treat her as your own?"

A sharp pain began to throb in my left temple at the thought of regarding Wickham's child as my daughter. I sighed and cast my eyes to the ground below.

"That…is more than I can offer." I struggled to find suitable words. "To feel affection for a child of Wickham's is beyond my command at present, but you have my word she will not be slighted in my house. It is common practice for a man of my position to rear his ward. The child will want for nothing, and she will, of course, have a place at the table with my own children."

Elizabeth inhaled sharply at my last words. "So, you do expect me to bear your children."

I looked up to meet her eyes. "Without question. I must have an heir —surely, you understand that—but…there is no need for haste. I shall allow you time to settle in the marriage. I will not make any demands before you are agreeable."

She rose and walked slowly towards the exit to the garden, her head down, her fingers playing nervously with the ribbon marking the place in her book. Neither of us spoke until she reached the gate.

"Will you give me an answer, Elizabeth?" I asked hesitantly.

She turned and gazed directly into my eyes. "Why are you doing this, Mr. Darcy? You owe nothing to my family or to me."

"I beg to differ. I wronged your family when I did not warn your father of Wickham's character the first day I observed him set foot in Meryton."

"I told you that is not your fault. I could have warned Papá after I read the account you gave me of Wickham's dealings with your sister."

I shook my head. "That is not the only error I committed. Other than my cousin Colonel Fitzwilliam, Charles Bingley is my closest friend, and I have sinned grievously against him. Because of my arrogance and conceit, I separated two people who love each other. Did you not declare that fact in similar words? If we marry, it will free Bingley and Miss Bennet to live the life they should have lived for over two years now. Also, it may provide the means by which your younger sister can find happiness."

"But what of your own happiness, sir? What do you forego by marrying me?"

I shrugged. "My sister is safely married. Our union will affect her little. As I said yesterday, Bingley does not have that option as long as Caroline remains unmarried and under his protection."

Elizabeth turned her head in that manner I had always found enchanting, and I thought her so lovely I could hardly catch my breath. "You failed to answer my question, sir. What about you? During the years since that day in Kent, have you not found someone to love whom you will lose by this sacrifice you propose?"

I gripped my hat tightly to keep my hands from reaching out and gathering her into my embrace. I wanted to kiss her with all the passion I had repressed for so long. Forcing myself to break our gaze, I turned aside for fear she would see evidence of my great need for her. "Miss Bennet, the woman I love does not love me. I relinquish nothing."

"Might you not somehow win her if you remain unattached? Are you willing to sacrifice that possibility?"

"Rest assured, if you consent to this marriage, I shall remain faithful to you. I shall not be an inconstant husband.

"I have no doubt of your integrity, sir," she said, so faintly that I had to step closer to hear her. "Still, I would not wish you to be unhappy."

She gazed up at me, her expression open and honest. My desire for her was so pressing that I felt myself begin to tremble. Compelling myself to look away from her lovely eyes, I walked ahead and pushed open the gate.

"As I said, my love remains unrequited, so no impediment exists to bar our marriage." As she walked by, her scent washed over me. "All you need do is say yes, Elizabeth."

Chapter Seven

A fortnight later, Elizabeth and I were married by special licence in Longbourn Church with none but her family and Charles Bingley in attendance. A strong blast of cold air had blown in the night before, and clouds had successfully thwarted the appearance of the sun.

At the announcement of my approaching wedding, Mr. and Mrs. Hurst and Caroline suddenly remembered an important social obligation in Town that caused them to depart Netherfield with unmitigated haste. I did not begrudge their unwillingness to attend the ceremony. In truth, I was relieved to see their carriage disappear through the gates, and I assured Bingley that I in no way suffered from the slight. On the evening before they left, Mrs. Hurst's half-hearted congratulatory expressions fell flat while Caroline did not even pretend to hide her displeasure. She spoke openly of the family's scandal and predicted my future wife would never be received in any prominent drawing room in London. When that threat failed to provoke a change in my decision, she resorted to her prior insinuations concerning Elizabeth and Wickham. I silenced her with the truth—that Elizabeth was not the mother of the child and that the babe was born to Lydia and Wickham—but I confess both my manner and words were harsh. I left not the slightest doubt in Caroline's mind that I would not tolerate further disrespect towards my future wife.

As for Wickham, two brawny Netherfield stable hands and I routed him from the county with naught but empty threats on his part. I dismissed his remarks. He was a coward who preyed on young women but was far too fearful to face a man.

I suppose, from a woman's perspective, the wedding seemed a sad little affair, for faint celebration occurred other than a simple breakfast at Longbourn after the ceremony. Mrs. Bennet appeared to be the happiest person there, perhaps because she envisioned a life of prosperity for Elizabeth or, perhaps, she simply rejoiced that another of her daughters had married. At first news of her daughter's engagement to me, Mrs. Bennet had immediately planned a large wedding, but her daughters and husband soon convinced her that would not do. It would be best for us to marry quickly and quietly, drawing as little attention to Longbourn as possible. Elizabeth and I were to leave for London directly, taking the child with us.

Bingley, of course, remained more than cheerful, for we had talked late into the night preceding the ceremony of how the day's transaction would eventually free him to pursue Jane Bennet's hand. I urged him to exercise patience until talk died down and the scandal of the child's birth faded. However, I doubted my friend would tarry long before another wedding took place in Hertfordshire. He simply could not hide his adoration for Elizabeth's sister.

Concealment of my own deep feelings towards Elizabeth proved the most difficult task for me on our wedding day. Joy flooded my heart at the thought of making her my wife. The moment she joined me at the altar, I pressed my lips together to refrain from smiling like a simpleton. She appeared solemn, slightly hesitant when repeating her vows, but resigned. Her reluctance dampened my elation somewhat, but like any fool in love, I refused to believe I could not win her affections once we were husband and wife.

My conceited assurance did not endure for long.

I had arranged for the child and her nurse to travel in the servants' carriage with our luggage, for I longed to be alone with my bride on the trip to Town. The babe had other ideas. Upon seeing Elizabeth boarding a different carriage, she began to bawl with unending furore, causing such bedlam that Elizabeth insisted she ride with us. I bit my tongue, hoping this was not an indication that the remainder of my carefully made plans were not to be. Instead of sitting by my side, Elizabeth placed the child on the seat beside her. There, she petted and soothed her while an image of Wickham laughing at my disappointment danced in my head.

"I am sorry Fan is peevish today," Elizabeth said, once she had lowered the child's volume to a level whereby we might converse. "For some reason, she has always preferred me over Maggie, although the girl has tended her since Fan was six months old."

I made a mental notation: *seek out excellent baby nurse first thing in the morning!*

For at least three-quarters of the journey, Elizabeth cared for the child while I sat across from them, wishing that a great need for sleep would overpower Wickham's daughter. I told myself to be patient, knowing full well I did not possess that particular virtue.

At least I might gaze upon my wife—*my wife!* I could not believe the dream I had harboured for so long had come true, but there sat dearest, loveliest Elizabeth with no need for a chaperone, no need to leave her after a few hours' visit, and—with luck, someday soon, hopefully—no desire on her part to separate herself from my presence.

How long had I wanted her? I thought back over the years, wondering when I began to love her, but I could fix neither upon the day nor the hour. It seemed she had drawn me to her in some unaccountable manner from the first time she turned her head and gave me that saucy look only she could give. Her amused smile had contained a mixture of sweetness and pertness I found irresistible. Neither did that smile fail to hide the challenge flashing from her fine eyes. That earliest encounter had provoked a burning desire in me I doubted would be quenched even on the day I died.

One might ask why Elizabeth had accepted my proposal, for it was evident she was not in love with me. Intelligence, however, she certainly possessed, as well as a practical nature. My arguments in favour of a marriage of convenience had made sense to her, I suppose, for she had waited less than a day before agreeing to be my wife. I was surprised at her insistence on being present when Mr. Bennet and I wrote up the marriage contract. Neither the amount of her pin money nor any other personal provision concerned her. She merely needed it declared in writing that I would always provide for the child. I thought Elizabeth Bennet the most extraordinary woman I had ever met and the most bewitching.

"There, I believe she rests easy at last," Elizabeth said, drawing me back into the present.

"And but a few miles from London," I replied.

"So soon?"

Had I discerned a hint of anxiety in the tone of her voice? I knew not the cause, but I hastened to reassure her. "All should be prepared at my townhouse. The servants have been alerted to our arrival."

She did not answer but, rather, seemed to sink back against the seat as she turned her gaze to the passing landscape.

This is a fine state of affairs, I thought. Now that the child no longer interfered, I could not think of a single subject upon which to converse.

How long will she come between us? I wondered. Seemingly unaware of her actions, Elizabeth continued to smooth back the babe's curls as she slept. For the first time, I examined the child's looks. She was pretty enough, I supposed, plump and healthy. She had inherited Lydia Bennet's chestnut-coloured hair and comely features, but when the little girl smiled or raised her eyebrows in surprise, there was no mistaking Wickham's imprint. *Will I ever be able to hold her in any regard, seeing that she will always remind me of him?*

After clearing my throat, I sat forward and gazed out the window. "The season changes quickly. I predict winter will be upon us within days."

When Elizabeth remained silent, I sat back, but I kept my eyes on the woods outside our carriage—anything to keep from staring at her.

THE MEAL THAT NIGHT WAS SHARED BY TWO ILL-AT-EASE PEOPLE SITTING across from each other and saying little. Of course, when first we arrived, Elizabeth had remarked upon the grandeur of the house and its fine furnishings, but after being introduced to the staff, she had hurried above stairs with the nurse and the babe. I did not see her again until we entered the dining room. I inquired after the child and was told that the large house frightened her, but she had eaten her supper and, hopefully, would not give Maggie much difficulty when put to bed. After that topic had lapsed, neither of us said anything more for the remainder of the meal. Even the delicious aroma of roast beef failed to elicit any comment from my new wife.

Why could we not talk to each other? Where was Elizabeth's sparkling conversation?

After dining, I escorted her into the drawing room and asked whether she would play on the pianoforte, but she declined with such emphasis that I did not insist. I had just poured her a glass of sherry when she suddenly rose from the chair upon which she perched like a bird eager to fly away.

"Thank you, no," she said. "I do not care for sherry tonight. I find myself so tired that I beg you to allow me to retire early."

"If that is your wish," I said, but I could not mask the disappointment in my voice. "Far be it from me to keep you from your bed."

She looked up quickly and frowned as though I had angered her.

"I shall accompany you although I am not yet tired."

Her eyebrows rose. "Then, why should you go with me?"

"To find the book I brought from Netherfield. By now, my valet has finished unpacking. Since you do not care to sit with me, I shall have to content myself with the *Lyrical Ballads* of Wordsworth and Coleridge."

"I do not retire to avoid your company."

"Do you not?"

She raised her chin. "I am truly weary. The day has been long and eventful."

By that time, we had reached the stairs, and I stood back so she might ascend before me. A curl or two had escaped her hairpins, and I watched the dark wisps caress her neck as I followed her. Thoughts of my hands doing the same flooded my mind. Of a sudden, she stopped mid-flight and turned to face me.

"Am I not entitled to some time to myself?"

"Do you begrudge me climbing the stairs with you?"

"Of course not, but I fail to understand why you think that I attempt to avoid your company."

I passed her by and proceeded up the stairs. "I suppose I am somewhat vexed."

She hurried after me. "But why? What have I done?"

Opening the door to my chamber, I walked in before answering. Elizabeth remained in the hall. "This evening—this day—has not transpired as I hoped it would."

"Lest you think otherwise, let me assure you, it has hardly fulfilled the dreams of my wedding day either!" With that, she entered her chamber and firmly shut the door.

So much for our wedding night! Angrily, I slammed the door to my room and hoped she heard it. After fuming about the chamber for some time, I calmed myself and began to search for the book. It had not been left on the bedside table or on the small desk. It was neither on the table beside my chair nor in my dressing room. After scouring the shelves in the closet, I pulled out the trunk, even though I knew my valet had emptied it. As expected, there was nothing inside.

At length, I opened the door to the sitting room only to find Elizabeth in a chair before the fire, unpinning her hair. She wore a soft pink robe that fell open to reveal her bare legs. I started, stood in place, my mouth open, and my eyes unable to avoid devouring the beauty she had exposed.

"Mr. Darcy!" She dropped the pins and hastily reached for the robe to cover herself. "How dare you enter my sitting room without knocking!"

I swallowed. "It is my sitting room too."

"What?"

"This suite of rooms has a shared sitting room."

"I do not believe you!"

I frowned. "I am not in the habit of being called a prevaricator, madam. This sitting room was designed for use by occupants of both bedchambers. I came in search of my book."

"Insupportable! Why would we share a sitting room?"

"Because, Elizabeth, we are husband and wife."

She blinked twice and remained silent.

"My father had this townhouse built to his design. We reside in the master suite of rooms. My parents enjoyed spending time...together." I stared at her, waiting.

Rising from her chair, she pulled her robe even closer to her body. "We may be married, but we are hardly husband and wife. When you asked for my hand, you promised me that you would wait until I was willing before prevailing upon me."

I walked across the room and picked up my book of poems from the table beside the sofa where my valet had placed it. "And I have no intention of breaking my word, but I hardly consider entering a joint sitting room in search of reading material as *prevailing* upon you." I glanced at her and struggled to repress a smile in spite of my annoyance.

An expression of injured indignation covered her countenance. Her breathing was laboured, and I watched her search to find a proper retort. Her cheeks had pinked. I knew they would turn red if she knew what I was thinking. She was adorable, and I wanted to kiss her more than I wanted to breathe.

"For the time being, I shall forego the use of this sitting room." She turned towards the door to her chamber.

"Very well. But if you happen to change your mind, be assured that I am not opposed to sharing it with you. Or, I suppose we could organise some sort of schedule. You could have it for so many hours in the morning, while I prefer the evening. If you think it necessary, I can have signs printed that we could hang on the doorknobs. Perhaps *'Occupied'* or *'Stay Out'!* Which would you prefer?"

She opened the door, glared at me, and slammed it behind her.

The phrase, *"I wish you joy,"* suddenly echoed through my mind. How many times had it been offered to us, the happy couple, hours earlier on this same day...this day of supposed delight? If the first day of our marriage was to end in this manner, what lay ahead?

I rang the bell for my valet, and when he appeared, I asked for a bottle of brandy. By the time he returned, I had changed my mind. Angrily, I departed the sitting room, made my way through the bedchamber, and down the stairs. At the door, I donned my coat and hat and walked out the door to my club.

"Shall I call for the carriage, sir?" a servant asked.

"No, I shall walk. Fresh air seems particularly inviting tonight."

SOME HOURS LATER, I RETURNED, THIS TIME BY HIRED CARRIAGE. IN TRUTH, the hour had grown so excessively late that I did not trust the streets of London. Although I had imbibed more than enough spirits to ease the disappointment I had suffered earlier, I did not consider myself inebriated.

"Impertinent woman," I muttered to myself, for I had failed to blunt the anger that yet possessed me.

Earlier at the club, while nursing my pain with generous doses of liquid comfort, I had alternately cursed Wickham and blamed Elizabeth: Wickham for straddling me with his offspring and Elizabeth for failing to appreciate the honour I had given her.

After all, had I insisted upon my marital rights? No, I simply desired to spend the evening in her company. How could my request be considered excessive? Why could she not look upon me with a more sympathetic nature? Why, any other woman of her meagre means and in her family's ruined circumstances would fill her position as fast as lightning flashed across the sky outside the carriage window. And any other woman would be grateful —particularly grateful—to me, the man who had single-handedly saved her family. She would welcome me into her bed on our wedding night. She would smother me with kisses, nestle into my arms, and offer her body willingly.

But not Elizabeth! No, not Elizabeth! But for her desire to help her sister and Bingley, I doubted she would wear my ring or bear my name. And I knew deep in my gut that it would be a long time before she entered my bed, if ever.

If I keep on like this, my countenance will be permanently Friday-faced by the time Elizabeth is willing, I thought. I detested self-pity and regretted having wasted the evening thus engaged.

Thunder roared when I stepped down from the carriage, and puddles had already formed on the wet cobblestones. I must have stumbled, for the footman offered to assist me up the steps, but I shook off his hand. Nonetheless, he extended the umbrella over my head until I reached the shelter of the vestibule where the butler hurried to take my coat and hat. I debated whether to read in my library or attempt sleep. I decided on the library.

"No need for your assistance tonight," I muttered to Rodgers who ran up the hall to meet me. "You may go to bed, for I shall not yet retire, and I need nothing more to drink."

He waited, hovering near the stairs until I looked up to wave him away. With surprise, I saw Elizabeth standing at the head of the staircase, wrapping that rose-coloured robe about her.

"Elizabeth?" I squinted, wondering why I saw two of her. "Is something amiss?"

She shook her head. "It is Fan. She continues to wake and cry, being in a strange bed. I shall go to her."

Of course, you will, I thought, and started to turn away.

"Have you been out at this hour, sir?" she asked. The words sounded like an accusation.

I looked up again and narrowed my eyes when I saw the expression on her countenance. Straightening my shoulders, I lifted my chin in defiance. "I have."

She said not another word but simply turned on her heel and walked away from me towards the nursery.

How dare she question where I had been when she had fled my company almost immediately following our meal and then raised such an outcry about my blameless incursion into the sitting room! I supposed she could tell I had been drinking and that caused her disapproval. *So be it*, I thought, making my way to the library where I shut the massive oak doors behind me. The fire still burned, and I sank down into the nearest chair.

"Blast! I left the poems in my chamber." Although the room I sat in contained hundreds of books, I could think of nothing I wished to read, no familiar passage that might soothe my soul or bring me peace.

Had I made a terrible mistake in marrying Elizabeth?

Would the evening's experience be repeated the following night and all the nights to come? Should I continue to watch her flee my presence at the slightest excuse? Did she truly dislike me to that degree? During our brief engagement, I thought I had detected a bit of softening in her attitude, but perhaps it had been nothing more than a wish on my part.

For some time I sat, staring at the fire, watching the flames devour the logs until they broke apart into glowing embers. At last, my eyelids grew heavy, and I fell asleep. If not for the pain afflicting my neck because of my position on the couch, I might have slept there all night. I awoke in distress, rubbed my neck, and attempted to remember where I was. Naught but coals remained before me, and a chill overspread the room. While climbing the stairs, I heard the clock chime four times.

Surely, at this hour my thoughts will cease, and I can sleep in my own bed.

Rodgers had failed to leave even a singular candle lit inside my chamber, or perchance it had burned down, but I cared not. When lightning illuminated the room for a second or two, I could make out the location of the bed. I pulled off my jacket and unbuttoned my vest. I attempted to untie my cravat—silently cursing the blasted knot—until, at last, it gave over. I threw it on the floor along with my shoes. Not bothering to undress further, I reached for the bed. Thankfully, the servant had pulled the coverings back, and I fell onto the pillows, sighed, and closed my eyes.

I still yearned to hold Elizabeth. My need for her burned with such fervour that I even imagined that enticing fragrance of hers wafting through the wall separating our chambers.

If only...

THE FOLLOWING MORNING, I AWOKE WITH A POUNDING HEADACHE.

Elizabeth did not join me for breakfast, and I did not see her the entire day. If not for the child's infrequent sounds that drifted down from the nursery, I might have suspected she had left my house. Along with other matters, several letters from Pemberley's steward required my attention. My prolonged stay at Netherfield had caused not only pressing matters at my Derbyshire estate to mount up, but also various other correspondence. I spent most of the day confined to my study. However, I left the door open lest Elizabeth need or desire my company.

Ridiculous thought. When would she ever need or desire my company? "She will have to overcome that objection," I said aloud, "for we are married, and we will learn to abide each other's company."

Closing the book of accounts that I had pored over all afternoon, I noted the lateness of the hour and knew that dinner would be announced shortly. A servant answered my call almost immediately.

"Inform Mrs. Darcy that dinner will be served within the hour."

The man bowed and hastened from the room to carry out my order.

Why cannot wives behave in an obedient manner as servants do? Or, perhaps the question should be why cannot *my* wife behave in that obedient manner?

The rain had ceased, so I decided to inspect my small garden before dinner, for I disliked being indoors all day. I needed reassurance that at least part of my world yet existed as I ordered. In the early moonlight, I walked among the covered beds of bulbs, sturdy shrubs, and rosebushes and took satisfaction that the gardeners had done their work well. All had been either planted or trimmed back, prepared for the threatening frost. Gazing up at the sky, I saw snow clouds closing in, and I knew I would not see blooms again for many months. London was disagreeable at that time of year. December was upon us, and I longed to return to Derbyshire.

I shall take Elizabeth to Pemberley before Christmastide, I decided. Perhaps the sight of that magnificent estate might sway her heart where I had failed.

"Elizabeth, Elizabeth," I said aloud, wishing I could divine a way to reach her.

"Sir?"

I whirled around. Her voice! From where had it come?

"I am here," she said, "at the back of the garden.

I circled the line of shrubs to see her sitting on a bench, a book in her lap.

"Have you been here the entire time I wandered?"

She nodded.

"Why did you not speak?"

"I have little desire to converse with an angry man."

"Nor I with a resentful woman."

Her eyes flashed, and she put the book aside. "You think me resentful?"

"What else? You intimated that my presence annoyed you last night, and you have avoided my company all day."

She stared at me. "I have been much occupied with settling in and seeing to Fan. I did not purposefully evade your company. Besides, you have neither sought me out nor called for me. I supposed you did not care to after our disagreement."

"Is that the way it is to be?"

"Is that the way *what* is to be?"

"Do you intend that we live separate lives under one roof?"

"I fail to see that my actions during the first four and twenty hours of our marriage signify the manner in which we shall live for the remainder of our lives."

I clenched my teeth to keep from cursing. Must she speak with such coldness? I turned my back on her and pinched a discoloured leaf from the holly shrub. What sort of game did she expect us to play? The scene reminded me of my first unfortunate proposal to her in the parlour at Hunsford parsonage. She had confounded me that day in much the same manner.

I resolved to begin anew. "Elizabeth, we are married. Husbands and wives spend time in each other's company."

"So you said last night. I have not forgotten."

I ignored her retort. "They dine together; afterwards, they spend the evening together; they—"

"Sleep together?" She spat the words at me like a kitten with its fur standing on end. "Is that your complaint? Was that the reason you intruded on me last evening? You could have informed me that we shared a sitting room when first touring the house. You did not. You waited until I had disrobed and thought I was alone before disturbing my privacy. If I had known you shared that room, do you think I would have exposed myself in that manner?"

I closed my eyes. So, that lay behind all of this. I turned to look upon her and saw not only anger in her eyes but something more—distrust. Walking to the bench, I sat down beside her. She moved to the edge, leaving more than adequate space between us.

"You must allow me to apologize. I confess I never imagined you did not understand the arrangement of the suites."

"Come sir, I saw the expression on your face when you saw my robe lying open. You found me in disarray."

I could not keep from smiling slightly.

"And now you smile at my humiliation?"

I swallowed the smile. "I do not mean to cause offense, Elizabeth, but I cannot pretend that I did not find it...pleasant to gaze upon your beauty."

She rose, and naturally, I did as well. "I am your wife, sir. I expect to be treated with respect."

"I meant no disrespect. I meant to compliment."

"I do not expect to be used as you do your mistress."

What? "My mistress! Whatever do you mean?"

"I assume that is where you spent the evening since we both know it was exceedingly late when you returned."

Shock rendered me silent. How had her mind conjured up the idea that simply because I left the house, I had gone to a mistress? Such illogic puzzled me.

"You assured me I might expect constancy on your part if we married. I am not some dull-witted country girl. I know gentlemen often keep a woman. Because I am not yet willing to occupy your bed, does that mean you will not honour the commitment you made at the altar until I comply? If that is the case, sir, I must tell you it offers little persuasion for me to become the wife you desire."

"Insufferable!" I muttered, beginning to pace. Taking deep breaths, I steeled myself not to explode with the anger she had provoked within me.

Slowly, I turned to face her. "Madam, such personal deceit is abhorrent to me. I honour my commitments. I keep my word. Your assumptions are utterly false. Excuse me."

Turning on my heel, I strode from her side, heading for the house. At that moment, a servant entered the garden. "Dinner is served," he announced.

I stopped and turned towards the back of the garden. "Will you join me?" There was no answer.

At length, I walked through the door held open by the servant. Inside, I longed to continue through the front door and down the street, but instead, I marched into the dining room and took my place in the chair that the servant hastened to pull out from the table. "Serve the meal," I barked at him.

I sat as straight as though a poker had been inserted into my backbone while within I crumpled into a dejected mass of disappointment. *Think about anything, anything other than her,* I silently commanded.

The first course had been placed before me, and I picked up my soup spoon when I heard the soft rustle of a woman's skirts. Without a word, Elizabeth walked to the end of the table and took her place. Rising, I bowed briefly before returning to my chair.

So, I thought, *I have won the first round.*

"Pour the wine," I instructed the servant, "and bring Mrs. Darcy's soup course without delay."

She placed her napkin in her lap and raised her eyes to meet mine with an unwavering gaze. "I am pleased that the rain has ceased," she said.

"Yes," I said slowly, "the storm appears to have passed."

"For now, at least."

Chapter Eight

The lull in the storm continued throughout that evening. Elizabeth and I conversed over dinner—an uneasy, cautious conversation—but, nonetheless, a civil exchange of innocuous subjects such as the family history of the china settings on the table, my plans for us to eventually travel to Derbyshire, and various comments about the meal. I might have spoken in much the same manner with a mere acquaintance in any dining room in London society.

After dinner, Elizabeth reluctantly agreed to play the pianoforte for me, protesting that I would find her ability woefully inadequate. I encouraged her, asking that she sing as well. As a guest at Lucas Lodge years earlier, I had discovered she possessed a lovely natural voice, and I praised her at the conclusion of the song.

"Truly, sir, I know my limitations," she demurred. "Pray, do not insist that I continue."

"As you wish, but draw near the fire, for a draught has always persisted by those windows."

Sitting on the divan, she selected a book from the stack I had left on an adjoining table.

"I have a substantial library," I said. "You must feel free to avail yourself of its resources."

She gave me an arch look. "That does not surprise me. Is it not common knowledge that extensive reading is foremost among your requirements of an accomplished woman?" I smiled slightly, determined not to take offense at whatever she might say, but she was equally determined to pursue the subject. "Shall you list for me even more of the attributes this accomplished woman you spoke of at Netherfield Park should possess?"

I straightened my posture, for my neck cloth felt uncomfortably tight. "Honesty, good humour, and grace."

"And what of how she walks and talks and that certain unmistakeable air Miss Bingley insisted she must own? I recall at one time you agreed with her, that you also found those characteristics necessary."

I rose from the chair and poured two glasses of sherry. "What else do you recall from that conversation?"

"I might ask you the same question, sir."

I raised my eyebrows. "I remember how decidedly you put me in my place when you said, 'I am no longer surprised at your knowing *only* six accomplished women. I wonder at your knowing *any.*'"

She blushed slightly as she took the glass from me. "I marvel that you overlooked such impertinence."

"Oh, I do not think I overlooked it, but I confess your remark intrigued me. No woman had ever spoken to me in that manner."

Now it was her turn to raise her eyebrows as she tilted her head to the side.

I sat down beside her. "Did you know that I have always found that expression of yours particularly fetching?"

"Sir?"

"That movement you just employed—the way you turn your cheek and cast a glimpse from the corner of your eye."

Her cheeks turned rosier. "And…does that mean it pleases you?"

"It does," I said softly.

"Well, then, I must remember to use that expression when I beg for an increase in pin money."

I frowned. What did she mean? The amount in her personal accounts had been settled with Mr. Bennet in the terms of our marriage agreement, and he thought it more than satisfactory. Did she find the funds inadequate? If so, she had failed to raise objections before the wedding. I looked up when I heard her light laughter.

"Come now, sir, you must understand when I am teasing, or this marriage shall prove most tedious."

I AM SAD TO SAY THAT, IN MY OPINION, THE REMAINDER OF THE EVENING did prove tedious, for Elizabeth soon retired to her chamber. My wife slept in her bed while I slept in mine. Although I had promised I would not prevail upon her in an untimely manner, I found it increasingly difficult to abide by my promise. Why had I proposed such a heedless agreement? Knowing that naught but a small sitting room lay between us proved uncommonly cruel when, in the quiet of the night, I moved restlessly, unable to fall asleep. We had been married but two days, and already I regretted my rash vow to wait for her welcome embrace.

Blast it all! I want to sweep her up in my arms and bring her in here to lie beside me!

I sat up and held my head in my hands. I would never rest if I remained in that room—situated so near her and yet compelled to sleep apart for perhaps weeks or even months. Taking my robe, I departed the room and walked downstairs. Once again finding myself in the library, I lit a candle, grabbed a book, and lay down on the sofa facing the fireplace. The wind began to howl without, and I felt a chill seep beneath the windowsills. Rising with a sigh, I stirred the logs and watched them catch fire anew. I returned to my book and read until, at last, I fell asleep.

The servant awakened me early when she came in to lay the morning fire. I sat up, bleary-eyed and ill tempered, my back aching from reclining all night on a piece of furniture never designed to be used as a bed. That did not prompt me to climb the stairs and return to my chamber, however, for I felt too weary to move, as though I had not slept at all. Unknowingly, after the servant's interruption, I must have gradually succumbed to sleep once more as my heavy eyes closed, lulled by the warmth of the fire. It was late in the morning before I was awakened again and that time in a rude, unsettling manner.

"Fan? Fan, where are you?"

Through the haze of sleep, I heard a voice. Not yet able to open my eyes, I felt sharp pain all over my head. I struggled to consciousness and opened one eye. The child stood before me, her tiny hands tugging at my hair.

"Stop that!" I said, my voice loud and forceful before I knew it.

Immediately, her bottom lip began to quiver. She screwed up her eyes and let forth a scream that reverberated around the room.

"Fan!" Elizabeth cried, running into the library. "What happened?" The child ran to her and buried her face in her skirts, continuing to wail at such a tortured pitch that my head now began to throb.

Elizabeth picked up the child and whirled around to face me. "What did you do to her?"

Her demanding tone grated on me as I am none too pleasant first thing in the morning in general and was certainly not in a gracious mood at that moment. I rose, gathered my robe around me, and hastily tied the belt.

"You might ask what that child did to me, madam!"

"What do you mean?"

"I am not in the habit of being awakened by an unruly creature pulling my hair."

Awareness of what must have occurred washed over her countenance. "And is it your general habit to sleep in the library, sir?"

"No, but I am master of this house. If I choose the library for my repose, I should be able to sleep free of terror." I swept my hand through my hair, stood straighter, and prepared to leave the room.

"You can hardly blame a child of tender years for her curiosity. Perchance she thought you dead."

I saw how Elizabeth attempted to mask her smile, pressing her lips together tightly. I failed to find anything amusing about the scene.

"If I had been dead, that child's screams would have wrought a miracle, for they would have jolted me back to life. Excuse me." I bowed stiffly and stalked from the room.

Unaccustomed as I was to being the butt of anyone's joke, a growing resentment settled in my heart towards the child. If not for her, my marriage might be greatly improved. My wife's attentions towards me might be gracious and warm rather than mocking. If not for the child, I might have awakened in my own bed with my wife lying in my arms. If not for the child...

Oh yes, I began to resent Wickham's spawn. Unfortunately, as the weeks of my marriage passed, the deeper my resentment grew.

DURING THE SECOND WEEK WE RESIDED IN TOWN, I SECURED WHAT I considered an excellent nurse for the child. Clearly, the girl Elizabeth had brought from Longbourn would not suffice. Maggie could neither comfort nor control the child. Repeatedly, my wife's activities were interrupted to hasten to the nursery in answer to the shrill screams that discharged from the floor above. Time and again, I came upon the creature unattended throughout the house. In my study, I found her scattering the papers from my desk throughout the room. In the parlour, she destroyed the floral arrangement Elizabeth had created, pouring a vase of water onto the carpet. Imagine my shock when I entered my bedchamber and came upon her sitting squarely in the middle of my bed eating blueberries! Thoroughly stained, the coverlet had to be cut up for rags.

The blueberry incident caused me to rebuke the nursemaid until the silly girl burst into tears. Elizabeth objected to the strength of my lecture, but I failed to discern any fault on my part. If the child was allowed the run of the house, even to wander out into the kitchen unattended, Maggie was clearly irresponsible. Truly, it was past time for a change in supervision of the child.

"Perkins said you wished to see me," Elizabeth said, upon entering my study.

I rose from behind the desk and led her to a chair. "Yes, I have something to tell you that shall greatly benefit the household."

"Oh?" She sat near the edge of the cushioned seat and peered up into my face.

I returned to my place behind the desk and picked up a sheet of paper to which I could refer. "I have solicited and obtained the services of a professional baby nurse, a Mrs. Abernathy. She should arrive soon, and I have instructed Perkins to bring her to us."

When Elizabeth made no answer, I ceased reviewing my notes and looked up. I could not interpret her expression, for she appeared not to understand the words I had spoken. "Are you not pleased?" I asked finally.

"Pleased? Should I be pleased that you have gone behind my back and hired a person I have never met to care for the niece who is like a daughter to me?"

I frowned. "Behind your back? I beg to differ. Nothing was done behind your back."

"Did you not procure this woman without one word to me? Have you not promised her the position? Shall she not arrive with her bags in hand, ready to move in?"

"Well…yes, but still, I fail to see why you question my actions. I thought you would be relieved to have an accomplished person in charge of the nursery rather than that unsuitable girl you brought from the country who obviously is not fit for the job."

"Maggie is perfectly suitable. She has tended Fan since she was an infant."

"That may be, but in my opinion, her performance has been highly unsatisfactory." I could see from Elizabeth's expression that she would need to be reminded of the servant's faults. Thus, I launched into a detailed list of how the unqualified girl had allowed the child to disrupt our lives, especially mine. Surely, my wife could see the wisdom in my decision. "Children should be well-trained, and I have found a person who will teach your niece her proper place in this house."

Colour flooded Elizabeth's face, and she pressed her lips together in displeasure. I could see her struggle not to tremble as she rose from the chair. Clearly, I had not persuaded my wife to see my viewpoint. Instead, I had provoked her wrath.

"Her proper place! I see. I shall examine this person, sir, and if I do not find her warm and loving towards Fan, she will not touch my child."

"Warm and loving! Are those your only requirements for a nurse? Surely not! Even you, growing up without a governess, can see that a child in *my* house must be reared with more discipline. How can she take her place in society when she is allowed to grow up wild and untamed? She will embarrass us at every turn!"

Elizabeth shook her head from side to side before beginning to pace. "Wild and untamed? An embarrassment? Is that what you think of my sisters and me? Do you find our upbringing so lacking that it should warrant the humiliation you now inflict upon me?" Whirling around, she stalked towards the door.

How can she misinterpret what I said with such deliberateness? She has perverted my words into thinking I spoke of her or her sisters.

I quickly intercepted her, seizing her hand before she reached for the doorknob. "Wait! I would discuss the matter further."

As she turned to face me, she gasped in anger. I could not keep from watching her bosom rise and fall. I hastily raised my gaze to meet hers but not before she saw where my eyes had rested.

"Let me go," she cried, flinging her hand loose.

I held up my hands, spreading the fingers wide to show I would not touch her further. "I beg your pardon. I have no desire to make you cross. May we simply speak of this matter with some semblance of civility?"

"Of what is there to speak? You have stated your demands, and I have stated mine. They do not correspond. What benefit will come from further discussion?" Crossing her arms over her chest, she glared at me.

"Please," I said, attempting to moderate the harshness of my voice to a calmer tenor, all the while leading her back to her chair. When she finally sat down, I sat on the edge of the sofa nearest her lest she once again spring up at the least provocation. "Shall I ring for tea?"

She shook her head.

"Very well, but pray listen to me. In no way did I intend to cast disparagement upon you or your sisters. In truth, I fail to see why you took offense."

"You inferred because I grew up without a governess that my training lacked the necessary requirements to be reared in *your* house. I wonder you would marry such a *wild and untamed* person. Shall my savagery not also embarrass you?"

Suddenly, the likeness of a wild and untamed Elizabeth in my bed flooded my senses, and I could not speak as desire rushed over me. I quickly retreated behind the desk, seeking to quell the urgency of my feelings by placing distance between us.

Clearing my throat, I began again. "If I have caused offense, I offer my apology. You will never embarrass me, of that I am certain. I am proud that you are my wife. You are a woman any man would be fortunate to marry."

The look she gave me was puzzled, but at length, I saw it soften somewhat.

"Regardless, Elizabeth, we must be united. We have entered into this marriage with the agreement that we will rear your sister's child. It is plain to see you want her to be happy. That is well and good, for I do not wish her to be unhappy. I simply wish for her to learn her place so that our lives will not be constantly disrupted."

Lifting her chin, she looked straight into my eyes, and the former softening now vanished. "That curious turn of phrase crosses your lips again. Tell me, sir, exactly what is *her place?* The day you sought my hand in marriage, you said Fan would have a place at your table. Were you sincere? Or is she to be kept in the distant recesses of the house, brought out only on Boxing Day to greet the servants?"

I could not help but sit back, stunned.

"I fail to comprehend your harshness, Elizabeth. I have not the slightest intention of banishing the child to the attic! Nor am I placing her in the servants' quarters. I merely wish for order to be restored in my household. Is that too much to ask?"

She rose, and I naturally did too, stepping out from behind the desk so I might restrain her lest she bolted once more. We stood for some moments, silent and wary of one another.

"Of course, it is not too much to ask," she finally murmured, tossing her head, and turning her back to me. Gently, I reached for her hand and turned her around so I might look into her eyes. Her face remained lowered, but she did not withdraw from my touch.

"I fear I have conducted this business in a clumsy manner. I did not consider seeking your opinion before selecting a nurse. Prior to today, I have always handled matters solely on my own, for…I never had a wife before." I tenderly lifted her chin with the tip of my finger, relieved when she allowed me to do so.

She raised her eyes to mine. "Then I suppose I must be more patient with you during your apprenticeship." She smiled, and it caused me to smile in return. "I also ask that you allow me time to learn how to behave as a proper wife."

"Indeed."

"I am willing to employ an open mind when I meet the nurse you have selected if you are willing to dismiss her if I do not approve her ways."

"Fair enough."

She turned to depart the room, but still she did not take her hand away, and so I walked beside her to the door.

"But, sir, you must be more lenient with Fan. We have uprooted her from the only home she has ever known, and do recall that she is less than two years of age. I suspect your own child will prove just as contrary at such a tender age." She turned her head to the side and looked up at me in that special way of hers, and I felt my heart melt into a puddle at her feet.

With a brief curtsy, she was gone.

My own child—a child of yours and mine, Elizabeth!

The thought warmed my heart throughout the remainder of the day.

WHEN WE MET MRS. ABERNATHY, THE WOMAN APPEARED…DISCIPLINED, a nurse who would not abide foolishness. I heartily approved of her, of course, but Elizabeth questioned her at length as to her methods and manners of tending children. Seeming to reserve judgment, she sent for the child to join us in my study.

Maggie soon entered the room, carrying the babe in her arms, although she squirmed to loosen her hold, pushing her nurse's hands away. Elizabeth indicated the girl should release her, and we watched the child examine Mrs. Abernathy from head to toe. Being a tall, stout woman, she may have appeared formidable to the small girl, but she did not cower. Instead, she moved to Elizabeth's side and took her hand. I could see by Elizabeth's expression that she entertained misgivings, but then Mrs. Abernathy sat down in a chair and beckoned the child to her side.

"So, you are Miss Fan, are you? I understand you have just moved into this house. It must be rather unsettling for one so young. Come sit with me, and tell me how old you are."

She reached down and placed the child upon her lap. I steeled myself, fully expecting to hear her unbearable screams burst forth, but to my amazement, the child leaned against Mrs. Abernathy's ample bosom and began to play with the gold watch hanging from a chain 'round her neck.

"She will soon be two years old," Elizabeth offered, "and ia terribly spoilt, I fear. She was the only little one in my father's house with three, sometimes four, doting aunts to wait upon her hand and foot."

"Do not fear, Mrs. Darcy, I have dealt with spoilt children many times over the years. I shall soon have her minding her manners. It simply takes a firm hand—"

"A firm hand?" Elizabeth blanched.

"—and a loving nature. I possess both, so Fan and I shall get on fine. Now, Mr. Darcy, have we concluded our business? If so, I would like to retire to the nursery and inspect this little lady's chamber, as well as my own."

I questioned Elizabeth with a look, and when she nodded, I rang for the servant to carry the nurse's bags.

"Shall I come with you," Elizabeth asked, "just to ensure Fan behaves?"

"Of course, madam, if you wish, but there is little need, for I feel certain I have the situation under control." She turned to Fan's nurse from Long-bourn. "Maggie, is it?"

"Yes, ma'am." The girl bobbed an awkward curtsy.

"Come along then. I shall outline your duties once we are above stairs." Placing the child on the floor, she held firmly to her hand as she led her towards the hallway. She paused at the door. "Shall you accompany us, Mrs. Darcy?"

Elizabeth shook her head. "No, I think you have things well in hand."

When the door closed, she turned to me. "I beg your pardon for my former objections. I should have known you are an experienced employer."

"You approve of Mrs. Abernathy?"

"I do, but still, I pray you will consult me before you undertake any more actions on Fan's behalf."

"Then I would take this opportunity to speak, for I propose a swift move that will affect the child as well as you."

"A move, sir?"

"To Pemberley, as we discussed before. I have a great desire to be rid of the city, and I wish to spend Christmas in Derbyshire."

"Is there any special reason to travel so quickly? I had hoped to visit my relations, the Gardiners, before leaving Town."

I frowned, for I dreaded having to meet more of Elizabeth's connexions. "And in what part of Town do they reside?"

She swallowed, and for some reason, seemed to stand straighter as though she anticipated her request would be met with disapproval. "In Gracechurch Street. My uncle is in trade, so I do not ask you to call upon them, but I feel it only fitting that I do."

I, of course, knew perfectly well the location of the Gardiners' house, recalling how I had earlier travelled up and down that street hoping to catch a glimpse of Elizabeth. "We shall not depart until Monday next, so you should have adequate time to call upon them. I fear my business affairs will prevent me from joining you."

Looking up, I saw my rejection had stung, but she said nothing more, quietly nodded, and walked from the room. I sat down behind my desk and allowed my head to lean back against the chair. How could I tell her that I wished to leave Town lest Elizabeth bear the wrath of my own relations? Upon hearing of my marriage, Lady Catherine had written me a scathing letter, berating me for polluting the family, betraying my cousin Anne, and personally wounding her for all time. I fully expected her to descend upon us within days. I had not yet heard from my uncle, the Earl of Matlock, but I assumed he would also disapprove my choice of wife before even meeting her.

We had entertained but few other guests and had not received any invitations. No more than three wives of gentlemen I considered friends had called upon Elizabeth. Their visits had been brief, and although my wife did not complain, I surmised the women had only come out of curiosity. They had mentioned the child, calling her my ward, but they could not conceal their astonishment. Why had a newly married couple acquired a small child so quickly? Elizabeth had returned the calls, but when I asked about the visits, she said little. If she had felt slighted, and I feared that she had, that fact only added impetus to my desire to whisk her away to my home in the country. I knew the people of Derbyshire, and they knew me. They would treat my wife with the respect she deserved, ward or no ward. They would honour her as mistress of Pemberley.

Three days later, Elizabeth set out on her mission to Gracechurch Street. I still felt rather guilty for not attending her, but in truth, I did have a conference scheduled with my barrister and several tasks to complete before we departed London on the following Monday.

The day was unpleasant, chilly, and damp. I was surprised to see Mrs. Abernathy and the child leaving with my wife, for I knew the nurse did not approve of taking her charge out during inclement weather. Elizabeth, however, informed me that her aunt longed to see the little girl before we left Town for fear she would not recognize her by the time we returned. If that was said to provoke guilt on my part, it did not.

I spent the morning at my desk and stopped shortly before tea, pleased I had answered the stack of correspondence and sifted through the other transactions that required my signature. After the meal, I intended to leave directly so that I might call at the attorney's office before the day ended. I wished to be home when Elizabeth returned, for with each passing day, I longed to be in her presence more and more.

Donning my coat in the front hall, I reached for my hat held by a waiting servant when the door was opened and in surged a whirlwind of anger—Lady Catherine de Bourgh, accompanied by her brother, the Earl of Matlock, and his son Colonel Fitzwilliam.

"Darcy!" she shrieked. "There you are!"

I attempted to welcome my family, but I doubt my words were heard over my aunt's discomposure and resounding affliction. She swept past me into the drawing room, followed by my uncle. I caught a hasty look from my cousin, his eyebrows aloft in obvious warning. Unable to take time to remove my coat, I was obliged to follow my guests. I signalled Perkins to shut the doors behind us and directed him to have more tea delivered.

"Tea? I have no wish for tea!" Lady Catherine thundered. "I would have a word with you, Nephew, a serious word!"

I bade them be seated and sank down on the chair across from my aunt. "I trust you are in good health, Aunt, and you, as well, Uncle."

"Neither my health nor that of my brother is of importance, although mine is, naturally, excellent. We are here to discuss the dreadful news being bandied about in the streets where even strangers talk of it."

"And what news might that be?" I asked, although I knew full well to what she referred.

"The rumour of your unfortunate marriage! Tell us it is untrue, Darcy. Tell us that you could not possibly have married my vicar's little country cousin. Why, she has no money, no title, and her connexions—" She rolled her eyes and sighed dramatically. "She has none to speak of—none I wish to speak of. And if that were not enough, I understand you have taken in her sister's child born outside of wedlock. Of what can you be thinking? Surely, you cannot throw away your good name with so little regard. What of Pemberley's future and the reputation of our family?"

"Is it true, Darcy?" the earl interjected. "Tell us at once before Catherine becomes ill."

She shot a dark look in his direction. "I have not the slightest intention of becoming ill. Illness does not dare befall the likes of me."

I cleared my throat. "I fail to see how news of my marriage should predispose anyone to sickness."

"That depends upon whom you have married," the earl said.

"I married Elizabeth Bennet of Longbourn in Hertfordshire."

My uncle rose and began to pace while my aunt's brows drew together and her eyes narrowed into slits before she spoke. "So, it is true. Oh, how the shades of Pemberley shall be polluted!"

"I beg to differ, Lady Catherine. I am a gentleman. My wife is a gentleman's daughter, and Elizabeth will preside over Pemberley with grace and skill. I have done nothing I regret."

"And what of your engagement to Anne?" Lady Catherine demanded. "Have you chosen to forsake your obligations to your family?"

Perkins walked in at that moment with the tea cart restored, and Colonel

Fitzwilliam took the opportunity to proclaim it was just what we all needed. He indicated that the servant should pour a cup for Lady Catherine.

"I told you I have no desire for tea," she roared. "Take that away immediately!"

Perkins looked to me for guidance, and I waved him aside but told him to leave the cart. As he closed the door behind him, Fitzwilliam took the poured cup and began to stir in sugar.

"Well, I find myself in need of something warm and soothing as it is quite nasty today," he said. "Father? Darcy?"

We both shook our heads. I appreciated Richard's attempts to ease the situation, but I knew it must be dealt with, that my aunt would insist upon satisfaction.

"Darcy," the earl said, "you have not addressed Catherine's question. What of your engagement to Anne?"

"I never offered for my cousin. Hence, I have broken no vow."

"But...it was a peculiar situation. It was assumed," Lady Catherine sputtered. "It was the fondest wish of your mother, and I have been waiting—that is, Anne has awaited your formal proposal for some time. I thought the singular cause for delay was your needless frolic through the Mediterranean that went on and on, and now that you are back, I expected you to call on us and set a wedding date. How can you say you have broken no vow?"

"Because I have not, Aunt. A wish, though fondly desired, does not a proposal make."

She opened her mouth to speak and then closed it as though gritting her teeth. "This—this is not to be borne! It will not do!"

"Aunt," Richard said, "are you certain Anne expected Darcy to propose? She has never mentioned it. In truth, last summer she told me that she hoped not to marry at all."

"Anne does as she is told. Unlike some in this room, she knows her duty."

"Do you speak the truth, Darcy?" my uncle asked. "Have you never spoken of marriage to Anne?"

"Never, sir."

"Then, Catherine, you have misled me. I came here ready to defend Anne's honour, but I no longer find any basis upon which to proceed. It seems this engagement has resided in your imagination and nowhere else."

"Insufferable! My sister and I dreamt of uniting our children and their houses. Surely, our expectations must be considered."

"If I may state the obvious," Richard said, "your expectations cannot be considered now, for Darcy has affirmed that he is, indeed, married."

"And to the worst possible choice!" Lady Catherine cried.

At that moment, I looked up to see Elizabeth standing just inside the door, still wearing her coat and holding her bonnet in her hand. The look on her face left no doubt that she had heard the last words spoken. Immediately, I rose and hastened to her side, holding out my hand. "Elizabeth, I did not see you there. Come, you must meet my uncle."

She allowed me to lead her to my guests, whereupon she curtsied before Lady Catherine, my uncle, and cousin but said not a word. I introduced the earl, explaining he was Fitzwilliam's father and Lady Catherine's brother. Clearly, he was surprised at my wife's beauty, and he bowed slightly in greeting. Richard kissed her hand and smiled broadly, having met her previously at Rosings. Lady Catherine's face froze.

"Miss Elizabeth Bennet," she said.

"Mrs. Elizabeth Darcy, ma'am," she corrected.

"So, you have prevailed." She rose, drawing herself up like a stuffed partridge. "You have used your arts and allurements to draw my nephew in and secure yourself a wealthy husband, have you not? Let me tell you this: you are not welcome at Rosings Park, nor shall you ever be."

"How unfortunate," Elizabeth said, "that you must leave us so soon. Shall I ring for your carriage?"

"My carriage awaits without. I have no need of your services." She glared at me once again and then stalked towards the door. "Come, Brother."

"I shall return with Richard," he said.

Turning, she fixed her eyes upon him. I took the opportunity to speak. "Lady Catherine, since you refuse civility to my wife, I am forced to state that, until you do, I shall no longer call at Rosings. As to any future invitations for your company either here or at Pemberley, that is entirely dependent on Mrs. Darcy's inclination. Good day."

Only the slightest of tremors escaped her shoulders as she pierced me with hostile eyes. "Very well, Darcy, but be warned: you will reap what you sow. Rearing a bastard in your house will taint your name for generations."

Chapter Nine

Although my uncle and cousin stayed behind after Lady Catherine's departure and their visit could be described as pleasant—the earl growing more and more pleased with my wife as the hour passed—I sensed Elizabeth was truly shaken by my aunt's displeasure. After my relations bade us farewell, she made to hasten from the room, but I could not let her go.

"Elizabeth, will you sit with me for a moment?"

"I am rather tired," she said, her eyes lowered.

"Naught but a moment, I promise."

Reluctantly, she walked back into the room, never once lifting her face to meet mine.

"I must apologize for Lady Catherine's rude behaviour."

"There is no need."

"I feel there is. She chose words meant not only to hurt but to wound deeply, and I can see they have affected you."

"She is a great lady, sir, one who is accustomed to speaking her mind without question."

"That may be, but it does not excuse the infliction of pain on the innocent. She should not have spoken to you in that manner. Never again will I allow anyone to speak to you in that way."

My words appeared to cause Elizabeth more sadness, for she still would not look at me. "Do you not fear her warning will come true, that rearing my sister's child will disgrace your good name?"

"A man's name is not ruined by good works, and I see providing a home for a needy child in a favourable light."

"But Fan is…illegitimate, and she is Mr. Wickham's child. Lady Catherine spoke the truth; gossip will abound. And despite your good intentions, we both know you are not pleased to have *his* child in your house."

I poured a cup of tea before answering. "'Tis true I would have preferred any child other than Wickham's, but would it be cause for gossip? Momentarily, perhaps, but not for long. There are more important people in London to talk about than I."

"But you have broken with your aunt. Will you not regret your hasty decision in the future? She is your family."

I placed the cup and saucer on the table and sat down beside her, whereupon I reached for her hand. "You are my family now, Elizabeth, and I do not regret it or anything else."

Slowly, she raised her eyes to meet mine. "Not even losing the woman you loved?" she whispered.

I frowned, at first unable to comprehend of whom she spoke.

"I have not forgotten. You said the woman you loved did not love you. Surely, you cannot help but regret that."

"Ah, yes. Well, things change, and I have never been one to brood over implacable situations. I am resolved to build a life with you."

"But a life without love is a dear price to pay."

How I longed to tell her that she was the woman I loved, that I would do all in my power to make her love me! I knew she was not ready for such a pronouncement—that it would send her dashing from the room—so I repressed my desires once more.

"Have you not also paid a heavy price? I have never asked you, but I assume you also have forsaken the chance for marriage to a man you love. Was there someone, Elizabeth…is there someone else?"

Her eyes widened at my question, and she looked away. "My family's position during the two years past has banished thoughts of marriage for any reason, much less for the luxury of love. Besides, I have married for love." I sat up straighter. "I love Fan, and because of you, she now has a home."

I smiled. "She does, and I must say I have another love as well. There is Pemberley, the home I have loved since I was a lad. I propose that we banish all unpleasant thoughts from our minds and concentrate on the journey upon which we are to embark. Have the servants completed packing your belongings?"

With the change of subject, Elizabeth's posture visibly eased as though a weight had been lifted from her shoulders. "Not yet, but all will be ready by Monday morning. I confess I anticipate the trip with pleasure. I have long desired a return to Derbyshire."

We rose, and I escorted her to the door. "And soon you shall, my dear."

She looked up at my words. "'My dear'? That is what my father calls my mother. I suppose we are becoming an old married couple."

I smiled as I watched her climb the staircase. *Not quite, Elizabeth, not quite.*

On Saturday, a post arrived for Elizabeth that altered our plans to proceed to Pemberley. Jane Bennet wrote, imploring her sister to return to Longbourn for the Christmas season.

Papá has taken to his bed with an illness that will not abate. The doctor says it is his heart and that he must have peace and quiet in which to rest. Mamá wails from morning to night in fear that he will die and we will be uprooted from Longbourn the following day. Our father has little chance to obtain the peace and quiet ordered by Mr. Jones. Will you not prevail upon Mr. Darcy to bring you to Hertfordshire for at least the holidays? I know it will cheer Papá and perhaps lessen our mother's fears.

Upon quitting her reading of the letter aloud, my wife raised her eyes to mine, hope evident therein that I would relinquish my desire to return to Derbyshire and agree to Jane's request.

"I fail to see how the addition of our family and servants will bring peace to your father's house," I said. "On the contrary, we should prove a great disruption."

"Not if we stay at Netherfield," Elizabeth said.

"At Netherfield?"

"You and I...or perhaps I could visit my father alone and attempt to calm my mother."

"Definitely you, for I cannot fathom how my presence would bestow calm upon your mother."

"Reassurance from you would alleviate her fears of being abandoned should we lose my father, would it not, sir?"

I am certain my eyes widened in alarm. "Are you suggesting that your mother and sisters would reside with us?"

Elizabeth shook her head. "I would not presume that far, but I do know you will not allow them to 'starve in the hedgerows,' as Mamá often proclaims."

"Of course not." I rose from my desk and stirred the logs in the fireplace. "Do you truly fear your father is near death?"

"I certainly hope not!" She stood and began to fidget with the letter in her hand.

"Forgive me, Elizabeth. I did not mean to speak with so little regard for your feelings."

"Papá has had these spells before, but with proper rest, he has always recovered. If I can assist Jane in soothing our mother, I believe all will be well. Will you not write to Mr. Bingley and ask whether we might stay at Netherfield?"

I sighed, but naturally I agreed and sat down to pen the missive. Upon receiving Bingley's prompt reply within four days, we thence departed London—not for my beloved estate, but rather for Hertfordshire, a county I had not planned to visit for some time.

NOT ONLY DID BINGLEY GREET US UPON OUR ARRIVAL AT NETHERFIELD, but we found his sisters and Mr. Hurst in attendance as well. My friend's family had descended upon him for Christmastide, and we had only added to his household. Bingley, however, met us with obvious delight and ushered us into the drawing room, whereupon he immediately ordered refreshments.

"Mr. and Mrs. Darcy!" Mrs. Hurst greeted us, affecting pleasure at renewing our acquaintance. She and her sister simpered and fawned over me, directing but slight conversation towards my wife. I instinctively moved closer to Elizabeth. The entire room knew that neither Louisa Hurst nor Caroline Bingley had ever cared for her, and I hoped my wife would not wish to give them the satisfaction of knowing our marriage was not all that it appeared.

"And how do you find London society, Eliza?" Caroline finally said, somehow unable to temper her voice until the simplest phrase sounded like a sneer. "I suppose you must have been inundated with callers and invitations, being the new bride of such an imposing gentleman."

Knowing full well that Caroline suspected few callers had welcomed my wife, I opened my mouth to counter, but Elizabeth spoke first.

"Lady Catherine de Bourgh called but a few days ago, and I found the Earl of Matlock's company exceedingly pleasant," she said with a smile. I thrilled when she tucked her hand within the crook of my arm and moved so near our arms touched. A current of delight shot through every sense of my body with that mere contact.

So, I was right! She wishes neither Caroline nor Louisa Hurst to learn we are not married in every sense of the word. Nothing could have pleased me more.

Caroline's face fell in disappointment, but she would not relent. "And have you entertained many of the *ton* as is the custom of new brides?"

"I fear we have not," I interjected, "and the fault is mine."

Elizabeth glanced up at me with wonder in her eyes.

"I am a selfish beast, for I have wished my wife to devote herself to me alone these first few weeks of our marriage. Elizabeth has graciously agreed to postpone entertaining until I am satisfied, but"—I smiled down at her —"that may take some time. I have waited such a long while for my bride that it may take months before I am willing to share her with others."

"That is selfish of you, Darcy," Bingley said while Caroline turned away, her countenance more embittered than before.

"I do not mind, Mr. Bingley," Elizabeth said, "for I wish nothing more than to please my husband."

"Ah, tea!" Mrs. Hurst said, obviously relieved to change the subject with the arrival of the servant bearing the tea cart.

A short time later, Elizabeth excused herself, pleading the necessity of changing for dinner, and within a few moments, I took the opportunity to follow her.

"Of course," Bingley said. "I shall have Andrews escort you to your chambers. Naturally, Darcy, since you are no longer single, I have altered the choice of rooms to accommodate you."

"Naturally," I murmured, wondering what I should find above stairs.

Imagine my surprise when Bingley's servant led me into the appointed bedroom, and therein I discovered Elizabeth directing her maid as she unpacked her trunk.

"Yes?" Elizabeth asked, looking up at my arrival. "Did you wish to see me?"

The Netherfield servant followed me into the room, assisting my valet to carry my bags into one of the two adjoining dressing rooms, whereupon he opened the wardrobe to put away my clothing. Immediately, I understood. Knowing we were married, Bingley assumed we would share the spacious suite, for it was designed for two people—two people who were man and wife.

"Ah," I said, hesitating. "Might I speak with you privately, Elizabeth?"

I dismissed the servants with a simple nod in the direction of the door. Upon their departure, I noted the look of apprehension on my wife's face. A sense of dread overtook me, mingled with a slight anticipation of hope. I walked to Elizabeth's side and spoke softly, lest itching ears remained in the hallway.

"It appears Bingley has ordered his servants to place us in the same chambers. We are married, after all, and he thinks…"

Acknowledgement appeared in her eyes. They grew quite big and round as her eyebrows rose. "I see. It is a simple mistake and one you should be able to resolve."

"This suite is exceedingly large with the adjoining sitting and dressing rooms." I gestured towards the area beyond her. She turned and surveyed it before raising her gaze to meet mine once more.

"It is lovely and shall prove more than adequate for *my* needs."

I took a deep breath and squared my shoulders. "I believe it should prove adequate for *both* our needs."

The incredulous look on her face told me that she would not agree easily to what I intended to propose.

"Elizabeth, do you wish Bingley to know our marriage is in name only?"

"Why should he know?"

"Servants gossip."

"But…it is quite appropriate for husbands and wives to have their own chambers."

"True, but rarely when they have been married the few short weeks that we have. The first flush of passion would normally cause them to share intimate quarters early in the union."

Her cheeks grew rosy, and for a moment, she could not face me. "But that is not our situation for we…are not in love."

I struggled to conceal that one of us was. "And, we must consider that not only Bingley will hear we prefer separate rooms," I said carefully, "but also the Hursts…and Miss Bingley."

Awareness swept over her countenance.

"That...would be unfortunate," she said slowly. "However, I do not see how we can share these rooms. There is but one bed. How can we possibly —where would you sleep?"

I moved near the bed and struck a pose pretending to survey the size of the furniture in great detail. I walked back and forth as though I were measuring the width.

"I do believe this bed is larger than most. In truth, it is as large as the bed I possess at Pemberley. I have an idea. If we were to place a pillow between us—a good, stout pillow—might it not give us the separation we desire and yet present us as normal newlyweds?"

She walked to the bed and stood beside me. "A pillow?"

I nodded.

"Shall a pillow provide enough separation? Sharing a bed—even one of such generous proportions—is still an intimate affair."

I raised one eyebrow. "You fear waking up in my arms? Well, we certainly cannot have that happen." I took a few steps back and forth as though deep in thought before speaking. "I do not know your sleeping habits, Elizabeth, but I am a fairly light sleeper. Do you toss and turn and ramble over the entire bed?"

I could see my question startled her. "N-n-no, not so far as I am aware."

"Well, if you happened to...stray in the night towards my side of the bed—"

"I would do no such thing!"

"Not with intention, of course, but we must allow for all possibilities. Now, if you did roll towards me, with a sizeable pillow between us—a great, plump pillow—the object would awaken you, would it not?"

She did not answer but nodded.

"Then, I think we have happened upon a solution that should allay your fears and yet satisfy any misplaced curiosity on the part of Caroline Bingley. Yes, with the aid of a pillow, I believe we may sleep comfortably on separate sides of this bed."

Elizabeth said nothing, but her breathing grew shallow as she stared at the bed.

"So, shall I call the servants and direct them to resume the unpacking of our belongings?" I asked, striving to sound matter-of-fact.

The silence between us grew to fill the room. At last, she whispered, "Yes."

I turned and strode towards the door.

"But sir…"

"Yes?"

"I shall require privacy when dressing and undressing."

I smiled slightly. "As will I."

When I walked out the door and down the stairs, I noted my step grew lighter along with my mood. That night, I would share a bed with Elizabeth! The thought set my senses on fire and sent my spirits soaring.

Now, if only I could bring myself to leave that blasted pillow in its place!

NEVER DID AN EVENING CRAWL LIKE OUR FIRST NIGHT AT NETHERFIELD! Bingley's chatter droned on and on, but I failed to follow much of what he said. My mind played on but one idea—sharing a bed with Elizabeth. Bingley's sisters insisted on exhibiting at the pianoforte, but when I suggested that Elizabeth play, she refused.

"Forgive me, but I am not myself tonight. I do not think I could concentrate upon the music."

"You are worried about your father, are you not?" Bingley asked.

"I am. I plan to visit him directly on the morrow."

Caroline sniffed. "If you are that concerned, I wonder you did not go tonight."

"She would," I broke in, "but, as you know, the hour was late when we arrived, and I would not have my wife unduly tired."

Elizabeth glanced up at me. Was it gratitude I saw in her eyes because I once again defended her against Miss Bingley?

"I also need to be here for Fan. She is often frightened by new places and requires my attention."

"Oh?" Caroline responded. "Did transporting the girl to London cause her to suffer terrors?"

"She—"

I interrupted the conversation for the second time. "The child settled in quite well within a reasonable length of time."

Elizabeth laughed. "My husband is too kind. I fear Fan did disrupt the household at first, but now she has seemingly found her place."

"I noticed she calls you Mamá," Mrs. Hurst said. "And does she call you Papá, Mr. Darcy?"

Before I could answer, Caroline rose, stretching her neck in disapproval.

"Of course not, Louisa! How could you suggest such a thing? Should Wickham's child consider Mr. Darcy her father? What a ridiculous idea!"

I laid my book aside and walked to the fireplace. "The child is now my ward, Miss Bingley. I signed the papers before we left Town. We have become a family." Although my comments were directed at Bingley's sister, my eyes were upon Elizabeth.

She held my gaze for a lengthy moment, and then rising, she walked towards the door. "Speaking of Fan, if you will excuse me, I believe I should make certain she is settled for the night."

I supposed with Elizabeth's absence that Caroline would prevail upon my attention, but she grew strangely quiet and retreated to a remote corner, whereupon she picked up a book. I know she did not read it, for as I took a turn about the room, I saw she held it upside down.

Ah, Caroline, I mused, *if only there were a man for you. How much easier your brother's life would be; in truth, how much easier all our lives would be.*

ELIZABETH DID NOT RE-JOIN US THAT EVENING. THUS, THE TIME SPENT IN the drawing room grew ever more tiresome for me. At length, Mrs. Hurst awoke her husband, and they, along with her sister, offered their goodnights. I lingered over my drink, and Bingley kept me company. We discussed his estate affairs, and I counselled him on two projects on which he asked my opinion. On the whole, I concluded my friend had grown in maturity and was capable of sound decisions regarding his holdings.

As the hour grew late and I searched for a reason to delay going upstairs to give Elizabeth time to retire, I broached the subject of Bingley and Miss Bennet.

"She continues to be the sweetest angel God ever created," he raved. "Darcy, I know not how much longer I can refrain from making her my wife."

"What about talk among the community? Has the gossip abated somewhat since I married Elizabeth and removed Lydia's child from Longbourn?"

"Your marriage has consumed Hertfordshire! At first, no one would believe a man of your stature would condescend to marry a woman from a family that has borne such shame, but I believe the Bennets are overcoming the rumours that have beleaguered the family since Lydia ran off with Wickham."

"Good. That is as it should be, and I am sure inviting them to your ball aided in the change."

"Perhaps, but Darcy, you have paid the ultimate price. I know you had no intention of marrying one of Mr. Bennet's daughters until you saw how much in love I am with Jane. You are a friend above friends, and I shall always hold you in the highest regard for making this great sacrifice."

I sighed. How could I go on deceiving my friend? "Bingley, I—"

He held up his hands to silence me. "Do not deny it. You are the truest of friends, and I thank you from the bottom of my heart. I have every hope that 'twill not be long until I may ask Jane for her hand, and I owe it all to you." He rose, and we shook hands.

"You give me far too much credit."

"No, Darcy, I will not hear it."

I could see he was in earnest. "Very well. Although I do not agree with all you said, I will consent to the fact that we are true friends, and I hope we shall remain so."

"We shall," he repeated. "We certainly shall."

At last, I climbed the stairs and opened the door to the chamber Elizabeth and I shared. Having imbibed freely of Bingley's port, I hoped the effects of the liquor would enable me to fall asleep quickly. I knew full well that dwelling within such intimate quarters with Elizabeth would test my resolve. It would take everything within me to refrain from reaching for her in the night.

I had already dismissed my valet, so as quietly as possible, I undressed in the dark and slipped into bed. I confess I could not help but hope that the obstacle between us would not be there. I was disappointed to find the largest pillow I had ever felt placed squarely in the middle of the bed.

Elizabeth made not the slightest noise. I could not even hear her breathe, and I wondered whether she lay there still awake; or perhaps, I worried, fear had caused her to find a bed elsewhere despite our agreement. As I settled myself beneath the covers, her scent drifted over me, and I breathed a sigh of relief to know she was there, that she had not fled from my side. As always, her perfume awakened that same desire deep within me, that yearning I struggled so mightily to suppress. Tossing about, as I had suggested Elizabeth might do, would disturb her, so I forced myself to lie still. Try as I might, I could not keep from turning my head towards her. Like a magnet, her presence pulled me in her direction, and I longed to take her in my arms.

As my eyes adjusted to the dark, I could not refrain from raising myself to lean on my elbow so I might see over the pillow. Her light form curved beneath the coverlet, her dark curls fanned out across her pillow, and I could just make out the line of her profile. I leaned closer to observe her lips pursed together. How easy it would be to touch those alluring lips with my own. Her gentle breath made not a sound, but I could see the rise and fall of her breasts as she slept.

Oh, Elizabeth, can you not sense how much I love you, how much I want you?

She stirred and turned her face away, and immediately I lay back down. I thought her movement appropriately familiar, as though she could feel what I had fancied. I closed my eyes. Would she ever come to love me, or was that more than I could expect? She knew I wanted an heir, so she must anticipate our coming together eventually. The thought of such coupling flooded my body with a need so warm I was forced to throw off the covers. I turned on my side away from her, willing my mind to dwell on another subject. But, it was useless. With her presence so tantalizingly near, I could think of nothing other than Elizabeth.

If and when she did come to my bed willingly, would I be able to disguise the wealth of my love for her? For that was what it was. Not only did I desire her; I loved her with a love that shook me to the depths of my soul. Never had I felt for any other person the magnitude of feelings I had for Elizabeth. I would have given all I owned, all I would ever own or care for, my very life for her. And if by some blessed favour, she loved me back…such happiness I could not envision.

I could only dream, and mercifully, dreams finally came to me.

Chapter Ten

I awakened before dawn the next morning. Slipping quietly from beneath the quilt, I hastened into the dressing room and put on my clothes without calling for the services of my valet. I wished to leave the chamber before Elizabeth awoke and thus afford her the privacy she desired.

In truth, that was not my wish. If I had my way, I would have remained beside her. I would have watched her sleep as the early light spilled through the windows and then awakened her with a kiss, but I knew that was not to be—not yet. Silently moving through the chamber, I reached for the doorknob so my wife might dream in peace.

"Is that you, sir?" Elizabeth whispered.

I stilled, my hand in mid-air. "It is. I did not mean to wake you."

"Is it morning already?"

"Yes." I remained in place, unsure whether to turn and face her. "But still quite early. You need not rise yet. The fires have not even been lit."

"May I ask why you have risen at this hour?"

Slowly, I turned to see her sitting up in the bed. "I thought—that is, I assumed you would prefer me to do so."

She laughed lightly. "That will hardly satisfy the servants, will it? I thought this pretence was for their benefit—that they should see us sleeping in the same bed. If you vanish almost before dawn, will that not cause gossip?"

I walked towards the bed in an unhurried manner. "I confess I had not thought of that. Your argument is valid. Shall I return to bed?"

Instinctively, she leaned back, pulling the bedclothes higher. "I...do not think that necessary. But you might light a candle and remain in the room until your servant comes to help you dress."

I fumbled in the dim light until I had secured a single taper and, after several attempts, managed to light it. Never had I felt clumsier.

"Oh, you have already dressed," Elizabeth said as I lifted the candle and carried it to the mantel.

"I could hardly wander the halls of Netherfield otherwise."

"Of course not," she murmured, smiling again. "But will your manservant not find it strange you did not need his services?"

I sighed. "We appear to be going to great lengths to satisfy the servants. I suppose I could remove my coat."

"Yes, and untie your cravat as well."

I slid my coat off and untied the neck cloth, making a strong attempt to appear nonchalant, as though I did that sort of thing in Elizabeth's presence every day. "I may as well remove my waistcoat," I said, as I unbuttoned my vest, slinging each article of clothing across the back of the sofa. "There now, does my state of undress meet with your approval?"

I took several steps closer to her side of the bed and was pleased to see she continued to smile. Then, my heart skipped a beat as she beckoned me to come closer. Sitting up straighter, she leaned forward and patted the side of the bed, indicating I should sit there.

Light had brightened the room sufficiently for me to see how her gown lay precariously close to the edge of her shoulders, and her curls streamed down her back all in a tumble. Dear God, she was breathtaking in the morning, her countenance fresh and dewy! I could hardly breathe when she raised her hands to my neck.

"Let me open your shirt." She loosened the button from its loop and pushed my shirt open. "There, you almost look as though you slept here. One more touch." With her hand, she mussed my hair, causing it to fall across my forehead, and then she laughed. "Now, the servants will see that we are both, indeed, in need of assistance, and all will appear natural between us."

I did not know what to say. Her actions surprised me to such an extent that I could not think. I feared any words I spoke might come forth as babble.

Just then, we heard movement in the hall. Instantly, I reacted.

"You forgot one final necessity," I whispered as I leaned across Elizabeth. Her eyes grew wide. Grabbing the pillow that had separated us throughout the night, I tossed it across the room, where it landed upon the chaise. Her eyes danced, and she stifled a giggle as though she thoroughly enjoyed our artifice.

At that moment, the servant knocked softly and then opened the door, carrying a fresh supply of logs for the fireplace. Elizabeth's maid followed closely behind. Both servants bobbed a curtsy and halted within the doorway.

"Beggin' your pardon, sir," the older maid said. "Shall we return later?"

Slowly, I returned to a seated position. "No, go about your duties. All is well."

I could not but see the knowing look that passed between the servants as they busied themselves laying the fire and filling the ewers with hot water. I continued to stare at Elizabeth, and she did not break our gaze, that enchanting smile still playing about her lips.

"Well, sir, if I am to call upon my father, I suppose we cannot lie abed all morning, can we?"

"No, that is why I rose early," I replied for the servants' benefit. "I knew you wished to call at Longbourn as soon as may be." I stood and looked around the room. "Is Rodgers on his way?"

"Yes, Mr. Darcy," Elizabeth's maid answered. "He's fetching fresh towels." She looked towards the hall door just as my valet entered. Shortly thereafter, I was ready to depart the chamber. Leaving my dressing room, I saw Elizabeth had risen and secluded herself behind the closed doors of her boudoir. I stared at the rumpled bedclothes and regretted the fact that we had done nothing more than sleep side by side.

At least she awakened smiling, I thought.

ELIZABETH LEFT NETHERFIELD SHORTLY AFTER BREAKFAST, CAUSING MISS Bingley's mood to lighten immediately. When she and Mrs. Hurst proposed I join them in a walk about the garden, I hastened to announce I was joining Hurst and Bingley in some sport.

"Why, then, shall we not join the men, Sister?" Caroline asked.

Bingley's eyebrows shot up. "Join us, Caroline? You and Louisa have never expressed an interest in shooting prior to today," he said.

"I have no desire to shoot, Charles, but I am in need of exercise, and a good tramp through the woods with all of you sounds delightful. Do you not agree, Louisa?"

Naturally, Mrs. Hurst nodded and exclaimed she was all anticipation at such a novelty.

I directed my frown towards Bingley, but he did nothing more than shrug his shoulders and rub his hands together. Hurst simply harrumphed and strode out the door.

Thus, some half hour later, the five of us, along with the stable hand and the dogs, set out for what can only be described as an unusual day's activity.

The day was bright, and the blue sky hosted a scattering of white clouds. A heavy dew still lingered on the grass, and I wondered that Caroline and Louisa cared to subject their skirts to the damp, but apparently they took little notice of it. The ladies were busy chattering the entire time we made our way through the fields.

Upon reaching the first stile, Caroline hurried to walk before me, reaching out her hand for my assistance in climbing the step. Fortunately, Bingley stood on the other side to help her descend. When Mrs. Hurst attained the top of the stile, she uttered an annoying squeal. I gritted my teeth and bit my tongue. I wondered whether either of Bingley's sisters had ever deigned to walk on ground not previously landscaped or paved with stones.

How dissimilar were they from Elizabeth! Had she walked with us, I could imagine the bloom colouring her cheeks, her expressed joy at being out in the fresh air, and her delight and appreciation of the surrounding countryside.

"Oh, wait! I have a burr in my gown," Caroline cried. "Pray, someone remove it before it tears my silk."

Bingley hastened to help his sister while I walked on, catching up with Hurst who had marched ahead some distance. At last, we arrived at our stand. Bingley cautioned the ladies to remain far afield of us, which they did, I am thankful to report. However, each time we shot a bird, they burst forth in a volley of clapping and shrieking. Needless to say, the number of pheasant we had uncovered soon vanished along with every other bird within five miles.

At the end of the fruitless day, my fellows and I returned, thoroughly dissatisfied, while Mrs. Hurst and Miss Bingley exclaimed that they were exhilarated by the outing. When they expressed an interest in joining us the next day, I am ashamed to admit that all three of us men said, "No!" at the same time and in an alarming tone of voice.

"But why ever not?" Caroline asked.

"Sport is a man's activity, Caroline," Bingley replied. "And besides, you must consider your complexion. Hurst, do you not believe my sister's face is growing somewhat *tanned* from being so long in the sun?"

Mr. Hurst simply grunted, but Caroline became highly agitated. "Tanned? Oh, no! Sister, Sister, let us repair to our chambers and have the maid fetch our lotions at once!"

I could not help but smile at Bingley as the ladies hurried across the park and into the house.

"I did not see *that* much sun today," I said quietly.

"As much as my sister values her complexion, it behooves me to urge caution," Bingley answered with a shrug and a grin.

Upon entering the house, Maggie bobbed a curtsy before me. "Beggin' your pardon, Mr. Darcy, but Mrs. Abernathy is not well."

"Is she in need of the physician?" Bingley asked.

The maid appeared nervous. "She says it's nothin' serious, but—"

"But what?" I asked. "Say what you mean, girl."

"It's Miss Fan, sir. She got away from me, and I can naught find her nowhere."

"Blast!" I hastily dropped my coat, hat, and gloves in the manservant's hands. "Where did you last see her?"

"On her bed, sir. She was taking a nap, and I...well—"

"Yes?"

"I...uh...had to leave the room for a few moments. When I returned, she was gone. I've searched the house, but like I said—"

"You cannot find her," I finished, gritting my teeth for the second time that day. "Has Mrs. Darcy returned from Longbourn?"

"No, sir," the maid said.

"Well, the little one cannot have gone far," Bingley offered. "Let me call some of the servants, and I am certain we will uncover her."

"Do not be too sure of that," I said grimly. "She has a talent for hiding where you least expect her."

Some two hours later, I found the child curled up asleep inside Elizabeth's wardrobe on a pile of her best gowns. She had wadded them up and made a sort of nest for herself.

When I opened the wardrobe door, she awakened with a start and began to wail.

"What have you done?" I said. My voice must have sounded harsher than I intended, for I truly was relieved to have discovered her unharmed. Stooping down to her level, I attempted to speak in a softer tone. "There now, do not cry. All is well."

I stared in unbelief as she held out her little arms to me. "Up, man," she sobbed.

Rather surprised that she did not even know my name, I picked her up, gathered her into my arms, and somewhat stiffly attempted to pat her shoulder. "There, there, no harm done." I rose and carried her to Elizabeth's boudoir chair, whereupon I sat down and placed the child on my lap. She sniffed and sucked her thumb while her shoulders continued to shudder with the remnants of sobs.

"Tell me," I said slowly, "why did you make a jumble of your aunt's gowns?"

She raised her eyes to mine and mumbled something.

"Here, let us remove your thumb. I cannot understand you." Gently, I pulled her hand from her mouth. "Now, what did you say?"

"Mamá gowns."

"Yes, those are Elizabeth's gowns. Why did you pull them down?"

"Smell Mamá."

"Ah," I said, smiling, for I certainly understood the allure of Elizabeth's scent. "Did you miss Aunt Elizabeth? Were you looking for her?"

Screwing up her face, Fan began to cry anew. "Want Mamá!"

"She is coming back from Longbourn soon. Do not cry. Your eyes will be red. Let us find Maggie." I stood up and carried her from the dressing room into the bedchamber.

"No Maggie. Mamá!"

Just then, Elizabeth threw open the door from the hallway and hurried into the room.

"Fan! Oh, you found her! Thank God!" Holding out her arms, Elizabeth took the child, who was only too happy to seek refuge in my wife's embrace. Maggie, along with several of Bingley's servants, stood in the doorway, and Elizabeth quickly left the room, returning the babe to the nursery.

Once the bedchamber was emptied, I walked to the fireplace and drummed my fingers on the mantel. The child really was rather cherubic. I could still feel her tiny arms around my neck and the warmth of her little body sitting on my lap. Yet, there was no excuse for the disorder she had caused at Netherfield. I sincerely hoped Mrs. Abernathy recovered on the morrow, for Maggie had proved just as inept as I had previously judged her.

Later, Elizabeth returned to dress for dinner. I had remained in our suite, engrossed in a new book I had bought before our journey. I looked up, relieved to see a small smile in answer to mine. She appeared tired, her shoulders drooping, with a look of apprehension reflected in her eyes.

"Has peace returned to the nursery?"

She sank down on the chaise across from my chair. "Yes. I am sorry Maggie allowed Fan to cause such a disturbance. If Mrs. Abernathy—"

"It matters not. The only consequence I can see is that your maid shall have to tend that pile of gowns the child slept on." At Elizabeth's look of wonder, I explained where I had found the little one and what she had done. "One cannot blame her for searching out the strongest reminder of you."

"I fear Fan possesses that same spirit of mischief her own dear mother owned. More and more, she reminds me of Lydia."

"Better her mother than her father," I said, to which Elizabeth nodded in agreement. "But I would discuss one matter with you. The child insists upon calling you Mamá. Do you think that wise? Should she not be instructed that you are not her mother but her aunt?"

Elizabeth pressed her lips together and picked up some needlework that lay upon the table nearby. She examined the stitches but did not withdraw the needle to resume the work. "It is hardly unusual that she calls me Mamá. Every child needs a mother, and since hers is gone, I suppose I have taken her place."

I closed my book and laid it aside. "But is that proper? I find it curiously unsettling."

"And why is that? Have we not taken her to rear as our own?"

Our own?

"Did I not hear you tell Caroline Bingley we were a family? And in a family does not a child need parents?"

"I agree that she needs guardians."

"But not parents." A frown knit her brows together. "Why is that? Do you dislike Fan to such a degree that you would deny her the comfort we might provide?"

I rose and poured myself a glass of water. "I do not dislike the child. In truth, I find her rather endearing—undisciplined, but still—" I coughed, clearing my throat. "It is just—"

"Just what?" Elizabeth said, leaning forward. I could hear the irritation in her tone.

I turned to face her. Gazing into her eyes, the truth struck me. "It is just that I never thought to hear any child call you 'Mamá' but mine."

There, I had said it. My heart beat faster. I saw the expression in Elizabeth's eyes change. She blinked several times as though my response had been the last thing she had expected to hear. An uneasy silence filled the room.

Had I said too much? Revealed my feelings too soon? I wanted to know, and yet, I feared the answer.

At last, I walked into the dressing room and rang the bell for my servant. By the time he had aided me in dressing for dinner, Elizabeth came from her boudoir, clad in a soft rose gown that caused her skin to glow, all semblance of weariness washed away.

I opened the door to the hallway and waited for her to walk through. I offered my arm, and looking up, she smiled and placed her hand thereon.

"How did you find your father?" I asked as we descended the stairs.

"He was glad to see me although he is still weak. He hopes to rise from his bed by Christmas Eve, and Mamá insists we join them at Longbourn for dinner."

"Do you think that prudent?"

"I think it would lift my father's spirits to see us all together, for he questioned me at length as to whether I was happy."

"And what did you tell him?"

"That I am fairly well satisfied with my situation and that you have not yet beat me more than once a day."

Horrified, I stopped and stood perfectly still until I heard her giggle and saw the sparkle in her eyes.

When will I ever learn? I wondered, sighing and shaking my head.

THE BEAUTY OF THE CHRISTMAS SEASON IN HERTFORDSHIRE COULD HARDLY equal that of Derbyshire, although I must say the festivities proved far livelier than any I had celebrated at Pemberley during the past seven or eight years. Only a faint dusting of snow littered the ground and rooftops, while I remembered with longing how majestic my snow-covered estate had reigned in years past during the month of December. Still, I recalled the last Christmas Eve Georgiana and I had spent there as quite subdued.

I trusted my sister would spend a joyful holiday in Lancashire at the estate of her new husband's family. She had written of their plans to travel and, once again, expressed her desire to meet my wife. I had assured her by return post that we would welcome them at Pemberley once we were able to leave Hertfordshire. I longed to see my sister and marvelled anew at how quickly our lives had changed in a matter of months. Had it only been this past September that I had escorted her down the aisle, and now we both were enveloped into the bosoms of our respective new relations? A year ago, I never would have foreseen spending Christmas as the guests of Mr. and Mrs. Bennet!

Gaiety and high spirits ruled at Longbourn. The small house fairly swayed to and fro with music, singing, and laughter. Candles glowed in abundance, generous displays of food and drink filled the table and sideboard, and widespread merriment ensued. Mr. Bennet felt well enough to descend into the throng, much to the delight of his daughters and guests. Made comfortable in his favourite chair and tucked in with pillows and blankets, he was indulged at every whim with eager participation by Jane, Elizabeth, or Kitty. Mrs. Bennet's voice penetrated the ceilings with her various exclamations, laughter, and exuberant displays of hospitality. It was evident that she enjoyed playing the hostess, especially since Bingley had accompanied Elizabeth and me—along with her grandchild, of course.

We had spent the day at Netherfield in the usual felicitations of the holiday, but upon news that the invitation to dinner at Longbourn for that evening had been extended to all of us, Caroline developed a headache, and Mrs. Hurst declined to leave her sister. Naturally, her husband remained behind, once he was assured Bingley's cook would prepare a feast for them and his glass would not be allowed to go empty. I wondered that Bingley did not feel obliged to remain with his family, but he seemed all too eager to board the carriage with us.

I had questioned the propriety of taking the child as I knew the hour would grow late before we returned, but Elizabeth assured me that her family had made a special plea to have Lydia's little girl present upon such a joyful occasion.

"My mother said that Fan's presence would be a bit like having Lydia there," Elizabeth said. "She still misses her greatly. Christmas was always such a happy time when all my sisters were at home, and with Mary and her husband unable to make the journey, my family needs the pleasure Fan naturally adds."

Upon arrival, I learned Mr. and Mrs. Gardiner and their children had also journeyed from London for a visit as well as Mrs. Bennet's sister and her husband, Mr. and Mrs. Phillips, from Meryton. I had met the attorney Phillips and his wife previously, of course, but I was pleasantly surprised when introduced to the Gardiners. Elizabeth's uncle seemed an intelligent man, quite the opposite of his two sisters in demeanour and very successful in his business interests from all accounts, while Mrs. Gardiner possessed as genteel and polished a manner as any lady in society that I had encountered. I soon perceived why Elizabeth was fond of them, and I found myself regretting not having made their acquaintance while in London.

"I understand you are the master of Pemberley in Derbyshire," Mrs. Gardiner said. "I grew up in that county, and I do love it so."

"It is my favourite place on earth," I responded. "Where, precisely, did you live?"

"In the village of Lambton."

"I know it well."

"And who that lives in Derbyshire could fail to know of Pemberley? My husband and I delighted in touring it with Elizabeth when last we visited the county."

"Elizabeth has seen Pemberley?" I was shocked, for my wife had never mentioned it. "When did that trip occur?"

"Some years past, sir," Mr. Gardiner answered. "I am surprised Elizabeth did not tell you! We invited our niece to tour the Lake Country with us that summer. Alas, my business prevented an extensive holiday, and thus, we contented ourselves with Derbyshire." He continued telling how they had also visited Dovedale and Matlock.

"But you saw the house?" I repeated.

Mrs. Gardiner nodded. "Your family was away, but the housekeeper, Mrs. Reynolds I believe, said we were welcome to view the mansion."

"Yes, yes, of course. I only regret I was not there to receive you. When, exactly did you say your visit occurred?"

"I believe it was the summer after you had first met Elizabeth here at Longbourn," she replied.

"Ah, yes, I had already made plans to go abroad by that time. A pity, a great pity we did not meet then. You must return and allow me to welcome you properly and show you the place myself. Do you care for fishing, Mr. Gardiner?"

"Indeed, I do," he answered emphatically.

I then went on to commend the virtues of my well-stocked ponds and lake, and I asked him to join us at Pemberley later in the summer and participate in the sport. He seemed somewhat taken aback by my words, but both he and Mrs. Gardiner graciously accepted the invitation.

At the close of the evening, Kitty and Jane begged to have the child spend the night. Mrs. Bennet added her voice, and even though Elizabeth questioned whether the added noise would harm her father, the family would not be dissuaded. Thus, my wife and I returned to Netherfield with Bingley and left Maggie to care for the little girl.

"I fail to see how your father shall recover with a houseful of people," I said. "Did not the doctor prescribe peace and quiet for his patient?"

Elizabeth laughed. "He did, but Jane says Papá seems much improved since we have arrived. Besides, the Gardiners were to go home with my Aunt Phillips, so that will lessen the number considerably."

"Mr. and Mrs. Gardiner are fine people," Bingley said.

"They are," I added.

To this, Elizabeth turned and faced me. "What is this? You find some of my connexions worthy?" With a smile, she turned towards Bingley and raised her eyebrows, which made him laugh.

"No one who meets them could fail to find otherwise. I regret I have neglected to do so until now. I have invited them to visit Pemberley in the summer."

"Indeed?" Elizabeth sounded shocked.

"Capital idea, Darcy!" Bingley said. "Mr. Gardiner and I discussed fishing for some time at the table, and I believe he is proficient in the sport. He should take great enjoyment in your estate."

Elizabeth remained silent for the remainder of the ride, but I could feel her eyes upon me as the carriage pulled into the drive at Netherfield. Did I dare hope my overtures towards her family might thaw our own relations a bit further?

Chapter Eleven

We had tarried long over the Christmas celebrations at Longbourn, and the hour was late when we climbed the stone steps and entered Netherfield. Bingley asked whether I cared for a drink before bed, but I could see he was as tired as I. In truth, I had little desire to imbibe more that evening, but I knew I should afford Elizabeth time to retire in private. As I opened my mouth to accept, Elizabeth took my hand.

"It is so late. Shall we not go up?" she said.

Surprise rendered me speechless. What did that mean? Could it possibly be the invitation I longed for?

"Of course, you should," Bingley said. "We have enjoyed more than our share of amusement this night, have we not?"

Elizabeth smiled at him, and I followed her up the stairs like an idiot struck dumb with delight. Inside our chamber, I soon learned she offered no more than kindness.

"I regret you have been forced to wait so long to retire each night," she said, as we walked through the door. "If you would linger a bit in your dressing room, I shall have my maid hasten with her duties, and I will be able to get into bed without prolonging your delay. You have been more than patient tonight, putting up with my family."

"Very well," I murmured, entering the adjoining room. I could think of nothing else to say, for I sought to hide my disappointment. Rodgers assisted me in dressing for bed rather quickly, gathered up the discarded clothing and towels, and waited for me to walk through the door before him. Instead,

I dismissed him with a gesture, explaining I wished to peruse my wardrobe and make the next day's selection.

"Yes, sir," he answered, obviously dumbfounded, for I had never made such a statement in all the years he had served me. "Shall I fetch a selection of coats for your examination, sir?"

I waved him aside again. "No, no. I prefer to...inspect them on my own."

After the servant departed the room, I shook my head. *He must think I am in my cups!* I sank down on the settee, regretting I had not taken a book to read from the bedside table. How long should I wait? I had no idea the length of time Elizabeth required to undress. More than once, I rose and strained to listen at the door, but I heard neither sound nor movement from the bedchamber. At length, I decided sufficient time had passed.

Opening the door, I cleared my throat to announce my entrance just in time to look up and see Elizabeth standing by the bed, slipping off her robe. With a quick glance over her shoulder in my direction, she darted under the eiderdown quilt, but not quickly enough, for I stood transfixed, every nerve on fire at the sight of her beautiful, light figure clad in nothing more than a thin gown of fine ivory lawn.

"I—beg your pardon," I said, swallowing hard. "I failed to estimate adequate time."

"All is well, sir. I am secure beneath the covers as you can see."

When she smiled, I could feel anxiety flow out of me. Walking to my side of the bed, I kept my back to her while disrobing and then swung my legs up under the sheets and lay back.

"Shall you blow out the candle?" Elizabeth said.

"Of course." I sat up and extinguished the light. Now we were in darkness save for the faint moonlight that glimmered through the window, bathing the room with inconstant shadows.

"Shall we say good-night, sir?"

That was the last thing I wished to say. I wanted her to remain awake, to converse with me, to allow me to declare how I loved her and wished her to be my wife in every way...but I did not voice my desires.

"Are you very tired?" I asked, instead.

"In truth, I am not. I find myself filled with elation from the evening's festivities. Are you?"

"Sleep is the last thing on my mind."

"And what is on your mind, sir?"

Oh, you must not ask me that question, Elizabeth!

I cleared my throat. "I wonder why you never told me you had seen Pemberley."

"Did I not?"

"No. And I find myself somewhat disappointed."

"In what way?"

"I had hoped the first time you saw the house, I would be the one to guide you through it."

I could feel her smiling. "I am certain I saw but a small portion of your home, for your housekeeper took us on an abbreviated tour. I look forward to viewing the entire mansion through your eyes."

"Were you pleased by what you saw?"

"Pleased? Who could fail to be other than pleased by Pemberley? I believe I should be very happily situated living there."

"I long for us to go."

"I regret my father's ill health postponed our trip."

I turned on my side to face her, but the large pillow between us prevented my seeing her countenance, so I raised myself up on one arm. "Elizabeth, do not be regretful. We are where we are needed.

"That is generous of you," she said, turning to face me. Reaching forth, she placed her hand upon the pillow, and slowly I dared to place mine over hers. When she did not protest or attempt to withdraw her hand, I raised it to my lips.

"Happy Christmas, Elizabeth."

"Happy Christmas, Fitzwilliam," she whispered softly. I then lay back, and we said no more that night, but my heart sang. Oh, it sang to the heavens above! At last, she had called me by my Christian name.

GARLANDS OF HOLLY GRACED THE SANCTUARY OF LONGBOURN CHURCH on the following morn, their red berries bursting forth with colour among the dark, polished wooden fixtures. As we entered the building in observance of the Christmas service, I noted it was crowded with parishioners, the pews swelling to unusual numbers. Ample room for us existed, however, for Mr. Hurst had remained abed, having indulged in Bingley's Christmas spirits far too freely the night before. Elizabeth and I followed Bingley and his sisters to their seats, and I saw the Gardiners had joined the Bennets across the aisle. Mr. Bennet, of course, did not attend, but Bingley leaned forward to smile at Miss Bennet, who blushed in return.

"I love the Christmas story," Elizabeth whispered.

I nodded and smiled, attempting to return my thoughts to the words spoken by the vicar. I confess my mind had strayed far from Bethlehem. I wondered when I might possibly broach the subject of our departure from Hertfordshire. Speaking of it the night before had only sharpened the need within my heart to see my home again and to experience the renewal of spirits that inevitably occurred upon first glimpse of the magnificent land-scape. And after the closeness with which Elizabeth and I had bid each other goodnight, I yearned to make her the mistress of Pemberley.

Glancing down upon her, I felt satisfaction to see that she wore the Christmas gift I had bestowed upon her that morning. A pendent hung from her neck containing a perfect rose-cut amethyst surrounded by a circle of diamonds. It caressed the soft hollow of her neck, and I envied its placement. I recalled how she had gasped with delight upon opening the beribboned box to discover the necklace nestled within.

"It is exquisite, Fitzwilliam," she had said without pretence, and I could tell she had been truly pleased.

She had asked me to secure it 'round her neck before we left for the church, and I confess my hands lingered longer than necessary while fastening the clasp. I wanted to cover all of her in jewels, and my thoughts meandered down that happy path for the remainder of the sermon.

The congregation rose to sing the closing hymn, pulling me back to my surroundings. With the final "amen," we filed outdoors. The earlier snow clouds had vanished, and heaven had blessed us with a day filled with sunshine.

"Mr. Bingley, Mr. Bingley!" Mrs. Bennet cried, pushing her way through several people to reach our side. "Was that not a beautiful service, and is this not a glorious Christmas morning?"

"It is, ma'am," Bingley said, smiling anew at the sight of Jane being pulled along behind her mother. "It truly is."

"And how shall you spend the rest of the day, sir? Do you have special plans for the afternoon?"

"No...that is—"

"Mamá," Elizabeth said, taking her arm, "we shall most likely enjoy a quiet day after the excitement of last evening."

"Oh, was it not lovely?" the woman declared. "I said to Mr. Bennet this very morning, 'Mr. Bennet, if only every night could be as enjoyable as the last!'"

Jane sighed and beseeched her sister with her expression.

"How is Papá faring this morning?" Elizabeth asked quickly.

Mrs. Bennet waved her hand as though to dismiss her daughter. "Oh, well enough. He is not near as sick as he pretends to be."

"Mamá!" Mrs. Bennet's daughters exclaimed in unison.

"I am glad to hear he is well," Bingley said. "I feared that entertaining a crowd might have taxed Mr. Bennet's strength."

Of a sudden, Mrs. Bennet's eyes widened, and I swear it looked as though a light appeared over her head.

"Now that you mention it, Mr. Bingley, my husband does need his solitude. I was just thinking, if only the girls and I might absent Longbourn a bit longer and allow him time alone to recover, what a fine thing that would be."

I heard Caroline's exasperated sigh behind me and frantic whispers directed towards her sister's ear, but Bingley's countenance lit up as though Mrs. Bennet had struck a match to it.

"Then why not join us for breakfast at Netherfield? Would that not give Mr. Bennet the solitude he needs and afford us a jollier celebration if we are all together?"

"Oh, Mr. Bingley! That is true gentlemanly behaviour if I have ever seen it! Girls, is that not the perfect solution and so good of Mr. Bingley? We shall be delighted to accept your invitation, sir."

Caroline groaned, but Mrs. Hurst put on a weak smile and attempted to play the welcoming hostess as we turned to board the carriages.

"What about Fan, Mamá?" Elizabeth said. "She remains at Longbourn. Will she not bother our father with her noise?"

"Oh, little Fan shall be well attended. Maggie is there to see to her, and you can come home with us afterwards to fetch her. Come along, girls. We must not keep Mr. Bingley waiting."

An elaborate Christmas breakfast had been ordered, and fortunately, the cook had prepared more than required to feed Bingley's extra guests. It almost made me wonder whether my friend had contemplated the idea of inviting Jane Bennet and her family before her mother constrained him to do so. Nonetheless, the meal progressed as one might expect with that assortment of people confined to the dining room.

Mrs. Bennet sallied forth with unexplainable effusions of pleasure over every dish on the table—all attributed to Bingley's inestimable worth, naturally. Caroline contributed veiled barbs when she made the rare attempt to converse. Mrs. Hurst pretended all was well but for the raised eyebrows she directed at her sister each time the mistress of Longbourn opened her mouth to speak. Jane Bennet blushed continually, and Elizabeth, after trying to stem her mother's conversation, eventually ceased and sat back to observe as I did. All the while, Bingley reigned over the table with unending charm and amiability. If anyone might overlook the unsuitability of the situation, my friend was the man to do so.

"I wonder I do not see one sprig of mistletoe hung about the house," Mrs. Bennet said as we made our way into the drawing room at the close of the meal. "You know, Kitty sought out the best glens in the county in which it grows long before the holiday arrived. Next year, she must gather some for Netherfield, Miss Bingley."

"By all means," Caroline said.

"I always say, 'What is Christmas without a bit of mistletoe?' Is that not right, Jane? And besides, Mr. Bingley, it allows for a stolen kiss or two, does it not?"

Now, it was Bingley's turn to blush. Fortunately, Mrs. Hurst had tables set up for card games, and she diverted Mrs. Bennet's attention by asking her to play. Mr. Hurst had joined us for breakfast, having recovered sufficiently while we worshipped, and he was eager to participate in the afternoon's activities. With Caroline as a reluctant fourth, the game afforded Bingley and Jane a period in which to talk. Naturally, Elizabeth and I visited with them while Kitty Bennet picked out a tune on the pianoforte. She was not as well acquainted with the instrument as her sister Mary, a fact I did not know whether to rejoice in or regret.

At length, I called for the carriage to transport Elizabeth to Longbourn to fetch the child, causing her mother and sisters to prepare to take their leave also. I knew Elizabeth worried that her father had overexerted himself the evening before, no matter how her mother dismissed the idea, and she would not rest until she saw for herself he was well. When her mother continued to dawdle and delay departing, Elizabeth looked up at me.

"Shall you see me off?"

"Of course. Give your father my best wishes."

I took her elbow and escorted her from the room, precipitating Mrs. Bennet following her daughters to their vehicle at last. After many good-byes, they were set to leave. From the window of the carriage, Elizabeth asked, "And what shall you do with the rest of the day?"

"Most probably a good ride before the weather turns too dreary, as I feel the need to be active."

"I think that a splendid idea."

BINGLEY ASKED ME TO ACCOMPANY HIM TO THE STABLES TO INSPECT A NEW colt that had been born in the early morning. We both were pleased the Christmas pony appeared healthy, and after Bingley conferred with the stable hand, we mounted up and left Netherfield for a long ride. We raced our horses up and down the meadows for a considerable time, and I revelled in the brisk air and exercise. By the end of the day, the clouds had returned, snow began to fall lightly, and we were ready to return to a warm fire and steaming cups of mead.

I was more than eager for my wife's presence, but she stayed long with her family and did not come in until after dinner. Thus, I was forced to endure the evening without Elizabeth's company. When I refused to join the card game, Caroline declared she was not in the mood for games either. Instead, she occupied herself by parading about the room, often sighing with deliberate affectation. When that failed to produce any response from the company present other than a smile from her sister, she exhibited herself at the pianoforte for three-quarters of an hour. Her performance was executed without fault, and I was much relieved that doing so forced her to remove herself to the opposite side of the room.

I could not help but feel some sympathy for Bingley's sister, for she seemed a wretched soul. Caroline wanted a husband, but she needed to alter her demeanour in order to attract men other than fortune hunters. Had I not realized the need for an alteration in my own outlook before I understood why the woman I loved would not have me? Yes, I could sympathize with Caroline, but I knew not how to come to her aid.

Instead, I wished my wife would return, and at last, Elizabeth walked into the drawing room. My heart swelled at the sight of her. Bingley asked about her father, and she replied he was tired but none the worse for enduring the excitement of the night before. Bingley invited her to join our company, but she refused.

"I must decline tonight, sir, as I have brought Fan back with me, and I fear Maggie will encounter difficulty putting her to bed, for she is still excited from being at my mother's house. I pray you will excuse me."

"Of course," Bingley said.

"Shall I come with you?" I asked.

Surprise reflected in her eyes, but she quickly masked it with a smile. "If you wish."

"Then, I shall bid you all good-night," I said to my host and his family, "since I have been deprived of my wife's company this afternoon." From the corner of my eye, I saw Bingley smile and shake his head.

I knew I appeared besotted with love, but it was true. I was so hungry to be with Elizabeth that I would even walk to the nursery with her! My presence flustered Maggie, but I justified my unusual action by making inquiries as to Mrs. Abernathy's health.

"I am somewhat improved, Mr. Darcy," the woman herself announced, entering the child's room from the adjoining chamber. She walked slowly and with the aid of a cane.

"We are glad to hear that," Elizabeth said, "but you must not become fatigued, lest the fever returns."

"Indeed," I echoed and then cast my eyes upon the child. "Well, young lady, have you had a busy day?"

Elizabeth looked up, seemingly amazed at my interest. The child had been washed and dressed for bed by that time, but she clung to her aunt.

"That will be all for now, Maggie. I shall put Fan to bed."

The maid bobbed a curtsy and disappeared through the open door.

"I regret that Miss Fan caused a disturbance while I have been indisposed," Mrs. Abernathy said. "I hope it did not inconvenience the household unduly when she was supposedly *lost*. I fancy this little girl delights in exploration. In my experience, I find it shows an intelligent, inquisitive mind."

"I can bear witness to that," I said emphatically, but seeing a frown flicker across Elizabeth's brow, I explained. "I feel certain that, with your guidance, Mrs. Abernathy, she may use her natural talents in a more advantageous manner."

"She surely will, Mr. Darcy. And soon I will take charge fully once again. For now, I shall bid you adieu for the evening." Mrs. Abernathy made her exit, and Elizabeth tucked the child into bed. I took the opportunity to look about the room, noting it contained various dolls and numerous toys.

"Shall you say your prayers, Fan?" Elizabeth asked the child.

"No."

"But you know how to pray. Have I not taught you since you uttered your first words?"

"No pray."

"Fan, you always say your prayers before going to sleep. Here, Mr. Darcy and I will help you. Simply repeat after us." Elizabeth knelt before the bed, and she glanced up at me. Surely, she did not suggest that I kneel as well! When she fixed her gaze upon me, reluctantly I lowered myself to my knees and joined her.

"Gentle Jesus, meek and mild—" Elizabeth said, and when neither the child nor I said a word, she turned her head slightly towards me, waiting.

Clearing my throat, I repeated the phrase I had learned in childhood.

"It is your turn, Fan," Elizabeth prodded.

"No pray—talk!"

Elizabeth pressed her lips together, and I shook my head.

Typical of Wickham's child!

"Now, listen here, you will obey your Aunt Elizabeth!" I said more forcefully than I intended.

The child began to wail, and Elizabeth quickly rose and took her into her arms. "There, there, Fan, do not cry. Mr. Darcy did not mean to frighten you."

Feeling awkward, I rose to my feet and prepared to leave the room, but Elizabeth shook her head, nodding towards a place beside her on the bed.

"Mean man," the child said between sobs.

"What man? Mr. Darcy? Oh, no, Fan, he is not mean. He is most kind. Remember how he found you when you were lost? How he held you until I came?"

The child snuggled closer to Elizabeth, and her tears ceased as quickly as they had begun.

"Would you like for him to hold you again?"

Oh, no! I felt as out of place as ever I had, and my last desire was to hold the child, but hold her I did, for after staring at me for some time with her great brown eyes, she crawled into my lap. I attempted as best I could to soothe her, but I held her at arms' length, once again stiffly patting her shoulder.

"Talk," she repeated.

"What shall we talk about?"

"Maggie man." She looked up at me as though I was supposed to understand her gibberish.

Elizabeth reached over and wiped the last of her tears away with a handkerchief. "Maggie is not a man. She is a girl."

The child shook her head. "Maggie man!"

Elizabeth glanced at me, but I certainly did not understand. I suspected Mrs. Abernathy's previous determination of the little girl's intelligence had been far too hasty.

"Maggie is a girl like you and me. Mr. Darcy is a man." Elizabeth gestured towards herself and then towards me. "You must not say Maggie is a man."

"No! Maggie man!" The child began to squirm, and I could feel my patience growing thinner by the moment.

But wait, I suddenly thought, perhaps it was not the child who did not understand, but Elizabeth and me.

"Do you mean Maggie *and* a man?" I asked hesitantly but in as gentle a voice as I could manage. "Did you see your nurse with a man?"

She began to bob her head up and down, and a smile appeared on her little face. So unexpected was its appearance that I could not help but smile in return. I had not known communication with a child, when it actually took place, could produce such a feeling of well-being.

Elizabeth smiled and clapped her hands. "You have solved the riddle! Three cheers for Mr. Darcy!"

The child laughed in delight and clapped her hands, as well. "Maggie and man," she proudly announced.

"The nursemaid must have a suitor," I said, handing the child back to Elizabeth. "Most likely, it is one of the stable hands here at Netherfield or even at Longbourn."

"Yes, most likely. Now, Fan, you must go to sleep, for it is past your bedtime. Shall you say your prayers like a good girl?"

The child nodded and yawned, snuggling down beneath the quilt. Once more, Elizabeth led her in the nursery prayer, to which she made unintelligible stabs at repetition. With a quick kiss goodnight, Elizabeth rang the bell for the maid to return and stay with the child until she fell asleep, and we made our way to our chamber.

At the door, I hesitated about going in with her, but she seemed content for me to do so. After all, we had said our goodnights to the company within the drawing room, so it would seem rather strange if I joined them again.

"Shall I pour you a sherry?" Elizabeth asked as I followed her into the sitting area and stood before the fireplace.

I nodded. "And will you join me?"

"I will."

As she prepared our drinks, I poked at the fire, stirring it up into a good blaze.

"I wonder at the wisdom of retaining that nursemaid, Elizabeth."

"What do you mean?"

"Obviously, she must have spent time dallying with some fellow in the child's presence. God knows what the little one may have seen."

She handed me my glass. "I doubt Maggie would do anything untoward when Fan is close at hand, but if you wish, I will speak to her. I certainly do not see the need to dismiss her, though. She came to us about six months after the babe was born, and I do believe she loves Fan. I admit, at times, she is somewhat lax in her duties, but a child cannot have too much love."

The firelight enhanced Elizabeth's beauty as she stood before me. Her skin appeared softer and more luminous than ever. "No," I said, smiling, "no one can have too much love, be they child or man."

Instantly, her countenance altered, and she looked away.

"Fitzwilliam," she said slowly, "I am aware our marriage is not based on love but necessity. And I am grateful you have allowed me to wait to consummate our union. Even so, I am sensible that a man has certain needs, and I wish you to know I am trying...I truly am trying to reach that point."

Every part of my being caught fire! *Will she offer herself to me this night?*

"And I wondered..." Her voice trailed off, and a blush swept across her cheeks.

"Wondered?" I prompted, my voice emerging an octave deeper.

"Perhaps, if we began slowly."

"Slowly. I am certain I can do that." The words rushed out far too fast before I could contain them.

Turning, she lifted her eyes to my mouth but not my eyes. She could not meet my gaze.

"Could we—begin simply with some small sign of affection?" Her words were barely more than a whisper.

"And what might that sign be?" I said. "A kiss?"

The blush on her cheeks turned darker.

I swallowed. *Is it possible for me to kiss her and yet restrain myself?* I wanted her more than I had ever wanted anything in this life.

I needed time. I downed the sherry in one gulp. I walked to the table, and using both hands, I carefully placed the tiny glass thereon. Only then did I turn to face her.

"A kiss goodnight, Elizabeth. I will not go further...unless you desire it. You have my word."

Her bottom lip trembled as her gaze travelled upward to my eyes. Almost immediately, she lowered her head and turned her back to me. Was my desire too plain to see?

Silently, I walked closer until I could have reached for the tiny curl that caressed her neck. "I do believe a kiss goodnight would be a favourable way to begin," I said, amazed my voice did not tremble and betray me.

When her only response was an intake of breath, I placed my hands on her shoulders and gently turned her around to face me. She still would not meet my eyes, and so I lifted her chin with the tip of my finger. Steeling myself to move with caution, I bent my head and lightly—oh so lightly— touched my lips to that pink rosebud of a mouth I had sought for so long.

"Goodnight, Elizabeth," I said softly. She opened her eyes, and I could see relief settle over her.

"Goodnight, Fitzwilliam."

I DID NOT REMAIN WITHIN ELIZABETH'S PRESENCE—IT WOULD HAVE BEEN unbearable—so I strode directly to Bingley's library. I rang for brandy, and I confess that I swallowed the first glass without stopping and then poured another. Never had I felt more drained. I might as well have broken a horse or fought a duel. It had taken every ounce of strength I possessed to content myself with but one chaste kiss. The taste of Elizabeth had inflamed my passion so that I know not how I escaped the room without revealing my need for her.

Were we progressing or not? I hardly knew.

The fact that she had not refused my kiss must be considered a good sign.

I rejoiced in that small step, but then I remembered the relief I had seen manifest in her eyes afterwards, and disappointment set me back on my heels. Would she ever come to me with a desire that matched my own, or would it only be in grim fulfilment of her marital duty?

Acknowledge the truth: her need for you will never be as great as yours is for her! "If she ever needs me at all," I muttered aloud.

I put down my glass and resolved it would be the last that night. I had no desire to become like Hurst. After stirring the fire, I picked up the candle and held it aloft so I might study the niggardly selection of books on Bingley's shelves. I almost laughed aloud, for other than a few issues of the almanac, most every book I picked up contained poetry—and not just any poems, but verses of love written to woo and win a lady's heart.

It came as no surprise. Had not Bingley made falling in and out of love his occupation in life? I wondered how many of those books he had studied before calling on various ladies. Had he memorized lines with which to win Jane Bennet?

I ran my fingers over the line of titles. *Hmm, my friend reads far too much Byron!*

I certainly did not need that poet's enflamed verses that night. I needed something dull, something as far from love as I might find. Spying a volume of Wordsworth, I carried it back to the sofa. A steady examination of nature's beauty would surely calm the fires raging within me.

I allowed the book to fall open and read the first verse on the page.

> *She was a Phantom of delight*
> *When first she gleamed upon my sight;*
> *A lovely Apparition, sent*
> *To be a moment's ornament;*
> *Her eyes as stars of Twilight fair;*
> *Like Twilight's, too, her dusky hair;*
> *But all things else about her drawn*
> *From May-time and the cheerful Dawn;*
> *A dancing Shape, an Image gay,*
> *To haunt, to startle, and way-lay.*[1]

---

1 *She Was a Phantom of Delight*, William Wordsworth, 1804

Groaning anew, I slammed the book closed and tossed it aside. Had I forgotten Wordsworth could be romantic? It was hopeless. I could not escape. I was possessed by Elizabeth. I saw her everywhere, even in the description the poet had composed years earlier.

I truly had been *startled* the first time she passed before me, turned her head to the side and smiled in that impertinent manner. I was *waylaid* by the desire for her that soon followed, that I had fought against, helpless to conquer; and I was now *haunted* by a love I never imagined could pierce my heart with unending need.

Chapter Twelve

I awoke the following morning alone in bed. Sitting up, I reached for my robe and heard a fire crackling and spitting in the fireplace and the clink of a china cup being replaced in a saucer.

"Good morning," Elizabeth said from across the room. "Will you have some coffee?"

I rose, wrapped the dressing gown around me, and walked towards the sitting area. She was resting on the settee, still clad in her gown and robe, with her bare feet tucked up beneath her. Her face bore that warm, sleepy expression I loved, the very picture of intimacy, and her dark hair curled all about her, falling down her back and shoulders, asking to be stroked. I steadied my hands when I took the cup from her, steeling myself not to forego the coffee and reach for her curls.

"Did you sleep well?" I said, sitting beside her.

"I did. I fear you did not, however."

"Did I disturb you?"

"No, but I heard the clock strike three bells before you returned to our room."

"Forgive me. I thought you would be asleep. I went in search of a good book."

"And did you find what you sought?"

I sipped the coffee. "Not particularly."

"I hope some challenge did not prey upon your mind, causing your distress."

I wanted to shout, *"You are the challenge preying upon my mind! Do you know how much anguish you cause by expecting me to content myself with one kiss before bedtime when I desire to carry you to that bed and—"*

146

But...I did not. Instead, I dismissed her concerns and changed the subject. "This is rather pleasant, is it not—lingering over a bit of coffee before joining our hosts at the table?"

Elizabeth's eyes sparkled, and when she smiled, the entire room lit up. "It is. I confess I did not anticipate that marriage could be like this."

I looked up. "Like this?"

"This snug, cosy beginning to the day. I feared we might never feel this comfortable with one another. I believe we owe Mr. Bingley our gratitude."

"Bingley?"

"By forcing us to share this suite of rooms. I think it has lessened the distance between us in this marriage of convenience, do you not?"

I nodded. "And he has not the slightest idea of what he has done."

She laughed then, and I exulted in the enchanting display of her pleasure.

AFTER BREAKFAST, HURST AND BINGLEY INVITED ME TO MARKET TO LOOK at a new fowling piece that Hurst desired to purchase.

"The gun promises improved accuracy," Hurst said, and then he went on to harangue the present arms he owned, blaming them for his poor shots.

Elizabeth planned to join her sisters at the milliners in Meryton, so we four travelled together into the small town. She had extended the invitation to Bingley's sisters, but they had received new sheet music from Mr. Hurst's sister, and they preferred to practice a duet on the pianoforte.

"Do not forget we are invited to Lucas Lodge for dinner tonight," Elizabeth said to me as we parted on the street. I nodded and assured her I was aware of our plans. By that time, Bingley had met up with Jane Bennet, and Hurst grew impatient before, at length, we separated my friend from the object of his attention.

"Did not Miss Bennet look uncommonly pretty this morning?" Bingley said, continuing to glance over his shoulder, as we walked towards the gunsmith's.

I smiled while Hurst grumped along, bemoaning the time he thought we had wasted. Inside the shop, Bingley spied a Manton-style double-barrel like mine, and he declared that, if his brother bought the shotgun, his luck in the field would soon change for the better. Hurst picked up the piece and examined it in detail while I wandered over to another display of ornately carved long fowlers. I deemed the curly maple quite fine, nigh to excellent.

"May I help you, sir?" the store clerk asked.

I shook my head slightly, intending to dismiss him.

The man did not walk away but continued to hover close by. He cleared his throat several times and re-aligned the bags of gunpowder. I wondered why, for they had already been placed in orderly rows.

"Begging your pardon, sir," he said, "but might you be Mr. Darcy?"

I looked up, wondering at his question. "I am," I said.

"May I have a word alone, sir?"

"And you are?"

"John Morehouse, owner of this shop." He led the way to a quiet corner away from the others. "I was wondering, sir, whether you might know the whereabouts of a man called Wickham."

A chill ran down my spine, and I gave him a piercing look and lowered my voice before I spoke. "Why should I?"

The man appeared embarrassed, for he could not meet my eyes. "My boy said—"

"Your boy?"

"Yes, sir. He cleans up around the Black Stallion, and he said you paid him to run a message to Wickham some time back. I need to know whether the fellow is still anywhere 'round about."

I took a deep breath. I now remembered the young lad to whom I had given a farthing to find Wickham when he came to Meryton on my instructions.

"Has he harmed your son?"

Morehouse's shoulders drooped, and his mouth turned down at the corners. "Not my son, sir, but he owes me a great deal of money."

Inwardly, I groaned. Why had I ever thrust Wickham upon this village?

"Would you know where I could find him, sir?" the man pleaded. "Is he a friend of yours?"

"He is no friend of mine. As to his whereabouts, I ran him out of the county over a month ago. I assume he returned to London where he has adequate means to disappear. Even if you should find him, I am sorry to say he will not make good on his obligation. His habit is to leave debts wherever he goes."

"I know that now, sir! I've been here less than six months, so when the man came into my shop, I had little reason to distrust him. He took one of my finest pistols."

"Do you normally allow a man to take merchandise without making payment?"

"He said he wanted to try it out—to make sure it'd line up straight. I took him out back where I've set up some targets so he could test the gun. I watched him fire a few shots, but another customer walked in about the same time. Expect it was a good three-quarters of an hour that I spent with the other man, so I put my boy in the yard to keep an eye on Mr. Wickham. He got the better of him, though. Asked him to go fetch some gunpowder, and when the boy returned, the thief had vanished. I sought him all over the village, but he was nowhere to be found, and no one's seen aught of him since."

I looked out the window, squinting at the glare caused by the sunshine reflected on the glass. "That must have occurred some weeks back before I sent him away. I fear you must write off the bill as one that will never be collected."

"But that's just it, sir. It wasn't weeks back that it happened. He was here just four days ago. That's when he took the gun."

At those words, my senses sharpened. "I cannot fathom why he should return. He has no friends in the county."

I started to rejoin Bingley and Hurst but turned back before leaving the corner in which we stood. "Mr. Morehouse, if by chance you discover Wickham remains in the area, send word to me at Netherfield Park. I will do all I can to aid you in recovering what is owed."

"I will, sir, and I'm much obliged."

Hurst made his purchase, and we departed the shop. An uneasy feeling settled about my shoulders like a heavy bag of stones. What could possibly draw Wickham back to Hertfordshire? Whatever the reason, I feared it signalled trouble.

WE MET ELIZABETH AND HER SISTERS AS THEY DEPARTED FORD'S. BOTH Miss Bennet and Kitty carried hatboxes, but my wife only had a small package. Bingley gazed with adoration at Jane Bennet while Elizabeth explained to me that she had not gone into the small shop to make a purchase but merely to offer her opinion of the bonnets her sisters planned to buy. However, she did find some lovely scarlet and green ribbons to grace her niece's hair.

"I suppose you have now filled your boudoir with turbans from the finest shops in London," Kitty said.

Elizabeth glanced at me in embarrassment, but I answered for her. "In truth, Miss Kitty, your sister bought very little in Town, but I hope in the future she will purchase whatever her heart desires."

"La, Lizzy," Kitty replied, raising her eyebrows towards her sister, "how fine a lady you will be with such a generous husband."

Hurst's impatience to return to Netherfield Park appeared obvious as he stomped about, loudly clearing his throat. At length, he announced he would await our company in the confines of the carriage. Elizabeth bade farewell to her sisters, and reluctantly, Bingley parted from Miss Bennet, but not without a promise that he would see her at Lucas Lodge that evening.

Upon arrival at Netherfield, Hurst collected his hounds and a servant to accompany him into the fields to try out his new acquisition. He called on Bingley and me to go along, but I had promised Bingley a game of billiards before tea.

"Shall you join my sisters, Mrs. Darcy?" Bingley asked Elizabeth.

"After I look to Fan's whereabouts," she said. "We have been gone so long that I feel certain she will want my company."

With a slight smile at me, she walked in the direction of the nursery. I stood watching until she rounded the corner and vanished from my sight.

"Ah, my friend," Bingley said, "I see the passion has not yet waned from your marriage. Your gaze still lingers on your pretty wife as though you were not even joined together."

I took a deep breath and turned to follow him into the game room. *If you only knew, Bingley!* Sometimes I wondered whether my desire for Elizabeth would ever be satisfied.

THAT NIGHT, AFTER DRESSING FOR DINNER, I ESCORTED ELIZABETH FROM our chamber to the top of the stairs. She wore a new silk dress of blue, and I revelled in her beauty. I was about to tell her how lovely she was before we descended to the second floor, but we were interrupted by the nursemaid.

"Begging your pardon, ma'am," she said. "I thought you ought to know that Mrs. Abernathy's fever came back. She likely will stay abed all day tomorrow."

Elizabeth frowned, as did I. "I am sorry to hear that," she said. "Can you manage alone, Maggie?"

The girl bobbed her head up and down.

"That means," I added, "that you keep your charge in sight at all times. Do you understand?"

"Oh, yes, sir, I do. But I wondered whether I might take Fan outdoors tomorrow? She gets so tired of being in the nursery all day."

Elizabeth smiled. "Of course, she does. If the weather remains mild, certainly you may take her out for some air. The gardens of Netherfield Park provide adequate room for her to run and play, but mind that you dress her warmly."

"I will, ma'am, I will." She curtseyed again, and I assumed the interruption was ended, but instead, she remained in place, fidgeting with her apron.

"Is there something else?" Elizabeth asked.

"Yes, ma'am, it's just that, Fan—she's already abed. And, sometimes, when you come in late to bid her goodnight, I have a devil of a time settlin' her back to sleep."

"I told Fan goodnight before I began dressing."

"Then there's no need for you to come to her bedside when you return tonight, ma'am, because it's sure to be late."

"Thank you, Maggie. Your concern is appreciated."

I moved in a somewhat restless manner, for the girl continued to dawdle. Would we never be rid of the simpleton?

"And, you know, ma'am, little Fan wakes right early. If you come to the nursery in the morning, most likely we'll already be outside."

"Very well."

"Oh, good, ma'am!" For some reason, the girl appeared unusually relieved. "I'll take good care of her. I promise!"

"Of course, you will." Elizabeth looked from the girl to me with a question in her eyes.

"Return to your duties," I said to the maid. "The time is upon us, Elizabeth."

The girl bowed again and then hurriedly left for the nursery. I offered my arm to my wife, and we began our descent down the stairs.

"Did not you find that conversation rather strange?" she said.

"I have always found that girl strange."

LUCAS LODGE WAS ALIVE WITH GUESTS BY THE TIME WE ARRIVED. AFTER travelling in two carriages, since Bingley's sisters and Hurst had also decided to accept the invitation, we were ushered from our conveyances and up the steps into Sir William's house by his waiting servants. I recalled a previous occasion when Elizabeth and I met on the path leading to this house. Scandal forbade her calling on Lady Lucas. I rejoiced that our marriage had erased that unfortunate state.

On this night, Sir William and Lady Lucas welcomed us, and I noted that a good number of Meryton citizens filled the rooms. Mr. and Mrs. Phillips soon joined us, and Elizabeth greeted her relations. I was pleased to observe the Gardiners had not yet returned to Town. At least, there would be one intelligent gentleman with whom I might converse.

"Lizzy! Mr. Darcy!" Mrs. Bennet cried from across the room, waving her fan excitedly.

With a quick glance in my direction, Elizabeth made her way through the throng to her mother. I turned to speak to Bingley, but he was already deeply engrossed in conversation with Miss Bennet.

I saw Mr. Long approaching, and contrary to all inclination, I stood my ground and spoke with the man. We were soon joined by his wife, accompanied by, of all people, Mrs. Collins of Hunsford Parish. I was surprised to see her until I remembered that she was the daughter of Sir William Lucas.

"I understand you are recently married, Mr. Darcy," she said. "Allow me to wish you joy. I am glad to see that a man of such stature has finally captured my dear Lizzy's heart. I trust she will—" She broke off speaking, obviously startled by an action elsewhere in the room.

When I followed her line of vision, I saw her husband frantically motioning her to his side. At the sight of my eyes upon him, he straightened, sniffed, and turned his back.

"I—forgive me, sir," Mrs. Collins said. "I beg to be excused." She curtseyed and strode across the room, whereupon her husband seemed to scold her, although I could not hear his words.

I found myself amused that a man of so little consequence would cut me publicly out of fear of his patroness, Lady Catherine de Bourgh. Did he think my aunt had spies everywhere, even in his father-in-law's house? *Ah, well, let him play his games,* I thought. It saved me the inconvenience of listening to him.

Picking up a glass of punch, I made my way to the edge of the room, observing that Elizabeth was now surrounded by friends and family. I sipped the drink and turned to gaze out the floor-length window. Met only by my own reflection and the lights of the room behind me, I sighed, wondering why I could not find more than a few persons in attendance with whom I wished to converse. This change I thought Elizabeth had wrought in me did not come easily.

Resolving to do better, I raised my head to turn back to the room, when the sudden image of Wickham appeared before me! I was so shocked I almost dropped the glass in my hand. I whirled around, thinking he stood behind me within the lodge, but he was not there. It was then I realized he must have been without, close beside the window where I stood.

I disposed of the glass on a nearby table and hastened across the room to the closest door. Running outside, I peered through the dark but saw naught but the drivers and footmen standing beside the carriages. I motioned to one of the men to bring a torch and hastened around the circumference of the house, paying particular attention to the window where I had seen Wickham. He was gone, however, nowhere to be seen.

I questioned the drivers and footmen to no avail. No one had seen any stranger or anyone lurking. Had I imagined it all?

At length, I returned to the drawing room, shaken and out of breath. My first thought was to seek refreshment, but at that moment, dinner was announced. I searched the room for Elizabeth, and upon reaching her side, I escorted her to the table.

"Are you well?" she asked.

"Perfectly," I replied, attempting to calm myself and appear at ease.

"You seem short of breath."

"I just returned from outdoors. Needed a bit of air." I smiled, hoping she would accept my explanation. I seated myself beside her, and with great relief, I found Mr. and Mrs. Gardiner opposite us, whereupon he and I conversed on the latest fishing techniques while dining. Elizabeth enjoyed her aunt's company, and I hoped she would not return to her previous questions. I had little appetite, however, and could not refrain from glancing over my shoulder from time to time.

Afterwards, Caroline Bingley and Mrs. Hurst were persuaded to entertain us on the pianoforte, and the company was suitably impressed with their exhibitions. Some of the younger people desired to dance, but neither of Bingley's sisters deigned to play for them. Maria Lucas took their place, and we were subjected to her efforts on the instrument.

Arriving back at Netherfield, Elizabeth and I joined Bingley and his other guests in the drawing room. Caroline and Louisa began their usual critique of the company from whom we had just parted. Bingley poured me a brandy, and I took my place at the hearth.

"Mrs. Darcy," Caroline said, "was not that your cousin's wife I saw in earnest conversation with you? I do believe Mrs. Collins is not well, for her complexion is drawn and wan."

Louisa nodded. "I noticed it too. I do hope she is not ill."

"She suffers from a condition that will right itself within six or seven months," Elizabeth said.

"Ah," both sisters said knowingly.

"'Tis a shame Mr. Collins has fallen out of Lady Catherine de Bourgh's favour, is it not?" Caroline said.

"I did not know you had learned of that," Elizabeth replied somewhat apprehensively.

"Oh, but we did, my dear," Louisa said. "Mr. Collins prevailed upon us to hear his sad tale. It seems the great lady is not as pleased with your marriage to Mr. Darcy as you led us to believe."

Elizabeth straightened her back, and I saw fire in her eyes, an indication that her temper was rising.

"I have little experience with Mr. Collins," I said, "but I suspect he has but superficial knowledge of my aunt's pleasure or displeasure."

"Oh no, Mr. Darcy," Caroline said, "the vicar stated it in the most precise language. Lady Catherine does not approve of your alliance. In fact, he told me that he had been forbidden even to speak to you or Mrs. Darcy."

"Unfortunately," Elizabeth said, "my cousin oft-times misunderstands situations. Most likely, he has caused offense in some way and does not wish to bear the blame."

"I agree," Mr. Bingley added. "Pardon me, Mrs. Darcy, but I find the man somewhat thick."

I smiled, for I had rarely heard Bingley criticize anyone. "I tend to agree," I said. "In one area, though, he has been wise. Mr. Collins has chosen a wife of excellent quality, as have I." I lifted my glass towards Elizabeth, and Bingley joined me.

"Charlotte is as fine a person as I have ever known, and we have been friends since childhood," Elizabeth said. "Her family has been more than generous with their friendship."

Caroline sniffed and rolled her eyes. "Sir William puts on airs, thinking himself more than he is. Why, when we first made his acquaintance, he dared to offer to introduce Louisa and me at court. As though we needed his introductions! It is obvious from his circumstances that he made his fortune in trade, if one might presume he owns a fortune."

"True," her sister said. "Lucas Lodge is most unhappily situated, for it is terribly small. I question why they held a party there tonight. I know the press of the crowd discomforted me more than once." Caroline nodded in agreement.

Elizabeth rose, her chin held high. "Sir William has always been a kind, generous host, whatever the size of his house. I pray you will release me, as I find myself grown weary."

"Of course," Bingley said, rising to bid her goodnight while his sisters simply nodded and smiled at each other under their raised eyebrows.

"I shall join you, my dear," I said, placing my glass on the table and offering her my arm.

In our chamber, Elizabeth instructed her maid to ready her nightclothes in the adjoining dressing room, but she chose to stand before the fireplace, clasping and unclasping her hands.

"You are distressed," I said, walking around the settee to stand before her.

"Sometimes, I cannot abide Mr. Bingley's sisters! Must they cast a contemptible eye on my friends and family? Why can they not be more like their brother who is always amicable and pleasing?"

"Caroline and Louisa can be petty, but do not allow their remarks to trouble you."

"I am not troubled for myself but for you. I fear our marriage has brought you nothing more than discredit in the eyes of the world."

I reached for her hand, and she did not seem to mind when I brought it to my lips. "I entered this union with my eyes wide open. Do not fret, Elizabeth. I am not complaining."

She gazed into my eyes, and I saw the worry disappear. "You truly are a good man."

My heart turned over to know she entertained such a thought.

She smiled again. "I should dress for bed. The hour is late."

Rising, we must have both realized at the same moment that I still held her hand in mine.

"Shall you content yourself with a kiss upon my hand tonight?" she said in a teasing manner.

"I think not," I murmured, as I raised my hands to her face. Her eyes closed when I leaned down, and I allowed my lips to meet hers and linger somewhat longer than they had the night before. It was like kissing the softest of rose petals, yet the rose was alive and warm. Naught but the greatest resolve forced me to content myself with a kiss. Slowly, I released her mouth, but I still held her face in my hands as I gazed into her eyes.

"Shall I go?" she whispered.

I nodded, but still I stood there, unable to move.

"Goodnight, Fitzwilliam."

Reluctantly, I let my hands fall. I could not bid her goodnight. I dared not speak, for I knew, until I had gained control over myself, that I was in danger of declaring my love for her then and there.

In my dressing room, I rang for Rodgers and instructed him to bring water with which to wash before helping me undress.

"And Rodgers," I added, "do not heat the water,"

"Cold water, sir, in December?" He raised his eyebrows.

"Utterly cold."

He picked up the pitcher and walked through the side door and down to the rear staircase. I loosened my neck cloth and sank down upon the chaise, laying my head back. Thoughts raced through my head—thoughts of Elizabeth, naturally, of the evening we had just spent together, but also concern about the news I had learned in Meryton concerning Wickham.

Why was he in Hertfordshire? Could he be plotting some sort of devilment, and if so, would it affect Elizabeth's family? Did he know Elizabeth and I were at Netherfield? Had I actually seen him outside Lucas Lodge peering through the window at us? I knew he did not want his daughter, so she could not have provoked his return. His debts were legendary throughout the village. What would possess him to dare make an appearance in a place where he would be hounded by his creditors?

"It is either a woman or a fortune," I said aloud. Perchance, Wickham knew of an heiress residing nearby and planned to ingratiate himself with her. I chastised myself for not paying closer attention to the guests at Sir William's dinner that night. If a newcomer had made an appearance at the party, I would not have known, for I had remained aloof most of the night but for my conversation with Mr. Gardiner and obligatory words with others.

I threw the loosened neck cloth aside and rubbed the back of my neck. I wondered whether I had been less than truthful with Elizabeth when I said her rebuke had changed me, for seldom did I find it less than painful to perform with strangers or even acquaintances. In truth, I rarely made the effort. Had I effected only the slightest of alterations to win her hand? Had I remained that arrogant, prideful man she had accused years ago?

And to speak of the truth—when had I become a deceitful man who plotted behind the scenes? I had lied to Elizabeth, her family, even Bingley to accomplish my wishes.

"Would you still deem me a good man if you knew all I have done, Elizabeth?" I said aloud.

No, if Elizabeth ever learned I had thrust Wickham upon her family, had approved, even conceived the idea that he should take the child from her, she would not forgive me. That fact I knew as well as I knew my own name.

I sighed and rubbed my hand across my eyes. Rodgers appeared with the requested water and filled the basin. Rising, I splashed my face, and the cold sharp sting felt like the slap in the face I deserved.

Chapter Thirteen

The following day began with unanticipated delight.

The first image to greet me upon waking was that of Elizabeth lying on the opposite side of the bed, her eyes wide open and a smile gracing her countenance. The detestable pillow that customarily lay between us was curiously absent.

"Good morning, Fitzwilliam," she said softly.

"Morning," I mumbled, pinching my arm to make certain I had not entered another dream. I glanced at the foot of the bed. "Where is the pillow?"

"I threw it across the room. I awakened early and knew the servants would soon be knocking at the door."

I searched her eyes, hoping for some further declaration. "But you did not rise from the bed."

"I confess I do not wish to shiver about in an unheated room."

"I shall ring for a servant to light the fire." I started to sit up, but she placed her hand on my arm.

"Not yet," she said, smiling again.

"Oh?" My heart began to beat in double time.

"I would rather just lie here and be lazy." She stretched her arms above her head and turned onto her back.

"And do you wish for solitude to indulge your fancy?"

She shook her head slowly from side to side, turning her eyes to meet mine.

I reached out for her hand and brought it to my lips. "May I fulfil any other desire of your heart?"

She turned back on her side to face me once again. "I wish to awaken as a normal married couple would."

"And in what manner might that be?" My voice had deepened.

She laughed lightly. "I truly do not know. Having never awakened beside any man but you, I find myself woefully ignorant. I assume husbands and wives discuss the day before them—that sort of thing."

"The day before them…pos-si-bly," I said, stretching out the word.

"But not probably? Then, tell me, what might a married couple discuss upon awakening?"

I struggled to maintain my composure. Could my young wife truly be that innocent? "Elizabeth, I doubt married couples engage in many discussions in bed, especially when they have been married as briefly as we have."

Her eyes widened, and she pursed her lips, unaware that her action kindled even more desire in me.

"Oh," she whispered, a blush caressing her cheeks. "I understand."

I smiled, waiting.

"My, you must think me a silly goose! I never thought—"

"Have no fear. I shall not inflict my attentions upon you. If you want to discuss the day before us, I am willing to do so."

We lay silent for a while. She avoided my eyes while I could not refrain from caressing every inch of her face and hair with mine. How could a woman be that lovely first thing in the morning? I felt certain my hair was tousled, and the bristle on my face that had grown during the night was now prominent.

Of a sudden, I realized I still held her hand in mine and I had been stroking small circles on her palm. Yet, she had not withdrawn it. I kissed the inside of her wrist, and she raised her eyes to meet mine. I reached out and placed my hand on her cheek. "Dear God, but you are something to behold in the morning."

"Fitzwilliam—"

"Yes?"

"I think it best if I get up."

I swallowed. "If you must." I traced the tender curve of her cheek lightly with my fingers before reluctantly withdrawing my hand.

Sitting up, she swung her legs over the side of the bed, and surprisingly, she did not seem to mind that I continued to watch her. She turned her head and glanced at me over her shoulder. I held my breath. What would she do next? With lightning speed, she leaned over and kissed me.

"Good morning again, Fitzwilliam," she said with another smile. Throwing her robe around her, she vanished into her dressing room.

"Good morning, Elizabeth," I said to the silent room. I lay there in bed with a silly smile on my face that insisted on returning no matter how many times I attempted to suppress it.

I ARRIVED AT THE BREAKFAST TABLE BEFORE ELIZABETH. CAROLINE AND Bingley greeted me, and shortly thereafter Mr. and Mrs. Hurst entered the room.

"I say, Darcy, you seem unusually cheerful this morning," Bingley said.

When I merely smiled in response, Caroline sniffed and abruptly changed the subject. She announced that she and the Hursts planned to depart for London on the following day.

"We have endured the savagery of country society far too long. I yearn for stimulating conversation and the gaiety that abounds in Town. Shall you be joining us soon, Mr. Darcy? I believe you stated that Mr. Bennet's health seems sufficiently restored, so surely Eliza can bear to leave her father."

"I would not say his health is restored, Miss Bingley," I said, "but it is improved. For that, my wife and I are thankful. As for London, I believe we will not visit at this time of year. I am for Derbyshire."

"Ah, Derbyshire," Mrs. Hurst joined in. "How you must long to return to your estate, for surely it is the loveliest place on earth. We do hope to receive an invitation to enjoy its beauty in the near future. You recall, do you not, that you were forced to cancel our previous excursion to Pemberley when you and Charles went abroad?"

I lowered my eyes. "Of course, and I regret it even yet, but as to when I can arrange a visit, I cannot say. I have been absent for so long that I do not know what I shall encounter upon my return."

"But your staff is highly skilled and reliable, are they not, sir?" Caroline said. "I wager that you will find all exactly as you left it."

"That is my fondest wish."

At that moment, Elizabeth entered the room, and after rising to escort her to her place at the table, I searched her face to ascertain whether her happy mood had altered. She greeted those at the table and smiled at me somewhat uncertainly, as though shyness now afflicted her after her earlier impetuous kiss.

"You appear none the worse for the late hours we kept last night, Mrs. Darcy," Bingley said. "I would say your countenance fairly glows this morning. Do you not agree, Darcy?"

"I do." My friend stated the obvious, for Elizabeth's eyes shone brightly, and her cheeks were truly luminous. She wore a pale yellow gown that accented her figure in precisely the correct manner. I encountered great difficulty removing my gaze from her long enough to continue my meal.

"Thank you," she said while moving to the sideboard and taking a plate. I served her from the platter of eggs, and when she nodded, I added a piece of bacon.

"Mr. Darcy informs us that you will soon leave for Derbyshire," Mrs. Hurst said.

"Oh?" Elizabeth turned to face me.

"My plans are not definite. Naturally, it depends upon the state of Mr. Bennet's health."

"My father is feeling better," she said, "and I hope we may journey to Pemberley in the near future."

"I fear when you do, you may find yourself overwhelmed, Eliza," Caroline said. "Pemberley is a great estate, the likes of which you have probably never even seen, much less presided over."

"Actually, I have visited the place, and I look forward to making my home there."

Caroline held a forkful of sausage in the air, her mouth agape. "*You* have been to Pemberley? I am shocked! When did this supposed visit take place, for I understood you have resided in Town since your wedding?"

"We have," I said. "Elizabeth, however, was introduced to my country estate more than two years ago."

"Indeed?" Mrs. Hurst said while Caroline placed her fork on the plate, left the food uneaten, and abruptly closed her mouth.

Neither Elizabeth nor I explained the reasons for her presence in Derbyshire, but I could see the curiosity bubbling between Bingley's sisters.

After breakfast, we all repaired to the drawing room—but for Hurst, who departed for the stables. Bingley announced he wished to call at Longbourn that afternoon, and Elizabeth said the same.

"Charles," Caroline said, "must you call on Jane Bennet again? I would think you might care to spend one day with your sisters. After all, we leave on the morrow."

"Yes," Mrs. Hurst said, "or you and Mr. Darcy might wish to join Ambrose in some sport. This will be his last day to bag those precious birds."

"Well," Bingley said, "I suppose I should aid my brother in trying out his new gun. Darcy, are you game?"

I turned to Elizabeth. "Shall I go with you to Longbourn? I am willing if that is your desire."

"Oh, leave Eliza to us," Caroline said, rising to link her arm in Elizabeth's. "Shall we take a turn about the room while you tell us all about your visit to Pemberley?"

The look that passed across Elizabeth's face made it plain that this was the last thing she wished to do. "I thank you for the invitation, Miss Bingley, but since we are to leave Netherfield soon, I know my father will insist on my presence today."

Caroline withdrew her hand and turned away, frustration evident in her expression.

"You need not come, Fitzwilliam, for I know you would much rather be outdoors. I would ask, however, that you keep account of Fan for me. Maggie was to take her for an outing in the gardens, but I do not wish for her to grow fatigued."

"Very well, but allow me to escort you to the carriage." I took her arm, and we walked out of the room. After she donned her spencer and bonnet, we descended the stone steps together.

"It is a beautiful day, is it not?" she said, looking about. "You have chosen well in selecting to shoot today. I yearn to have a good, long tramp in the woods. Soon, the weather will grow bitter, and we shall be confined inside for the winter."

I glanced up at the sun that had broken through the clouds. "Why not return early and join me in a short walk before evening? Would you like that?"

"Oh, I would, I truly would." She graced me with a smile so sweet that my heart turned over in my chest. I bent my head close to hers, and it was all I could do not to place my lips upon hers. Instead, I contented myself with a kiss upon her hand before handing her into the carriage. "I shall not stay long," she whispered.

"Walk on!" I called to the driver and watched the carriage depart the park. I could not recall when I had been in such high spirits.

BINGLEY AND HURST CALLED FOR ME TO JOIN THEM IN THE FIELDS SHORTLY thereafter. I thought about running up to the nursery first, but I contented myself with the thought that the child was probably being fed and put down for a nap. I certainly did not wish to disturb her routine. And I knew my visiting her quarters without Elizabeth would somewhat fluster that goose of a maid and most likely the little girl. I resolved to delay complying with my wife's request until I returned.

The birds were in short supply, the majority having already flown south. That fact did not prohibit Hurst from shooting at everything that moved, and he succeeded in killing three rabbits, which he gave to the stable hands for their supper. He was delighted with his new gun and spent more time singing its praises than he did aiming at the sky. I had never heard the man speak to that extent in all the years I had known him.

Recalling the previous day's visit to the market when Hurst made his purchase reminded me of the shopkeeper's dilemma and the troubling fact that Wickham had returned to Hertfordshire. I confess the renewal of my worries about the scoundrel interrupted my attempts to shoot. As a result, I walked back to the house with nothing to show for my efforts.

We entered Netherfield through a side door to store our weapons and leave the dogs to be fed. After handing my hat and greatcoat to a servant, I headed for my chamber to wash my hands before going to the nursery to see about the child. I did not reach my chamber, however. Before I opened the door to the bedroom, two maids and Rodgers met me, all three running down the hall in my direction.

"Sir," Rodgers said, "you are needed in the nursery most urgently."

"I intend to go there as soon as I have freshened up."

"Beggin' your pardon, sir," one of the maids said, breathing hard, "the need for your presence is pressing."

"And why is that?"

"'Tis the little 'un, sir," the other maid cried. "She's gone missing!"

I groaned. *Not again!* "She cannot have wandered far. Where have you searched in the house?"

"Everywhere, sir," Rodgers said. "And the grounds, as well."

"Well, where is the nursery maid—Maggie? She should have some idea where she last saw her."

"That's just it, sir. We cain't find Maggie neither." The maids eyed each other nervously.

I frowned, and brushing past the servants, I headed down the hall. As I strode into the nursery, I heard Elizabeth's voice coming from Mrs. Abernathy's bedside. Without knocking on the adjoining door that stood ajar, I entered the chamber. The older woman remained in bed, her voice sounding hoarse when she attempted to speak.

"Elizabeth," I said.

My wife whirled around and ran to my side, grasping both my hands in hers, a look of fear on her face. "Oh, Fitzwilliam, at last! We can find neither Fan nor Maggie anywhere!"

"Have you searched our chamber and your dressing room? You know that is where I discovered her the last time she disappeared."

"I went there immediately when told the news upon my return." She shook her head. "She is not there. When did you last check on her?"

I swallowed, a sinking feeling descending upon me. "I...that is—"

"I have not seen or heard the child since last night," Mrs. Abernathy whispered.

"Last night! Did you not give the nursemaid her instructions this morning?" I demanded.

"Fitzwilliam," Elizabeth said, "Mrs. Abernathy is quite ill. I sent for the physician a half hour ago."

"I fear, sir," the older woman said, "that my fever was severe last evening, so much so that it caused me to be derelict in my duties. I barely recall Maggie giving the child her supper. That was the last occasion upon which I spoke to her. I confess I was too sick to rise this morning and have slept most of the day. I recall the maid lighting the fire and fetching me fresh water, but I had no appetite and told her not to bring a tray of food."

"But you say Maggie lit the fire this morning."

"No, sir, one of Mr. Bingley's servants saw to it. I have not seen Maggie since early last evening before you and Mrs. Darcy went out." Her cough began with such intensity that Elizabeth cautioned her to refrain from speaking. She assured her the physician would arrive soon. After ringing the bell for a maid, she instructed her to remain at Mrs. Abernathy's bedside.

Elizabeth and I walked out into the hallway, and I turned to face her. It was time to confess the truth. "I must tell you that I neglected to check on the child. I thought she was napping, and I planned to look in on her as soon as I returned from the fields. I pray you will forgive me, Elizabeth."

She shook her head. "It is not your fault. I should have sought her out in the park before I left for Longbourn. I assumed she was playing, and if she detected my presence, she would beg to accompany me. I was selfish, for I wished to spend some time with my father unencumbered. Thoughts of leaving him for Pemberley provoked me to think only of myself."

I was relieved Elizabeth did not blame me, but it did not absolve me of guilt. Where could the child be, and where had that silly maid disappeared?

In the drawing room, we met with Bingley, Hurst, and Bingley's sisters. In an unbelievable turn, Hurst appeared interested in the search, perchance because he possessed a penchant for hunting. The ladies expressed naught but superficial concern.

We discussed various plans for dividing up the large house, and Hurst suggested Bingley draw an outline of Netherfield's arrangement—a creditable idea I never would have thought the man capable of conceiving. After Bingley complied, he called his entire household staff together and issued assignments to search the house thoroughly once again. Elizabeth, Bingley, Hurst, and I each took a section as well.

"Caroline and I will remain in the drawing room," Mrs. Hurst said, pouring cups of tea for herself and her sister, "in case the child should wander in here."

"Look under beds, inside armoires and closets, under desks and tables, in every nook and cranny," I instructed the servants. "Remember, this is a small child, and she can squeeze into places we would not ordinarily consider."

As we dispersed to our assigned destinations, I took Elizabeth's hands in mine and raised them to my lips. "Do not be alarmed, for we will find her," I said. She nodded, unable to speak.

"I told everyone to meet here in the hall outside the drawing room within two hours unless we find little Fan before then, and I feel certain we will, Mrs. Darcy," Bingley said. "I feel very certain that...we will."

Some two hours later, however, we assembled in the designated area empty-handed. By that time, fear reigned in Elizabeth's eyes, and a feeling of dread settled about me. I glanced out the tall windows and estimated that ne'er but a half hour of daylight yet existed. We needed to search the grounds immediately. After adding Bingley's outdoor servants to our search party, we once again set off to look for the child. I bade Elizabeth remain indoors and rest, but she would not. She selected the park and hurried out the door before everyone.

By the time darkness fell, we had gathered beside the stone steps at the entrance to Netherfield. Again, no one had seen a trace of either the child or her maid. Since both were missing, it was assumed by all that Fan and Maggie were together.

"Bingley, we must expand the search beyond Netherfield Park," I said. He agreed and directed that torches be lit. Hurst worked with him once again in dividing the surrounding countryside before giving the stable hands, gardeners, and menservants certain places to look. Tears filled Elizabeth's eyes.

"Fitzwilliam, where can she be?"

"We will find her. You must go in now, for the night air is dangerous. I would not have you catch a chill."

"No! I will continue to search."

"Elizabeth, I will not allow it. The weather is taking a turn for the worse, and the men say snow will fall before morning. I cannot have you out in this weather."

"I know this countryside as well as I know the back of my hand. I will not become lost, and I have walked in snow many a time."

"But not at night," I said, shaking my head back and forth. "You must remain here. I insist."

She stamped her foot, her hands clenched in fists. "How can you expect me to stay here when my child is lost? At least let me go with you."

"I can cover a lot more ground on horseback than on foot, but I will be severely hampered if I must worry on your behalf. Elizabeth, you will obey me in this. You will not leave Netherfield tonight!" When she did not reply other than to glare at me, I took her face between my hands. "Promise me."

I would not release her until she yielded to my demand. "Give me your word. I cannot leave until you do."

At last, she closed her eyes and nodded slightly.

"Good," I said.

She placed her hands on my arms. "But what will I do here? I shall go mad!"

"Pray…and if you are willing, give me a kiss before I go." Once again, she closed her eyes, and I reached down and met her lips with mine. I cared not that servants, Bingley, or Hurst could witness our intimacy.

"Find her, Fitzwilliam," she said.

"I will." I swung myself onto the horse the servant held ready and waiting. After seizing a lighted torch, I met Elizabeth's eyes for one last look and put the spurs to my steed.

Instead of spending time combing the woods, I rode fast and hard to Longbourn. While searching Netherfield, for some reason the child's earlier words about the nursemaid and a man nagged at me. If I was correct and she had tried to tell us that Maggie had a beau, the first place I wanted to search was Longbourn's stables. If the witless girl had arranged a tryst with one of the hands, surely he would have bragged about it to his friends.

Upon arriving at Mr. Bennet's estate, I did not call at the house, for I hoped to avoid informing the family that Lydia's child was missing. I feared what the news might do to Mr. Bennet's health, especially when I knew his wife would become hysterical. I rode directly to the stables and asked that all the men assemble. They, of course, knew my identity and that I had married their young mistress. They appeared willing to answer my questions.

Unfortunately, none of them had seen either the child or the nursemaid last night or that day. I walked among them, searching their eyes for the truth, but I did not detect signs of falsehood in any of them.

"Ain't none of us seen the little 'un, sir," the man called Stephen said. "We're all partial to the wee girl. Might we join the search party?"

"We can use your assistance," I said, "but I am forced to inform Mr. Bennet, as he is your master. Make preparations, wear your warmest clothing, assemble your torches, and I shall return shortly."

Leaving my horse with the men, I walked up to the house, dreading what was to come. The housekeeper ushered me into the parlour, where I found Mr. Bennet reading the newspaper while his daughters kept him company. I was relieved Mrs. Bennet had retired to her chamber early that night. The family was surprised at my visit but welcoming, and when I requested a private audience with Mr. Bennet, he led me into his study. I noted how stooped his shoulders had become. Jane lingered in the antechamber, obviously nervous for her father. Before closing the door, I beckoned her to join us. I needed her calm demeanour, lest my news proved too taxing for the gentleman's health.

My precautions were not in vain. Upon learning the child was missing,

Mr. Bennet sank back in his chair and clutched his chest. While Jane tended him, I attempted to reassure him that the little one could not have wandered far and asked his permission to direct his stable hands to search portions of the woods. Naturally, he agreed, and leaving Jane to see to her father, I prepared to make my departure.

"You will send word the moment you find Fan, will you not, Mr. Darcy?" Miss Bennet said, her eyes large with concern.

"I will."

"And my sister? How does she fare?"

"Elizabeth is fearful, but she is well. I will find the child. You have my word." I held her gaze with my own, willing her to believe against my own doubts.

"I pray you will, sir," she said with conviction.

"We are depending upon you, Mr. Darcy," Mr. Bennet said.

THE CLOCK CHIMED THREE BELLS WHEN I ENTERED NETHERFIELD, MY very bones weary from the hours I had spent in the saddle, and my heart heavy because I had not kept my word. I had not found the child. Bingley awaited me in the outer hall, obviously just as tired. One look into each other's eyes told us neither of us had encountered success.

"Come into the drawing room, Darcy. I shall pour you a brandy."

Entering the room, I saw it was empty. "Where are the others?"

"You are the last to return," Bingley said, handing me the snifter.

"And Elizabeth?"

"I urged her to retire an hour ago with the promise I would have her awakened the moment the little girl returned."

I sank down into a chair and stared at the fire before me. "Where can she be, Bingley?"

He shook his head sadly. "I have instructed the men to begin the search anew at first light. You must have struggled to find your way through the trees with the clouds setting in."

"It has begun to snow." I leaned forward and raked my hand through my hair.

"Well, if it covers the ground sufficiently, at least we will have the advantage of more prominent tracks."

I looked up to meet his eyes. "How long can a babe survive in this weather?"

He had no answer. "You must rest, Darcy. We both must if we are to leave at daybreak."

We rose and climbed the stairs together. I considered stretching out on Bingley's couch in the library in order not to awaken Elizabeth, but seeing faint light below the door to our chamber, I turned the knob. Inside a single taper shed a dim glow, but it proved enough to see my wife, still clad in her dress, lying on the bed, covered only by a light throw. The fire had gone out, leaving the room chilled.

Treading lightly, I picked up the side of the eider down quilt on which she lay and gently placed it over her sleeping body. She stirred, and I froze, hoping she would not awaken, but alas, it was not to be.

"Fitzwilliam?" she said, sitting up. "Where is Fan? Did you find her?"

When I shook my head, tears filled her eyes and spilled down her cheeks. My heart ached to see her anguish. I gathered her into my arms where she cried against my chest. Slowly, I led her from the bed into the sitting area where I placed her on the sofa, and then I poked at the coals in the fireplace until they caught anew and gave us some small amount of warmth.

"What time is it?" she asked, wiping her face with her hands.

"Nigh on to four. We shall set out again at first light."

She rose and stood beside me before the fireplace. "This time I *shall* go with you."

When I opened my mouth to protest, she placed her hand upon my lips to silence me. "Do not forbid it, for I insist."

I took her hand from my mouth and held it between mine. "We will discuss it later, but for now, we must rest."

"Yes, you must be greatly fatigued. Come, get into bed."

"I must wash and change first," I said, but she would not have it.

"There is not enough time. Lay upon the bed, and I will fetch blankets to warm you."

She began to pass before me, but I caught her hand. "Not unless you agree to sleep too."

"I will try."

While she collected the coverings from the armoire, I discarded my coat, jacket, and boots. Untying my cravat and taking off my vest, I stretched out on top of the bed while Elizabeth arranged the blankets. Then stepping out of her slippers, she crawled onto the opposite side. I extinguished the candle on the stand next to me and turned on my side facing her. I could not recall a time when I had felt such exhaustion.

The pillow is missing. I thought about rising to fetch it, but weariness kept me tied to the bed. She had nothing to fear from me tonight. I closed my eyes and began to drift off when I heard her sobs. Her sorrow tore at my heart, and I could not bear it.

"Elizabeth," I said softly.

"Forgive me. I do not mean to keep you awake, but I am so afraid for Fan."

"Elizabeth, come to me. Let me hold you."

She hesitated but a moment and then moved across the bed and into my arms. I gathered her close and held her until, mercifully, sleep overtook us both.

Chapter Fourteen

The day had just dawned when I awoke with a start. *Something is wrong!* For a moment, I could recall neither where I was nor what had happened, and then I looked down to see Elizabeth asleep on my shoulder. Like a dreaded blackness, the truth descended upon me. The child was missing, along with her maid. No one had seen them for more than four and twenty hours.

I rubbed my hand across my brow and felt Elizabeth stir. Although she moved slightly, she did not awaken. I gazed at this woman I loved who now lay in my arms, a scene I had dreamt of for years. I watched the whisper of her dark lashes caress her cheeks as she slept. Instinctively, I reached out and smoothed back the errant curl that had fallen across her forehead.

"Wha…Fitzwilliam?" She opened her eyes and met my gaze. "Is it daylight?"

"Yes," I said, as she moved away from me, leaving my empty arms suddenly cold. We both rose from the bed. I shook my head, attempting to clear away the murky haze caused by too little sleep. Ringing the bell for the servants, I stepped gingerly onto the cold floor, avoiding the clothes I had discarded a few hours earlier.

Elizabeth wrapped a blanket around her shoulders before she disappeared into her dressing room.

One glance out the window did not lift my spirits. Snow fell like unending streams of shattered white feathers, and I knew the child's chances of survival grew slimmer by the hour. Not bothering to wait for Rodgers, I dressed, left the chamber, and hurried towards the dining room.

Therein, I met Bingley and Hurst. Foregoing time to sit down, they stood by the sideboard, fortifying themselves with hot coffee and muffins. Once we had eaten, we joined the servants assembled in the stables to renew our search efforts and make assignments. Many of the areas had already been explored the night before.

"Go over every acre of ground again," Bingley said. "We may have overlooked much during our ramblings in the dark."

"Make certain you look in low places or abandoned shelters," I said, "anywhere the maid might have sought refuge for the child and herself."

Bingley authorized the use of his entire stable of horses, and it took but a short time for the men to mount up. The remainder set out on foot, laden with provisions to sustain them throughout the day. Carrying clothing that bore the scents of the maid and child, they led the hounds. The dogs were alive with excitement, their shrill yelps building into a crescendo of noise.

I told my servant to bring my horse to Netherfield's front steps to await my departure and then returned to the house to see Elizabeth before I left. I expected to find my wife either in the drawing room or at breakfast, but I was surprised to meet her coming out the front door, clad in her heavy coat, wool bonnet, and boots.

"Say now!" I said, turning her around and escorting her back into the house. "Just where are you going?"

The frown she gave me answered my question. "You know where. To seek Fan and Maggie."

"Elizabeth, that is insupportable. It is snowing and has done so all night. The wind threatens to increase. If drifts mount up, you will be unable to walk. I shall order the carriage to take you to Longbourn."

Horror crept into her face. "Do they know?" When I nodded, she closed her eyes in dismay. "Papá! What will this do to him?"

"He has borne it with great courage, and Jane is there to comfort him, but your presence will benefit him even more, especially once your mother is told."

"You kept it from Mamá?"

"Most likely, she knows by now." I explained how I had escaped her notice when informing Mr. Bennet the night before. "You will be sorely needed there."

"They have Jane and Kitty. I can be of greater assistance by helping with the search, for I know places around here that you do not."

"Such as…?"

"I have travelled this countryside all my life. I will not give over." She folded her arms and stood her ground, but I refused to be outdone, not when it came to Elizabeth's well-being.

"You must ride. I shall have a horse saddled immediately."

She opened her mouth, and her eyes widened. "I…I do not ride."

"Then you cannot search. Look how the snow continues to fall!" I gestured towards the window. "You will flounder about and be lost in a drift in no time. Would you have us abandon our search for the child to look for you?"

"I…have never floundered about, nor have I been lost." She attempted to argue, but her tone had lost its certainty.

"Elizabeth, even a trained tracker could get lost in this weather, and it grows worse as we speak. We are wasting time. You must either go to Longbourn or remain here. Otherwise, I shall be unable to leave you and search for the child. Can you not see the wisdom in my argument?"

She turned away and paced back and forth, but at last, she gave in. "Very well, call for the carriage," she said. "I will go to Longbourn."

As I helped Elizabeth into the conveyance, I handed her a note I had penned to her father. "This will alert Mr. Bennet as to the areas Bingley's servants are searching. He can proceed with directing his men to other regions. I have suggested we enlarge the expanse of woods we explore. Perhaps he can enlist the villagers to join us. I shall ride into Meryton directly and spread the news to the townspeople."

"God willing, someone has seen Fan by now," Elizabeth said, her eyes misting over.

I nodded before kissing her hand. "God willing."

ELEVEN HOURS LATER, I RECEIVED THE RANSOM NOTE.

For eleven hours, the good people of Hertfordshire had scoured the county, risking their health and livelihoods. Many had left their places of business unopened all day. Others had remained out after dark until, exhausted from the weather's onslaught, they had returned as I did, empty-handed and with an air of defeat.

I was not that surprised to receive the note; I almost expected it.

That morning when I had ridden into Meryton, I had scarce begun to alert the various merchants about the missing child when Mr. Morehouse came running up the street from his gun shop.

"Mr. Darcy!" he called, and I turned aside from speaking to the owner of Ford's millinery establishment to join him. "I've news for you—news of Mr. Wickham."

"Speak up," I said quickly.

"My boy has seen him."

"At the Black Stallion where your boy works?" I glanced down the street at the pub. "Is Wickham there now?"

"No, sir. Just this morning he boarded the early coach bound for London. I aimed to walk out to Netherfield to tell you, but the weather—"

"Did he stay the night in Meryton?"

"Evidently, sir. My boy doesn't work reg'lar, so he doesn't know how often the man comes into the pub, but on his way to work this morning, he saw Wickham walk out from the inn and catch the coach."

So, it had not been my imagination or even a guilty conscience! Most likely, Wickham had been peeping in the windows of Lucas Lodge the night we were in attendance. But why? Should I even take time to seek an answer? Something nagged at me that I should—that Wickham could possibly have something to do with the child's disappearance.

"Might I speak with your son?"

"Of course, sir," he replied, leading the way into the public house.

After finding the boy in a back room, unpacking cartons of whiskey, his father brought him to me, whereupon I questioned him as to whether he saw Wickham with travelling companions—in particular, a young woman and small girl.

"No, sir," the boy said, darting a glance towards his father, his eyes big with wonder. "Am I in trouble, Da?"

"No, no trouble, Tim. Just tell the gentleman what you know."

The boy swallowed. "The man called Mr. Wickham didn't have nobody with him, sir, but he was in a frightful rush. Kept looking over his shoulder, he did, and when the coach came late, he cursed the driver."

"Did you see him leave?" I asked.

"No, sir, I ran to get me Da 'cause I knew he owed him money, but the man was itching to leave, so I'm sure he climbed on the coach."

"By the time I got out here," Mr. Morehouse said, "the coach had left, and I've not seen hide nor hair of Mr. Wickham since."

I thanked the man for his assistance and from there moved to speak to the owner of the Black Stallion, questioning him at length as to whether he had seen Wickham in his establishment and whether he had observed him with a woman or a child at any time. I found the answer to both questions disappointing. Wickham had frequented the place the night before, and he had been alone, playing long at several games of chance and amassing sizeable winnings by the close of the evening.

That paid for his fare back to Town, I thought.

Questioning the innkeeper gave me no additional information. However, both men were much alarmed about another incident that took place during the night. It seemed that their tills had been emptied, along with those of several other merchants. I wondered whether Wickham had now added burglary to his crimes.

"And there's some thief about what helped hisself to my larder yesterday," the innkeeper said. "I'm missin' a loaf of bread, half a side of ham, and a crock of fresh milk!"

Since no one had seen Wickham with Maggie or the babe, I decided to return my efforts to what was most important: finding the child. But why had Wickham been in Meryton, and what would have caused him to lurk about Lucas Lodge? Those questions badgered me throughout the long day's search.

Thus, when I returned to Netherfield at the end of the day, weary and downhearted, I met the news of the ransom note with dread but not complete surprise.

After bathing and changing into clean clothing, I joined Bingley, Hurst, and his sisters in the drawing room. Elizabeth had sent a message saying she would stay at Longbourn that night as her family was distraught, and although I missed her, I was relieved she was not in attendance when the distressful news came upon us.

"Mr. Darcy," Caroline said, "you have missed dinner. You must be famished. I shall have Cook send up a plate for you immediately."

I murmured my thanks as I sank into a chair before the roaring fire. Even after soaking in a hot tub, my toes felt as though they suffered from frostbite.

"Did you tell Mr. Darcy about the note, Caroline?" Mrs. Hurst said.

"Oh, no, here it is." She picked up an envelope from a nearby table and handed it to me with her usual flourish. "It has your name on the outside, although I must say it arrived in a most peculiar manner—at the back door of all places."

"The back door, you say?" Bingley asked, looking up from stirring the fire.

"Yes. One of the kitchen girls said she found it on the floor as though it had been slipped under the door. Is that not strange?"

"Strange, indeed," her brother replied.

I broke the seal and opened the page, trepidation welling up within me. Sure enough, it was as I feared.

Darcy,

I have the child.

We had a bargain, and you failed to honour it, but now you will. If you wish to conceal the truth of what you have done from Eliza, and if she ever hopes to see her niece again, you will hand over the fortune we agreed upon.

Your search for her will turn up empty, so do not waste your time. Wait for further notice of when and where you are to deliver the funds.

—GW

I sensed the colour drain from my face. I felt as though I had been punched in the gut. I smashed the page between my hands and balled it up in my fist. If Bingley had not restrained me, I would have hurled it into the fire.

"Darcy, what is it?" He blocked my arm just as I raised it. "Are you ill?"

I shook my head, sank down in the chair from which I had risen, and laid my head back.

"You have obviously received bad news," Hurst said, rising from his seat and pouring a glass. "Have some brandy."

I took the drink, but I could not swallow it. As a servant wheeled in a cart, the smell of food assaulted my senses. I waved it away, for I knew I could not keep it down.

Wickham has the child! The rogue has possession of that innocent little girl. What had I brought to pass?

Unknowingly, Bingley had taken the note from my hand. "Darcy, may I read this?"

I raised my eyes to see him hesitate before attempting to smooth out the wrinkled page. I nodded. I could not keep it from him or anyone else in the room.

Reading it aloud, I heard the gasps of Mrs. Hurst and Caroline and the oath Hurst uttered, but all I could think of was the pain I would see in Elizabeth's eyes once she knew what Wickham and I had done.

BINGLEY, HURST, AND I CONFERRED FOR SOME TIME THAT NIGHT. AFTER expressing their horror, the ladies had retired at Bingley's suggestion. Naturally, the men had questions about the wording of the note, in particular, "the fortune bargained for" to which Wickham had alluded. I attempted to dismiss it, but then Bingley offered an explanation as he saw it.

"The man remains bitter that he did not receive more in exchange for the living your father left him. And he threatens to blacken your name with even more lies to Mrs. Darcy. That is it, is it not?"

"I...hardly know," I murmured.

Why did I not tell the truth? Why did I not confess what I had done, how I had convinced Wickham to return to Hertfordshire and claim his child by promising him money? I could not. I needed to tell Elizabeth first.

"Where do you think he has hidden the child?" Hurst asked, swirling his drink.

"In London. He has friends there who will protect him, or so he thinks." I went on to relate the news that Wickham had been seen in Meryton early that morning boarding the coach to Town. "I must travel to Town with all haste."

"I shall go with you, Darcy," Bingley said.

"No," I replied. "I will send an express to my cousin. With Fitzwilliam's resources, I will have enough help. You must remain here, Bingley, for I feel certain the Bennets will be in need of your presence."

After writing a quick letter to my cousin, I bade my friends goodnight. I would send the note to be posted, even at that late hour, and then direct Rodgers to pack a bag for me. Bingley walked with me into the great hall where he signalled for a footman to deliver the note.

"Make certain it is taken tonight," I said to the servant. He nodded and turned to leave, but before he did, I called him back. "Are you not the man I sent to Longbourn earlier this evening to inform Mr. Bennet of our lack of success?"

"Yes, sir."

"And how does the gentleman fare? Is he ill?"

"No, sir, he did not appear to be."

"And Mrs. Darcy? Was she well?"

"I didn't see Mrs. Darcy, sir."

Bingley said, "What about Miss Bennet? Was she with her father?"

"Yes, sir. I saw all the ladies and Mrs. Bennet sitting in the drawing room —all except Mrs. Darcy."

I wondered at that statement. Where was Elizabeth? It would have been odd for her not to be with her family. Keeping company with them had been her purpose in going.

"Are you the one who brought Mrs. Darcy's note back from Longbourn tonight, her note informing me that she would spend the night with her family?"

The servant frowned. "Mrs. Darcy gave me a note, sir, but not tonight. It was early this morning when I served as footman on her carriage."

"Mrs. Darcy gave you a note *this morning* stating that she would not return to Netherfield tonight? Is that correct?"

"I assume that's what it said, sir. Of course, I didn't read it, but it's the only message I've carried from Mrs. Darcy." He looked away, opened his mouth as though he would say more, and then closed it.

I took a step closer. "What is it? Do you have further information about Mrs. Darcy?"

"It's not my place, sir."

"I tell you it is your place. Say what you will, man."

He swallowed. "This morning, Mrs. Darcy directed the carriage to stop some mile and a half from Longbourn. That's when she gave me the message."

"Why would she stop the carriage that far from Longbourn? What are you saying?"

The footman grew agitated, his eyes darting back and forth between Bingley and me. "She asked me not to say, sir."

"You will say," Bingley said, "or you will be relieved of your position this night!"

The servant took a deep breath. "Mrs. Darcy climbed out of the carriage and told us to return to Netherfield."

I raked my hand through my hair. "You mean you did not deliver Mrs. Darcy to her father's house? You are telling me you left her on the road in the snow?"

"She ordered us to do so, sir. Sully pleaded with her, but she told him to drive on."

"Why did you not stay with her?" Bingley demanded.

"She didn't wish it, sir. She ordered me to carry Mr. Darcy's note to Mr. Bennet and then return here with her message."

I began to pace. "Of all the blasted, foolhardy things to do! Elizabeth is wandering about out there in the snow, Bingley!"

Bingley directed the footman to have the driver summoned immediately and to see that my letter to Fitzwilliam was sent by express post. After questioning the servant called Sully and confirming the footman's story, I ordered him to fetch the carriage and take me to the fixed location where he had left Elizabeth.

Fear consumed me! *How long could Elizabeth survive on foot in this weather?* I had ordered the driver not to spare the horses, and although he drove at breakneck speed, I still wished to travel faster. We had gone less than two miles when the carriage slowed. Wondering why my commands were being thwarted, I peered out the window into the dark. The moonlight reflected an endless white landscape as far as the eye could see.

"Whoa!" Sully shouted, causing the carriage to stop abruptly.

Before the footman could do his duty, I thrust open the door and leapt onto the road. "Why the devil have we stopped?"

"Up ahead, sir," Sully said. "There's somethin' lyin' by the side of the road."

My heart racing, I ran in the direction he pointed and saw her curled up in a ball.

"Elizabeth!" I knelt and gathered her into my arms, holding her tightly, and repeating her name over and over.

"Fitzwilliam?" she said weakly.

"What happened? Are you injured?"

"My ankle—I turned it." Her coat was wet, her bonnet missing, and she shook with uncontrollable tremors.

I picked her up and carried her to the carriage. Aided by the footman, I climbed aboard and sat down, placing her on the seat beside me. Gently I lifted her feet off the floor so she reclined against me.

"Did you find Fan?" Elizabeth asked, her voice a hoarse whisper.

I shook my head.

"Fitzwilliam, I—"

"Hush, do not attempt to speak." I turned her about until I could hold her in my arms.

"Cold, so cold," she said, her teeth chattering.

I leaned forward and grabbed the rugs the servant had placed in the carriage, wrapped them around her, and then held her tightly against my body. With one hand, I rubbed first her arm and then her back, attempting to stroke some warmth into her. Her hair hung in wet ringlets all around her face. Beginning to cough, she held her throat as though it hurt. I placed my lips against her forehead, wishing I could breathe for her.

"To Netherfield without delay!" I called in a loud voice, and the carriage lurched forward.

"Wait!" Elizabeth cried with more strength than I expected. "We must not leave, for I may have found Fan!"

I shook my head and made no attempt to alter my command. "No, no, she is not here. We must see to your injury."

"But I have something to show you, something of Fan's! In my pocket." She buried her hand in her coat and pulled forth two damp strips of scarlet and green cloth.

"What is this?"

"Fan's hair ribbons. I bought them for her at the milliners in Meryton. See the notches? I cut them in that manner before I gave them to her only a few days ago. And I found them in the snow near Cutter's Wood."

"Where is Cutter's Wood?"

"About a mile from here off the road through the trees. Jane and I played there as children. I remember a hidden glade in the forest where we gleaned walnuts until Papá forbade us to tarry there because of what he called hidden dangers."

She stopped to cough, and although I cautioned her to rest her voice, she would not.

"The land around Cutter's Wood varies from most of Hertfordshire. There are numerous gullies where ruffians might hide, and an open cave existed at one time. A pool of water within the cave seeped out and ran down the nearest channel, forming a steep rocky ravine. Papá had the entrance to the cave blocked off with huge stones to discourage anyone from hiding there. He attempted to tear down the old hut that lies not far from the cave, but I know for a fact it was still standing last year. I happened upon it on one of my walks. The windows were broken, there were holes in the roof, and the door sagged dreadfully. All four walls were intact, though."

When I did not respond, she went on. "Do you not think it possible that Maggie and Fan may have taken refuge there? I tried to climb down to the cave, but that is when I slipped on a rock and fell."

Chills ran up my spine to think of her out there, helpless and alone. "How did you get back to the road?"

"'Twas hard going, but I knew if I were to remain alive, I needed to find help before dark. I thought I could make my way to Netherfield, but my strength failed me."

I took her by the shoulders and raised her up, pulling her close. "You could have died, Elizabeth! Do you realize that?" My voice came out with more force than I intended.

"But I did not die. I am here. Pray, direct the driver to turn the carriage around and let us go back. I can show you the way through the wood!" She raised her voice, causing her to cough again. "We have lost precious time. Let us make haste, as there is not a moment to lose!"

"You are not going anywhere other than Netherfield."

"But Fan may be in Cutter's Wood!"

"I think not."

"Why?

I gritted my teeth, hating the thought of revealing Wickham had possession of the child. And, at that moment, I was spared the task, for we had arrived at Netherfield. We were immediately besieged by servants assisting us in departing the conveyance and making our way into the house. Upon seeing Elizabeth was hurt, Bingley dispatched a servant to fetch the physician with all haste.

I carried my wife up the stairs to our chamber and gently placed her on the chaise in her dressing room. All the while, she peppered me with questions.

"Later," I said, "after you shed those wet clothes and soak in a hot tub." I withdrew as the maids began to assist her.

In the hallway, Bingley questioned me at length as to where I had found her, and I attempted to answer his inquiries, all the while pacing back and forth, worrying that Elizabeth's injuries might be more grievous than she thought.

"Have you informed Mrs. Darcy that Wickham has the child?"

I stopped abruptly and shook my head. "Not yet. Where is that blasted physician?"

At that moment, the maid signalled to me from the dressing room to transport Elizabeth to her bed.

"I shall send up Mr. Jones the moment he arrives," Bingley said as I closed the door to our chamber.

Striding into Elizabeth's dressing room, I saw she was clad in a gown and robe, her hair loosened and brushed, cascading about her shoulders. She held up her arms and clasped them around my neck as I lifted her from the stool on which she sat. The scent of fresh lavender from her bath clung to her skin. Although she now felt warmer to me, I noticed that she continued to tremble. Placing her in the bed, I pulled the quilts up and tucked them securely around her body.

"Shall I call for more blankets?" I asked. "You are shivering."

Shaking her head, she snuggled into the quilts and pulled them up around her chin. "It is not from the cold but the ordeal."

"Bingley has sent for the doctor, and he should be here before long."

"Oh, must he come? I do feel better."

I had been leaning over her and straightened up as though to leave.

"You are not going, are you?" she said, catching my hand in hers.

"You are exhausted. I thought to allow you rest until the physician arrives, but if you do not wish me to leave, then—"

"I do not wish it. Pray, remain here and tell me of Fan."

The maids departed the room, carrying the wet clothes and towels, just as another entered bringing a tray. Bingley had sent up hot tea and a light meal, but Elizabeth would not eat. She took the steaming cup and held it in both hands. "I am too weary for food."

"You would do better with a hot toddy," I said. "Shall I order one?"

"Not now. Sit with me. Tell me why you insisted Fan is not at Cutter's Wood? How can you be certain?"

I had walked to the fireplace to stoke the logs into a larger blaze. At her request, I turned to see an expression of fear and hope mingled in her eyes. I felt a tightening in my chest.

Crossing the room, I sat down on the bed. "Elizabeth, you never should have taken off on your own! You are an intelligent woman. Can you not see what a foolish endeavour you attempted?"

She handed me the cup. "Why do you change the subject and avoid giving me an answer when I ask about Fan? I know something has happened.

Tell me, please!"

I rose from the bed, turning my back towards her, wishing I could flee from the room, wishing I could do anything other than the task that lay before me.

I took a deep breath. "Wickham has taken the child and is holding her for ransom, most likely in London."

I heard Elizabeth cry out, and when I turned, I saw what I dreaded most—the look of utter horror on her face. It was no more than I expected nor less than I deserved.

Chapter Fifteen

A knock at the door announced the arrival of the physician, Mr. Jones, and after a thorough examination, he wrapped Elizabeth's ankle and pronounced it severely bruised but not broken. He was also concerned about her cough, although he considered the fact she did not have a fever to be a good sign.

"I shall leave a sleeping draught for the pain. You must remain in bed several days, Mrs. Darcy," he said. "Walking will only cause the foot to swell and delay your recovery."

She nodded, but I knew that the moment the man left the room, my wife would wish to rise. As expected, she did. Throwing off the quilts, she reached for her robe, but I was quicker.

"No, Elizabeth," I said, snatching the garment. "You heard Mr. Jones as well as I did." I replaced the covers over her and tossed the robe across the room onto the chaise.

"How can I remain abed when Wickham has Fan?" she demanded. "And when and how did you learn this dreadful news? Pray, Fitzwilliam, tell me everything."

I took a deep breath and revealed the sad facts. "I received a ransom note tonight here at Netherfield. One of the girls in the kitchen found it on the floor by the back door. Evidently, Wickham either slipped it under the door or had someone do it for him."

"Where is it? What does it say?"

I glanced about the room. "I must have left it with Bingley. It simply states that Wickham has Fan, and he demands money for her return. The amount and place of delivery will be revealed when he is ready to do so."

"That is monstrous! How could Wickham treat his own child like a pawn to be bargained for?" Elizabeth fell back against the pillows as though someone had struck her. "I thought him wicked, but I never dreamt he could act in this manner."

"I could."

"But he was here in the area, so why do you think he has left? He might yet be holding Fan at Cutter's Wood!"

"He was seen in Meryton this morning boarding the coach to London. I feel certain he has hidden the child somewhere in Town." I related all that I had learned from Mr. Morehouse and the innkeeper. "He may have been in Hertfordshire for several days. I could swear I saw him outside Lucas Lodge the other evening."

She leaned forward. "Lucas Lodge! Why would he be there?"

"To keep his eye on me and to insure we were all away from Netherfield. I suspect he took the child that night."

Her eyes grew darker, magnified by fear. "And Maggie? He must have taken her too."

I looked away and pressed my lips together. "Do you recall our conversation with the child when she talked about Maggie and a man?"

"You think the man was Wickham."

I nodded. "He could have been lurking around Longbourn when your mother and sisters came to Netherfield for breakfast on Christmas day. That would have provided adequate time for him to charm Maggie and persuade her to run off with him."

"The same way he persuaded Lydia," Elizabeth said sadly. "But I do not understand! Why would Maggie agree to take Fan with them?"

"Only the maid knows the answer to that question."

A servant entered bearing a tray with the hot drink I had ordered for my wife. Although she refused at first, I remained firm. I reached for the bottle of medicine the physician had left on the table.

"Do not dose the toddy!" she protested, growing agitated once again and beginning to cough. "I must have a clear mind."

"Mr. Jones prescribed it for the pain."

Elizabeth shook her head. "My ankle does not hurt badly. If I need the remedy in the night, I shall ring for Sarah. Please, do not insist."

"Very well, but you must rest now."

"I have so many more questions. How shall I ever sleep?"

"I have questions as well, but they will have to wait for morning light. The doctor ordered rest, and rest you shall if I have to stand watch over you."

A sigh escaped her as she lay back on the pillow. "I could never sleep with you standing guard."

"Then I shall leave you. Goodnight, dearest wife." I bent over and kissed her forehead, and she reached up and touched my cheek with her hand.

"You promised you would find Fan."

"And I vow to keep that promise."

AFTER DESCENDING THE STAIRS, I WAS SURPRISED TO SEE THAT BINGLEY and Hurst remained in the drawing room. I had returned to the room to secure the ransom note and read it again. Why, I know not, for I could have recited it from memory, so seared into my brain was its threat.

Bingley asked after Elizabeth, and he was visibly relieved to learn she had not suffered serious harm. When I asked for the note, Hurst handed it to me.

"I have been examining the scoundrel's words, Darcy," he said, "and it appears this man Wickham wishes to injure you. Did he take the child for the money or to cause difficulties between you and your wife?"

"Both, I would presume," I said. "Primarily, he acts out of greed, but there is no love lost between us. Our history is murky at best."

"That makes the man doubly dangerous."

"I agree," Bingley said. "Wickham could do anything, Darcy. Who knows whether he will return the child to you even if you give him the fortune he asks."

"He does not want Fan," I said.

"How do you know this?" Hurst asked.

How do I know? Because I brought this situation about! I thought. But I did not say that, for I still had not yet confessed to Elizabeth my part in this scheme gone wrong. "His is not the behaviour of a man who wishes to rear a child even though he is her natural father. Wickham needs money, and he will do anything to secure it."

"I understood he had made his fortune," Bingley said. "He told Mr. Bennet that was the reason he was now able to care for the child."

"It has been my experience that Wickham loses money more quickly than he gains it."

"Shall you return to Town as planned?"

I nodded. "But not until the morrow. I must make certain Elizabeth does not grow worse during the night."

"I still think I should accompany you."

"Bingley, I thank you, but you can assist me far better by remaining here and seeing to it that my wife is afforded the care she needs. And, as I said earlier, I feel certain the Bennets will benefit from any comfort you can offer them."

"Louisa and I will remain, also," Hurst said. "She will be needed to see to Mrs. Darcy."

That surprised me, for I knew Caroline and her sister had planned to return to Town. Hurst had shown unexpected character throughout this ordeal, and I found my estimation of him improved.

The men retired for the night, for by that time, it had grown exceedingly late. I did not return to my chamber. Instead, I sat before the fire until morning, my eyes fixed on Wickham's ransom note, my brain wondering how quickly I could find him, and my heart broken from the knowledge of what I would be forced to tell Elizabeth with the dawn.

As THINGS CAME ABOUT, I DID NOT MAKE MY CONFESSION TO ELIZABETH that morning. God knows, I tried, but it was not to be. She was sound asleep when I entered our chamber, and her maid sat beside the bed, looking somewhat drowsy as well. Sarah rose to depart the room upon my arrival, but not before informing me that Elizabeth had awakened in pain about four o'clock. The maid had given her a dose of the sleeping draught. Because of the medication, no matter what I did, I could not rouse her.

I did not try very hard, for she slept the sleep of the innocent, and I knew she needed rest more than she needed to hear my sad tale. There would be time enough in days to come for all the distress it would cause. After dressing and taking the bag Rodgers had packed, I simply kissed Elizabeth's cheek, left the brief note I had written on the pillow beside her, and boarded the carriage for London.

Upon reaching Town, I met with Fitzwilliam, who had received my express early that morning. We conferred for some time and agreed to call in

Harrison, the dependable man who had aided me in finding Wickham some months back. My cousin also had trusted men in his unit who would be pleased to support us in combing the London abyss Wickham called home.

"We shall find him, Darce," Fitzwilliam said, "and he will lead us to the little one. The man is not clever enough to elude all of us. I doubt it will take more than a few days."

I longed for Fitzwilliam's prophecy to come true, but it did not.

A week passed without results. We had immediately sought out Mrs. Younge, but she had left the city, and no one seemed to know or would reveal where she had gone. None of the gambling dens, taverns, or lodging places on that end of Town sheltered Wickham, nor had anyone seen him for weeks. Perhaps, the scoundrel had grown cleverer than we thought.

I wrote to Elizabeth daily—hopeful, confident letters—that did not reflect the growing fear that disturbed my sleep through the long nights. Why had Wickham not contacted me? The more time that passed, the more I worried about the condition of the child. Had she even survived the first night's abduction? A tremor ran through me at the thought of the little girl out in that weather! Surely, even ignorant Maggie knew enough to protect her young charge from the elements. What was I thinking? The maid was unable to keep up with the child inside the house!

Bingley had promised he would send word whether Wickham left another note for me at Netherfield. I had received but one letter from my friend, lamenting the fact that there had been no further message from Wickham. Bingley did say that Elizabeth's belongings had been packed, and she had returned to Longbourn. That caused me concern as I knew she would be more comfortable in Bingley's establishment than the cramped chamber she would inhabit at her father's house. On the other hand, I understood her need to be with her family at such a troubled time.

What I failed to grasp was why Elizabeth had not answered any of my letters. While confined to her bed for at least three or four days, surely she had opportunity to write. I expected her to share her worry and fear with me, but for days and days, I had eagerly sifted through my mail seeking a post addressed by her hand, only to be disappointed.

I missed Elizabeth terribly! A hole the size of a boulder inhabited my heart. I was an empty cavern of a man, and my need for Elizabeth bounced from wall to wall in an endless echo.

IN ADDITION TO MY WORRY, THE GUILT I CARRIED WEIGHED ME DOWN until at times I felt I could no longer bear it. I had taken to leaving my house after dark and walking alone through the streets of Mayfair. One night I found myself outside St. George's Church in Hanover Square. I stared up at the imposing edifice and remembered how many Lord's days I had worshipped within. Images of Georgiana's wedding flashed before me, and with the memory appeared the vision of seeing Elizabeth across the street that fateful morning.

I turned and gazed at the now empty walk and yearned for her to be standing there, looking up at me, her fine eyes glistening in the torchlight. Would I ever see love for me reflected in those eyes? *Not likely*, I thought, *not after what I have done.*

Candlelight flickered from within the church as a couple emerged through the door, bidding goodnight to the old curate, Mr. Wynne, with whom I had shared an acquaintance through the years. He began to withdraw, but upon seeing me, he stopped.

"Did you desire to see the rector, Mr. Darcy? He has left for home, but I can fetch him," he said.

I shook my head but did not move to depart.

He looked uncertain. "Perhaps you wish to pray?" He nodded his head in the direction of the sanctuary.

"Yes, thank you," I murmured, passing through the door he held open.

"You are always welcome at St. George's, sir. Evensong has concluded, but the church remains open every night until eight bells." With a nod, he disappeared into the sacristy.

I entered a pew at the back of the church and sat down on the hard, oak bench. I stared up at the heavy canopy shading the pulpit and thought of how many sermons I had heard in years past. In the light of His word, how would God judge the sins I had committed? I wanted to pray, to beg His forgiveness, but the words would not come. I did not feel worthy to be in His presence.

Within moments, I bolted from the pew and pushed through the massive front door. Outside, I gasped, gulped in the night air, and walked briskly down the street away from the church.

The following night, however, I found myself there again, and every night thereafter for the better part of a week. Something drew me to the house of God, something inexplicable. I still did not find it easy to pray, but a presence in that great house of worship beckoned me to its fount of blessings. One evening, I joined the congregation of parishioners and listened to the choir sing the canticles. I bowed my head when the rector prayed, and I paid heed to his reading of the scriptures. I appeared like any other man in the congregation, and yet I was not, for my head was bowed low with the transgressions I had wrought.

If only I had never sought out Wickham in the first place…if I had never inflicted him on Elizabeth's family…if I had never considered myself smarter and wiser than others, then the little one might still be sleeping safely in her bed at Netherfield. How could I live with myself when I had brought harm to that innocent babe?

On what was to be the final night I went into the church to pray, I arrived later than usual and found the sanctuary empty. I slipped into the pew at the rear that I had come to think of as mine and bowed my head. I wrestled with my conscience in the familiar pattern now well established. When at last I could find no words to voice the anguish that besieged me, I cried aloud.

"Help me!"

Unknowingly, I had uttered the words in none too low a voice. Within a few moments, I sensed the presence of someone nearby. Looking up, I saw the old curate standing in the nave, an expression of concern in his eyes.

"Are you well, sir?" the stooped elder said. He took a few steps across the stone floor towards the pew. "No, I can see that you are not."

How could he see that? I had not responded to his question. My heart was too full of torment to speak.

"Would it help if I listen? There is no one here but us, and I am well-acquainted with keeping a confidence."

When I lowered my head and remained silent, he entered the pew and sat down. Neither of us said a word for several moments. He removed his spectacles and rubbed his hand across his eyes.

"Mr. Darcy, I have assisted the rector here at St. George's for a great many years. Every week I see people enter the assembly dressed in their best with their Sunday morning faces in place. I rarely see anyone at less than their finest. For the most part, they smile and appear pleased to be here. Rarely does a man walk through the door looking as you do."

What did he mean? What was amiss in my manner?

"When a man haunts this house night after night with agony in his eyes," he said, "he reveals an urgent need whether that is his intent or not. Will you share with me why you cry out for God's help?"

"Do we not all need His help?" I said rather shortly.

"We do, sir, we do." He nodded his head up and down. "And sometimes, we need the comfort of another human voice."

I shuddered and leaned back against the pew for support. "I need much more than comfort. I need forgiveness, redemption, and the ability to make things right."

"God offers all three, sir, as you well know."

"I accept God's grace, and I am grateful, but how will I ever receive pardon from those I have wronged?"

The old man leaned towards me. "Deep within, I believe you are harbouring great secrets. Have you no one with whom to share them?"

Slowly, I shook my head. "My guilt is such that I have difficulty admitting it even to myself, let alone baring my soul to another."

"Shall I remind you again that I can keep a confidence? Only you and I... and God will ever hear the words we speak tonight. Will you not unburden your heart?"

I looked up to meet his eyes. The compassion shining forth was evident, and for some reason, it unleashed a torrent within me. That night, I confessed all to that elder churchman—how I had fallen in love with a woman I deemed unsuitable, how I had brought a despicable man back into her family's life, hoping to make the woman's situation one I could tolerate, and how I had married that woman under false pretences, unable to be honest with her about my feelings for fear of rejection. I told of the resentment I had harboured against a blameless child and how I had arrogantly depended upon my wealth and position to secure what I wanted, no matter the consequences. And now, that same arrogance had caused the child and all who loved her to be held hostage by a scoundrel's greed.

"Even if I find the little one, how will my wife ever forgive me?" I cried, burying my head in my hands.

I felt his hand grip my shoulder. "Do not surrender to despair, Mr. Darcy. You must believe."

"How? If I lose Elizabeth, I lose everything that matters to me in this life!"

"Does your wife love you?"

I shook my head. "I hardly know. Her manner towards me has grown softer lately, but once she becomes privy to my misdeeds, how can she love me?"

"Ah, there is no accounting for a woman's heart. God has given it more tenderness than a man's. You must pray for the courage to confess all to her and beg her forgiveness, and I shall pray that she will."

I sat back, feeling spent. "Thank you, Mr. Wynne."

"All is not lost, sir. Have faith." He rose, and I followed him, bidding him goodnight at the door. As I walked home, somehow I felt lighter, as though a small part of the ponderous weight I carried had been lifted from my shoulders.

On the eighth day of January, I awaited Fitzwilliam in my study. We met early each morning to discuss the previous day's investigation and make plans to enlarge the search.

When a servant entered, I assumed it was to announce the colonel.

Instead, he said, "Mr. James Barlow of Hanover Square to see you, sir."

Surprised, I rose to greet an acquaintance I had not met with for some time. I welcomed him and bade him sit down.

"Darcy, I come on a strange mission," Barlow said. "The truth is I have put it off because it seems incomprehensible."

Naturally, my curiosity was piqued. "Go on," I urged him.

"Unbeknownst to me, my wife's maid, Polly, has been harbouring her sister in my house for the past week."

Why should Barlow tell me of problems with his household staff, I wondered.

"Not only is her sister there, but she has brought a young girl with her. When I discovered this, I called them to account. I could tell from her manners and dress that Polly's sister is a young woman who had obviously been in service, but the child with her, however, wore clothing of marked wealth.

"I questioned the woman at length. In the beginning, she said her husband was coming for her and the child, but she refused to give his name. She said she needed a place to stay for only a short while, but when I asked the whereabouts of her husband, she could not say. I found the entire situation highly suspect."

"As would I."

The servant brought in the tea cart then, and we ceased talking while acquiring our steaming cups.

"I must ask what this has to do with me, Barlow," I said, once the servant left the room.

"I am coming to that. I questioned my wife's maid privately, and when I threatened her with the loss of her position if she dared tell an untruth, she relented. It seems that Polly's sister is not married. In truth, she said she worked as a nursery maid for you, and that she foolishly eloped with a man Polly fears has no plans to marry her at all."

I leaned forward in my chair, all my senses heightened!

"To make matters worse, it seems the child does not belong to this maid, but is the natural daughter of the worthless man who is playing with her affections. Darcy, I do not know whether I have arrived at the whole of the story or not, and thus, I have come to you for answers. Do you know of a former servant who may have worked in your nursery?"

I rose and took a step nearer my guest. "Her name—I must have her name! Could it be Maggie, and is the child called Fan?"

Barlow looked astonished. "Why yes, I believe those are the names I heard. Do you have knowledge of all this?"

I nodded, beginning to pace. "I do. Oh, yes, I do! The child is my ward. She was taken without my permission from Netherfield Park in Hertfordshire almost two weeks past, and the man Maggie hopes to marry is concealing the child's whereabouts from me until I pay a king's ransom. Where are they? Where is the child?"

"Why, I never!" Barlow's chin dropped, as he rose from his chair. "I cannot believe such daring! And—and to think they have been secreted away in my servants' quarters all this time. Of all the insufferable wickedness!"

"Where is the child? Barlow, take me to her, I beg of you!"

"Yes, yes, of course," he sputtered. "Without delay, Darcy!"

UPON OUR ARRIVAL AT BARLOW'S TOWNHOUSE, HE SENT FOR MAGGIE AND Fan to be brought into the drawing room. I could not sit still, so great was my apprehension that the maid had somehow escaped with her before we arrived. But no, the door opened, and in walked little Fan clinging to her maid's skirt.

With one look at me, terror filled Maggie's eyes, and she turned to run from the room, but not before I had crossed the length between us and demanded she stay. With Barlow's butler barring the door, she could no longer elude her fate. In the excitement, I saw Fan's lower lip begin to quiver.

Stooping low, I held out my arms. "Fan, shall you come to me?"

She hesitated but a moment and then ran into my arms. "Up, man," she demanded, and I obliged her request, my heart offering prayers of thanksgiving as I felt her chubby little arms encircle my neck.

"What shall I do with this one," the butler asked Mr. Barlow.

"Hold her in the kitchen for now, Johnson. Do not let her leave the house," his employer answered.

While Johnson removed the maid from the room, I carried Fan to the window and showed her the sun shining brightly without. "I am so happy to see you," I murmured.

She peered into my eyes. "Mamá?"

"Yes, we will see Mamá soon. I promise."

I held Fan in my lap for some time, reluctant to let her out of my sight. I smoothed back her wayward curls that insisted on falling across her brow and laughed when she reached up and attempted to do the same, running her little fingers through my hair. She appeared well. Her face and clothes were clean, and she had not grown thin.

"Mamá?" she asked again.

"Soon," I said, pulling her close to my heart.

A short while later, Barlow called for one of his trusted maids to take Fan to the nursery. With the promise of milk and biscuits waiting, the child took the servant's hand and followed her up the stairs. Still, I stood at the foot of the staircase watching until I heard the click of the latch on the door. Barlow and I then made our way to his library, whereupon he instructed Johnson to fetch Maggie.

She was obviously frightened, and I could tell from her puffy eyes that she had been weeping. I had no compassion to waste on her, though. I struggled to control my temper. Her sister, Polly, had walked in with her, and the younger girl clung to her arm with both hands.

"Tell the gentleman what you done, Maggie," Polly said, her tone none too mild as she prodded her sister forward. "Go on with you. There's no use tryin' to hide it now."

In a halting, sniffling manner, the girl answered my questions and laid bare the events that had transpired in Hertfordshire, beginning on Christmas Eve. My assumptions had been correct. Wickham had met Maggie at

Longbourn on Christmas Eve night. While Fan remained in the parlour enjoying the festivities with us, Mrs. Bennet's cook had sent Maggie to the stables with Christmas pudding for the hands. On her way back, she met Wickham, who wasted no time in persuading her into sneaking out to meet him again after she put the child to bed.

On Christmas Day, when everyone was gone other than Mr. Bennet and while he rested, Maggie had entertained Fan outdoors when Wickham came on the scene again. He soon convinced her that he loved his child. Upon her return to Netherfield that night and after her charge fell asleep, she had once again crept from the house for a tryst with the scoundrel. Wickham courted her with affection and pretty words she had never heard before, and it did not take long before he convinced the foolish girl to run away with him.

"He said we'd marry and have bairns of our own. He'd put Fan in a school for gentlemen's daughters so I wouldn't have to keep her anymore, and we'd have plenty of money," Maggie said. "I'd get a new dress and bonnet, and I wouldn't have to work in service ever again!"

Maggie had alerted Wickham that we would be gone from Netherfield on the night we visited Lucas Lodge. Once we left the house, she was to pack a bag for the child and herself and meet him on the lane outside Netherfield. Fortunately, she stuffed a blanket into the valise. Wickham took them to a remote part of the woods and hid Maggie and Fan in a small, deserted hut.

"Where is the hut?" I demanded.

She cowered down beside her sister, but at her urging, finally replied. "Don't know, sir. We walked in the dark."

"Didn't you tell me it weren't far from the London road?" Polly asked.

Maggie nodded. "That's where George told us to meet him the next morning real early."

"Do you mean to say he left you and the child alone in that hut all night?"

Again, the girl nodded. "He had to go to Meryton for food and money. He came back late and gave us the food, but he only stayed a bit. It was terrible cold. I remember it began to snow something fierce. Me and Fan huddled under the blanket all night, but leastways we had ham on bread to eat and milk to drink. Once her stomach was full, Fan quit crying and went to sleep. I listened to that wind moan all night, though. George said he'd be coming for us in the coach what goes to London. I done just what he told me. I got to the road early, but it was powerful hard carrying Fan through the snow. Made me all fagged out.

"We waited and waited, and finally I seen the coach coming, but it didn't stop for us. Went some distance 'fore the horses slowed. I couldn't carry Fan anymore and had to drag her along behind me. She was crying by the time we reached George, and all he did was stand there by the side of the coach, watching us! Lazy bugger!"

Upon reaching Town, Maggie soon learned her dreams of marriage would have to wait. For several days, they moved from room to room. When she told Wickham that her sister worked in Hanover Square, he had promptly deposited her and the child at Barlow's kitchen door and told her he would be back as soon as his business matters were arranged. She had not seen him since.

At the completion of her tale, the room grew eerily silent for a few moments. The only sound to be heard was Maggie's sniffling. It was as though neither Barlow nor I could absorb all that had happened. How had Fan survived that night in a deserted hut without heat in the midst of a snowstorm? Only God knew!

I had paced back and forth during the girl's recital, and now I clasped my clenched fists behind me and walked directly to the maid, bearing down on her with vehemence in my gaze. She ventured but one brief glance at my face before dropping her eyes to the floor.

"Maggie, what possessed you to do such a thing? Has Mrs. Darcy ever mistreated you?" I demanded.

She shook her head and mumbled, "No, sir."

"Why would you return evil to the Bennets, a good family that employed you for almost two years? Surely, you heard from the other servants at Longbourn how Fan's natural father left her mother before she was born. Why would you listen to George Wickham and steal my ward?"

"George said she's his child. He told me *you* stole her from *him*."

"Girl, remember to whom you speak," Barlow thundered. "I have known Mr. Darcy for years, and he is not a man to be accused of such a crime."

I turned back to the maid. "You understand that Wickham never intended to marry you, do you not? He used you to barter a ransom from me. He has no money, and he wants neither you nor the child."

Maggie began crying anew, and something within me faintly regretted that I had crushed her dreams with such severity. At a nod from me, Barlow had the butler take both maids back to the kitchen.

"What will you do with her?" Barlow asked after the door closed.

I shook my head. "I cannot keep her in my employ."

"Certainly not! I would not have such a dishonest person among my servants. I even wonder at retaining her sister. Mrs. Barlow, however, holds Polly in particular regard—says she knows just how to curl her hair and soothe her bad headaches, which I regret to say, occur with regularity."

"I see no need to rid your house of the maid. Polly urged her sister to tell the truth."

"She did hide the girl and the child for nigh on seven days."

I shrugged. "They are sisters. 'Tis not often family loyalty can be trumped by allegiance owed to an employer."

"True enough," Barlow said, nodding. "I say, Darcy, let me take care of the matter for you. I will question Polly further. Mrs. Barlow says the maid's parents work a small farm south of Town. If nothing else, I can have Maggie returned to her father. She will be far from both Hertfordshire and the North Country where you live, and you will be free of her."

I expressed my gratitude to Barlow and asked for Fan to be brought to me.

"What will you do about this rascal, Wickham?" Barlow asked as he walked with us to the front door.

"Wait to hear from him and proceed from there," I said. He wished me luck. I picked up Fan and carried her to the waiting carriage.

Back at the townhouse, I took Fan to the nursery myself and put her down for a nap, sitting beside her on the bed until her eyes closed. My housekeeper suggested a young maid called Annie would serve as a suitable nurse until I made other arrangements. The girl had worked in my house in Town for some time, and the housekeeper assured me that she was honest and reliable.

After sending messages to Fitzwilliam and Harrison, I met with them in my study for over an hour. They were as amazed as I to have the child safely returned. We discussed what to do about Wickham but reached no satisfactory conclusion.

At last, I rose from behind the desk. "I know but one thing to do. I must return to Hertfordshire and reunite my wife and child."

Both men nodded. "We will continue our search for Wickham here in Town," Fitzwilliam said. "But Darce, you must be ever vigilant that he does not reappear at Netherfield or Longbourn."

I HAD ANNIE RIDE IN THE CARRIAGE WITH FAN AND ME. THE SERVANT must have wondered at my break with convention, but I cared not. I resolved not to let the babe out of my sight until I placed her in Elizabeth's arms. Annie carried sweets for the little one and small toys she had found in the nursery. Fan ate but a few bites of the tart and then left the maid's side and climbed into my lap.

"Mamá?" she said, looking up at me, her brown eyes bright with anticipation.

"Yes, we are going to see Mamá."

Her face broke into a smile, causing mine to do the same. "Love Mamá."

I nodded. "I know you love Mamá."

She reached up and patted my cheek. "Love Papá too."

And at that moment, I lost my heart for the second time.

Chapter Sixteen

Darkness prevailed when the carriage pulled up outside Longbourn. Fan had fallen asleep in my arms. Her head lay nestled against my chest while her tiny hand rested in mine. I did not need to knock at the door. Mr. Bennet heard our arrival and met us there surrounded by his wife and daughters.

Great excitement and uproar ensued at the sight of little Fan! Hugged and kissed and passed from grandmother to aunts, she at last found solace in Elizabeth's embrace. Tears of joy and numerous questions abounded for some time while I related the story of how I had found the child. I did not fail to notice that Elizabeth appeared unusually quiet. She devoted her attention to Fan, not once directing a comment or question towards me. She extended neither words of welcome nor gratitude while her family lavished praise upon me for my success.

She knows, I thought.

After an hour had passed in which Fan was petted and fussed over and allowed milk and scones with jam, Elizabeth announced that it was far beyond the little one's bedtime. She and the maid I had brought from Town led her to the nursery. I took the time to answer Mr. Bennet's penchant for detail as to exactly how I had discovered the child's whereabouts. On several occasions during the recital of events, Mrs. Bennet called for her salts, and eventually, she declared her need to retire to her chamber. Jane and Kitty accompanied their mother from the room just as Elizabeth returned to the parlour.

"Ah, Mr. Darcy, here is your wife," Mr. Bennet said. "I know you have much to discuss, so I too will make my way to bed. Tonight, I think I shall sleep at last. Welcome back, and once again, let me say well done."

He shook my hand before I watched him climb the stairs and heard the latch click when he closed his door. Turning towards Elizabeth, I saw her back to me, her shoulders rigid, her posture unyielding. I did not advance into the room but remained near the doorway.

"Are you well, Elizabeth?"

Slowly she turned in my direction, and I could see the displeasure in her eyes. "Am I well? That is all you have to say to me: Am I well?"

I cleared my throat. "I hardly know what to say. I perceive you are angry."

"Oh, you perceive that, do you? How discerning you are!"

I took a deep breath and walked farther into the room. Raking my hand through my hair, I passed by her to stand before the fireplace. She followed and sat down on a chair some distance away.

"When were you going to tell me?" she said.

I blinked several times but remained silent.

"When were you going to tell me the nature of this bargain you entered into with Wickham?"

I looked up quickly. "You read the ransom note."

"Oh, yes. The day you left for Town, Caroline and Mrs. Hurst paid me a visit in my chamber on the pretext of inquiring after my health, but Caroline was only too eager to bring the note to my attention."

I must have left it in the drawing room the night I had spent sitting on the couch staring into the fire. Now, I recalled how carelessly I had thrown it aside. "Is that why you removed yourself to Longbourn?"

"I wished to be with people who love me—people I can trust."

I winced, for her words stung, as I knew she considered me neither. "Elizabeth, will you listen while I tell you what happened?"

"Can I believe you will speak the truth?" Her gaze was direct and filled with hostility.

"You have my word."

"And does *your word* mean anything?"

I felt heartsick at the distrust I heard in her voice. "I never intended for any of this to happen. Last October, when Bingley and I returned to Hertfordshire, we were horrified to hear what Wickham had done to your family during our absence. I, in particular, suffered greatly, knowing that, had I been here at the time instead of traipsing across the Mediterranean, I might have saved Lydia. I could have forced Wickham to marry her."

"And how could you possibly have done that?"

"The man will do anything for money."

"Oh, I know that well enough. He will even steal a child!" She turned her head away, and I could see with what difficulty she struggled to control her emotions.

"If I could have persuaded Wickham to marry Lydia, all would have been well. Instead, I returned to find your entire family in disgrace. Even though it was too late to help your youngest sister, I was determined to make the scoundrel honour his responsibilities. I knew he had no money, but I could finance the child's education. My plan was for Wickham to take his rightful place as Fan's father, place her in a school, and disappear from her life. I would see to it that she was reared appropriately and secured proper employment when she became of age."

Elizabeth rose. "So, *you* are the one who brought him back into our lives. You conceived this entire scheme to take Fan from us and place her under that wicked person's protection!"

"Under *my* protection, Elizabeth, never Wickham's. I would not have left her at his mercy. He did not want her! But I needed him to remove her from Longbourn."

"Why? Why was it ever your prerogative to have any say over Fan? And do not tell me it was done for Mr. Bingley and Jane, for I do not believe it."

I walked across the room to the window and stared out into the night. The moon had vanished behind the clouds, and I saw nothing but blackness. I kept my back to Elizabeth as I spoke. "It was partly for Bingley, but mainly for—" I broke off, unable to finish.

"Go on. For whom?"

I turned and faced her. "For you, Elizabeth. I did it for you."

She had been pacing, but at my words, she stopped and stood perfectly still, appearing taken aback.

"For me? Your meddling caused Wickham to propose to me! It made you and me to marry without love." The tone of her voice mocked me, and her eyes did the same.

"That was never part of the plan. Wickham concocted that idea on his own, and once I learned of it, I cancelled our agreement and ordered him to leave the county."

She folded her arms across her chest and raised her eyebrows. "If you sought to rescue me from disgrace, why not just offer to marry me? Why did Wickham have to propose before you felt compelled to act?"

I swallowed and cast my gaze to the floor.

"Ah," she said, "we both know the answer, do we not? It was Fan. It was not only Mr. Bingley who needed Fan to be removed from our family but you as well. The great Mr. Darcy could not bear the thought of making an alliance with such a discredited family!" She uttered a disgusted laugh. "And now you find the joke is on you. Here you are, not only married to a woman you do not love but saddled with the responsibility of rearing Wickham's child. Just what did your schemes merit?"

She emitted a great sigh. Her bowed head and rounded shoulders signified her despair. I feared she now repented of entering into our union. I walked to her side and reached for her hand, but she snatched it from me and held it aloft.

"No!"

I began to turn away, but I could not let it be. "I have wrought this disaster. I thought only of myself and my pride and superiority. Foolishly, I believed my wealth could solve everything. I have been selfish since I was a child, raised in arrogance and pride. And until now, I...I never knew myself."

An expression of disbelief covered her face. "It seems I do not know you, either, sir. You once told me you were a man who abhorred deceit. How could you have lied with such abandon?"

I closed my eyes in shame and shook my head. "I know not, Elizabeth. I was given good principles to live by but left to follow them in pride and conceit. Yet, until recently, I strove for honour. Why did I fail? I cannot give you a creditable reason, for reason had nothing to do with it. I have been like a man possessed, driven to obtain the one prize I desired and willing to do anything to get it. I did not set out to lie, but one falsehood led to another. Before long, I had gone too far and could no longer see my way out."

A period of silence followed, a period during which Elizabeth twisted the handkerchief she held round and round. I saw the turmoil within reflected in her posture and her actions.

"Why did you not at least warn me about Wickham, tell me that he might possibly continue to do us harm?"

"Because, fool that I am, I did not consider the degree of his desperation.

I ran him out of Hertfordshire after you agreed to marry me. I never dreamt he would return and conceive this evil plot to take Fan from us."

"Where is he now?" Her eyes had grown wide with alarm once more.

I shook my head. "I do not know. I plan to ride to Netherfield on the morrow to discuss the matter with Bingley and Hurst."

"You may as well go tonight. There is no reason for you to remain here."

I inhaled sharply. She wanted me gone from her presence.

"Very well, if you are certain."

"I am certain." She averted her face and would not look at me.

After walking to the anteroom to secure my coat and hat, I said, "I will instruct Mr. Bennet's steward to keep the stable hands on alert around the vicinity of the house. Do not allow Fan outdoors."

She nodded.

"Goodnight, Elizabeth." When she did not reply or even turn to look at me, I exhaled deeply and left the house.

I FOUND BINGLEY ALONE AT NETHERFIELD. MR. AND MRS. HURST, AS WELL as Caroline, had departed for Town that morning. Since they were no longer actively searching for the child in Hertfordshire and since Elizabeth had gone to stay at her father's house, Hurst could not persuade the ladies to remain in the country. Bingley listened intently while I related the details of finding the child. He was surprised but much relieved to hear Fan had been safely returned to Longbourn.

"But why have you come at this late hour, Darcy? I would think you could not bear to be parted from your wife."

"I came to inform you of the child's recovery and to inquire whether Wickham has left any further notes for me at Netherfield."

He shook his head. "Not one word in all the time you were gone. Can it be the man has given up his nefarious quest?"

"I doubt that. No, something has occurred to cause this delay."

"Does the scoundrel know you have found the child?"

"As of yesterday, he did not. And Barlow promised to send word if Wickham showed his face around his house. No, I believe Wickham is ignorant of recent events, but why, I cannot fathom."

"What will you do about him?"

I shrugged. "There is little I can do until he appears again." I went on to tell how Fitzwilliam and I, along with the men who aided us, had searched throughout London for days and yet found not a sign of the man.

Bingley rose from the chair in the drawing room and walked to the hearth where he added a log to the fire. "I wonder you do not take your family to Derbyshire for safekeeping. Surely, you might protect them to a greater degree on your vast estate than either here or at Longbourn."

With my back to Bingley, I raised my head to study the ceiling. Would Elizabeth ever consent to travel to Pemberley with me now that she knew all I had done? It was the question that tore at my heart. I did not care to discuss my marital woes with Bingley. Even though we were friends, it felt disloyal to Elizabeth to speak of such private pain with anyone other than her. It was evident she had not shared her anger at me with her family, for they had demonstrated gratitude towards me and none of her animosity. Until I learned the reason behind my wife's actions, I would refrain from telling my troubles to Bingley.

"When I shall travel to Pemberley is not a decision I can make tonight," I said. "I find I am far too weary. May I impose upon your hospitality and stay the night? I fear that all of Longbourn has already retired, and my return would simply interrupt the peace."

Bingley naturally agreed, and we soon parted to our respective chambers. Rodgers quickly had a fire lit in the room and the bed turned back. After assisting me to disrobe, wash, and prepare for bed, he left, and I felt profoundly alone.

In that room we had shared, I suffered the absence of Elizabeth most acutely. Her things were missing from the nightstand. Her books and needlework no longer graced the table beside the settee. I made my way into what had been her dressing room and groaned aloud at the bareness of the counters. No lotions or bath salts remained, no brushes, mirror, or ribbons —nothing at all to indicate she had ever inhabited the chamber. Opening the armoire, I almost cried out to see not one of her gowns left behind. The faintest trace of her scent yet lingered in the empty wardrobe, and I wished I could crawl inside as Fan had done and recover some small part of her I had once enjoyed.

On the morrow, I awoke with a dull headache and delayed going to breakfast. I requested a pot of tea sent to the chamber and spent the remainder of the morning in seclusion. By mid-day, the affliction had lifted slightly. Just as I departed my room, I was astonished to meet Elizabeth, Fan, and Annie climbing the stairs.

"Papá," Fan cried, escaping the maid's hand and running towards me, her arms outstretched. She threw herself around my legs and then leaned her head back to smile at me. "Up, Papá!"

Naturally, I bent down to comply with her command. I kissed her cheek before she laid her head upon my shoulder. When I looked up, Elizabeth appeared shocked. I spoke to her, and she responded woodenly, still watching the continued affection the child bestowed upon me.

"I am surprised to see you here," I said hesitantly.

She recovered her composure. "I have come for Fan's things and to collect Mrs. Abernathy."

"I trust she is well now."

"She is fully recovered."

The child turned and stretched forth her hand towards Elizabeth. "Mamá!" Elizabeth crossed the distance between us and reached out to take Fan from me, but that was not the little girl's wish. With one arm, she clasped Elizabeth's neck while keeping the other arm firmly around mine, drawing the three of us close. "Mamá and Papá," she announced with a triumphant squeal.

Losing her balance, Elizabeth swayed and fell against me slightly. I instinctively reached out to steady her, placing my hand at her waist. She stiffened, and within moments, we parted in a somewhat awkward way. After motioning for Annie to take Fan, Elizabeth gazed at the floor, the walls—anywhere but my eyes. Within moments, they walked up the hall to climb the stairs to the nursery. I felt chilled, as though the warmth in the house had disappeared.

Three-quarters of an hour later, I sat in Bingley's drawing room, leafing through his newspaper when a servant entered the room and extended a small salver before me. I picked up the note and Bingley, who had been struggling to compose a letter at the desk, turned in my direction.

"Early for the post to arrive," he said.

"Didn't come by post, sir," the servant answered. "Molly come across it layin' on the floor by the kitchen door when she was sweepin' up."

Bingley arose and, waving the man from the room, walked towards me. "Is it from Wickham?"

By that time, I, too, had risen. I broke the seal and opened the single page. "It is."

"Shall you read it aloud?"

I nodded.

Bring ten thousand pounds and a horse to Cutter's Wood at four o'clock today, and I will tell you where to find the child. Come alone. None of your tricks, Darcy, or you will never see the girl again.

— GW

"Cutter's Wood!" I looked up to hear Elizabeth's voice. Evidently, she had entered the room as the servant left. "That was where I suspected he had taken Fan! Did I not tell you that I found her ribbons on the main road nearby?"

"Mrs. Darcy!" Bingley said. "I did not know you were here, but I suppose you have come to collect your husband. I fear he has been laid low with a headache all morning, and now this message from Wickham may cause its return." He bowed before her and then turned back to me. "But Darcy, ten thousand pounds! The rascal expects you to hand over ten thousand pounds? What an insufferable addle pate!"

"Surely, you will not go," Elizabeth said, her eyes on mine. "Now that we have Fan, why should you meet with him?"

"I will. I must be done with Wickham, or he will continue to plague us."

"But he is dangerous! You know not what he might attempt to do."

"Mrs. Darcy is correct," Bingley said. "You must not see him alone. I shall go with you."

I shook my head. "This is between Wickham and me."

"Come now, man, you do not mean that. It is an imprudent plan."

"Mr. Bingley is right. You must have someone with you." Elizabeth's brow was furrowed.

"You heard what Wickham said. I am certain he will keep watch, and if I walk into the woods with Bingley at my side, the rogue will vanish, only to attempt to seize Fan again when we least expect it. I refuse to live with his threat hanging over her head. I will go alone."

Bingley clasped his hands behind him. "At least let me follow. I can bring several of the hands from my stable. We will remain a mile or two back until you enter the forest. Then we can make our way quietly through the trees and be there if you need assistance."

"No, Bingley, it will not do. I cannot hazard the chance of Wickham taking flight."

"You do not know Cutter's Wood," Elizabeth said. "Allow me to go with you, for I can lead you directly there."

I fixed my gaze upon her. "Under no circumstances!"

"But why can I not be of service in this matter? Fan is my child."

"She is *our* child," I said, "and this is my responsibility. I will protect her and you with my life."

I knew not the meaning of the look that passed between us. She seemed to implore me with her expression not to engage in this undertaking. Was I hoping for too much? Was her concern the same apprehension she would feel for anyone contemplating a situation fraught with danger, or did she care for me in spite of the wrong I had done?

She folded her arms across her chest and raised her chin. "You do not know the way to Cutter's Wood."

"Then you will draw me a map," I said in a matter-of-fact manner.

She shook her head. "I will not. I refuse to be a party to your endangerment."

I was amazed at her stubbornness. "Elizabeth, be sensible. How else shall I keep the appointment?"

She shrugged. "As long as you remain foolhardy, I suppose you will not meet with Wickham."

I pressed my lips together. She may have thought our wills equal, but she did not know the strength of mine. I would not expose Elizabeth to Wickham's desperation.

"Then I shall find someone who can direct me to the wood. I feel certain some of Bingley's staff has heard of it, and if not, there is always your father or Miss Bennet. You do recall you told me how you and Jane played there as children, do you not? And how your father forbade it in fear of ruffians? It will be simple enough for either of them to draw me a map."

"I am afraid he has you there, Mrs. Darcy," Bingley said.

Clutching the ransom note, I headed towards the door to question Netherfield's servants but not before observing Elizabeth stamp her foot as I passed by.

"Very well," she said. "I will tell you how to reach the wood, but you are the most wilful man I have ever known!"

AN HOUR BEFORE THE APPOINTED TIME TO MEET WICKHAM, I MOUNTED my horse at Netherfield's front door. Bingley stood on the stone steps, the concern on his face apparent.

Mr. Bennet's carriage remained in the yard, and his driver and footman stood nearby. After drawing the map, Elizabeth had surprised me when she had not returned to Longbourn before I left, for it could not have taken that long to pack up Fan's belongings. Perchance, Mrs. Abernathy required more time to prepare her trunk.

Could it be that my wife cared enough not to leave until she knew I had returned from my task unharmed? All that was within me hoped the latter reason kept her there.

"Proceed with caution," Bingley said.

I glanced up at the nursery to see Elizabeth at the window. She did not wave nor did I, but I held her gaze. With a nod, I urged the horse forward and, within moments, galloped through the gates of Netherfield. Fortunately, the weather had cleared. I welcomed the warmth of the sun overhead, for the air remained brisk. How would Wickham react when he learned I had found Fan? I had taken but one means of persuasion to cause him to see things in a rational manner, and it was not ten thousand pounds.

Elizabeth had given me clear directions. I proceeded down the London road for an estimated three miles, looking for the huge fallen oak she had noted. Sure enough, it lay not ten yards off the main pathway. I remained on the horse until the trees grew dense and then dismounted, looping the reins securely over a branch. With a quick glance behind me to make certain no one had followed, I entered the wood.

A faint trail wound in and around for more than a mile. I could see the appeal for Elizabeth to explore the path, for every tree and shrub native to the countryside grew in abundance. Eventually, the foliage parted to reveal a clearing. An old dilapidated hut sat in front of a formation of boulders. The rocked-up cave lay near a precipice that looked as though it fell some distance below. Mr. Bennet had been wise to forbid his children from play-ing near the ravine. The decline of the rift and the possibility of the cave serving as a hiding place for the lawless made the secluded area no place for his young daughters.

I skirted the clearing, looking for signs of Wickham. I approached the remains of the hut and peered through a broken window but saw no one inside. Suddenly, he emerged from the cave, slipping through a narrow opening at the side where the stones had been pulled loose.

"Ah, Darcy, prompt as always. I trust you will be as complaisant with the rest of my demands." He walked a few steps from the cave while I chose to remain a fair distance from him. I noted he limped, and I detected a haggard air about his person even from afar. "Do you have the money?"

"I have the child."

He gave a short laugh. "Do not think me a fool. You have no idea where the child is!"

"I found her in Hanover Square at the home of an acquaintance of mine, Mr. James Barlow."

Wickham's mouth fell open. "How—how did you find her? That ignorant maid—she came to you, did she not? I should have known the chit did not have the sense to keep her mouth shut."

"The maid lacked the sense to refuse you. How could you have exposed Fan to the bitter weather? She could have died, forced to spend the night in that hut!"

Wickham swore and slapped his fist into the palm of his hand. "What do I care? The brat has brought me nothing but trouble since I learned of her birth. I should have known you were out to gull me. I should have heeded my own counsel when you first came up with your senseless scheme." He began to cough, coming nigh to doubling over from the severe spasms.

"That last remark is one you and I can agree upon. It was an ill-conceived plan and one of which I am thoroughly ashamed. I rue the day I ever summoned you into Fan's life!"

Wickham looked up, his eyes narrowing. "And I suppose you would not wish for your wife to ever learn of your intrigue, now would you?"

I remained silent.

"Give me the money, and I swear she will never hear it from my lips."

"For how long? Until you spend the last farthing and return for more? You must think me a defective to believe you will not continue to make threats. No, Wickham, I will not give you the ten thousand pounds you seek."

"Then why should I not reveal your plot to your wife?"

"Because I have already told her."

Once again, his mouth fell agape. He began pacing slightly, favouring his right leg. "And did you tell her *all*, Darcy? Did you tell her how long you coaxed and begged to convince me to go along with this plan? Did you tell her how much money you promised me if I would rid Longbourn of the brat?"

I nodded. "But you know as well as I that it was never ten thousand pounds."

"It should have been!" He began to cough again. He was obviously ill and looked as though he had suffered a wound to his leg. What was he contemplating? It was much like watching a snake darting its head about, looking for the best place to strike. Of a sudden, he stood still. Looking up, his eyes passed over me towards the woods behind, and an expression of recognition and then mockery descended over his face.

"Tell me, Darcy, did you tell the lovely Eliza that it was your idea for me to propose marriage?"

"That is a lie! And you will refer to her as 'Mrs. Darcy'!"

He tried to laugh, but the effort resulted in another round of coughing. When, at length, the paroxysm lessened, he continued. "I knew you wanted her the first time I saw you together more than two years ago. You never fooled me. We grew up together. As youths, we were confidants. I knew the moment I saw her that Eliza Bennet was the woman you would pursue. How I laughed to see with what disdain she beheld you! And as for me—within days of our meeting, she believed every word I fed her against you. I had her in the palm of my hand like that." He snapped his fingers. "And I could have had my way with her whenever I chose."

"Shut your filthy mouth!" My hands balled up in fists, I started towards him when he reached within his coat and pulled out a pistol.

At that same moment, I heard a woman's cry behind me. As I whirled around, my heart began racing to see Elizabeth standing there, her eyes huge with fear, her hands reaching out to me.

"Elizabeth!" I immediately ran to place myself in front of her, attempting to shield her from Wickham.

He stretched forth his arm, aiming the gun straight at us, and began to laugh once again. "Did you not know she was there all along? She heard it all. Wonder how warm your marital bed will be tonight…that is, if you ever see your bed again."

He resumed pacing but did not lower the pistol. "And tell me, Eliza, what do you think of your husband's aim to banish the brat to a school? Has he convinced you it is best for all, especially him?" He snorted in derision. "If he survives today, believe me he will do his utmost. The last thing he will tolerate is rearing my bastard in the hallowed halls of Pemberley!"

With one hand behind me, I reached for Elizabeth, and she placed both hands in mine. "Let her go, Wickham. This is between you and me. She has nothing to do with it."

He made no reply, simply ceased walking and stood there, holding the firearm in place.

"Let her walk away," I said. "We can settle this between us."

"The only way this will be settled, Darcy, is for you to give me the money. Eliza is not going anywhere, and neither are you until I get what I want."

I glanced over my shoulder and pulled her closer to me. She did not resist. I turned back to Wickham. "I did not bring money, but I brought something else."

"I want nothing you have to offer other than money!"

"There is a ticket in my coat. I bought passage for you to sail to Virginia on the next ship that leaves Portsmouth. Most likely, it will not depart for several months, but if you are willing to start over in a new country, I will stake you three thousand pounds on the day you leave."

He began to cough anew. "Three thousand pounds—the exact sum you gave me in place of the living I was promised at Kympton! You can see how long such a paltry sum lasts. No, I will have none of your fimble-famble! I will not be cheated again, Darcy."

"You appear to be ill, and what has happened to your leg?"

"Never mind my leg. The worst of my malady has passed, and the wound is nothing more than the upshot of some coxcomb in Uxbridge who lost at cards last week and accused me of cheating. Neither infirmity will take down George Wickham, nor will you."

"I will see that you are cared for until you heal. Truly, you do appear in need of a physician, but with luck, you will be well enough to sail by early summer. In Virginia, you can begin afresh. I understand the lands to the west are vast beyond our imagination. Prices are cheap, and a man can make a good living there with such a start."

"Once again, you have it all planned, do you? But when have I ever cared to make my way in that manner? You propose a perilous journey, and once I make land, hard work awaits. I prefer an easier life. Besides, I have no desire to leave the country of my birth. I have no use for your ticket. I want what I demanded. You either pay me, or Eliza can live in fear of losing her niece whenever I take a notion to play the loving father."

I was breathing heavily by that point, for I grew more and more enraged at the thought of how his threats must be frightening Elizabeth. Quietly, I released her and whispered, "When I move towards him, drop to the ground."

"Do not encourage her to run, Darcy."

"I did not. But you are going to have to shoot me to end this. I have made my offer, and you have made yours. We have reached an impasse. One of us must yield."

Slowly, I began to walk towards him. His eyes flickered back and forth, and he waved the gun about as he edged backward away from me.

"Stay where you are! You think I will not fire, but I will!"

"Will you, George? Will you kill your boyhood friend?"

"You were never my friend. You were the son and heir, too great for the likes of me."

"We *were* friends, but you have forgotten. You laid aside all that my father tried to teach you."

"Your father"—he stopped to cough—"always telling me to be more like you. Study harder, George! Be more diligent, George! I could never be like you. No matter what I did, I would never inherit Pemberley or be the favoured son. You were always there, Darcy, showing me up in every way!" His agitation grew the longer he talked. His voice became more ragged, and as I advanced, he continued to retreat. "You think I will not fire this pistol, but you are wrong. You should fear me because this time I hold all the cards."

Slowly, I extended my left hand. "Give the gun to me."

Wickham looked about, his eyes wild, but he refused to lower the weapon. "No, stay back, Darcy. Stay back—"

Suddenly, Wickham tripped over a fallen branch lying behind him on the edge of the ravine! He fell backward. I ran forward, hoping to catch him, when I heard the blast of the pistol and felt the bullet tear into my shoulder! The searing pain burned like the fires of hell, knocking me to the ground.

The last sounds I heard were Wickham's cries of terror as he tumbled onto the rocks and Elizabeth's screams echoing against the boulders behind the hut.

Chapter Seventeen

When I awoke, the first thing I saw was Elizabeth's face—her beautiful, tear-stained face—hovering above me, and I wondered what had caused her to weep. I wanted to take her in my arms and say, "Do not cry. All is well."

With a jolt, I remembered where I was. I heard the voices of men nearby and cast my gaze beyond her. Bingley stood within a few feet, directing Mr. Bennet's driver and footman. I thought I must have entered a strange dream, for the footman had removed his shirt. How extraordinary! Then, Bingley knelt beside me.

"Mrs. Darcy, we must turn him so we can bind up the wound," he said.

"Yes," she answered and took my head in her hands. I tried to smile, for I was pleased to feel her hands upon my face, but then gut-wrenching pain caused me to groan aloud, and I slipped into the blackness once again.

The second time I awoke, Mr. Jones's face appeared above me. *No, no,* I wanted to say, *return Elizabeth to my side!*

"Ah, very good, Mr. Darcy," the physician said. "You have come back at last." He placed his hand on my forehead and nodded. "The fever has lessened. Make certain he drinks the tea I ordered."

"I will, Doctor," Elizabeth said. I could hear her voice, but I wished to see her. *Move away!* I wanted to shout at the man standing between us.

"I will return on the morrow." He nodded in my direction and, at last, departed the room.

Elizabeth appeared beside me. "Fitzwilliam, can you speak to me?" she asked tenderly.

"Are…are you unharmed?"

"You are the one who has been shot."

I looked past her and saw I now lay in my bed at Netherfield. Moving slightly, I grimaced at the burning sensation in my arm.

"Lie still. Mr. Jones removed the bullet from your shoulder."

It seemed difficult to get enough air, and I could hear the sound of my own laboured breathing. After a few moments, though, the pain eased somewhat. "Wickham?" I managed to gasp.

Elizabeth looked down, tightly pressing her lips together. She shook her head. "He is gone."

"Gone?"

"He broke his neck when he fell down the ravine."

Shock silenced me. I closed my eyes and turned my head away.

"There was nothing to be done," she said. "My father's footman climbed down the precipice, but he must have died immediately."

"I did not want that. For all Wickham's faults, I did not wish him dead."

"Of course not."

The door opened, and Bingley entered and approached the bed. "I heard the good news from Mr. Jones! Darcy has returned to us, and not a moment too soon."

"How—how long has it been?" I asked.

"You have not been awake for two days," Elizabeth said.

"Two days during which your wife has rarely left your side. You are a lucky devil, Darcy."

I smiled slightly. "Exceedingly."

She did not smile in return but rose from the chair next to the bed. "Shall you relieve me, Mr. Bingley?"

"Certainly."

"But you will come back?" I said, my eyes following her every move.

She nodded. "I will not be far."

After closing the door behind her, Bingley sat down and leaned forward. "Are you too weary for conversation? Shall I let you sleep?"

"No, no. Evidently, I have done nothing but sleep." I moved, hoping to sit up but grimacing instead. The pain was too great.

"What is it? Shall I fetch the nurse?"

I fell back against the pillow and shook my head. "No, have patience with me." Raising my uninjured arm, I rubbed my hand over my face, feeling the bristle that now covered my chin. "Tell me all that has happened, Bingley. How did you come to be there? Who brought Elizabeth to Cutter's Wood?"

"She brought herself for the most part."

When I frowned, he settled back to relate the events that had transpired since Wickham's gun had gone off and I had fallen to the ground. As soon as I announced my intention to proceed to Cutter's Wood, Bingley and Elizabeth had privately entertained notions of following me, but neither informed the other. After I rode through the gates of Netherfield, Bingley marched to the stables and ordered his horse saddled. Elizabeth, meanwhile, had rushed down the stairs from the nursery, boarded her father's carriage, and directed Mr. Bennet's servants to follow me, keeping a safe distance behind so I remained unaware.

Elizabeth reached the site after I had disappeared into the trees, whereupon she ordered the reluctant servants to remain well back in the wood while she walked ahead alone. Bingley arrived in time to hear the shot and Elizabeth's screams. Within moments, he and Mr. Bennet's servants raced through the forest to find her kneeling over my motionless body.

"I feared you had been killed," he said.

"I remember seeing you there, but I thought I was in the midst of a nightmare. For some reason, Mr. Bennet's footman had removed his shirt."

"We used it as a tourniquet."

"I must see that it is replaced."

Bingley chuckled.

"What about Wickham? Elizabeth said he died."

He nodded, his expression turning sober. "He hit his head on a large rock, and his neck snapped like a twig. When we examined him, we found he also had a deep gash in his leg, but that was an older injury. It appeared to have been inflicted by a knife. The wound looked diseased, as though it had begun to fester."

"The result of a dissatisfied card player, according to Wickham."

"Ah, that is not surprising. Upon our return to Netherfield, I sent some of my men to Cutter's Wood to recover the body. It was no easy task hauling him up that rocky slope, I warrant." He lowered his eyes, and I sighed, picturing the scene.

"Is there anyone I should notify? Did he have any family?"

"His parents died several years ago," I said softly. "Wickham had no one… other than the child he did not want."

"'Tis a nasty business, Darcy." He rose from the chair. "But thank God it is over, and now you must rest and regain your strength to heal this wound. I am sure Mrs. Darcy will return before long. Do you need anything before I go?"

"No, but allow me to thank you for all your assistance. You are truly a good friend, Bingley."

He smiled and made his exit. A nurse, evidently on orders from Mr. Jones, entered the room and brought fresh water. She poured me a glass and helped me sip from it. All the while, I kept watch on the door, hoping for Elizabeth's return.

TEN DAYS LATER, IN WHAT HAD BECOME HER CUSTOM, ELIZABETH ENTERED the chamber early in the morning. She was surprised and not a little distressed to find me dressed and sitting in a chair beside the fireplace. The look on her face expressed her alarm.

"What are you doing out of bed?" She hastened to my side and placed her hand on my forehead.

"The fever is gone. I have had none for five days now. And I have lain in that bed until I can bear it no longer!"

"Where is that nurse? I will have her head! And how did you manage to dress?"

"Spare Mrs. Simpkins, for I am the one who dismissed her. And I rang for Rodgers, who always does as he is told without question."

An expression of annoyance settled about her countenance. "Unlike his master?"

"Elizabeth, have pity. I feel well—but for the disuse of this blasted arm —and I cannot abide playing the invalid one more day."

"Mr. Jones said you were to remain in bed two full weeks."

"What does he know? I wager he has never been shot and has no idea how it feels."

She shook her head and took the empty cup and saucer from my hand, refilling it from the teapot on the table. "Have you eaten?"

"No, and I would prefer to break my fast at the table like an adult."

She smiled at my attempt at levity. "Even though you act the child?"

"Even though," I said, smiling in return. She was concerned I would prove too weak to walk down the stairs, but I assured her that, with her assistance, I would be successful. I wore my left arm in a sling, so at the staircase when she insisted I lean on her by placing my right arm around her shoulder, I was an obedient patient and did not prove uppish in the least.

Bingley was overjoyed to see me, and I was much relieved to note the sun had lifted the morning fog and now streamed through the dining room windows. After the meal, Elizabeth attempted to persuade me to return to my bed, but I prevailed and spent an hour in the drawing room, where I read the newspaper on my own for the first time in days.

During my confinement to the sick bed, Elizabeth had spent much time reading to me, not only the news but also passages from my favourite books and some of her own. She had played the dutiful wife, plumping my pillows, feeding me from her own hand before I could sit up, and making certain I drank the dreaded tea Mr. Jones had prescribed. The nurse tended my bandage and other tedious duties, but it was Elizabeth's presence that had restored the colour to my face.

We had not spoken of what had transpired between us since that angry night at Longbourn, for she would not allow it, saying it would wait until I had healed. Nor would she have me speak of all Wickham had said during our confrontation at Cutter's Wood. She had agreed, however, to speak of Fan and the change she had witnessed between the child and me. Two days prior, she had even allowed Mrs. Abernathy to bring Fan to my chamber but took great caution that the little one did not clamber up on the bed as she wished.

Seeing the child had done me great good like a medicine. I had not realized how hungry I was to view her sparkling brown eyes and hear the infectious giggles that frequently erupted. And when she called me 'Papá,' it warmed my heart much like it had done upon hearing it for the first time.

THREE DAYS LATER, I ANNOUNCED I WOULD SOJOURN OUTDOORS. ELIZAbeth immediately protested, but I would not be dissuaded.

"Bingley's steward warns that the weather will grow worse on the morrow. I must breathe fresh air before I am imprisoned again."

"It is still late January," Elizabeth said, "and it is not warm."

"Warmer today than tomorrow. I wish to walk in the garden for a short while."

"Will you allow me to accompany you?"

I smiled. "By all means."

Donning the great coat Elizabeth insisted I wear was not easy, for I could place only one arm in a sleeve and had to drape the heavy garment over my afflicted limb. Still, I was grateful to walk in the garden and feel the sun on my face.

We strolled the paths lined with shrubs and trees for some time before Elizabeth suggested we return to the house, but I chose to tarry awhile, sitting down on one of the stone benches.

"If you are tired or cold, you must go in," I said. "I shall be perfectly well."

"It is for you I am concerned. This bench is damp. Shall I fetch a rug?" When I shook my head, she frowned. "You must not become fatigued."

"I will tell you when I have done enough."

We sat in silence for a few moments, and I wondered whether I dared approach the great encumbrance that lay between us.

"Elizabeth," I said finally, "you have spent the past weeks caring for me with devotion, but I can no longer forego the axe that hangs over my head. We have to speak of the wrongs I have committed. I must know the opinion you now harbour towards me in your heart."

She stared out across the length of the garden for several moments before turning to face me. "I have already heard your confession. I do not see any need to belabour the unpleasantness."

"You expressed your anger with me quite clearly at Longbourn, but do you not wish to add to it? Shall you not rebuke me as I deserve?"

"Would that remove your guilt?"

I shook my head. "No, but at least it might arouse my natural defences."

The briefest of smiles flickered across her face before it vanished, and her grave demeanour returned. "I have borne witness to your suffering, Fitz-william. During those two days you lay in an insensible state, you cried out against yourself repeatedly—vile, despicable accusations. I saw how your conscience afflicted you. Nothing I say could equal the torment you have already imposed upon yourself."

"It does not compare to the danger into which I placed Fan or the anguish

I caused you. Elizabeth, I truly regret all that I brought upon you and the child. Can you forgive me?" I raised my eyes to meet hers.

She gazed at me for some moments before speaking. "That is my fondest wish."

"But you cannot." My heart fell, and I allowed myself to sigh aloud.

"At times, I think I have forgiven you, and then the slightest memory will transport me back into the midst of it, and I find myself growing angry anew." She stared off at the distant woods that encircled Netherfield. "In truth, I do not know myself."

I looked at the ground. What was there to say?

"I do have questions," she said at last. "Have you planned all along to send Fan away to a school as Wickham claimed? Shall you deny her the right to be raised at Pemberley?"

My face darkened at the memory of that accusation. "No! By the time we were wed, I knew neither she nor you would be content if you were parted. I married you with every intention of rearing Fan under my own roof. You must believe me when I declare Wickham's statement false."

The apprehension reflected in her eyes seemed to diminish visibly with my reassurance. "I will rely upon that declaration," she said.

I breathed easier, thinking I had put her fears to rest. "Are you now content? Have I answered all questions to your satisfaction?"

She looked up at me, and I could not discern what her expression conveyed, for she neither smiled nor frowned. "I would ask you one more. Did Wickham speak the truth at Cutter's Wood? Did you want me for your own when first we met?"

"I hardly know. I found you intriguing the moment you crossed before me at the assembly ball, and you glanced at me with that arch smile. Most likely, I did feel the attraction, but fool that I was, I fought it with all that was within me. I thought myself too far above you, too disparaging of your connexions, too proud to admit I could need someone as I came to need you. At length, I could not deny the feelings you awakened within me. I found I was in the middle before I knew that I had begun."

Her face softened, her lips parted, and I needed to kiss her in the most desperate way.

I gathered my courage and reached for her hand, and thanks be to God, she did not draw it away. "Do you not see how it is with me?" My voice broke.

"Why did you not tell me all this when you proposed at Longbourn?"

"How could I? If I revealed the depth of my feelings, I feared it would drive you away."

She frowned. "Why do you say that?"

"Why?" I could not believe she could ask that question. "Because you spurned my declarations of affection at Hunsford! I remember all too well, and I promised you I would not renew those avowals. I am painfully aware you do not return my feelings."

She rose from the bench. "But you—" Twisting her hands, she faltered. "You said you loved another!"

I smiled sadly. "I said I loved a woman who did not return my love—the one truth I uttered among all my lies. That woman is you, Elizabeth, only you. Always."

I rose, and she turned away as though she might leave me there. I gazed at her back and clenched my good hand into a fist, struggling not to reach out and undo the mass of dark curls tied up with pale yellow ribbons. When, instead of running, she faced me at last, I saw with surprise that her eyes had misted over with tears.

"All this time I thought you loved some other woman. I thought you married me out of pity."

I shook my head. "Selfish desire but never pity."

She took my fist in her hands and unfolded each finger, and I felt it hard to breathe. "Perhaps desire, but also out of nobility."

I frowned. Why would she ever consider me noble?

"Once Fan was born, no honourable man offered to marry my sisters or me and take the child into his home. The curate that wed Mary made her promise no one in his parish would ever learn she had an illegitimate niece living in her father's house."

"'Twas a difficult situation, especially for a man of the cloth."

"Yet not too difficult for you—even though you did go about it in the worst possible manner!"

I closed my eyes, thinking the subject had returned to my misdeeds, but when I looked up, I saw her smiling. And when she turned her face to the side in that manner I loved, I began to smile as well.

FOUR WEEKS LATER, MR. JONES PRONOUNCED MY SHOULDER SUFFICIENTLY healed to travel. No longer was I required to wear my arm in a sling, for which I could not have been more thankful. Plans were made to leave Netherfield for Pemberley, and I anticipated the journey with gladness.

Much had occurred during my convalescence. Bingley asked Jane Bennet to marry him, and she, naturally, accepted. Great rejoicing occurred, and we spent numerous occasions with the Bennets, during which Mrs. Bennet planned the wedding with ever-flourishing details. They were to marry in April. Bingley insisted that we return for the ceremony, and I readily agreed.

Elizabeth and I had made gradual progress in making peace between us. I am not certain how much involved her journey towards forgiveness of me —for we had not discussed the subject again—and how much was due to my growing relationship with Fan.

The child besieged me with affection whenever we encountered each other, and I returned it in kind. I know not whether it was her own winsome nature or the threat of losing her that had untied the knots in my heart. I simply know she brought me constant delight. I discovered she possessed a keen intelligence and a natural curiosity. I took pleasure in hearing each new word she learned to pronounce, and when she crawled into my lap begging for a story, I was more than pleased to read to her. I began to wonder why I had ever considered her a burden.

And Elizabeth did not fail to notice.

Mrs. Abernathy had long since fully recovered from her illness, and her influence in the nursery had its desired effect. Although Fan still had much to learn, she responded well to the training the nanny provided, and the household was no longer subjected to tantrums or sudden disappearances. Elizabeth and I spent many an hour discussing our hopes for Fan, knowing full well that the circumstances of her birth hindered our greatest dreams but certain we might find ways to insure she lived a full, happy life in spite of her tragic beginning.

The evening before we were to make our departure, the Bennets came to dine with us at Netherfield. Mr. Bennet's good health, I was pleased to note, had returned. If his heart survived the celebration his wife was planning for Bingley and Jane, I felt certain he would enjoy many more years. Although Elizabeth's parents were saddened that we were leaving, their anticipation of the marriage of their eldest daughter lessened the regret of parting.

"You must come and visit us at Pemberley," I said at the end of the evening while they wended their way towards the waiting carriage.

Elizabeth added her hopes that they would make the journey, and our invitation threw Mrs. Bennet into throes of exhilaration. It took a full half hour for her to walk through the front door and down the stone steps. I assured Mr. Bennet that I possessed a well-stocked library at Pemberley, and he thanked me for the unspoken assurance that he might have a place to escape his wife's exuberance during the proposed visit. Amidst tears and kisses, at length Elizabeth's family boarded the carriage, and Bingley called to the driver to walk on.

Returning to the drawing room, Bingley poured sherry for the three of us and proposed a toast. "May your journey be safe and uneventful, and may you begin your life at Pemberley with God's every good blessing."

"And may you and Jane have a long and happy marriage," I returned.

"Hear, hear," he said, and we all sipped our drinks.

Not long afterwards, Elizabeth and I bade Bingley goodnight as we planned an early start on the morrow. Outside our chambers—for Elizabeth had not returned to my bed since I had been injured—I took her hand to kiss it goodnight, when she indicated she was not ready to part. I was surprised but gladly stepped back for her to enter my room.

Walking in, she surveyed the area as though seeing it for the first time. She ran her hand lightly across the foot of the bed and over the back of the settee before approaching the fireplace. I followed, wondering at her actions, for her countenance did not reveal her thoughts.

I reached her side and paid ever more careful attention to her expression. "Elizabeth?"

"I wished to see this place again, to remember all that transpired within these walls."

"And what do you see?"

She laughed lightly. "My shock on the day of our arrival when we realized Mr. Bingley had placed us in the same chamber."

"And I suggested we make the best of it."

"By sharing the bed! Where is that pillow? Whatever happened to it?"

I laughed. "It seems to have vanished, but it served its purpose."

She looked up to meet my eyes and held my gaze for several moments. Then walking towards the mantel, she picked up a book I had left there. "Mr. Bingley forced us to come to know each other in this room. We learned each other's tastes, not only in literature and poetry but other things as well."

"And they often corresponded, did they not?"

She nodded. "We discovered how to converse without one of us retreating from the room. And you even made some progress with Fan."

"I remember the day I found her asleep in your wardrobe. I wanted to scold her and hug her at the same time!" We laughed in unison. "That was the first time I held the child. I cannot believe I had refrained from even attempting to know her until circumstances forced me to do so."

"Fan was Wickham's child. You had much to overcome, and I confess I did not account for the gravity such alteration in your feelings required. I could have been more patient with you."

"No," I said, stoking the fire. "I was a man who acted the child. I behaved in a selfish manner. You must have thought yourself mother to more than one babe."

She lifted an eyebrow. "Perhaps, but you have had to endure a most reluctant bride, have you not? You have shown great forbearance in waiting, Fitzwilliam."

I felt my heart begin to race. "I would do anything for you."

Again, she held my gaze for several moments. "I remember that dreadful night you carried me in here after I had turned my ankle."

"I hope to never relive that experience!"

"Nor I to see you brought in insensible after being shot. I feared you might die!" She lifted her face towards mine.

I took hold of her hands. "You nursed me back to health. For that I will always be grateful."

She grew even more serious, a pensive expression covering her face. "We did grow closer here before those terrible things tore us apart, did we not?"

"We did...until you learned all I had done." I dropped her hands.

"Our intimacy was founded on dishonesty. That is not the basis for a true marriage. Perchance, it took all the horror we experienced to bring us to this moment."

"I fear I have ruined everything that was good between us, and I will regret my actions all the days of my life."

"But not all is ruined...for what has been done can be undone," she said softly.

"What are you saying, Elizabeth? Have you forgiven me?"

A frown creased her brow, and she ran her hands up her arms as though she were chilled. "You did not deserve my forgiveness. You deserved the anger I held against you. You cannot deny it."

"I have no wish to deny it. I deserve neither kindness nor compassion from you."

She stared at me. "When I learned you and Wickham had conspired together, I—I tried to hate you!" A sob escaped her, and she placed her fist to her lips. "But I could not. For all your false actions, Fitzwilliam, I could not hate you."

I held my breath. I had come closer to losing her than I feared.

"In spite of all you had done, I followed you to Cutter's Wood. I still—"

I took several steps until I could see her face. "Why did you follow me? Was it no more concern than you would have offered any fool rushing headlong into danger?"

"I wish I could answer yes."

I took hold of her. "Then why?"

She refused to look at me, but I would not be dissuaded. I caught her chin with my finger and gently raised it. She would face me; I would not release her until she did. Slowly, she raised her eyes to meet mine.

"Tell me. Why could you not hate me? Why did you not leave me to face Wickham alone? I have to know, Elizabeth."

She searched my piercing stare as though she searched my soul. "Can you not guess? Is it not easy to see? Because...I love you," she whispered.

I heard myself inhale deeply and catch my breath.

She shook her head and cast her gaze to the floor. "Heaven help me, I love you, whether I should or not."

I breathed her name and gathered her into my arms, placing her head on my chest. I could feel her resistance, her disinclination to give herself completely, but little by little, I discerned she was yielding until at last she surrendered into my embrace. Our hearts beat in unison as I cradled her. Slowly, she raised her face to meet mine. I placed my lips on hers, and all the strain I had borne for so long flowed out of me. I had found my way home after a tumultuous voyage. Again and again, I captured her mouth. I wished for this ecstasy to go on and on, but it was not long before she pulled away.

Clasping hands, we stood at arms' length. "Not yet. Not here, Fitzwilliam. This room is haunted with too many ghosts. Let us begin anew at Pemberley."

I swallowed, attempting to conceal my disappointment, but if she was not ready, I would not press her. I wanted our first time together to be perfect. I wanted to give her everything her heart desired.

"As long as you promise we will begin anew, I can wait."

"I promise."

I kissed her hand and opened the door to the hall. I watched her walk away from me until she entered her chamber. Looking back over her shoulder, she smiled ever so slightly and closed the door.

Chapter Eighteen

I led Elizabeth through the doors of Pemberley on the twenty-sixth day of February.

From the moment I realized I loved her, I had wanted to carry her off to Derbyshire. I had longed for her to see my ancestral home through my eyes as my wife. As our carriage first reached the rise in the long road leading up to the house, I watched her face intently. Upon her glimpse of Pemberley, she smiled, and I beamed with pride.

"When I saw the estate over two years ago," she said, "I recall that my uncle had the coach stop on this very spot so we could enjoy the view."

"And are you pleased to return as mistress of the house?" I asked.

Layers of white outlined the branches of the ash trees before us, while the snow-covered moors leading up to the folly loomed behind the house in an unspoiled, almost primeval vista. Elizabeth gazed over the landscape as though captivated by the prospect. "I do not believe there is a house to be found wherein I could be more pleased."

I struggled to tamp down my elation, for I felt as though I might burst with pleasure. I reached for her hand and held it tightly within mine.

Having sent a rider ahead to alert the household of our arrival, I was glad to see Mrs. Reynolds, the housekeeper, had assembled the indoor staff to meet us. They were lined up in an orderly fashion. I thought the magnitude of that number of servants might overwhelm Elizabeth, but whatever she may have felt, she did not falter and graciously acknowledged each one's welcome.

We arrived late in the evening near dusk. I decided to delay my wife's tour of the house until the morrow. After dining on a light supper, she wished to visit the nursery and make certain Fan was settled. The child had behaved better than I expected on the long trip, adjusting without too great a fuss to the unfamiliar inns during the nights we spent on the road. Following the incident with Wickham, Fan had suffered from night terrors for a few weeks, but gradually they had lessened and almost disappeared. Pemberley, however, was vast indeed compared to Netherfield. Elizabeth feared the size alone might alarm the little one.

"I suppose your steward is in urgent need of your company," she said after supper. "Do not feel it necessary to accompany me."

I bowed as she left the dining room but then reconsidered. It was far too late for a long working session with Mr. Yates, and I had travelled on too great a journey of my own to slip back into my old ways. I bounded up the stairs two at a time until I reached the nursery floor just in time to hear Fan's plaintive little voice.

"Where Papá?"

"He is here," I announced, striding through the door.

Fan raced to meet me, threw her arms around my legs, and raised her mop of chestnut curls to gaze up at me.

"Up, Papá!"

Happily, I picked her up, and I did not miss the smile it provoked from Elizabeth.

"I thought you were to meet with Mr. Yates tonight."

"On the morrow," I said over the child's head. "Important things must come first."

I sat down on Fan's bed, and she placed her hands on my face to claim my attention. "Papá house?"

"You are correct. This is Papá's house," Elizabeth said. "It is called Pemberley."

"Pemmey," she echoed.

I laughed to hear her attempt to pronounce the word. "Pem-ber-ley is not only my house, but it is your house too. Yours and Mamá's."

I looked up to see the delight shining in Elizabeth's eyes that bespoke her gratitude.

On our way from the nursery to the drawing room, I led Elizabeth through the gallery of portraits, for she expressed a desire to visit it again. I pointed out various ancestors, my mother's and father's separate images, and the painting of Georgiana completed prior to her wedding. She nodded and made appropriate answers but continued along the hall until she stopped beneath the large painting of me.

She studied it for some time.

"I recall seeing this on my previous visit."

"You must have hurried past it, hoping to banish the image of a man you did not wish to recall."

She shook her head, still staring at the portrait. "You are mistaken. My feelings were quite the opposite. I found myself entranced by your smile."

I glanced up at the painting and saw nothing that should catch anyone's fancy.

"It was the same expression I had seen you bestow on me, although rarely, I must admit." She turned from the portrait to observe my expression. "I confess I stood here for some time. Mrs. Reynolds and my aunt and uncle had already walked into the next room before I realized they were gone."

I was perplexed and did not know how to answer. "What are you saying, Elizabeth?"

"You are not the only one who did not know when your feelings began to change. At Kent, I thought I despised you, but after reading and re-reading your letter, gradually all my former prejudices began to fall away. I recognized I did not know your true character. And standing here before your portrait, I had to accept the truth of my own inclination. I wanted to know you, and I longed for you to come back into my life."

"But when Bingley and I met you again on the road to Hertfordshire, your manner was quite cold."

She lowered her head to look at the floor, and we walked towards the staircase. "You had been gone for a long time, and as you know, our lives had changed. By then I bore the burden of shame. All hope you would seek me out again had died after the disgrace that had befallen my family. I could not imagine you would ever come to Longbourn again. When we met on the London road, it was by accident, and besides, you must remember that I thought you married."

She took my arm as we descended the stairs, and I closed my hand over hers. "And all the while I feared you were Fan's mother. Oh, let us not return to those days and those thoughts!"

"No, we must think only of the past as its remembrance gives us pleasure."

WE SPENT MUCH OF THE REMAINDER OF THE EVENING IN MY LIBRARY, FOR Elizabeth expressed a wish to visit it. She studied the titles on the books for some time. I studied her.

I could not dismiss the past as easily as she did. Was I mistaken in my belief? Had she also concealed her true feelings when I proposed at Longbourn? I recalled she had spoken little. Her uppermost concern had been that Fan would have a home with us. Otherwise, she asked the reason I wished to marry her, and whether someone else lived in my heart. Had she remained silent to hide the change in her feelings? Could it be she loved me even then?

"Will you show me your favourite books?" she asked, rousing me from my thoughts.

I smiled and led her to the section nearest the window. "I am afraid you will find these well worn."

"Meaning they are well loved." She selected three she wished to read when she retired, and I took that as a signal our time together was drawing to a close.

"You must be tired. Do you wish to go to your chamber?"

"I am weary, but I have one more request."

"Name it, and it shall be yours."

"Show me the music room again. I do not think I have ever seen a pianoforte as exquisite as the one you gave Georgiana."

"Ah," I said, leading her down the hallway. "I fear you will be disappointed, for I ordered the instrument shipped to my sister's new home shortly after her wedding."

Her face fell, but when we entered the room, I saw the light return to her eyes. "But what is this? Another strikingly handsome piano!"

I smiled. "I ordered the pianoforte that belonged to my mother returned to the music room. It is old but still in tune."

"It is lovely," she said, running her hands over the polished wood.

"Do I ask too much of you to play tonight?"

She looked up. "Perhaps one song before bed."

I pulled open a drawer on the chest nearby. "Shall you select from this stack of music? It seems Georgiana left a large collection behind."

She shook her head. "Allow me to play the only tune I truly ever learned."

I sat down on the settee across from the pianoforte and gazed upon her as she played and sang.

> *What is this yearning, these trembling fears,*
> *Rapturous burning, melting in tears?*
> *While thus I languish, wild beats my heart,*
> *Yet from my anguish I would not part,*
> *You who have tasted love's mystic spell*
> *What is this sorrow naught can dispel?*[2]

My heart began to beat faster while she sang, for her pure, untrained soprano lifted my spirit higher than any aria sung by a prima donna. I could not keep from smiling, and when she finished, I strode to her side. Taking her hand, I kissed it.

"Charming," I murmured, sitting down on the bench beside her. "Shall you tell me why you chose to learn that particular song?"

"Mary taught it to me before she married. I had heard it when visiting the Gardiners in London. A gifted artist presented it much better than I at a concert we attended, and I was determined to hear it again even if I had to be the one to perform."

"A determined spirit that now benefits me, for I shall wish to hear it again and again."

Elizabeth laughed. "I fear you will regret that statement. I must apply myself and learn another, for listening to the same song will drive you mad."

"Why did that song provoke your interest? Did you fancy yourself in love at the time?"

"In truth," she said, hesitating somewhat, "I could not account for the feelings the music stirred within my breast. Perhaps, my inability to do so is what drew me to the verse. It expressed my confusion."

I pressed on. "And when, may I ask, did those confused feelings afflict you?"

She did not answer for several moments, and quiet reigned in the room. At last, she raised her face so that I might see her eyes. "After I read your letter at Hunsford."

---

2 "Voi Che Sapete" from Mozart's *The Marriage of Figaro*, 1784

I drew in my breath. Her love had begun years before I proposed at Longbourn!

Without warning, she rose from the bench and changed the subject. "Did you know that the slight smile that graced your face while I sang is the image of the one in your portrait?"

Rising, I took her hands in mine. "I know but one truth, and that is you have made me more certain of my decision than ever before."

"And of what decision do you speak?"

"To make you mistress of Pemberley, for clearly, you were born for it."

I could tell that my words pleased her. She lifted her face to be kissed, a task I was more than ready to complete. When I released her, she sauntered towards the window. Drawing the drapes aside, she gazed through the glass. I joined her and noted how the moon illuminated the white park covered in snow.

"'Tis enchantment," she said softly.

"Truly," I murmured, gazing at the soft curve of her cheek and the ivory lustre of her throat. "I find it hard to cast my eyes upon any other."

She looked up and understood that I did not speak of the prospect without. Blushing slightly, she lowered her eyes and turned her head in that manner I loved.

"I feel like a bride."

"And is this our wedding night?"

We gazed into each other's eyes for several moments as though neither of us could speak.

"Shall I come to you?" I asked, my voice deepening. When she did not answer, I felt my spirits drop. "We said we would begin anew at Pemberley." Still, she did not answer. "I know the hour is late and the journey difficult. If you are too tired—"

She dropped her eyes then and turned to leave. I stared at her as she crossed the room, silently willing her to turn back to me. Why did she not answer? At the door, she smiled over her shoulder. "As you wish."

What did that mean? I wanted to ask, but she had already departed the room. Hastening after her through the door and up the stairs, I saw her disappear into her chamber that adjoined mine. Her maid entered through the side door into her dressing room, carrying a pitcher of warm water. I walked into my room and rang the bell for Rodgers. He, too, delivered warm water, pouring it into a basin in the dressing room, and I hurriedly washed off the stains of the road.

Clearly, my wishes were more than she meant, I thought. She would not welcome me into her bed that night, for had she not said earlier she was weary? But that last smile and those haunting words—what did they mean? Perchance, it was time I acted, that I showed her the man I was. If that meant revealing a husband besotted with love who could not wait one more night, then so be it.

After donning my dressing gown, I entered my chamber, wondering whether Elizabeth had yet climbed into her bed. I had just walked towards the door that separated us when a faint familiar scent swept over me. Did I want her so much that I imagined the fragrance drifting through the walls? I shook my head, wondering whether desire had driven me mad. For some unaccountable reason at that moment, something made me turn and glance over my shoulder.

There, to my amazement, lay my wife—in my bed!—her curls dark and loose across the white pillowcase, a sweet smile playing about her lips. And there, between where she and I would sleep, sat the largest, plumpest pillow I had seen in all of Pemberley!

I turned and slowly approached her. "Elizabeth?"

"Yes?"

"You are in my bed."

"Is this not where the mistress of Pemberley sleeps?"

I swallowed. "It is."

"Then, am I not where I should be?"

"You are." I stepped closer, keeping my eyes on that tantalizing smile. "But pray tell me, why is this insufferable pillow yet placed between us?"

"More than once this evening you have remarked on the long journey we have endured and how tired I must be. I assumed you were weary as well. I placed the pillow on the bed lest my presence disturb your sleep."

Although her expression was all innocence, I could tell from her tone that she was toying with me. I sat down on the bed and leaned across the large impediment between us. Once again, my voice lowered of its own accord. "You have disturbed my sleep for years, and there is not a pillow large enough to solve the problem."

She sat up, resting on one arm, and leaned her face dangerously close to mine. Her eyes sparkled, and the bedclothes fell away so that I saw how her gown exposed the delicacy of her lovely shoulders. "Then what do you propose we do to resolve your problem?"

In one immediate, forceful move, I grabbed the pillow, walked across the room, unlatched the window, and pushed the glass open. With a mighty heave, I cast the hated cushion out into the night and watched it sail across the lawn.

From across the room, I heard Elizabeth giggle. Turning, I saw her pull back my side of the quilt and sheet, smooth it with her hand, and beckon me to her side. It took not a moment longer for me to cross that room and, at last, truly join my wife in our bed.

SOMETIME IN THE NIGHT, I AWOKE WITH A SMILE ON MY FACE. I REACHED for Elizabeth only to discover I was alone. I blinked several times until my eyes became accustomed to the darkness. When I searched the chamber, I saw my wife perched on the window seat, her arms wrapped around her legs drawn up beneath her gown as she stared out into the night. I rose, shrugged into my dressing gown, and walked across the room.

I called her name softly as I made my way to her side. "Is something amiss?"

She looked up, smiling. "How could anything in this chamber be amiss?" She leaned against me when I embraced her. "I woke up and could not go back to sleep."

"You are shivering." I sat down and pulled her closer. She snuggled into my arms, and I kissed the top of her head. "What has captured your interest without?"

She laughed softly. "That poor pillow. It landed precariously near the pond."

"In the morning, I shall go out and drown it."

That caused her laughter to break forth in a stream of joy. "But, Fitzwilliam, it is a perfectly good pillow. Why should you destroy it?"

"Anything that separates you from me belongs at the bottom of the pond!"

She reached up and pulled my face down to hers. Placing her lips on mine, she kissed me slowly and deliberately. "Nothing shall ever separate us again."

"Nothing?" I said, nuzzling her ear.

"Nothing," she murmured, twining her fingers through my hair.

"Then I shall take you back to my bed, for I am cold. If I am there and you are here, we will be separated, and that cannot be. Agreed?"

"Agreed."

I picked her up and carried her to the bed. By that time, I was thoroughly awakened too, so we spent no little time together enjoying the pleasures of marriage before falling asleep wrapped in each other's arms.

ELIZABETH AND I HAVE NOW BEEN MARRIED FOUR AND TWENTY YEARS. IF possible, she has grown even dearer and lovelier as time has passed. In truth, my heart races as rapidly at the sight of her today as it did all those years before.

Our union has not always been perfect, for we have both proved somewhat headstrong in our opinions, but we are happy. When we disagree, which happens occasionally, it is because we speak before we consider the consequences. The quarrels that result produce hurt feelings and necessitate apologies, but they always conclude in displays of affection. We have gone to bed angry, but not for long, for we do not sleep apart. Without a pillow to separate us, we never fail to find our way into each other's embrace.

Our families have undergone alterations. Georgiana and Harry have a daughter, the image of my sister, and a son who has become her favourite. He has inherited both her love of and talent for music. They spend many happy hours together at the pianoforte.

Elizabeth's parents have gone on to their reward, but not before seeing Kitty marry a fine man from London who found employment with Mr. Gardiner. Mrs. Bennet died a happy woman, having secured husbands for her four surviving daughters.

Caroline Bingley remains unmarried. She spends most of her time with Mr. and Mrs. Hurst, preferring their house in Town to that of her brother in the country. We rarely see them, an occurrence about which neither Elizabeth nor I have ever complained. I regret to say that age has not softened Caroline's features, but rather drawn the taut lines of her face downward into a sour expression, replicating the bitterness in her heart.

I would have to say the same for Lady Catherine de Bourgh but for the kindness of my wife. With the birth of our first son, Elizabeth extended an invitation to my aunt to visit us at Pemberley, which Lady Catherine promptly declined and none too politely. Elizabeth refused to be daunted by the hateful reply. She waited until James, our next son, was born, whereupon she issued a second invitation. When the third son's birth and third invitation were not acknowledged, I thought the situation impossible to solve and advised Elizabeth to concede defeat. She, however, refused to give over. Sadly, it took the death of my cousin Anne and the birth of our fourth son for Lady Catherine to wait upon us in Derbyshire.

Upon receiving a post from Richard warning that Anne was on her deathbed, Elizabeth had insisted I travel to Rosings. It was the first time I had visited my aunt since our marriage. I kept my stay brief and left shortly after the funeral, well before the Earl of Matlock or Fitzwilliam ended their visits. I was shocked at how Lady Catherine had aged. I had never pictured her old and fragile, but my wife knew I would find her thus.

"A mother cannot lose her only child," she said, "without reflecting that deep wound in her visage. You must make peace with her now, dearest, while there is still time."

When Lady Catherine arrived on our doorstep some eight months later, Elizabeth was prepared. She did all she could to make my aunt's visit pleasant, including shielding her from Fan's company as much as possible. Other than having the three oldest join us for meals, all of the children cut a wide path around Lady Catherine. They were more than willing to avoid the elderly woman who chose to judge everyone by her prejudiced standards.

At that time, Fan was twelve years old and beginning to bloom. I had ordered music and drawing lessons added to her education, and Fan showed a natural aptitude for art. Elizabeth could not account for the talent, for she said it did not come from her side of Fan's heritage.

One day, Lady Catherine happened upon the girl. Fan worked at her easel near the north window of the conservatory to catch the light. My aunt did not speak to her but walked behind and observed her work.

"Heed the shadows, girl," Lady Catherine said. "You need more than light to reflect a true image."

Fan held forth her brush. "Will you show me, your ladyship?"

My aunt looked her up and down but said nothing. Taking the brush in her hand, she dipped it in the grey paint from the palette held by the girl and applied it skilfully behind the figure on the canvas.

"Follow my lead." She handed the brush back to Fan, who worked diligently to copy Lady Catherine's example. "There, you have it."

Elizabeth, who had witnessed the encounter and related it to me, experienced such shock that she had to sit down in a far chair at the edge of the room. Lady Catherine continued to demonstrate correct technique to Fan for nigh onto an hour.

"That is sufficient for today," she said in conclusion. "I shall teach you again on the morrow."

Turning, she observed that Elizabeth remained in the conservatory. "The girl has a bent towards art. She should receive the very best instruction. I will send Edwin Marsh to you from London. With his training, she will develop her artistic eye properly."

Elizabeth expressed her gratitude as she accompanied the lady into the drawing room. When they sat down together, Lady Catherine looked down her nose at her and sniffed. "As I recall, you do not draw."

"Neither my sisters nor I showed any ability in that area."

"It appears to be the one good trait she inherited from her natural father."

"I did not know Mr. Wickham painted."

Lady Catherine raised her eyebrows. "I doubt that he did, but I do know his mother did not lack the skill."

Elizabeth's eyes widened. "Did you know Mrs. Wickham, ma'am?"

"I saw some of her work when I visited my sister. Anne did all she could to encourage the woman to pursue her gift, for she showed an unusual fitness, but the steward's wife preferred to while away the majority of her time in the shops, spending her husband's wages before they were earned." She sipped her tea and peered over the teacup at Elizabeth. "You must watch for that singularity in the child and put it to bed forthwith. She must be encouraged to live a better life and overcome her earlier misfortunes."

"Fan has never shown any indication of that fault, ma'am. She is a sweet girl, and I believe she will grow up to be a worthy person."

"My, you still express your opinions decidedly, do you not? I see that has not altered since your marriage."

Elizabeth did not reply. I suspect she was too busy biting her tongue.

By the end of my aunt's stay with us, Fan had won Lady Catherine's heart. Their daily chapters in the conservatory exposed the older lady's better nature since she did possess certain artistic skills, and the young girl's innate charm could not help but soften her sad, lonely heart.

"You have done more than I expected with the child," Lady Catherine said before she prepared to board her barouche. "When I return, I will examine her again. Do not disappoint me."

We waved good-bye and watched until the last of the carriage could no longer be seen leaving the estate.

"That is the nearest thing to praise I will ever hear from Lady Catherine," Elizabeth said.

"It sounded more like a warning to me."

"What do you mean?"

"'*When I return, I will examine her again,*'" I said in a mocking voice. "Elizabeth, that means my aunt is coming back!"

AS WAS MENTIONED EARLIER, WE BECAME PARENTS TO FOUR SONS—ALL handsome, stalwart, intelligent young men—each of whom taxes my patience daily with some new trial.

My namesake, Fitzwilliam, has recently fallen in love for the first time. Like his father, I believe he has chosen a young woman who will challenge him, for he fears she does not care for him. I have urged him not to despair, and I related a bit of my own struggle in pursuit of his mother.

James, on the other hand, falls in love with a different girl every other month. I have sent him to spend some time with Bingley, hoping my friend's experience will prove enlightening and he will choose a woman of substance as Charles did. I am happy to report that the Bingleys gave up Netherfield and now live within a day's distance of Pemberley. This has led to many happy hours for my wife to enjoy with her beloved sister.

My youngest sons, Edmund and Thomas, are still at home and remain inexperienced in the throes of infatuation. They are both able horsemen, as are all my children, and my greatest parental task is insisting they forego riding for more profitable pursuits, such as their studies.

And then there is Fan, who has grown up to be a sparkling jewel in our lives.

I know not when I began to think of the child as my daughter. The seed may have been planted when she first called me Papá on the ride from London to Longbourn. At the time, I was reeling from all that had transpired in our lives, and I failed to appreciate the truth of the matter. It did not take long, though, before I found myself forgetting that Wickham had fathered her. As the years passed and she has grown into a beautiful, obedient but lively lass under Elizabeth's gentle guidance, I rarely think of Fan's natural parentage.

It is only upon the odd occasion when a certain expression lights up her eyes that I glimpse a trace of Wickham, and then it reminds me of the good days when we were youths laughing and playing together on the grounds of Pemberley. Elizabeth says she oft-times sees reflections of Lydia in Fan —her sparkling brown eyes, her mischief when playing with her brothers, and her instinctive love of life.

The circumstances of Fan's birth did alter my life in society. Shortly after our marriage, I discovered that Elizabeth would suffer if we spent much time in Town. Although a king might harbour his love child in *his* house, a gentleman of my standing would pay the price. Gossip plagued us the first few years, causing me to retire to the country for the most part. Eventually, however, the Darcys became old news when a more exciting scandal erupted. Thus, five years after our marriage, Elizabeth was accepted in the best drawing rooms in London. Her natural elegance and liveliness enhanced any gathering to which we were invited. Still, we both prefer the peace and simplicity of Derbyshire and spend the majority of each year there.

Gone are the days when I considered country society to be confined and unvarying.

WE CONTINUED QUITE CONTENT WITH OUR LIVES UNTIL FIVE YEARS AGO when it came time for our daughter to marry. I confess that I judged the young men who called as severely as though Fan were my own child. Not one of them was good enough! Finally, Elizabeth tenderly persuaded me to accept that Fan loved Edward Fitzroy, and she would not give him up.

Although she could not hope to marry a gentleman because of the circumstances of her birth, she had drawn the attraction of the son of the only attorney within thirty miles. The young man was a partner in his father's thriving business, and he would provide an adequate living for our little Fan. Grudgingly, I had to admit it was a good match.

The wedding took place in the month of June. The night before, Elizabeth and I stole away from the house for a walk in the moonlight. Kitty and her family had come for the celebration, as well as Bingley, Jane, and their children. Our house was filled with relations and the noise and commotion that accompany them. My mood had grown dour, for I suffered from a lack of time alone with my wife.

"Are not the roses perfect this year? It is almost as though they know we are having a wedding," Elizabeth said.

"They have performed adequately," I replied. My voice did not match the level of excitement of my wife.

She turned her attention from the roses to fix her eye upon me. "You are subdued this evening, dearest. Do you not anticipate the morrow with pleasure?"

I exhaled in a deep sigh. "My feelings are divided. It gives me satisfaction to witness Fan's happiness, but I can hardly look forward to giving her away."

"I can remember a time when that is precisely what you wished to do."

I frowned that she would bring up an old but unpleasant subject. "I had hoped those memories had faded by now."

"Oh, they have! Indeed, they are but faint recollections. At times, however, I take joy in reliving those days in my mind."

"Joy! How can you make such a statement?"

We approached a bench in the midst of the garden, and Elizabeth sat down. I braced my boot against the bench and leaned forward on one knee.

"The joy stems not from recalling the misunderstandings or—"

"My sins?"

She smiled. "Or *mistakes* committed by each of us. But joy does overtake me when I call to mind the slow dance you and Fan engaged in when you began to love each other. Those memories fill me with delight."

"If I had not been a fool, I would have loved her instantly. To this day, I cannot account for my stubbornness and resentment. How could I have felt that way towards an innocent child and one as charming as Fan?"

Elizabeth laughed. "As I remember, discovering your important papers strewn all over your study and blueberries staining your bed were not Fan's most charming moments."

The scenes flashed before me as though they had just occurred, and I smiled. Standing erect, I folded my hands behind my back and stared up at the night sky. "She has led me on a lively quest at times." I turned to gaze at Elizabeth and held out my hand to her. "Much like her mother."

She rose and leaned against me. "Do you regret I have not given you a daughter of your own?"

I frowned. "But you have. I could not ask for a lovelier child than Fan. I am proud of our sons, but Fan will always own a particular place in my heart. I am told that daughters stake that claim when they are quite young, and nothing can dislodge it."

"Yet now, she gives her heart to another man."

"And he does not deserve her."

"Edward is a fine man, and I believe they are suitably matched. I rejoice that they will be settled nearby."

"If Fitzroy decides to move her out of the county, he will have to deal with me."

Elizabeth slipped her arms around my waist. "Now, Fitzwilliam, you took me hundreds of miles from my father. If business causes Edward to move Fan from Derbyshire, you must understand."

"I must do nothing of the sort! Your father had daughters to spare, and I have but one."

She smiled. "Change comes to everyone. We must adapt, or I fear they will say we are old and set in our ways."

I grimaced. "I do not care for change. If it insists upon coming, I shall require a generous amount of comfort from you."

She turned her head in that way I loved. "And it will pleasure me to provide that comfort."

I took her face within my hands and kissed her sweet lips. "One thing must never be altered, Elizabeth."

"And what is that, my darling?"

"You must always, always love me, even if I grow into an ill-tempered old fellow."

She kissed me again. "That is a promise I can easily pledge. And I shall do even more. I promise to love the ill temper right out of you."

And she did just that. I confess at times, I become ill tempered just to have her keep her word, and she has never failed me, not even once.

The End

Acknowledgements

I would like to offer a fond, sincere thank you to each of the following:

- Debbie Styne, my funny, smart, creative editor who encouraged me years ago when I first conceived this story and who was willing to tackle the task again and smooth out the rough edges until my words became a book;

- Janet Taylor, whose talented artist's eye can visualize what I'm saying and translate it into a beautiful cover, and whose friendship is priceless;

- Michele Reed, Ellen Pickels, and the staff at Meryton Press who continue to maintain quality standards;

- L. E. Smith for her excellent beta reading and Cassandra Grafton for sharing her geographical knowledge of London;

- My dear family and friends who sustain me with their love and care;

- My readers and bloggers who continue to encourage me with comments and reviews; and

- Jane Austen, the genius who started it all.

CPSIA information can be obtained
at www.ICGtesting.com
Printed in the USA
FSHW01n1939090518
48060FS